'Of a⟶   ⟶ of a
long ti⟶ — *So Many Books, So Little Time*

CRITICAL ACCLAIM FOR *MURDER RING*

'A great murder mystery in its own right and highly recommended'
– *Fiction Is Stranger Than Fact*

'Smoothly professional fare from the always-consistent Russell'
– *Crime Time*

CRITICAL ACCLAIM FOR *BLOOD AXE*

'A great story with some interesting and unexpected twists and turns.
It ends with some scenes of high drama and a clever and surprising
outcome' – *Fiction Is Stranger Than Fact*

CRITICAL ACCLAIM FOR *KILLER PLAN*

'Her previous six novels featuring DI Geraldine Steel marked her out as
a rare talent, and this seventh underlines it' – *Daily Mail*

'I will be looking out for more from this author'– *Nudge*

'A fast-paced police procedural and a compelling read'– *Mystery People*

'Fans of the series will enjoy reacquainting themselves with Leigh
Russell's work'– *Crime Fiction Lover*

CRITICAL ACCLAIM FOR *RACE TO DEATH*

'Unmissable' – **Lee Child**

'Leigh Russell has become one of the most impressively dependable
purveyors of the English police procedural' – **Marcel Berlins,**

'As tense openings go, they don't come much better than this'
– *Bookbag*

'If you enjoy a well-written mystery with a well-constructed and thought-out plot line then this is the book for you… it is my BOOK OF THE MONTH' – *Crime Book Club*

'the story unfolds at a great pace and grips until the end'
– *Fiction Is Stranger Than Fact*

'Leigh Russell weaves a fascinating tale that had me completely foxed. Whilst the mystery is tantalising the characters also fascinate, so clearly are they drawn'– *Mystery People*

CRITICAL ACCLAIM FOR *COLD SACRIFICE*

'A complex mystery rich in characters, this new series promises some interesting times ahead for Ian Peterson' – *Promoting Crime Fiction*

'Russell's story telling was strong enough to keep me enticed right to the very end'– *Lloyd Paige*

'Ian Peterson as a character could potentially be just as good (if not better) than Geraldine Steel' – *Best Crime Books*

CRITICAL ACCLAIM FOR *FATAL ACT*

'a most intriguing and well executed mystery and… an engrossing read'– *Shotsmag*

'the best yet from Leigh Russell – she keeps you guessing all the way through and leaves you wanting more' – *Crime Book Club*

'another fast-paced and complex mystery – a fabulous read'
– *Fiction Is Stranger Than Fact*

'a truly great author… enough mystery and drama for the most ardent of mystery fans' – *Bookaholic*

'another corker of a book from Leigh Russell… Russell's talent for writing top-quality crime fiction just keeps on growing…'
– *Euro Crime*

'the plot is strong and the writing just flows with style and panache'
– *Goodreads*

CRITICAL ACCLAIM FOR *STOP DEAD*

'*Stop Dead* is taut and compelling, stylishly written with a deeply human voice' – **Peter James**

'All the things a mystery should be, intriguing, enthralling, tense and utterly absorbing' – ***Best Crime Books***

'A definite must read for crime thriller fans everywhere – 5 stars' – ***Newbooks Magazine***

'For lovers of crime fiction this is a brilliant, not-to-be missed, novel' – ***Fiction Is Stranger Than Fact***

'Geraldine Steel sticks out as a believable copper and *Stop Dead* flows easily' – ***Electric Lullaby***

'A well-written, a well-researched, and a well-constructed whodunnit. Highly recommended' – ***Mystery People***

'a whodunnit of the highest order. The tightly written plot kept me guessing all the way' – ***Crimesquad***

CRITICAL ACCLAIM FOR *DEATH BED*

'Earlier books have marked her out as one of the most able practitioners in the current field' – **Barry Forshaw, *Crime Time***

'*Death Bed* is a marvellous entry in this highly acclaimed series' – ***Promoting Crime Fiction***

'An innovative and refreshing take on the psychological thriller' – ***Books Plus Food***

'Russell's strength as a writer is her ability to portray believable characters' – ***Crimesquad***

'A well-written, well-plotted crime novel with fantastic pace and lots of intrigue' – ***Bookersatz***

'Truly a great crime thriller' – ***Nayu's Reading Corner***

'*Death Bed* is her most exciting and well-written to date. And, as the others are superb, that is really saying something! 5*' – ***Euro Crime***

'The story itself was as usual a good one, and the descriptive gruesomeness of some scenes was brilliant' – ***Best Crime Books***

CRITICAL ACCLAIM FOR *DEAD END*

'All the ingredients combine to make a tense, clever police whodunnit'
– **Marcel Berlins,** *The Times*

'A brilliant talent in the thriller field' – **Jeffery Deaver**

'I could not put this book down' – *Newbooks Magazine*

'An encounter that will take readers into the darkest recesses
of the human psyche' – *Crime Time*

'Well written and chock full of surprises, this hard-hitting, edge-of
the seat instalment is yet another treat… Geraldine Steel looks set to
become a household name. Highly recommended' – *Euro Crime*

'Good, old-fashioned, heart-hammering police thriller… a no-frills
delivery of pure excitement' – *SAGA Magazine*

'The critical acclaim heaped on Russell thus far in her literary career is
well deserved' – *Bookgeeks*

'a macabre read, full of enthralling characters and gruesome details
which kept me glued from first page to last' – *Crimesquad*

'*Dead End* was selected as a Best Fiction Book of 2012'
– *Miami Examiner*

CRITICAL ACCLAIM FOR *ROAD CLOSED*

'A well-written, soundly plotted, psychologically acute story'
– **Marcel Berlins,** *The Times*

'New star of crime fiction, Leigh Russell's chilling psychological thriller
is terrific and terrifying!' – **Clem Chambers**

'Well written and absorbing right from the get-go… with an exhilarating
climax that you don't see coming'– *Euro Crime*

'Leigh Russell does a good job of keeping her readers guessing. She also
uses a deft hand developing her characters, especially the low-lifes… a
good read' – *San Francisco Book Review*

'perfect character building… cleverly written… can't wait for
the next one' – *Best Books to Read*

LEIGH RUSSELL

CLASS MURDER

A GERALDINE STEEL MYSTERY

NO EXIT PRESS

First published in 2018 by No Exit Press,
an imprint of Oldcastle Books Ltd,
PO Box 394, Harpenden,
Herts, AL5 1XJ, UK

noexit.co.uk
@noexitpress

ISBN
978-1-84344-930-0 (Print)
978-1-84344-931-7 (Epub)
978-1-84344-932-4 (Kindle)
978-1-84344-933-1 (Pdf)

2 4 6 8 10 9 7 5 3 1

Typeset in 11.25pt Times New Roman
by Avocet Typeset, Somerton, Somerset, TA11 6RT
Printed in Denmark by Nørhaven, Viborg

To Michael, Joanna, Phillipa, Phil, Rian and Kezia

Acknowledgements

I would like to thank Dr Leonard Russell for his expert medical advice, and all my contacts in the Metropolitan Police for their invaluable assistance.

Producing a book is a team effort. I am fortunate to have the guidance of a brilliant editor, Keshini Naidoo. I am very grateful to Ion Mills, Claire Watts, Clare Quinlivan, Katherine Sunderland, Frances Teehan, Jem Cook and all the team at No Exit Press, who transform my words into books. I would also like to thank Anne Cater and her wonderful team of bloggers for organising my blog tour. I am grateful for their support which has been invaluable.

My final thanks go to Michael, who is always with me.

Glossary of acronyms

DCI   – Detective Chief Inspector (senior officer on case)
DI   – Detective Inspector
DS   – Detective Sergeant
SOCO – Scene of the Crime Officer (collects forensic evidence at scene)
PM   – Post mortem or Autopsy (examination of dead body to establish cause of death)
CCTV – Closed Circuit Television (security cameras)
VIIDO– Visual Images, Identification and Detections Office

Preface

He never forgot the first time the cat brought a bird into the house. A small brown creature, its wings were still flapping although its eyes were glazed above a beak that hung open. Warning him not to go anywhere near the dying bird, his mother chased the cat outside. He must have been about six or seven, young enough to obey his mother's command without question. Returning to the kitchen, she explained that the cat had intended to bring her a present.

'We feed Billy,' she went on, 'but it's still a generous gesture. He could have kept the bird for himself. That's his way of showing us he loves us. Cats aren't like people.'

Her last comment had puzzled him. Of course he knew that cats weren't like people. They had four legs, for a start, and they couldn't talk. Another time, the cat brought in a dead mouse. His mother scooped it up in a wad of newspaper, leaving a streak of blood on the lino. After cleaning the floor and washing her hands, she turned to him with a sour expression on her face.

'Don't be upset with Billy,' she said. 'He was bringing us a present.'

Far from upset, he had been intrigued and vaguely excited at the enormity of what Billy had done.

It was a hot summer, with blazing days that seemed to stretch out endlessly, a childhood summer where he fell asleep before the sun set, and woke to see it rising in the sky. Crouching in dry grass behind the garden shed, he spent weeks devising a box with a lid that snapped shut as soon as a frail stick holding it open was dislodged. Discovering that his homemade contraption had succeeded was one of the highlights of his early childhood. His breath caught in his throat when he first saw the box was shut. Concealed beneath a hedge behind the garden shed, he was pretty sure no one else would have stumbled on it. Only a small animal could have set off the mechanism that snapped the box shut.

His hands trembled with excitement as he picked it up. There was no sound from inside the box, no frantic scuttling of tiny feet, no outraged squawking from a trapped creature. Dreading that he would open it only to find it empty, he lifted the lid a fraction and peered inside. There was no movement in the box. He slid the lid across another fraction and cried out at the sight of a tiny beady black eye glaring up at him.

Slamming the lid shut, he collapsed on the ground, laughing hysterically. It was a while before he calmed down enough to consider his next move. He wanted to be brave and kill the mouse with his bare hands, but he was afraid of being bitten. Apart from the pain, mice carried all sorts of disgusting diseases. Sitting on the ground behind the shed, feeling the dry grass prickly against his bare legs, he weighed up his various options.

In the end he chose to kill it with a stick, pressing down against the creature's head until something cracked with a minute jolt rather than a sound. Spellbound, he watched a thin trickle of blood seep into the untreated wood. He couldn't explain what was happening, but he understood that something significant was taking place through a process he himself had initiated with his own hands inside a box he had made.

His mother's reaction when he handed her a dead mouse had been his first letdown in a life filled with disappointment.

'It's a present for you,' he told her proudly. 'I killed it myself.'

Her scream seemed to pierce his head. He was so shocked he dropped the mouse, which landed on the floor with a faint thud. Such a small sound for a dead body. His father came running into the kitchen. When his mother had recovered sufficiently to recount what had happened, his father scrubbed his hands before taking him into the living room and sitting him down.

'Where did you find the mouse?' he asked, his grey eyes sharp with concern.

'I trapped it,' he muttered, already less confident about boasting of his exploit.

'You mean you found it?'

He shook his head.

'Tell me exactly what happened.'

Pride in his accomplishment overcame his reticence as he recounted how he had set a trap in the garden and, after many attempts, had finally succeeded in catching a mouse.

'And the animal was dead when you found it?'

Something in his father's manner warned him to be cautious. 'Sort of,' he hedged.

'So you finished it off to put it out of its misery?'

He nodded. It was a weird way of describing his experience but even at such a young age he could sense it might be best to conceal his feelings. Later that day he heard his father explaining to his mother that he had wanted to end the creature's suffering.

'He said it was a present for me,' she replied in an odd stiff voice. 'He told me he killed it himself.' She burst into tears. 'If he had a little brother or sister to keep him company, he wouldn't be trying to copy Billy.'

He had often overheard his parents talking about wanting to give him a brother or sister. For some reason they were unable to do that. That was one of the disappointments of *their* lives but if they had bothered to ask him, he would have told them he was pleased not to have a noisy baby grabbing his toys, and hogging his parents' attention. They were better off as they were.

He never told either of his parents that the mouse had not only been alive, but completely unharmed, when he had caught it.

He hadn't expected the tiny creature to die so slowly. The memory made him smile. That, at least, hadn't been a disappointment.

1

THE ESTATE AGENT WAS apologetic about the state of the house.

'The paintwork needs touching up and the wallpaper's seen better days, but you can soon...'

'The wallpaper's not important,' he interrupted with an impatient wave of his hand.

Clearly heartened by his potential client's response, the estate agent continued. 'You're going to want to redecorate wherever you go. The windows will need replacing, eventually, but that's been taken into account in the asking price.'

The state of the house must have put a lot of buyers off. The agent tapped the window sill with one manicured fingernail finger as he spoke. Behind his fake grin his eyes were bright, alert to any sign of interest.

'The vendor might be persuaded to make a further reduction for a quick sale. It's been on the market for a while, at a higher price. He's only recently agreed to lower the asking price, so you've come along at just the right time. Once you've replaced the old windows with double glazed units, you'll hardly hear the trains going by.'

He nodded, but he wasn't really listening to the estate agent's chatter as he stood gazing out of the back window. The railway ran along the end of the garden. Beyond a thin screen of birch trees, trains travelled in a cutting below the level of the garden.

'You can't hear the trains at all from the front of the house, and it's a very quiet street, even during the day,' the estate agent assured him.

The house was set back from the road, with a high privet hedge shielding the front yard.

'It's very quiet,' the agent insisted, rubbing his white hands together and leaning forward, eager to close the sale. 'Once you've fixed the windows and seen to the damp, all you need to do is change the wallpaper and put a lick of paint around the place and it's going to look very nice indeed. You've got good sized rooms here. It's a real bargain. You won't find anything else this spacious at the price, not around here.'

He gave another nod to indicate he was listening.

'A lot of people like to buy a place that needs a bit of attention,' the agent continued, as though afraid the opportunity to sell the property would vanish the instant he stopped talking. 'It means you can have it however you want.'

'That's true.'

He didn't mention that he was in no hurry to decorate. Peeling wallpaper didn't bother him. What attracted him was something very different: a garden that wasn't overlooked from any direction. He waited a moment, telling the agent he wanted to hear a train go past the end of the garden. In reality, he wasn't interested in how much noise the trains made, only in whether their windows travelled below the level of his fence. He had to be sure he couldn't be seen by passengers rattling past.

The transaction was straightforward. He had already found a buyer for the house he had inherited from his parents. Moving in, he settled into his own private routine, content in his solitude. His demands were modest: to be left alone to pursue his hobby free from interference. Since he was a child he had listened to other people grumbling about their lot. Sometimes their complaints intrigued him. Mostly they amused him. The solution was so obvious. They just had to take whatever they wanted. He did.

Of course most people weren't as clever as him, and he had been fortunate in having a mother who was easy to manipulate.

His father had been more difficult. In the end the situation at home had become untenable. There couldn't be two of them in charge. But there had been a solution. There always was. He had laid his plans carefully for a very long time, watching and waiting, until at last the chance had presented itself. He found things usually worked out that way for someone who had the guts to seize opportunities when they came along. He had discovered he had the requisite courage quite early on in his life. It still made him smile when he remembered it. Everyone had been very sympathetic towards his mother, and very kind to him. They had all believed the fall had been an accident. No one had suspected a ten-year-old boy had been responsible for his father's death.

Over the years that followed he had honed his skill, so he knew what he was doing. The difficult part was to manage it without being caught. Once again, his patience served him well. He watched and waited until she was alone in her flat before slipping on his gloves and ringing the bell. His crude disguise of fake glasses, moustache and beard, were enough to mask his identity from the security cameras in her block. It was a simple matter to talk his way into her flat by convincing her he had been called to fix a dripping pipe because residents in the flat below had complained to the landlord that a leak was causing a damp patch on their ceiling.

'No one said anything to us about it,' the girl remonstrated.

He raised his eyebrows in feigned surprise. 'The landlord arranged it with your flatmate. It's not my fault if she forgot to tell you. But your landlord's going to hold you responsible for any further damage, if you refuse to let me in to fix it. It's no skin off my nose.' He gave a careless shrug. 'Let's hope your floor doesn't collapse.'

He almost smiled on seeing her worried frown. She believed every word of his story.

'You'd better come in, then,' she said.

He had come prepared, but he didn't have to use his own

weapon. The minute he walked into the kitchen he spotted a set of sharp knives on the worktop. A murder weapon that was already to hand would leave fewer clues for the police to follow up. As soon as she turned away he reached for the longest blade.

'Can I make you a cup of tea?' she asked, turning back to face him.

Without answering, he raised his arm and struck her a powerful blow in the middle of her chest. He felt the blade slide in and stop as it hit bone. Her blue eyes widened in shock and her mouth gaped open ready to scream, as he drew the knife out. Blood soaked her sweatshirt, cascading on to the floor. Before she could make a sound, with one swift movement he sliced across her mouth. Blood dripped from a macabre semblance of a grin that split her face. She staggered back against the worktop. Lunging forward, he slashed at her chest repeatedly, hoping the police would infer she had been killed by someone in a jealous rage, someone who knew her. A strange gurgling issued from her bloody lips as she sank to the floor, her sweatshirt drenched with blood. While he stood watching, fascinated, he barely noticed the knife slide from his grasp, the handle slippery with blood.

Whipping off his gloves, he pulled on a clean pair and bundled the wet ones into a plastic bag inside his rucksack, along with his bloody mac and trainers. There was no point in washing any of them. Traces of her blood would remain in the garments, and cling to the pipes of whatever washing machine he used, and to the seams and internal fabric of his shoes. Nor would he attempt to destroy the telltale clothes. Every time he moved them he risked leaving a trail for the police to follow, instead of which they would stay in the plastic bag, safely locked away where no one would ever find them. Too many killers were caught because they attempted to destroy evidence. That was stupid, because forensic examination could detect microscopic traces of blood and

DNA invisible outside of laboratory conditions. Far better to leave no clues.

Driving back to his lock-up garage, he started to plan his next outing.

2

GERALDINE WAS DOING HER best to feel pleased about her relocation from the Metropolitan Police force in London to the Major Investigation Team in York. Much about her move had gone well. For a start, she had found a tenant for her flat in North London straight away, and so far she liked what she had seen of the city of York. But she still wasn't sure if she had made the right choice. She had dithered briefly over whether to sell her London flat which would enable her to buy a small house in York, but she wasn't ready to make that commitment. Everything had happened so fast. She had only seen pictures of her rented apartment online. On arrival, she had been surprised at how spacious it was. The two bedrooms were perfectly adequate, and the large living room had a balcony with a stunning view overlooking the River Ouse. But the place belonged to someone else. It wasn't really her home.

After a week she was still finding it difficult to get used to her new bed. She had only just fallen asleep one night when her phone rang. Even though she was tired, force of habit quelled any temptation to ignore the call. She listened for a moment before climbing out of bed. After scrabbling frantically through her wardrobe to find something warm to wear, she set off. Although it had been a mild winter so far, the temperature in York in January was noticeably colder than in London. Freezing air hit her like a slap as she left the building. By the time she reached her destination, her car had barely warmed her up. Trying to control her shivering, she pulled on protective covering, and entered the house.

'Her killer was angry,' a scene of crime officer said when Geraldine had introduced herself.

'What makes you say that?'

He shook his head, looking around the confined space.

'Just because there's a lot of blood doesn't mean the attack was personal,' Geraldine added. 'He might be one of those sick people who enjoy carving people up.'

Her colleague's brow lowered in a scowl. 'That's true,' he admitted.

'And the killer could be a woman. At this stage we need to keep open-minded about everything.'

'But you have to admit it does look as if this was done by a man who was uncontrollably angry.'

'Admittedly her attacker was powerful,' Geraldine agreed.

'Yes, and it was a frenzied attack.'

'So you think she was killed by a man who was in a rage, and this was a crime of passion?'

'You think because that's a cliché it can't be true,' he replied.

She turned away from him to look at the body.

'There's a reason why things become clichés,' he added. 'It's because they're common, which means they're likely to be true.'

Geraldine looked around the blood-spattered walls and floor. 'I hope there's nothing common about a scene like this.'

She turned to gaze at the dead girl's bloody face. Her blue eyes were wide open, seemingly staring at the ceiling, her mouth stretched in a ghastly grin. Geraldine's gaze travelled to her chest which was drenched in blood from multiple stab wounds. Another scene of crime officer approached holding up a large evidence bag, and Geraldine was surprised to see a bloodstained knife inside it. This scene seemed to be full of clichés.

'You've got the weapon?'

The officer nodded. Above his mask his eyes crinkled in a smile. 'So it would appear.'

Geraldine returned his smile. Having the murder weapon should speed up the search for the killer. She took a quick look at the knife in the bag.

'The make is called Kitchen Devil,' the scene of crime officer said. 'There's a set of them in the kitchen. One of them's missing.' He held the bag up. 'It was lying on the floor beside the body where her assailant must have dropped it. The handle would have been slippery.'

Geraldine nodded. She had a similar set of knives in her own kitchen. With hard black plastic handles and sharp serrated blades they were useful, and very common. The murder weapon suggested the dead girl might have been the victim of a spontaneous attack, the killer seizing on whatever he could find, to assist him in his vicious attack. She knew she ought to resist drawing any conclusions from the scene, but she found it impossible not to try and piece together what must have happened.

'She might have been killed by a random opportunist,' she muttered tentatively, staring at the knife as though it could tell them who had used it to kill the girl.

She would have liked to stay longer at the scene, absorbing the setting and the atmosphere of the place while she waited to see what else the scene of crime officers might uncover, but she had to return to the police station in Fulford Road for a briefing. Leaving with what she thought would be plenty of time, she underestimated the volume of traffic around the centre of York and arrived with only minutes to spare. Dashing into the building from the car park, she found her colleagues already gathered in the major incident room. She had met a few of them since her arrival in York, but had only worked with one of them before. The detective chief inspector, Eileen Duncan, was probably not much older than Geraldine. Well built, with dark hair that was turning grey, she had a fierce look about her that Geraldine suspected might be an act to help her to maintain discipline. Briskly the detective chief inspector reviewed the facts so far.

The dead girl's name was Stephanie Crawford. She had grown up in the village of Uppermill in Saddleworth in West Yorkshire, where she had lived with her parents until she had moved to York a few months before her death. She had worked in a bank, and had shared a flat in York with another girl from her home village. It was the dead girl's flatmate, Ashley, who had found her body in the kitchen.

Ashley had been taken to the police station for questioning, leaving the flat cordoned off to minimise contamination. From what the constable looking after Ashley had said, it sounded as though she might be intending to return to her own family in Uppermill once the questioning was over. It must have been terrible, discovering her friend's body in their blood-splattered kitchen. Geraldine couldn't really imagine the shock she must have experienced. She was probably too traumatised to talk sensibly about what she had seen, but they had to speak to her and find out as much as they could before she went home to her family.

'Anyone have any thoughts on all of this so far?' Eileen asked in conclusion. 'Have I missed anything?'

Geraldine raised the possibility that the attack had been unplanned, since the murder weapon had been in the kitchen already.

'It's far too early to go jumping to conclusions,' a familiar voice responded. 'The murder could have been planned by someone who was familiar with the kitchen and knew in advance that the knife would be there.'

Geraldine couldn't help smiling at her former colleague, Ian Peterson, who had just spoken. She had chided him numerous times for jumping to conclusions, when he had been an eager young detective sergeant and she had been his detective inspector. Only now their roles were reversed: he was the inspector, and she was his sergeant. When the duty sergeant allocated their tasks, she was pleased and at the same time slightly nervous to see that she would be working with Ian.

She wondered whether he had requested her presence on his team, and how easy it would be for her to adjust to him being her senior officer.

3

ASHLEY LOOKED UP AS Ian and Geraldine entered the room.
'It was completely out of the blue,' she sobbed, before they
had even greeted her, as though death arriving unexpectedly
somehow intensified its finality. 'She was the last person on
earth to deserve this. I know Steph. We've been friends forever.
We were at school together.' She broke off again, and sniffed
loudly. 'She's always been so kind. She would never have hurt
anyone. Who could have done that to her?'

Ian introduced himself and Geraldine. 'Can you tell us what
happened?'

Ashley shook her head. 'I came home and went in the kitchen,
and she was just lying there. It was horrible.' Shuddering, she
dropped her head in her hands and sobbed uncontrollably.

Geraldine gazed at her shaking shoulders. She only looked
about twenty. The victim had probably been about the same
age. It wasn't entirely rational, but it always seemed more
upsetting when murder victims were young. So many years
of life had been snatched away from them. And for what? The
suffering caused by this meaningless loss of life could never
be assuaged.

'Who could have done it?' Ashley stammered. 'Why did it
happen? Why?'

Ian shook his head. 'I don't know. But we intend to find
out.' Leaning forward in his chair, he gazed intently at the
distraught girl. 'We'd like to ask you a few questions, if you
feel up to talking?'

Ashley nodded. 'I'll do my best, if it's going to help,' she mumbled. 'But there isn't much I can tell you. I wasn't there when it happened. I just came home and found her. Who did it? Why?'

'We don't know.' Geraldine repeated what Ian had just said. 'But we're going to do everything we can to find out who did this. First of all, did anyone else have a key to your apartment, apart from you and your flatmate?'

'No. Only us, and the man who owns the flat.'

The landlord was in Spain. He had already been questioned by local police. Shocked to hear that one of his tenants had been murdered on his property, he hadn't been able to share any information that might assist the investigation.

'Can you think of anyone who might have wanted to do this?'

Ashley shook her head.

'Did she have a boyfriend in York?'

'If she did, I didn't know about it.'

'You knew her before she came to York, didn't you?'

'Yes. We were at school together.'

She explained that she and her flatmate had moved to York only three months earlier. Geraldine and Ian already knew much of what she told them, but neither interrupted her. Geraldine wondered if Stephanie had been running away from someone. Three months might be enough time for a stalker to track her down.

'What brought you to York?' she asked.

'Stephanie was moving here so I applied for a transfer to York, and came here with her. We got this two-bedroomed flat. It was supposed to be fun… we were going to have fun…'

'What made her decide to come here?'

Ashley shrugged. Ian frowned as though Geraldine was posing the wrong questions, but she pressed on with her enquiry.

'Is it possible she was trying to get away from someone?'

Ashley looked startled by the suggestion, but she just shook her head.

'Can you think of anyone she knew before she came to York who might have wanted to harm her?' Geraldine persisted.

Ashley shook her head. 'No. She would have said. She did mention...' she hesitated.

'Yes?'

'It's probably nothing, but she did mention she had a violent boyfriend once, but that was a few years ago.'

'What was his name?'

Ashley shook her head. 'I don't know. I don't know. She didn't say. We were comparing notes, you know.'

'We're studying her phone and computer records,' Ian said. 'Would you recognise the name if you saw it? There might be a record of him somewhere.'

Ashley nodded. 'I'll try, but I don't think she ever mentioned anything else about him. It was just a casual conversation, you know.'

It seemed there was nothing more she could tell them. Urging her to contact them if she thought of anything else, they left her with a constable. The only possible lead they had was that the victim might have had a violent ex-boyfriend at some time in the past. It wasn't much to go on, but it was better than nothing.

Leaving the technical team to examine the dead girl's laptop and smart phone, Ian and Geraldine sat down in Ian's office to discuss the case before completing their decision logs. They both had the impression the attack had been personal. Certainly they hoped it had been. In a random assault, the killer might be more difficult to trace. Scene of crime officers were busy searching the apartment and the body was being examined by a pathologist. While they were waiting for more evidence, Ian wanted to speak to everyone who had been close to Stephanie. Her parents had been on holiday out of the country, but they had been contacted and were on their way back to England.

'They were only in France,' the borough intelligence officer told them, as though that made any real difference.

The years seemed to roll back as Geraldine found herself working on a murder case with Ian at her side once again.

'At least we have the murder weapon,' he said. 'And we know where it came from.'

'Which hasn't helped us. In fact, it's made things more difficult for us.'

'How so? We know the forensic team have confirmed the killer was wearing gloves, and they've found no match for the partial DNA sample they were able to find on the knife, but that would be the same with any murder weapon, and at least this way we don't have to spend time and resources searching for it.' He smiled. 'No time wasted lifting floorboards and digging up gardens.'

'But knowing it was already there means we don't know whether this was an unpremeditated attack by someone who was in the flat anyway, or an attack planned by someone who knew in advance that the set of knives was to hand in the kitchen, or a killer who turned up already armed and chose to use a knife that was there instead of the weapon he had brought with him.' Geraldine tried to conceal her impatience, but she couldn't help feeling that Ian was prioritising deployment of manpower over detection. 'Come on, you're not thinking about this, Ian. A weapon that was already there gives us no clues at all to the killer's identity.'

Ian frowned. Accustomed to being the senior officer in their working relationship, Geraldine hoped she hadn't been insolent. She needed to adapt to the fact that she was now Ian's sergeant, and she needed to make that adjustment quickly. She wondered if it had crossed his mind that relations between them could become awkward, if they weren't both careful. But he merely acknowledged her concerns with a nod and said nothing about her patronising tone.

He was keen to follow up the suggestion that the dead girl had once had a violent boyfriend. Having set a constable to look into the victim's past contacts, he ordered Geraldine back to her desk to write up her decision log. She was slightly taken aback by his peremptory tone and tried to remember if she had been similarly imperious towards him when *she* had been *his* inspector. She thought she had done her best to treat him as an equal, but when he had worked as her sergeant she had been older and more experienced than him. Now that their roles were reversed, she remained older and more experienced. Perhaps he was feeling insecure. All she could do was bite her tongue and behave as though she had never worked with him before.

Before they left the police station at the end of the day, Ian asked Geraldine to be present when the dead girl's parents identified the body the following morning. She was happy to agree. Although invariably painful, meeting bereaved family members sometimes revealed information about the victim's life which could make the encounter useful. Having finalised the arrangements, she packed up her things and left, relieved to return to the quiet solitude of her new flat.

Looking around her living room, she liked the fact that she had not yet accumulated any clutter. She had abandoned her few ornaments when she had moved, determined to keep her new flat as orderly as possible. It was part of her resolution to leave her life in London behind her. The solitary photograph she had of her mother was hidden away in the drawer beside her bed, and the one frame containing pictures of Celia and her family was displayed in the living room mainly for their satisfaction should they visit. Other than those few pictures and a small collection of books, everything in the flat was as functional and impersonal as it had been on the day she had taken up residence there.

Having seen numerous homes crammed with possessions, she was still surprised by the quantity of junk other people hoarded.

'Why do you keep all this?' she had asked her sister, Celia, one day.

'What?'

'All this stuff.'

Genuinely curious, Geraldine had pointed to a wall of shelving filled with vases, photos, books, magazines, random teapots and decorative plates, ornamental bookends, half-finished knitting, fossils and shells presumably collected from various beaches, a plastic box that Chloe must have made at school, together with all sorts of other bric-a-brac. Visibly indignant, Celia had been quick to point out that everything Geraldine dismissed as rubbish in fact had significant sentimental value, from their mother's favourite teapot, to Chloe's discoveries and handiwork.

'I couldn't part with any of it,' Celia had insisted.

Looking around her own sparsely furnished flat Geraldine felt pleased. She had the view through her window to look at; the river and sky were enough for her. She didn't need anything else. But her gaze moved to the photograph of her sister and her niece, and her thoughts drifted to the picture of her dead mother, hidden away beside her bed. She sighed. She was no different to other people who hoarded memorabilia from their lives. It was just that she had spent most of her adult life focusing on dead strangers who left her no souvenirs.

4

PEOPLE MADE SUCH A fuss, as though it was something out of the ordinary, when in reality anyone with a modicum of sense must realise that murders were commonplace. It just suited the authorities to hush them up. Their puppets in the media were no better. Most of the population were happy to buy into the fiction that, by and large, criminals were caught and locked up. It made everyone feel safe, which was good for maintaining order and helped protect the status quo. He didn't mind. He had no interest in exposing the truth. Far better to let people carry on believing the police had the situation under control. It meant people were less vigilant, and that made life much easier for him.

It didn't take long for the police to turn up, lights flashing and sirens blaring. Men and women in uniform leapt out of their vehicles, scurried in and out of the house, stopped passersby, and put up a cordon across the street. From an upstairs window a few doors away across the road, he had a clear view of what was going on. The following day he would be gone. He had only been using the place for the weekend, watching and hoping for an opportunity to find his victim at home alone. The owners of the house he had broken into could be back at any time, but he was banking on them being away for the weekend. In the meantime he had been careful. He hadn't removed his gloves, or touched anything in the place for fear of leaving a record of his presence. He had held his breath as he raced up the stairs and now stood by an open window, to minimise his breathing inside the house. Hopefully no one would ever discover he had been there, and the police would have no cause to search for a trace of the DNA he had inevitably left behind, in spite of his prudence.

The uniformed officers were irrelevant. He was only interested in the plain clothes detectives. They were the ones who would be hunting for him. A few of them had been and gone. Before he had time to slip away, a new investigating team appeared: a man and a woman, both tall; the man blond, the woman dark-haired. The man arrived first. Young, broad-shouldered, with a powerful physique, from across the road he looked more like a construction worker than a police officer as he marched up the path to the front door, exuding energy. The woman arrived shortly after him. From a distance her face looked pale and beautiful, but there was something daunting about her air of authority as she strode along the pavement and up the path to the front door. Clearly she was there on business. And what other business could take her into that house just hours after a young woman had been stabbed to death there? No doubt she was a police detective come to poke about at the scene of the crime, searching for clues.

He smiled as she disappeared through the front door. If she thought she was going to find anything that would lead her to the girl's killer, she was going to be disappointed. Although it was true that many murderers killed to vent their feelings, not everyone was that stupid. Ordinary murderers were quickly apprehended because they lost control of their emotions and made mistakes. The cunning killers, the ones who got away with it, were the ones who plotted their actions deliberately and carefully, leaving nothing to chance. So far everything had gone according to plan, but it was important not to become complacent. The slightest slip could lead to discovery.

As long as the police were looking for him, he had to stay one step ahead of them. He wondered how much they knew. From his post along the road, he was able to see everyone who entered and left the house. There was a period of commotion, then the front door closed for a while. After the flurry of activity, he grew bored sitting in the window for hours with the lights off, watching and waiting, but his vigilance paid off because at last the front door opened and the two detectives emerged. The man went rapidly back to his car but this time the woman walked along the drive slowly, no longer in a hurry. When she reached the gate she lingered for a moment. It looked as though she was going to turn round and go back in the house. Appearing to make up her mind, she carried on through the gate, back towards her car. Dashing down the stairs, he barely had time to leap into the car he had hired before she turned the corner and disappeared. He put his foot down.

On the face of it, stalking a police detective was a dodgy strategy, crazy even. But in addition to superior intelligence, boldness was a characteristic ordinary killers lacked. As was patience, for that matter. Although his plan might involve many more hours of tedious watching and waiting, it would be worth it. If she was not on her way there already, eventually the dark-haired detective would go home. The more information he discovered about her, the easier it would be to find out how much the police knew about him. If his plan worked, she was going to end up helping to protect the very person she was trying to arrest for murder.

5

GERALDINE WOULD NEVER HAVE left London had the move not been forced on her. She had been confronted with a stark choice: accept a demotion and move to another police force, or resign. She had chosen to accept the offer to relocate. Although this was hardly her ideal career path, she had broken the law in an attempt to protect her twin sister, hoping to rescue her from a life of addiction. Given the choice, she would do the same again. She felt she had no choice. Helena was her twin sister, and Geraldine had promised her dying mother she would take care of her. So far Geraldine's sacrifice appeared to have succeeded, and her sister had come through a rehabilitation programme. But Geraldine was aware that as a recovering user, her sister lived at constant risk of falling victim to her addiction again.

Now Geraldine was making the best of her new situation as a sergeant on a new team. The next morning she went to the police station to check in with Ian and attend a briefing.

'Well?' Eileen barked. 'You were there, Ian. Bring us all up to speed. What was your impression of Stephanie's flatmate?'

Ian cleared his throat. Geraldine was surprised to see he looked nervous. She had never noticed such hesitation in his demeanour when he had been working with her. They had always got on too well for that. Dismissing a flutter of anxiety, she hoped the same level of trust would develop between him and Eileen. Briefly Ian reported what he had discovered at the crime scene. He turned to Geraldine. She understood that he was waiting for her to comment but before she could start, a constable spoke.

'I've questioned the next-door neighbours on both sides,' she said.

Geraldine turned to look at the speaker. In her twenties, Detective Constable Naomi Arthur was blond and slender. Although they had only been briefly introduced, somehow Geraldine wasn't surprised to hear Naomi speak out without being asked. Young enough to be Geraldine's daughter, she displayed an air of forceful efficiency, and had already struck Geraldine as overtly confident. Ian didn't interrupt Naomi, and Geraldine had to wait in silence until the constable had finished her report. Naomi was succinct and clearly bright. She would probably soon be promoted to sergeant. Doing her best to suppress her bitterness at herself being demoted to sergeant, Geraldine felt a flicker of resentment at the prospect of being the same rank as a colleague so much younger and less experienced than herself. But it couldn't be helped. She had brought her disgrace on herself and had to put up with the consequences stoically.

After the briefing, Geraldine collected an unmarked police car and set off for the mortuary. Ian had told her only that the pathologist was pleasant and professional. Geraldine was happy to know very little about him. It would be easy to let Ian fill her in on everyone, but it was better to make up her own mind about the people she met. She found the hospital easily and made her way to the back entrance which led straight to the mortuary. A young blond woman let her in. Introducing herself as Avril, she led Geraldine along the corridor, chatting cheerfully.

'Jonah's not quite finished, but I'm sure he won't mind you coming along to see the victim now. He's very relaxed about things like that. He never objected to Ian coming along anyway, but everyone gets on well with Ian, don't they? Will he be coming along later?'

Geraldine gave a non-committal grunt.

'Don't worry about the parents,' Avril went on. 'They haven't arrived yet, but I'll look after them until Jonah's ready to let them view the body. She was quite young, you know, and I think she'd only been in York for a few months. Here we are.'

Geraldine drew her own conclusions about what Avril thought of Ian, as the young woman handed her a mask and pushed open the door. The forensic pathologist was humming to himself as Geraldine entered. He was a plump man in his forties, with ginger hair and pale freckled skin. When he glanced up, his blue eyes twinkled brightly at her above his pug nose.

'No Ian?' he greeted her.

Geraldine tried not to feel peeved that both Avril and the pathologist seemed disappointed to see her in place of her colleague.

'No, he was busy, but he sends his greetings,' she fibbed.

She knew that Ian avoided attending post mortems if he could. For a detective working on murder investigations he was surprisingly squeamish.

'Oh well,' the pathologist replied, smiling at her, 'he wouldn't have sent you along if you weren't up to the job. Jonah Hetherington, at your service.'

His tone implied that although he was prepared to make do with Geraldine, he would have preferred to see Ian.

'Geraldine Steel, Ian's sergeant,' she replied, stopping herself just in time from introducing herself as a detective inspector. 'So,' she went on, turning to the cadaver, 'what have you got for us?' There was a slight hiatus, as though she had spoken out of turn.

'We're looking at a young woman, barely out of her teens,' he began.

'She was twenty-two.'

'Exactly. She had no physical problems as far as I've been able to ascertain, and had suffered no serious injuries before this.'

He pointed to the white chest, scored with several lacerations.

'These are deep incisions,' he said. 'The murder weapon wasn't razor sharp, so it didn't slice easily through her chest. Whoever attacked her went at it with a will.'

'Would you describe it as a frenzied attack?' Geraldine asked, remembering her earlier conversation with Ian.

Jonah frowned. 'That's a very emotive word, and I'm afraid it's not for me to draw any conclusions about the motivation driving the attack. The blows the killer struck were extremely powerful, but it's impossible to say whether her attacker had been whipped up into a rage, or was just determined to make sure he killed her.'

'Perhaps he was enjoying himself,' Geraldine added.

Jonah threw her a curious glance before continuing. 'Any one of those injuries might have proved fatal without immediate medical attention, and even if she'd been attended to without any delay at all, she might not have survived the trauma.'

'How many times was she struck?'

'Seven, possibly eight. It looks as though she was slashed twice in the same place,' he added by way of explanation.

'Can you tell us anything about the killer?'

Jonah looked surprised. 'What do you mean? You can see what happened.' He indicated the body. 'She was stabbed to death.'

Geraldine paused. She was used to working with a pathologist in London who was happy to speculate, off the record, about the events at crime scenes. He would willingly share his theories about the physique and motivation of unknown killers. But it had taken time for Geraldine to convince him that she was discreet. Jonah had only just met her.

'We found a scraping of skin under one of her finger nails,' he went on. 'It wasn't hers.'

'Are you sure?' Geraldine asked with a rush of excitement. 'How long had it been there?'

'Since around the time of her death.'

'And it definitely wasn't hers?'

'The DNA analysis shows it was a man but there's no match on the database.'

Geraldine nodded, doing her best to hide her disappointment at the anonymity of the DNA sample.

'Was there any evidence of sexual assault or any sexual activity at all shortly before she was killed?'

'No, nothing.'

'Off the record, Jonah, can you give me anything else? I won't tell anyone.'

Jonah raised his eyebrows, but he was grinning. 'Off the record?' he repeated. 'You won't even tell Ian?'

Geraldine hesitated. Until recently she had been a detective inspector. She would have been seriously vexed if her sergeant had kept anything from her. Now she was hinting at doing just that. As an inspector her request wouldn't have been questioned. She bit her lip. She had to remember that she was now a detective sergeant, and needed to adapt her behaviour accordingly. Jonah winked at her, well aware that she was going to pass on to Ian any information she gleaned.

'I used to work with Ian, when he was a sergeant,' she said, hoping that her long relationship with Ian would inspire confidence in the pathologist.

There was no need to mention that she had once been Ian's senior officer, and that their roles were now reversed. After she had been working in York for a while, and her colleagues knew her, she wouldn't care so much if they found out what had happened. But for now she preferred to keep her recent history to herself. First impressions were difficult to shake off. She didn't want to start out with everyone knowing she had been demoted.

'The fact that we can analyse the DNA is good news,' she said.

He nodded. 'Yes, we should be able to learn something about the killer, even if we can't come up with a name. And look here.' Shining a bright light on the victim's face, he pointed to her cheeks on either side of her lips. A wound across the victim's mouth had been neatly concealed. 'We've patched her face up for the viewing.'

Geraldine nodded. The injuries to the victim's chest could remain hidden beneath the covers, but her parents would have to see her face to confirm her identity.

'She looked ghastly when she came in, enough to give anyone nightmares, and certainly not in a fit state for her parents to see her.'

Geraldine praised his handiwork.

'With any luck, they won't notice it,' Jonah said. 'She wasn't a pretty sight.'

'How did it happen?' Geraldine asked.

He shrugged. 'Our kindly killer slashed her across the mouth, while she was still alive and breathing. God only knows why.'

Before either of them could say anything else, the door opened and Avril came in to inform them that the victim's parents had arrived.

Jonah nodded. 'She's almost ready. Give me five minutes.'

'Right,' Avril smiled as she withdrew.

Geraldine wondered how they could remain so cheerful knowing a bereaved couple were in the next room, waiting to see their dead daughter. She always found the living more painful to deal with than the dead. At least they were at peace.

'After life's fitful fever she sleeps well,' she muttered.

'What's that?' Jonah asked.

'Nothing. Just something I remember from school.'

'Macbeth.'

Geraldine was surprised he recognised the quotation, but before she could respond he turned away. 'Time to get her ready.'

6

REMOVING HER MASK, GERALDINE followed Avril along the corridor and through a door marked 'Mortuary – Visitor Suite'. The room was delicately scented, with a few anodyne watercolours hanging on the walls and a vase of flowers on one of the tables. There was a drinks machine, and several boxes of tissues placed within reach of all the chairs. Everything had been thoughtfully arranged to support visitors' needs. But none of it offered much comfort to the people who came and sat there.

The victim's parents were younger than Geraldine had expected. Mrs Crawford was small and plump; her husband was tall and thin. They must have been very young when their daughter was born, because they couldn't have been older than their mid-forties now. Both of them were very pale. They were standing motionless, side by side, staring at the floor, ignoring the sofa and armchairs in the room.

'Mr and Mrs Crawford?' The door swung closed behind her. 'I'm Detective Sergeant Geraldine Steel. Can we sit down? I'd like to ask you a few questions.'

Mr Crawford stirred. Reaching out to grasp his wife's hand, he stared at the wall behind Geraldine's head.

'You don't know it's her yet, do you?'

Geraldine hesitated. 'We need you to identify her.'

She didn't say what they all knew, that this was just a formality. Ashley had found her dead friend in their shared kitchen.

'She'll be ready for you in a few minutes,' she added.

'But you don't know it's our daughter in there, do you? All you know is that a girl was killed in her flat. It could be anyone,' Mr Crawford insisted.

His eyes were bright with repressed desperation. Geraldine didn't answer.

'Do we have to go in there?' Mrs Crawford asked. 'I'm not sure... I don't think I can...'

Her husband pushed his shoulders back and straightened his back. Then he looked directly at Geraldine.

'I'll come with you,' he said. 'We need to know.'

'Don't leave me alone here,' Mrs Crawford stammered.

'Avril will stay with you,' Geraldine reassured her.

Leaving the distraught mother behind, Geraldine led Mr Crawford along the hushed corridor to view the body. Steeling herself to witness his grief, she was relieved when he merely nodded his head, too shocked to speak. His face remained fixed in an impassive glare. Only his eyes burned with unspoken grief.

'That's her,' he whispered at last, choking on the words. 'That's our Stephanie.'

In place of pity, Geraldine felt only an overwhelming relief that the wound on his daughter's face was no longer visible. Without a word she led him back to the visitors' lounge. His wife took one look at his face and broke down in tears.

'No, no,' she wailed, dropping her face in her hands and sobbing.

'I know this is difficult for you,' Geraldine said, 'but I need to ask you a few questions about Stephanie. We can do this now, or I can come and see you tomorrow.'

Mr Crawford put his arm around his wife. 'I'm sorry, but we can't talk right now. Please...' his voice broke.

Turning away, he buried his face in his wife's shoulder. After glancing helplessly at Avril, Geraldine withdrew.

The following morning, Eileen held a brief meeting to review the investigation so far. The main topic of discussion was the

DNA that had been discovered on the body. Even without a positive identification, the sample of skin could reveal a lot about Stephanie's attacker. Establishing the gender and ethnicity of the killer could help to eliminate suspects, when they had any, and with luck they would be able to positively identify her attacker.

After the meeting, Geraldine drove out to see Stephanie's parents in their home. The area of Saddleworth in the West Riding of Yorkshire was over an hour's drive from York through rugged countryside. It was an invigorating journey, all the more enjoyable because she was pleased to leave the confines of the police station in Fulford Road. It was early days, but so far working as a sergeant in York felt very different to being an inspector in London. She wasn't sure that anyone but Ian and Eileen knew that she had been demoted. No one appeared curious about her move out of London, but she felt compelled to stay on her guard at work. Probably no one would care, or even notice, if she addressed a fellow sergeant as though she was their superior officer, but it would be all too easy for her to gain a reputation for being haughty, if she wasn't careful. She had to keep reminding herself that she was no longer an inspector.

Uppermill was an attractive village of soft yellowish York stone nestling in a valley, the houses and shops dominated by a tall church steeple. A canal ran parallel to the main thoroughfare, set back from it. Passing a pub, Geraldine left the High Street and drove up a narrow road with cars parked on both sides. Reaching a Victorian civic hall, she turned right and stopped outside a row of terraced houses where the dead girl's parents lived.

Mrs Crawford answered the door looking drawn, and so pale that the resemblance to her dead daughter was uncanny.

'The paper reported she was stabbed several times,' Mrs Crawford said dully as soon as Geraldine sat down in the front room.

'She would have been killed by the first blow.' Geraldine feigned a confidence she didn't feel. It could have been true. 'She wouldn't have suffered.'

Mr Crawford entered in time to hear Geraldine's comment. 'I thought it took four minutes for a person to die,' he said, his face twisted in a sour expression.

'But she would have lost consciousness straight away,' Geraldine countered, as firmly as she could.

Desperately sorry for them both, she had no wish to be insensitive. Nevertheless, she had travelled a long way to speak to them and didn't want to leave there without answers to her questions. Instead of sitting down, Mrs Crawford went off to the kitchen to make tea. Geraldine suspected she wanted to avoid having to talk about what had happened.

'It's hit her very hard,' Mr Crawford muttered when his wife was out of the room.

It was hardly surprising.

Geraldine reiterated her condolences. 'I can't express my sympathy strongly enough, but at the same time we do need to find out who did this,' she said gently. 'We all want to see justice done for the sake of your daughter's memory. And until we have her killer behind bars, there's a chance he might attack another young woman. So we need to find him urgently.'

'You said he?'

'We don't know who did this. But we intend to find out.'

Mrs Crawford returned. She sat down, and began weeping silently. Mr Crawford was better able to control his emotions, although Geraldine could tell he had been crying earlier.

'We'll do anything we can do to help you find out who did this, won't we, Wendy?'

Unable to speak, his wife nodded her head.

'I understand you have a son?' Geraldine asked.

'Yes. But he's not in,' Mr Crawford replied. 'He's not often here.'

'He spends a lot of time rehearsing,' his wife explained,

stifling her sobs and smiling faintly. 'He's in a band with some of his friends from school. A rock band.'

'I might have to come back and speak to him.' Seeing Mr and Mrs Crawford exchange a worried glance, Geraldine continued, 'Is that a problem?'

Mr Crawford shook his head. 'Not at all.'

'It's just that he's – he's difficult,' his wife said. 'He's twenty,' she added as though that were sufficient explanation of her son's conduct.

'Did he and Stephanie get on well?' Geraldine asked.

There was an awkward pause, before Mr Crawford assured her his children had got on 'well enough'.

Despite their assurances that they wanted to help, the Crawfords had little to add to what Geraldine already knew about their daughter. She moved on to the subject of Stephanie's ex-boyfriends.

'Her flatmate, Ashley, mentioned that she had a boyfriend who was violent?'

The couple exchanged a worried glance. Mrs Crawford shook her head at her husband who looked at Geraldine helplessly.

'Not that we know of,' he replied. 'I don't know that he was ever violent.'

'If he was, she never said anything to us,' his wife concurred.

Geraldine asked them for a list of all their daughter's ex-boyfriends. According to her parents, Stephanie had been in a relationship with a man called Tony Palmer for three years. They had only recently split up, and shortly after that she had moved to York. She had been in two other brief relationships before meeting Tony, neither of which had been serious, according to her mother.

'They were still at school,' Mrs Crawford explained. 'They were just children. It was different with Tony. We could all see it was serious. When she went to live with him, we thought she was going to marry him.'

'She ought to have got that ring on her finger before she ever moved into his house,' her husband added bitterly.

'After they split up, she went off to York in a fit of pique,' Mrs Crawford said.

'She was hoping he'd run after her,' Mr Crawford added. 'If she hadn't gone off like that, this would never have happened.'

'We begged her to stay here, with us. She didn't have to go off to the city like that. She would have been safe here…' Mrs Crawford said. Her voice broke.

'What's Tony like?' Geraldine asked gently. 'I'm sorry to press you but we need to follow up any possible suspects. Do you think Tony could have been angry with her for going off like that?'

'Angry enough to kill her?' Mr Crawford shrugged. 'Tony seems like a cold fish, but I don't think he'd have hurt her.'

'I never liked him,' his wife added.

'You say that now, but you never had a bad word to say about him when they were together.'

'I thought he was going to look after her.'

'Do you know why they split up?' Geraldine asked.

'He dumped her for someone else,' Mrs Crawford answered sharply.

'You don't know that,' her husband said. 'No one saw them together until after Stephanie left Uppermill.'

'It was pretty soon after she went,' his wife snapped. 'It stands to reason he was seeing that cow before he and Stephanie broke up.'

Geraldine made a note of Tony Palmer's address, and left soon after that. Having reported the names of the other two men so they could be traced, she went to see Tony Palmer, wondering if he could be the violent ex-boyfriend Stephanie's flatmate had talked about. The dead girl's medical records had shown no injuries reported since she had broken her leg as a child, a history borne out by the detailed notes from the post mortem. If Tony had been violent towards her, he had been very careful to leave no trace of physical abuse. And if the Crawfords' account was accurate, it sounded as though Stephanie was the one who had reason to be angry with Tony, rather than the other way around. All the same, Geraldine was keen to talk to him.

7

THE WOMAN WHO CAME to the door was too young to be Tony Palmer's mother, but she looked too old to be his girlfriend. Her square shoulders were oddly out of proportion with her thin arms, giving her the appearance of a badly formed doll.

'A detective sergeant?' she repeated when Geraldine introduced herself. A wary expression flitted across her face. 'Is there some sort of problem?'

Geraldine explained that she wanted to speak to Tony Palmer. 'He does live here, doesn't he?'

'Well, yes,' the woman hesitated.

'Is he here now?'

'What's this about?'

Geraldine answered the question with another. 'Are you related to him?'

'I'm his girlfriend. We're not married, if that's any business of yours,' she added quickly. 'It's not a crime to live with someone. So what do you want with him?'

'I'd like to speak with him,' Geraldine repeated patiently. 'Is he here?'

When the woman hesitated, Geraldine took a step forward.

'Look, you can't come barging into my house like this without any warning...'

'Very well. In that case please tell Tony a patrol car will be outside your house in five minutes to pick him up and drive him over to the police station in York.'

She turned away and took out her phone.

'No, wait!' the woman called out. 'Wait right here! I'll tell him you're here.'

The front door closed. A few moments later it opened again to reveal a man in his early thirties. He had a delicate face with high cheekbones, and a pointed chin. Above his dark eyes, very thin eyebrows rose in surprise. Tall and slender, he moved with a grace that made him look effeminate. He turned to the blond woman at his side with a baffled expression. She shrugged and suggested that Geraldine must be mistaken.

'Are you sure it's me you want? I haven't broken the law,' he stammered.

'This is about your ex-girlfriend, Stephanie Crawford.'

He seemed to tense, instantly on his guard. It wasn't clear if that was because his current girlfriend was standing right beside him, or because he had something to hide.

'She's got nothing to do with us,' his girlfriend snapped. 'Whatever she's done, it's none of his business. Like you said, she's his ex. He doesn't know her any more.' She glared at Tony. 'You don't have anything to do with her any more, do you?'

Ignoring the interruption, Geraldine spoke to Tony. 'Stephanie's dead.'

'What?' He gasped. 'Stephanie's dead?'

'She was murdered,' Geraldine added softly.

'Murdered? What do you mean?' His expression of shock appeared genuine. 'That's not possible. I mean, I would have heard.'

'Why would anyone tell you? You don't have anything to do with her now. She's history,' his girlfriend said. She turned to Geraldine. 'That's terrible, but it's got nothing to do with Tony. He doesn't see her any more.'

'Wait, Amy. I want to know…' he turned to Geraldine. 'How did it happen?'

'Tony, it's got nothing to do with you…'

'I want to know what happened.'

Peevish rather than angry, he didn't strike Geraldine as an

aggressive man, but she knew how deceptive appearances could be.

'How did it happen?' he bleated.

'Can I come in?'

As she stepped into a narrow hallway, Geraldine turned to Amy and asked her to put the kettle on. With a scowl, Amy nodded and hurried away to the kitchen as Tony led Geraldine into an untidy sitting room, the carpet partly hidden under several piles of glossy magazines. Stepping over them, he sat down on one of two matching armchairs and invited Geraldine to sit opposite him on the other.

'What happened?' he repeated.

Briefly, Geraldine told him what she knew.

He frowned. 'Stabbed? But why? Who would have done that?'

'That's what we need to find out. Tony, can you think of anyone who might have wanted to harm Stephanie?'

He shook his head.

'Her flatmate told us that she once had a boyfriend who was violent.'

He looked surprised. 'What do you mean?'

'Tony,' she leaned forward and lowered her voice. 'If we discover anything in Stephanie's medical records that indicates she was injured while you were seeing her, or at some point after you split up...'

'You won't,' Amy said firmly, entering the room.

Geraldine glanced up at her as she placed a tray down on a magazine lying on a low table.

'Tony never raised a finger against that girl. He couldn't have. He's not like that. I should know. I live with him.'

'Thank you for the tea. I'd like to speak to Tony alone now, please.'

'Well, that's not going to happen. There's no way you're sending me out of the room in my own house, sergeant or no sergeant, so...'

'If we can't conduct our conversation here,' Geraldine cut in abruptly, 'then Tony will have to come to the police station in York so we can speak properly. Tony,' she turned back to him, 'you're not a suspect. But you did know Stephanie, and we're currently speaking to everyone who knew her. We'll need to speak to you as well,' she added, turning back to Amy. 'Would I be right in suggesting you had a grudge against Tony's ex-girlfriend? You don't seem comfortable with him talking about her. Perhaps you wanted her out of the way?'

'Oh for goodness sake,' Amy cried out. 'I never even met the girl, not to talk to. Are you going to treat everyone you meet as a suspect?'

'In a murder investigation, everyone who knew the victim is a suspect, yes,' Geraldine replied severely, 'and anyone who seems reluctant to assist us in our investigation is bound to attract our attention. Now, would you please let me speak to Tony alone? And then perhaps I can have a word with you? At the moment, I'm only here to eliminate you from our enquiries. So far there's been nothing to suggest either of you is under suspicion, apart from your unwillingness to assist the investigation.'

'Oh, all right,' Amy conceded disagreeably, 'you've made your point. I'm going.'

When they were alone, Geraldine invited Tony to tell her about his relationship with Stephanie.

He assured her the affair had ended by mutual agreement. 'We both agreed our relationship was going nowhere. Her parents were pressurising her to get married but neither of us was sure that was what we wanted. Not with each other, anyway. There wasn't any falling out, nothing like that. She wanted to move to York and see a bit of life...' he broke off, his voice trembling. After a moment he regained his composure. 'She thought I was a boring stick-in-the-mud because I was happy to stay here in Uppermill. But it's a beautiful place. Why would I leave? She said she wanted to experience life in the city. So she went ahead and got herself a job in York. She wanted me to go with her, but I think she knew deep down that was never going to happen.' He sighed. 'We just wanted different things. She was more than ten years younger than me. I think that had something to do with it. I'm thirty-five.'

Geraldine wondered if that was why he had turned to an older woman once Stephanie had left him. He seemed a reticent kind of man, tall and gentle and rather weak. She asked him to provide a DNA sample to eliminate him from their enquiries, but somehow she doubted that Tony was the killer they were searching for.

8

A HEAVY FOG WAS descending as Geraldine drove out of Uppermill. If she had brought an overnight bag with her she wouldn't have hesitated to check into the pub on the main street, since she had to return to the village the next day to speak to the dead girl's other ex-boyfriend. It occurred to her for the first time how very different working in York was going to be, compared to her job in London where volume of traffic was a problem, rather than distances travelled. Despite her reservations, the journey back to York wasn't too heavy going, although it was miserable. She was always able to see far enough ahead to be able to drive comfortably and although the roads were likely to be icy overnight, they had not yet frozen over. A faint sleety drizzle began to fall as she approached the city and she was pleased when she could stop and get out of the car to stretch her legs.

Focused on her driving, she had given her visit to Uppermill little thought on her journey. Back at her desk, writing up her findings, she struggled to report her conviction that Tony wasn't responsible for Stephanie's murder. As an inspector in London, she had grown accustomed to working with colleagues who were prepared to follow her instincts. Her former detective chief inspector had often been impatient with her for following her hunches before she had sufficient evidence, but even he had come to acknowledge that her gut feeling rarely let her down. Now, without the trust of her colleagues, she no longer felt the same confidence in her own instincts.

Weighing everything up, it seemed wise to be circumspect

in her comments about Tony Palmer. Avoiding insisting too firmly on her own impression, she focused instead on his good relationship with his new partner and his surprise on hearing about Stephanie's death, which had seemed genuine. She hoped Eileen wouldn't dismiss her comments as naive. Ian wasn't around, so she went home as soon as she had finished writing up her report.

On Monday morning she set off very early for Saddleworth once more. Peter Edwards, one of Stephanie's former boyfriends, still lived there. The other one had moved to America two years before her death and had not returned to the UK since. The young man she was going to visit lived in a village a few miles from Uppermill where he rented a room in a house on the main street. She hadn't called ahead, because she wanted to catch him off guard before he left for work.

Once again, it was a woman who opened the door. She looked about sixty.

'Yes, dear? How can I help you?' She smiled enquiringly at Geraldine.

When Geraldine explained what she was doing there, the landlady invited her in without any questions.

'Wait here and I'll call Peter down,' she said. 'He's upstairs in his room. At least, I haven't heard him go out yet.'

Leaving Geraldine sitting in a cosy front room, she disappeared. A moment later Geraldine heard her going upstairs. She returned with a young man in jeans and a crumpled T-shirt, who gave the impression he had just climbed out of bed and pulled on whatever clothes he had been wearing the previous evening. His feet were bare. Brushing his untidy fair hair out of his eyes, he sat down opposite Geraldine while his landlady bustled about putting the kettle on, making a pot of tea.

'I'll just pop some toast on, shall I?' she asked. 'Or would you prefer a tea cake?'

'I'm sorry but this isn't a social call,' Geraldine interrupted her. 'I need to have a word with Peter on his own. Thank you,' she added as the landlady poured them all a cup of tea.

The landlady left and Geraldine closed the door behind her before turning back to Peter who was blinking sleepily.

'What's this about?' he asked. 'Who did you say you were?'

Sipping his tea as she introduced herself, he seemed to wake up.

'A detective? What do you mean?'

As he registered what she was saying, his expression grew wary. He glanced guiltily around the room, as though looking for an escape route. Accustomed to being treated with suspicion, Geraldine didn't read too much into his reaction. Even people completely innocent of any wrongdoing could feel uncomfortable when she visited them at home in her official capacity. And few people she spoke to were completely innocent. She had heard many unforced apologies for petty misdemeanours while she had been pursuing murder enquiries.

'I haven't done anything wrong,' he began.

'I'd like to talk to you about Stephanie Crawford.'

'Steph?' He frowned. 'I haven't seen her in a while. I heard she's gone to York. Why? What's she done?'

While he wasn't particularly forthcoming, Peter soon convinced her that he knew nothing about Stephanie's recent history. His shock on hearing that Stephanie had been murdered seemed authentic.

'She was with this guy Tony Palmer,' he told her, obviously trying to be helpful. 'But they split up a while back, and he's with some other woman now.' He shook his head. 'I don't think he's got anything to do with it. Tony's a nice guy. A bit soft, but nice.'

'Tell me about your relationship with Stephanie.'

He shook his head again, helplessly. 'It was years ago. We were still at school. This has got nothing to do with me. And now I'm going to be late for work if I don't leave soon.'

His face had turned pale and he looked frightened. Ignoring his last comment, Geraldine continued with her questions.

'When did you last see her?'

'Shit, I can't remember. I mean, I haven't seen her since we left school, and that was nearly five years ago.'

'Where were you last Thursday evening?'

'Is that when it happened?'

'Just answer my questions, please. Where were you?'

He frowned. 'Having a pint, I guess. Yes, I went out for a few beers.'

'Were you with anyone?'

He shrugged. 'I wasn't drinking on my own, if that's what you mean. I was with a mate. And the landlord will tell you I was there as well.'

Making a note of the names of the men who could corroborate Peter's story, Geraldine left after taking a sample of Peter's DNA. The local pub was open and the cheerful middle-aged man behind the bar nodded when Geraldine showed him a photograph of Peter. She had taken it on her phone, but the landlord recognised Peter straight away.

'Course I know him,' he told her with an easy smile. 'He lives in the village. He's a regular here. Name's Peter. Nice lad. Is he in trouble?'

'No. Nothing like that. But can you tell me if he was here last Thursday evening?'

The landlord paused, thinking. 'Well, he did miss one evening last week but that must have been Monday, so yes, he would have been here on Thursday. He was having a beer with another local boy, if my memory serves. They're here together most evenings during the week.'

'What time did he leave?'

'Oh, they're here till closing, those two. It's the darts keeps them here. We run a team.' He smiled.

Geraldine didn't need to question Peter's companion to confirm his alibi. Thanking the landlord of the pub she left.

Normally she wouldn't have been disappointed by the outcome of her enquiries so far, but Stephanie had mentioned a violent ex-boyfriend to Ashley, and Geraldine had gone to Saddleworth with high expectations.

It felt strange to be driving back home to York. Her new flat was pleasant, with views out over the river from her kitchen and her sitting room. When the weather improved it was going to be picturesque. But she was a long way from London. She missed her family, and her friends on the Met, particularly her sergeant, Sam, to whom she had been close. Of course she had known that she was going to be hundreds of miles away when she had agreed to the move, but she hadn't anticipated quite how isolated she was going to feel in her new home. What was more disappointing was that she had overestimated the consolation of working with Ian again. No longer her sergeant, it was understandable he would appear more distant with her than he had been when they had worked together before. She should have realised that would happen. But she couldn't turn the clock back, and would just have to make the best of her new situation.

It was nearly midday by the time she arrived back in York. After lunch Eileen wanted the team to gather for a briefing. Aware that her opinions no longer carried much weight, Geraldine deliberated about her report. Apart from the DNA samples she had taken, everything she had to say was subjective. Tony and Peter had both given a plausible appearance of innocence, but that was just her opinion. It wasn't much to go on. Eileen wouldn't be impressed.

9

SHE WAS BACK IN Saddleworth. Good. It amused him to watch the police going round in circles. Having been to visit Tony Palmer once, she was off to talk to him again. She could question him for as long as she liked. It wouldn't help her. He alone knew the police were on a hiding to nothing; they were never going to find out who had killed Stephanie. But while they were busy running around, they were unwittingly giving away quite a lot of information. He smiled to himself. This was another attribute of a successful killer. In addition to his intelligence, boldness and patience, he was lucky. He smiled, acknowledging the truth in the saying that people made their own luck, because persistence was another quality that contributed to his success. He never allowed anything to stop him, once he made up his mind.

Yesterday he had suffered a temporary setback. Having followed the detective all the way back to the police station in York, he had lost sight of her. He had watched the exit to the police station for hours, but she must have gone home in a different car. He would have to look out for that, and not assume he could keep track of her through her vehicle. Undeterred, he had set out the next morning to try and pick up her trail again, and his tenacity had been rewarded when he had caught sight of her on her way back to Saddleworth. She had actually driven right past him as he was travelling back to the police station in York. Turning round as soon as he could, he had set off in pursuit, relishing the chase now that he had picked up the trail again so quickly. Casting about to find him, she had no idea that he was right behind her, like a pantomime villain.

Instead of going back to see Tony Palmer, she drove to the neighbouring village and stopped in a street off the main road where she rang one of the bells. He didn't recognise the woman who came to the door. It must have been someone who had known Stephanie. After about half an hour, the detective emerged from the house and drove off. He considered going to the house himself to find out who she had been speaking to, but he could go back there any time. He would be better off following the detective, and this time he wouldn't lose her. He had bought binoculars especially. He would have to be careful, scrutinising drivers leaving the car park at the police station, but with a little discretion he thought he could carry it off. It was just a case of being careful not to draw attention to himself.

In the event, he didn't need to wait outside the police station at all because the detective didn't go back there but instead drove along the A1036 and on to Bishopsgate Street, where she disappeared into an underground car park beneath a smart block of apartments overlooking the river. As he drove past he noted the position of the building. Finding a parking space, he hurried back, registering that there was a hotel across the road, which could be useful. Cautiously he trotted up a short flight of steps leading to the entrance to her block. A key fob was needed to open the front door, but it would be easy to gain access by following someone inside. Peering around the corner of the building, he could see a series of balconies. It looked as though her flat overlooked the river, which might offer him another way in.

Having learned as much as he could on an initial reconnoitre, he didn't linger. Discovering where the detective lived was enough information for one day. He would need to think through his next movements carefully. He wasn't reckless and had no intention of breaking in there unless it proved necessary. If his luck held, the police would never come anywhere near discovering his identity, and that was just how it should be. All he wanted was to be left alone to pursue his own agenda. It wasn't much to ask. Still, if he needed to learn how much they knew, now he had discovered where she lived he could easily find a way to slip into her apartment and have a look around. Going there while she was out during the day probably wouldn't help him much. She would carry her information around with her on a laptop or smart phone, besides which she was bound to have some sort of alarm system protecting her home while she was out. But he could go there one night and have a look around. Hopefully she wouldn't wake up. He was confident he would be able to overpower her if she did, but killing a police officer wasn't a good idea.

10

MISJUDGING THE BOTTLENECK SHE would encounter around the centre of York, Geraldine reached the Major Incident Room that afternoon with only seconds to spare. Everyone else was already there. Even though Geraldine wasn't late, Eileen raised her eyebrows when she entered, as though to make sure she knew her arrival had been noted. Geraldine felt herself squirming. She couldn't remember feeling so insecure at work since she had been a young constable.

Geraldine didn't understand the detective chief inspector's attitude. Eileen must be aware that until recently Geraldine had been an experienced inspector. To begin with Geraldine had thought Eileen couldn't mind that much about her demotion or she wouldn't have accepted her on the team. She was beginning to wonder if Eileen's hand had been forced. Perhaps the detective chief inspector had expected Geraldine to be more grateful to her for allowing her to relocate to York when she had to leave London. It would have been nice to clear the air, but Geraldine wasn't sure how to approach her senior officer, and she was afraid of making matters worse.

'Now, Geraldine,' Eileen said with an air of exaggerated patience, as though she had been waiting for her to arrive. 'You spoke to Stephanie's ex?'

Geraldine nodded. She had prepared for this. It was some years since she had been nervous reporting to a meeting of her colleagues. She could feel tension in her neck and shoulders as she cleared her throat and began to speak. Her anxiety about Eileen proved justified, as the detective chief inspector challenged her report on Tony Palmer.

'You had the *impression* he was telling you the truth?' she repeated coldly.

'Yes ma'am,' Geraldine replied, remembering just in time that she was no longer in the Met where all officers were addressed by their first names.

'Did he have an alibi for the time of the murder?'

'His current girlfriend said he was at home with her.'

'Hardly a reliable witness,' someone else commented.

'I think she was telling the truth,' Geraldine said.

'They could be in it together,' Naomi suggested.

'In it together or else she'd agreed to vouch for his alibi,' Eileen agreed.

'I'll have CCTV checked,' Geraldine said, concealing her irritation at hearing her views so readily dismissed. 'But I hardly see what motive they could have for coming all the way to York to kill her...'

A chorus of voices chimed in with different suggestions. Geraldine glanced at Ian, who was listening in silence. Apart from Geraldine, everyone appeared to agree with Eileen that Tony was the most likely suspect. Although Geraldine still believed he was innocent, she wasn't sufficiently confident in her assumption to repeat it. She could be wrong, and once she established a reputation for poor judgement, it might be difficult to change that perception among her new colleagues. So she kept quiet, fretting inwardly at her cowardice in failing to speak out in defence of her own opinion.

'Let's see what the lab tests show,' Eileen said briskly, referring to the traces of skin found under the dead girl's nail.

After the meeting, Geraldine set a team to check traffic records on the streets in and around Uppermill, as well as passengers leaving and arriving at local railway stations, for the twenty-four hours before and after the time of the murder. She also had any CCTV cameras close to Stephanie's flat checked. Any evidence that Tony had travelled to or from

York that day would disprove his alibi. In the meantime, she continued to research the dead girl's past, hunting for any clues to the identity of a violent ex-boyfriend. By the end of the day neither she nor the team had made any progress. It was early days, and there was no cause for despondency, but she couldn't help feeling impatient, convinced they were pursuing a pointless line of enquiry.

Geraldine was pleased when she spotted Ian leaving the police station. She ran out and had almost caught up with him as he reached the car park. She called out to him. Looking back, he stopped and waited for her. At the warmth in his smile, Geraldine felt the tension in her neck begin to relax, and when he suggested going for a drink, she agreed at once. They walked down to the street, turning right as they left the police compound to go to a nearby pub. The place was old-fashioned and slightly run-down but comfortable enough, in addition to which Ian assured her they could get a decent beer there. Geraldine wasn't bothered about that. She just wanted some friendly company for the evening.

She sat down at a table in a poorly lit corner. The pub was pleasantly warm and she took off her jacket and slung it over her chair while Ian went up to the bar. Watching him from across the room, she recognised a couple of constables chatting with the landlord. Unsociably, she hoped their colleagues wouldn't want to come over and join her and Ian. He appeared to exchange a few pleasantries with them, and share a joke with the landlord while he was being served but, to Geraldine's relief, the other two officers remained seated at the bar when Ian came over to where she was sitting. They drank in silence for a few minutes before they both started talking at the same time. Geraldine asked Ian what he made of the case, while he enquired about her first impressions of York. It was strange, making polite conversation about the town, almost as though she was talking to a stranger, when they had known one another for so long and had worked together so closely in the past.

She felt an unexpectedly sharp sense of loss, recalling how pleased she had been to see Ian on the rare occasions they had met up throughout the entire time they had been living two hundred miles apart. She had thought they had developed a genuine close friendship. Now they were working together again, she was beginning to suspect that she had built up unrealistic expectations about her relationship with her former sergeant.

'York seems very nice,' she replied. 'I'm sure it'll grow on me.'

'Yes, it didn't take me long to settle here. It's a great place to live. I'd choose York over London any day, mainly because of the people. It's much easier to feel lonely in London. They're a friendly lot up here, and you'll soon feel at home with the rest of the team.'

Geraldine avoided enquiring about his estranged wife for fear of upsetting him, but of course he hadn't been on his own when he had moved to York, and that must have made a difference. Instead she shifted the conversation around to their colleagues.

'What about Eileen?' she asked, lowering her voice. 'What's she like?'

He took a drink while he considered his answer. 'She can be tough,' he admitted, 'but she gets the job done. I have to say, I do like working with her. She's the sort of DCI where you feel you know where you stand.'

Geraldine wondered if he had ever used those words about her.

'And it's great finally being an inspector...' he broke off, embarrassed. 'Sorry, that was crass of me.'

'Oh, that's OK,' Geraldine replied cheerily. 'I'm happy to still be on the job at all.'

She hoped he wouldn't see through her fake smile, but he wasn't even looking at her. He was gazing towards the bar, his hand raised in greeting. Looking round, Geraldine saw Naomi grinning back at him. A moment later the constable came over to their table.

'Mind if I join you?' she asked, pulling a chair over and sitting down. 'So, how are you liking York, Geraldine?'

'It's fine,' Geraldine replied, returning Naomi's smile.

'Yes, I like it here. There's always something going on.'

There was an awkward pause.

'Well, I'd best be off,' Geraldine said, pushing her chair back and standing up. 'I've still got some unpacking to do.'

And just like that, her evening with Ian came to an end. As she walked back to the police station for her car, she remembered Ian saying it was difficult to feel lonely in York. She wished she could agree with him. Driving home, she questioned whether she had made the right decision. Instead of accepting a demotion to sergeant and relocating to York, she could have quit the force altogether and found something else to do for the rest of her life, but she had never really considered that. The trouble was, she couldn't think of anything else she wanted to do. After years of experience on the job, she was fit for nothing but her chosen career. She tried not to feel miserable about Ian, but she couldn't kid herself that she wasn't disappointed. She was glad no one else had known about her inflated expectations. Clearly she had misjudged their relationship, because Ian didn't seem to care that he had been joined by his former inspector. Geraldine had been a fool to think he would greet her with the open arms of friendship.

11

THE FOLLOWING MORNING IAN greeted Geraldine as she arrived at the police station.

'How did you get on with your unpacking? Get much done?'

'What? Oh, not really.' She smiled, pleased that he had remembered her parting comment from the previous day. 'Did you have a good evening?'

'Yes, it was all very nice. We had another beer and then went for a curry. You should have stuck around.'

'Thanks, another time.'

Geraldine smiled at the invitation, but she had an uneasy feeling Ian found her old and boring compared to Naomi, the cheerful young constable who would no doubt soon be promoted to sergeant, equalling Geraldine's rank.

'Cheer up,' Ian said, with a flash of his old sensitivity. 'Are you all right?' His gentle blue eyes gazed into her own dark ones. 'You look a bit down in the dumps. Problems with your sister? She's not using again?'

She shook her head, touched by his concern. 'As far as I know she's OK.'

'As far as you know? Don't tell me she doesn't keep in touch with you, after all you've done for her? If you hadn't stepped in to save her, the addiction would probably have finished her off by now, if her dealer hadn't got to her first. Not many people would do what you did for her. She could at least be grateful.'

'It's not that. She's just so far away, and I've been busy... it's OK, but you know,' she sighed. 'It's not always easy.'

'Plus, next to death and divorce, moving is supposed to be

the most stressful thing, isn't it? Or was that changing job?' Ian said. 'Anyway, you've done both. You've had a lot of change to cope with lately.'

'Change is always hard,' Naomi chipped in, stopping to join them in the corridor.

Seeing her stand beside Ian in a manner almost proprietorial, Geraldine wondered if there was something going on between her two colleagues. She recalled how Ian had been a magnet for the young female constables when they had worked together previously. Resolving to be circumspect in what she said about Naomi, she smiled at her. She hoped the constable hadn't heard Ian saying that Geraldine's twin sister was a recovering heroin addict.

'Exactly,' she replied. 'I was just saying to Ian that it's not always easy relocating. But it's not a problem. I'll soon get myself sorted. There's just so much to do all the time.'

'That doesn't matter. What's important is to focus on what needs to be done,' Naomi replied.

'Quite right. Let's not stand around nattering. Time to get on,' another voice chimed in.

Eileen had appeared from around the corner in the corridor. Clearly she had overheard Naomi's final remark, and possibly Geraldine's preceding comment as well. Geraldine wondered if Naomi had noticed Eileen's approach and had spoken up intending to be overheard. Such toadying might be predictable in an ambitious colleague. It was perhaps unfair to criticise Naomi for trying to impress her senior officers. In her own way, Geraldine had done the same, but she had sought to impress her colleagues by being effective at what she did, not by talking about how to go about it.

She suppressed a sigh at the thought that it didn't matter very much what Eileen thought of her. Promotion was no longer a possibility for her. She would remain a sergeant until she retired. Naomi might well be an inspector before that happened, if not a detective chief inspector. But her colleague's progress had no bearing on her own career. On the positive side, she still had a job to do. Without her work, her life would be empty. That hadn't changed. She made her way to her desk, telling herself she had spent enough time feeling sorry for herself. It was time to throw off her despondency and focus on her work. Sitting at her desk, she reviewed the situation so far before going to talk to the team which had been tracking Tony Palmer's movements on the evening of Stephanie's murder.

Two officers had been checking CCTV in the area. One was a burly middle-aged man. His colleague on the job was a small, neat, young woman. Andy shook his head when Geraldine enquired whether they had discovered anything.

'It looks as though he was at home all evening,' Daisy agreed, nodding. 'Unless he went out the back way. But he didn't drive to York and he wasn't on any train back to York that evening.'

Geraldine thanked them and left them still looking through film, but she didn't expect them to find any new information that might implicate Tony in Stephanie's murder.

'If he really was at home the evening of the murder, we're back to square one,' Ian said, when Geraldine went to see him. He was seated in his own office. Although it was very small, he didn't share it with anyone else. There wasn't enough room for two desks in there. Geraldine would have liked to reminisce about the days when he had worked as her sergeant, before their roles had been reversed, but this was not the time for nostalgia.

'What about the other two possibilities?' he asked.

Geraldine shook her head.

'Geraldine's been looking into Stephanie's exes, and drawn a complete blank,' Ian said when Eileen gathered the team together in the Major Incident Room.

Naomi turned to Geraldine. 'Never mind, it was worth a try. The obvious answer often turns out to be accurate, so you had to spend time looking into her ex-boyfriends.'

Geraldine felt herself bristle at her young colleague's

patronising tone. Telling herself Naomi was just trying to be nice, she hid her irritation as she answered.

'Ashley told us Stephanie had a violent ex so it was necessary to follow this up.'

Momentarily vexed for feeling the need to defend herself, she was nevertheless relieved when Eileen agreed with her.

She was still following up Stephanie's other ex-boyfriends when Ian stopped by her desk to ask if she was going to the pub for a quick drink.

'Or just a coffee?' he added.

She shook her head. 'I want to get this finished and then, to be honest, I've still got some things to sort out in the flat. I thought I'd get it all done by now, but this case came up so soon after I arrived that I haven't had much time to myself. I've hardly had any time off since this came up.'

Naomi overheard her. 'You don't have to work at weekends, you know.'

Ian looked as though he was about to say something, but he appeared to think better of it. Geraldine wondered if Naomi knew that she and Ian had worked together in the past. He knew how focused she became once they were investigating a murder. He used to be the same. Looking at him now, Geraldine felt uneasy. She had been blaming her sense of dislocation and the stress of moving for their strained relations, but she was beginning to suspect that Ian was the one who had changed.

'Well, I'm off,' he said. 'See you tomorrow.'

Driving home she told herself that she had no reason to feel miserable. Her recent dejection had just been a reaction to the challenge of moving. More important than her personal problems was the knowledge that a young girl had been violently killed and so far her murderer was evading capture. He could be a complete stranger to the police, or they might have already questioned him. Either way, they had so far failed to identify him. It was a pity the DNA profile they had from the scene of the crime was incomplete, but it was better than nothing. Sooner or later, they would track him down. Meanwhile, someone prepared to commit so brutal a murder could be a danger to the public. Instead of going straight home, as she had intended, she took a different route. Her dinner could wait. Right now finding Stephanie's killer took priority over everything else.

12

PETER KEPT HIS HOOD up at the station in York. The carriage was half empty. Finding a seat, he sat with his shoulders hunched and his head lowered, trying not to draw attention to himself. As the train hurtled through the darkness he glanced around furtively to check if anyone was watching him. As far as he could tell, no one there resembled the man who had been following him all evening, although it was impossible to be sure, since he had never seen his stalker's face. Nowhere felt safe. Out and about travelling, he felt as though everyone was watching him. Afraid that other people would consider his fears groundless, he hadn't mentioned his suspicions to anyone. His friends would think he was being needlessly paranoid, or worse. He could hardly blame anyone else for being sceptical when his own initial reaction had been to laugh at the idea that he was being stalked.

At first he had barely noticed the man who was following him. After a while it had struck him as odd that the man kept appearing, seemingly hanging about on Peter's street. Still, he had thought little of it, until the man had turned up outside his workplace. The idea that he was being stalked was ludicrous. The reality was terrifying.

Reaching his local station, he hurried out to his car. As he was driving home a fine sleet began to fall, droplets flickering across the beam from his headlights. He didn't think anyone was following him. It wasn't until he was climbing out of the car that he saw the now familiar figure, hat pulled down over his eyes, scarf pulled up around his chin, long black coat reaching down below his knees, standing motionless on the other side of the road. The orange glow from a street lamp fell across the side of his dark hat so that he looked more than ever like a photograph of an actor in an old film: a spy or a private investigator. Peter couldn't tell if the man had followed him all the way home from York, or had been waiting for him at Greenfield station. He was hardly likely to have been standing outside in the freezing cold all day.

Refusing to look round, Peter hurried towards his home, walking as fast as he could on the icy pavement. He was already through the gate and had reached the narrow path that led up to his front door when he changed his mind. The situation was becoming intolerable, and he had been a fool to put up with it even for a moment. He resolved to discover the stalker's identity for himself and put an end to the problem once and for all. Spinning on his heel he darted back out on to the street, pumped up and ready to confront the stranger and demand what the hell was going on.

There was no sign of the man. Peter looked both ways, peering through the darkness, but the mysterious figure had vanished. Uncertain whether to feel relieved or more unnerved than before, he went home. Closing the front door behind him, he was enveloped in welcoming warmth. His landlady kept the heating on all day and night, professing to suffer dreadfully from the cold. In his panic, Peter almost barged into her at the foot of the stairs.

'You're in a hurry,' she smiled. 'Are you going out somewhere nice tonight?'

Too worked up to answer, he shook his head. It took him a few seconds to compose himself, but she didn't seem to notice anything unusual in his demeanour.

'No, I'm not going anywhere,' he replied at last.

'I'll make us some supper then, shall I?' she asked. Plump and smiling, she bustled past him towards the kitchen. 'I'll put some lamb in the oven…'

Although she had no way of knowing about the danger he was facing, he was nevertheless irrationally offended by her ignorance of his plight. All at once he seemed to be suffocating in the warm air of the house, hemmed in by her cheerful hospitality. Without a word of explanation, he flung the front door open again and ran out into the night.

The street was deserted, but he had a feeling his stalker wasn't far away. Lowering his head as though that would shield him from view, he dashed down the road and slipped into the pub. He didn't think anyone had seen him go inside. Nodding at the landlord, he felt safe for the first time in days as he went to the bar and ordered a pint. He didn't know anyone else in there, although one or two people looked vaguely familiar. Had it been a Saturday evening the bar would have been packed. Raised voices would have been competing to be heard above loud music blaring out through the PA system. Sometimes there was a band playing. They weren't usually up to much but the landlord said he liked to support local talent.

Finishing his pint he ordered another one. He was beginning to relax. Already the memory of his mysterious stalker was beginning to fade, like a half-forgotten dream. He had obviously been mistaken. No one was going to be interested in following him around. By coincidence he had seen several men, similar in appearance, in the space of one evening. It was hardly surprising that he would have seen more than one man dressed in a long coat, hat and scarf, in such cold weather. By the time he left the pub it was dark, and he was feeling slightly woozy from downing a few pints on an empty stomach.

The night air was sharp and cold. Feeling queasy, he crossed the road and walked straight ahead, towards the canal. The towpath was deserted at that time of night in winter. After the warmth and colour and pungent smell of beer in the pub he would be able to think clearly in the quiet darkness by the water and, more to the point, no one would see him if he threw up there. Even the ducks had disappeared for the night. He could have been the only living man on the planet.

Until he heard soft footsteps on the path behind him.

Stifling a cry of alarm, he spun round. 'Who's there?' he called out, hearing his own voice quiver. 'Where are you? I know you're there.'

13

THE APARTMENT RENTED BY the victim was being carefully examined. Days after the incident, clues could still be discovered at a crime scene. Stephanie's flatmate, Ashley, hadn't left York but was staying with a neighbour on the floor above. She had gone back to work so Geraldine didn't go and see her until the evening. The door was opened by a woman in her forties. Hearing who Geraldine was, she introduced herself as Gloria.

'I had the room empty, with my daughter being away at college, so I checked with my daughter and she said it was fine to let Ashley stay until they've finished searching her flat. Although, what she'd want to go back there for...' she broke off with a shrug. 'Anyway, come on in. We're sitting in here.'

'I'd like to speak to Ashley on her own.'

Gloria looked slightly put out but she nodded and gestured towards the room where Ashley was waiting. Geraldine entered a neat square sitting room. The carpet was pink and white, as were the curtains, and the walls were painted white with a tinge of pink. The whole room gave an impression of warmth and homeliness. Coming in from the cold winter air outside, Geraldine immediately felt comfortable as she sank into a soft armchair. It would have been nice to put her feet up and turn the television on and simply relax. Making a mental note to buy a rug for the wooden floor in her living room, she smiled at Ashley.

'I had to go back to work,' she said, as though she felt the need to apologise for appearing to recover from the recent trauma so quickly. 'I couldn't stay in the flat. I mean, they wouldn't let me anyway, but I didn't want to be there right now, and I can't sit around here all day...' she broke off and glanced at the door which Geraldine had closed behind her when she entered the room. 'Gloria's very nice,' Ashley went on in a whisper, 'but she talks about her daughter all the time.'

'I want to ask you about something you told us,' Geraldine said, launching straight into the reason for her visit.

Ashley nodded when Geraldine mentioned the matter she wanted to discuss. 'Yes, I remember saying that.'

Geraldine breathed a silent sigh of relief. She had been afraid Ashley was going to say she had been confused.

'We're trying to trace this violent ex-boyfriend Stephanie mentioned to you,' she explained. 'Can you help us?'

'She went out with a guy called Tony for quite a while, but I don't think it could have been him. I mean, I don't think he ever hit her or anything like that.' Ashley frowned. 'Steph told me he was a bit of a wimp. I think she had the upper hand in that relationship. But they were together for quite a while and I think she was happy enough with him until they split up.'

'Why did they part company?'

'Oh, she was bored with him. They were just drifting on, you know.'

'So she finished it?'

'Yes.'

'Do you know how he felt about that?'

'According to Steph he just accepted it when she suggested they have a break. I think that was the final straw for her. He didn't seem to be bothered. From what she said, he wasn't exactly the passionate type. But,' she leaned forward, and her eyes narrowed, 'I think he was already seeing someone else, because he moved in with her before Steph and I moved to York. I mean, he didn't hang about!'

Geraldine noted down what Ashley told her. It didn't sound

as though Tony had killed Stephanie in a rage. If anything, she was the one who might have had cause to be jealous.

'What about Peter?'

'Peter?'

'Peter Edwards.'

Ashley looked surprised. 'Blimey, that was back in school. I didn't know he was still around.'

'Could she have been seeing him again?'

'No.'

'You sound very definite.'

'I would have known about it if they were.' Tears suddenly spilled from her eyes and coursed down her pale cheeks. 'Steph and I were close. She was a good friend.' She began to sob.

'Ashley, I'm sorry to press you,' Geraldine said after a moment, 'but you did mention that Stephanie had a violent ex-boyfriend. If it wasn't Tony or Peter, who was it? We really need to find this man and talk to him. Do you have any idea who it was?'

Ashley made a clear effort to pull herself together, blowing her nose and shaking her head, as though she could shake off her emotional outburst.

'I honestly don't know who she was talking about, really I don't. It was only a brief conversation. We were comparing notes on past boyfriends.'

'But you said you'd have known if she'd been seeing Peter, so didn't you know who else she was seeing?'

'We were best friends at school, and we've been very close lately, since she split with Tony and we agreed to flat share, but we did drift apart for a while after we left school. So she might have met someone then, before she went out with Tony, or maybe even while she was seeing him. But I don't know who. Like I said, we drifted apart for a while.'

Geraldine questioned her further, but she had nothing more to tell. It was beginning to look as though Stephanie's violent ex-boyfriend might have been nothing more than a piece of idle gossip. When Ashley had told Stephanie that she gone out with a violent man, her friend had responded with a similar claim that could have been groundless.

'So you really have no idea who it was?' Geraldine asked once more.

Ashley shook her head. 'She never said.'

The following morning, when the team met to discuss the case, Geraldine reported her discussion with Ashley. Naomi agreed that Stephanie might only have said that she had once had a violent ex-boyfriend because her flatmate had claimed that first.

'But why would she lie about it?' Ian asked.

'It's the sort of thing a girl might say,' Naomi explained. Seeing Ian look puzzled, she went on. 'She probably wanted be in with her friend.'

Ian remained unconvinced but Geraldine concurred, as did Eileen. There was little else to report. Door-to-door questioning of neighbours along Stephanie's street hadn't yielded any information. Most of them knew nothing about her. The same was true of the residents of the apartment block where she had shared a flat with Ashley. It was frustrating. All the police could do was wait for the results of the forensic search of the crime scene, and hope someone would come forward with a new lead.

When the briefing was over, Geraldine returned to her own desk in the busy open-plan office. She missed her quiet office back in London, but as a sergeant her situation was different. She could no longer expect privacy, but she didn't mind that too much. She never had trouble focusing when she had something to work on. Her problem now was that she had nothing pressing to investigate. She had been so sure that the violent ex-boyfriend was worth pursuing, but that lead seemed to have come to nothing. Ian was out at the crime scene, and she was stuck at her desk writing up her notes.

Just as she was settling down to work, she received a

summons. This was the first time she had been called in to the detective chief inspector's office. Since her demotion, Geraldine felt as though she had lost all her confidence. She wondered how much her former self-assurance had rested on the fact that she was an inspector, well on her way to further promotion. Now she was afraid that being summoned to the detective chief inspector meant she was about to receive a reprimand. With a sinking feeling, she walked along the corridor, wracking her brains to think what she might have done wrong. The detective chief inspector didn't ask her to close the door when she entered the office. Geraldine took that as a good sign. If a reprimand was coming, Eileen would have wanted to speak to her discreetly. Then again, Eileen might not care if another officer turned up and overheard her admonishing Geraldine.

'Ian's not here,' Eileen said.

Geraldine nodded, wondering what was coming next.

'Peter Edwards is in an interview room,' Eileen went on.

Relieved, Geraldine understood that she was being asked to go and talk to a potential witness.

'You've spoken to him before, so I'd like you to find out what he wants, if you can. The desk sergeant said he's been drinking, so let's see if you can get any sense out of him.'

Geraldine felt a surge of excitement. She might be about to hear a confession. Any concerns for herself forgotten, she hurried to the interview room.

14

IF ANYTHING, PETER LOOKED scruffier than Geraldine remembered him. She wouldn't have been surprised to see he was still wearing the same creased T-shirt under his coat. He hadn't shaved and his hair was dishevelled, and there was an unmistakable whiff of alcohol in the room. But the most noticeable alteration in his appearance was the expression in his eyes. Even though he was seated in an interview room in a police station, he started when she entered, and glanced up, wide-eyed, like a rabbit caught in headlights. Geraldine thought she saw him tremble.

'Peter,' she said, in as reassuring a tone as she could muster. 'You have something to tell me?'

He leaned forward in his chair, and she saw that his hands were shaking. 'I'm being followed,' he blurted out. It was the middle of the day, but his speech was slurred and he had clearly been drinking. 'Someone's following me. I think he might have followed me here.'

When he glanced around the room as though there might be someone hiding in the corner, she wondered what had happened to prompt his sudden paranoia. The last time she had seen him, he had appeared quite relaxed.

'Who's following you?' she asked him, when he didn't speak again.

He shook his head, his expression fearful.

'Peter, I can't help you if you don't tell me what this is about.'

He shook his head again. 'I don't know,' he whispered, although there was no one there to hear him apart from

Geraldine and a constable who stood by the door staring straight ahead, who might as well have been deaf for all the response he gave to what was said.

'What makes you think you're being followed?'

Peter took a deep breath and spoke more clearly. 'I thought I was imagining it at first, but every time I go out, he's there.'

He broke off, staring past Geraldine.

'Who do you see every time you go out, Peter?'

In random snatches, Peter explained what was worrying him. Piecing together what he said, Geraldine gathered that he had spotted a man standing across the road from the house where he was staying. Although he had seen him three or four times, he couldn't describe him. The man had been wearing a long black coat, with the brim of a hat pulled low over his brow, and a scarf wrapped round his neck and over his chin.

'I could only see his nose,' Peter said. 'He looked like a spy in one of those old films, you know.' Unexpectedly, he sniggered.

Geraldine didn't point out that it was hardly surprising apparel for someone standing outside in the freezing cold weather.

'I know you'd expect someone to be wearing a coat and hat and scarf in this weather,' he went on, as though he knew what she was thinking. 'But he didn't want me to see his face. I know he didn't.'

His face creased in consternation and his voice cracked. He looked down and coughed. Geraldine waited to hear what he would say next, but he didn't look up or speak. She was uncomfortably aware of the constable watching them impassively, and wondered fleetingly if he had been posted there to report back to Eileen on how her new sergeant was getting on. It seemed that Peter's paranoia was contagious. After a pause, she asked him what had convinced him that he was being watched.

'At first I thought it was a coincidence, him being there outside the house every time I went out.'

'How many times did you see him?'

He shrugged. 'Two or three times last week. I thought it was nothing to do with me, but then he followed me down to the canal last night. I thought he was going to kill me, but he was just watching me. He's always watching me.'

Geraldine frowned. 'Did you see his face when he followed you?'

'No, but I heard him.'

'So how can you be sure it was the same person?'

He stared at her without answering for a moment. 'What are the chances that different people would be standing on the pavement outside my house on different days, dressed in identical clothes?' he asked at last.

When Geraldine asked if he had any idea who could have been watching him, he glared miserably at her without speaking. She repeated her question.

'You think I'm imagining all this, don't you?' he replied at last. 'You don't believe me, but I'm telling you, someone's following me. You have to do something about it. I demand police protection.'

He was evidently making an effort to control himself, but his voice rose, betraying his agitation.

'Peter, why would someone be following you?'

'I don't know. I don't know.'

'Is there something you're not telling me?'

He shook his head.

'I'd like to help you, Peter, but so far all you've given me is a vague impression you have that someone might be stalking you. I need a lot more than that if I'm going to follow this up with any action.'

'You have to help me. You're the police. It's your job to protect me. You can't just do nothing.'

'Has this unknown person threatened you?'

'Not exactly, but he's following me. He must be intending to do something.'

Peter had become increasingly agitated while they had been

talking. When Geraldine repeated the suggestion that the stranger's appearance on more than one occasion might be a coincidence, he leaned further forward in his chair. Behind her, Geraldine heard the constable stir. She too leaned forward in her chair until her face was inches away from his and their eyes met.

'Peter,' she said gently, 'what's happened? You can tell me.'

She held her breath, trying not to inhale a nauseating smell of alcohol and sweat. If Peter's stalker was real, there was a chance he might be the killer. She was hoping to hear something that might help them trace the culprit, but Peter merely reiterated his fear that a man was following him.

'What makes you so sure it's a man, if you've never seen his face?'

He shrugged, and mumbled that it could be a woman. Unable to glean anything more from Peter, Geraldine could only reassure him that she would file a report.

'A report's not going to protect me, is it?'

Recalling Peter saying the stranger resembled an actor in an old film, Geraldine wondered whether the stalker was just a figment of his imagination. Nevertheless she treated his statement seriously. Filing a detailed report on it, she recommended that his house be kept under surveillance. Eileen was sceptical of Peter's claim, dismissing his fears with a shrug. She even suggested that Peter might have killed Stephanie himself, and was now projecting his terror on to strangers, believing they were watching him.

'The stress of guilt can play strange tricks on the mind,' she said.

'It might well have all been in his imagination, but he was scared.'

'And drunk. Well, Ian can talk to him tomorrow, if there's time,' Eileen said, 'although I doubt there's any more to this. But he'll have to come back here. I can't have Ian going all the way to Saddleworth on a hunch. And he'll have to be sober next time.'

Only Ian appeared at all interested in Peter's story. 'It's bothering you, isn't it?' he asked Geraldine.

'He's a very frightened man,' Geraldine replied.

'Murder is frightening, and disturbing, especially to those who knew the victim.'

Geraldine scowled at his condescension. 'This isn't my first case.'

She knew she was overreacting, but it was hard adjusting to her new position. Rather than growing accustomed to her demotion, she was feeling increasingly conscious of her lowered status.

'How's your sister getting along?' Ian asked quietly.

Remembering the reason for her demotion, Geraldine felt a weight of anger lift from her mind. 'To be honest, I've hardly spoken to Helena since I came to York, it's been so manic, what with moving and now this murder to investigate. I should have been to see her, I just haven't got the strength to cope with her problems right now. But I have called the clinic regularly to check, and she's still there.'

'That's good, isn't it?'

'Yes. I'd be gutted if all this was for nothing.'

Ian nodded. 'But whatever happens, even if she relapses and goes back to using, she'll always know you did everything in your power to help her to kick her habit. And what's more important, *you* know you did everything you could for her.' He smiled sympathetically. 'There can't be many people who would throw away a brilliant career to try and rescue a drug addict, like you've done.'

'She's my sister, Ian.'

'A sister you only met recently. You're effectively strangers.'

'We're identical twins. I didn't have a choice, Ian, not really.'

'That's what you say, but I'm telling you, I don't think many people would have done what you did. I'm not sure that I would have done it.'

'Is that because you don't think she'll be able to kick the habit?'

He hesitated. 'That's not what I'm saying.'

They both knew he was lying.

'I have to stay positive,' she said, speaking to herself rather than to him. But it was too late. The dull aching anger that had been haunting her swept over her again.

She turned away. 'She'll be out of rehab soon,' she muttered.

'That's a good thing, isn't it?' he repeated, but this time he sounded uncertain.

15

AFTER WORK THAT EVENING, Geraldine went for a drink with Ian. She couldn't tell him that she hoped Naomi wasn't going to join them again. Instead she suggested they go somewhere different.

'What's wrong with the Fulford Arms?'

'Nothing, but we went there on Monday.'

'That's because it's on our doorstep. It's comfortable enough, and the beer's good. I can't see the point in going anywhere else.'

She couldn't argue with him without admitting that she wanted to spend time alone with him. It wasn't that she was hoping any kind of romance might spring up between herself and Ian, but they had known one another for years, and he was someone with whom she could discuss her twin sister who was due to leave the rehabilitation clinic. She didn't feel comfortable disclosing details of her family to Naomi, who was still virtually a stranger to her.

It was Geraldine's turn to buy a round. Standing at the bar she glanced around and recognised a small group of her colleagues seated at a table. She nodded to them in greeting without going over to join them. Ian was sitting by himself when she took him his pint.

'You must be pleased Helena's going to go home soon,' he said as she sat down.

Geraldine shrugged, but before she could answer he turned away and looked over at the door.

He smiled, and Geraldine realised he was still looking towards the door. She glanced back over her shoulder and saw Naomi waving at them. Ian jumped to his feet and pulled a spare chair over to their table. Geraldine forced a smile as the young constable sat down and put her pint on the table.

'It's so cold out there,' Naomi grumbled, her eyes fixed on Ian. 'Winter's finally here with a vengeance. I think it's going to snow tonight.'

'They've had snow in London already,' Geraldine said. 'I was expecting the weather to be wintry far earlier around here.'

'Wait,' Naomi told her. 'When it gets bad here, it's really bad. You won't believe it.' She laughed, and Geraldine smiled at her.

They began to discuss the case. Geraldine kept quiet, listening to her colleagues. Ian thought Tony was the most likely suspect, and Naomi agreed with him.

'Geraldine doesn't think it was him,' Ian said, as though Geraldine wasn't there.

'Why not?' Naomi asked, turning to her.

'It's not that I think he didn't do it, it's just that I'm not convinced he did.'

Naomi looked puzzled. 'What do you mean? Have you got another suspect in mind then?'

'No, not really.'

'Then I don't understand. I mean, I don't see the problem with going after Tony.'

'It's quite simple. I'm not sure Tony killed her. Just because he's the only suspect, doesn't mean he's guilty.'

'Geraldine has a reputation for instinctively getting at the truth,' Ian said.

Naomi looked surprised. 'Have you two worked together before, then?'

'It was a long time ago,' he replied, moving the conversation back to the investigation. 'Of course, we're only surmising at this stage. But if he is guilty we'll find proof soon enough. It's only a matter of time. He won't escape for long.'

'Look at it another way,' Geraldine said. 'What makes you so sure he's guilty? It's not as though we've got any proof, in fact, all we've got to go on is that he used to be her boyfriend. Since they split up, she's moved to York and he's found himself a new girlfriend. He seems perfectly happy with his present arrangement. So what possible motive could he have for killing Stephanie? Surely if either of them was going to be jealous it would be her, not him? We can't pin this on him just because he used to go out with her.'

'But someone killed her,' Naomi said.

'And so far we've got nothing to go on,' Ian added.

'We need to look harder then,' Geraldine told them. 'We have to find evidence.'

'There doesn't seem to be any,' Ian said. 'We're having his house searched, and digging up the garden there, but so far nothing's come up.'

'His girlfriend must be happy,' Geraldine said.

'She's going crazy,' Ian grinned.

'What about the man's DNA found on the body?' Geraldine asked. 'That didn't come from Tony Palmer. So we know there was another man present when she was killed.'

Ian shook his head helplessly. A match had still not been found for the partial DNA profile that had been left under one of the dead girl's finger nails. All that they knew was that he was Caucasian, with dark hair and dark eyes.

'Dark hair narrows it down,' Ian said, with a scowl.

'It gets you out of the frame,' Naomi teased him, ruffling his blond hair.

Without a match on the database they had no way of identifying the dark-haired man.

'We don't even know the man whose DNA was found was actually there at the time of her death,' Ian pointed out. 'He could have arrived before the attack.'

'We need to find that man, whoever he is,' Geraldine insisted.

'And how do you suggest we do that?' Ian was sounding irritated.

They were all frustrated by the unidentified DNA. Samples had been taken from everyone who had known Stephanie, and so far none of them had provided a match.

'My money's on the ex,' Ian said after another pause.

'It's not his DNA,' Geraldine repeated. 'That has to be significant.'

'Ian's already told us what he thinks.'

Feeling increasingly frustrated by the ramifications of her demotion, Geraldine held back from suggesting that Naomi was only agreeing with Ian because he was the senior officer there. If she hadn't taken a foolish risk to save her twin sister's life, she would still be on track for promotion to detective chief inspector. But she didn't regret her decision. As for the consequences of her demotion, it was a bitter experience but she was learning to deal with her new circumstances. It wasn't as though she had much choice.

A few days had passed since she had last spoken to her sister. Leaving her colleagues in the pub, she went home and poured herself a large glass of wine before calling Helena's mobile.

'Hi, it's me.'

Although they had only recently met, on the death of their mother, Helena recognised Geraldine's voice straight away. She reminded Geraldine that she was due to leave the rehabilitation clinic soon.

'What are you planning to do when you leave there?'

'That depends on you, really.'

'What do you mean?'

Even though Helena had been in rehab, Geraldine didn't want her twin coming to live with her. As a recovering heroin addict, her life was very different to Geraldine's. She was immediately reassured by Helena's reply.

'I'm hoping to go back to my old place. It's still empty.'

'What's to stop you?'

Helena hesitated. 'There's the rent for starters. Mum used to help me out with that. There's what I still got of the money she left, but that's going to run out, innit?'

'What about housing benefit?'

'I can't claim.'

'Why not?'

'They're only letting me leave the clinic because I said I was going to family.'

'What family?'

'You. You're my family now.'

'I'm living in a one-bedroomed apartment,' Geraldine lied.

'No, no!' Helena interrupted her, 'I'm not coming to live with you! Bloody hell, I'm not moving to wherever it is you've buggered off to.'

'Then I don't understand...' Geraldine broke off as she realised what Helena meant. 'Are you asking me to pay your rent?'

'So you'll do it?'

'How much is it?'

Geraldine didn't mention that she still owned a two-bedroomed flat in Central London. The rent she received was enough to cover her mortgage and other expenses of keeping the flat. With that and her salary she could afford to cover Helena's rent as well as her own, but she didn't rush to offer to support her. She had already done so much for Helena, it might be time to expect her to cope independently. But the spectre of Helena reverting to her habit silenced her.

'Well? You gonna help me or what? I know you got the dosh because you're paying for this place. But I'm done with rehab. I'll be getting out soon. So, what's it to be, sis?'

Geraldine frowned. Although the clinic's fee was more than Helena's rent could possibly amount to, Helena was only ever going to be at the clinic for a few months. Committing herself to paying her sister's rent might become a permanent obligation. As though listening to someone else speaking, she heard herself say that would be fine.

'But I'll pay the rent directly,' she added quickly.

There was no way she would risk handing over that amount of money to a recovering heroin addict.

'You don't trust me,' Helena snapped. 'After all I been through in this bloody place, you still think I'm going to blow your dosh on smack.'

Geraldine sighed. It would have been nice to get some thanks for agreeing to cover Helena's rent.

16

MORE OF THEM SHOULD have been killed by now. With so many potential victims to choose from, there could have been more deaths. He was spoiled for choice, really, but he needed to take his time and select his targets carefully. Only by controlling his feelings could he maintain his success. If he was clever, he would never have to stop. And he was clever. He was very clever. Far too clever to be caught. He took a deep breath and made a conscious effort to control his frustration. It would be easy to become complacent, watching reports of his exploits in the media, and be tempted to rush into his next attack.

Despite the vast array of resources at their disposal, the police were clueless about his identity. They said they had several people 'helping them with their enquiries', but they hadn't approached him yet. All the same, he had to remain on his guard. He was aware of the risks he took. That knowledge kept him safe. Because he hadn't finished yet. He had barely begun. It might take a long time for him to achieve his goal, but he could be patient. In the meantime he had to protect himself. There must be no possibility of discovery.

He had spent a long time thinking up a safe way to dispose of any evidence that might lead the police to discover his identity. It was crucial to get this right because, however careful he was, once his bloody clothes were discovered his arrest would be inevitable. The blood of his victims would be easy to identify, and his DNA was bound to be all over the clothes he had worn when killing them. At first the problem had seemed insurmountable. Puzzling over what to do had delayed him for months until, in the end, he had come up with a simple solution.

Once he had worked out how to avoid discovery, Stephanie had been easy to dispatch. Killing was never a problem. As soon as she opened the door he had slipped through it before she could stop him. Safely inside the flat, he had left no doubt that her murder was intentional. A violent attack was necessary to send out the right message. Afterwards he had been careful to leave the building without attracting attention, slipping away to dispose of his clothing where no one would ever find it. There had been no one around to see him emerge from an abandoned lock-up garage, washed and in clean clothes, the bloody evidence of his work tied up in a black bin bag in the back of his van.

Not even a week had passed since he had killed Stephanie, and he wasn't planning to find another victim just yet. There had been a lot of fuss about her murder in the local media, so he was keeping a low profile. He had been mulling over who to choose as his next victim, trying to pick an easy target from her group of friends at school, when an opportunity turned up out of the blue. Not far from Stephanie's family home one evening, he nearly drove straight past a man leaving the pub. Just in time he recognised Peter and pulled into the kerb to see where he went.

Obviously tipsy, Peter staggered down towards the canal, and he followed with no clear plan in mind. He did his best to move around silently, but Peter heard him and hurried back to the road. Back on the street he had to seize his chance or lose it.

'No, no,' Peter waved one hand at him dismissively. 'I don't need a lift. I want to walk.' He was so drunk he could barely string his words together in coherent sentences. 'Go away. I want to walk.'

There were no other vehicles on the road.

'It's going to rain,' he insisted softly. 'You might as well jump in. Are you going home? It's on my way.'

It wasn't strictly speaking a lie because it was going to rain, although possibly not that evening. Peter craned his head back and stared at the sky. Satisfied with his scrutiny, he lowered his gaze.

'Says who?' he demanded. 'What do you want? Who are you anyway? I don't know you.'

'Get in and I'll drop you home. I'm a police officer,' he added vaguely. 'Anyone can see you've had a drop too much and we can't have you getting in trouble, can we? You might wander into the road and have an accident.'

'How do you know where I live?'

'You're going to tell me and then I'll take you home. Come on now, you're in no fit state to be wandering around the street on your own.'

'Going to rain,' Peter mumbled as he clambered into the van.

He still hadn't made up his mind what to do, exactly, but when Peter fell asleep almost as soon as they drove off, he realised this was too good a chance to pass up. Driving at a steady pace, he waited until they were out of the built up area before putting his foot down. From time to time he glanced at his passenger who was sound asleep and snoring gently. Reaching a deserted spot he drew up, taking care not to drive off the tarmac to avoid leaving tyre tracks. Jumping out, he ran round to the back of the van to grab his knife, before dragging his befuddled passenger out on to the road.

'What you want?' Peter asked, arms and legs flailing in protest at being manhandled so roughly. 'Let me sleep, will you? Fuck off.'

For a moment it looked as though it would be impossible to shift his unwitting victim away from the road and into the fields. Every second they remained at the roadside he risked being spotted by a passing motorist.

'Come on, this way,' he urged.

'Where are we going?'

'Come on, just keep walking.'

'I want to lie down.'

'You'll soon be able to rest. Now come on, I told you, I'm taking you home.'

As they left the road behind, Peter seemed to come to his senses. 'Where the fuck are we?'

But by then it was too late. Catching sight of the knife, he raised his hands to protect his head and bellowed as the blade struck his forearm. He staggered backwards, stumbling and crying out in pain. With a second swipe the blade sliced through his throat and he sank to his knees, shaking, his voice reduced to a gurgle. Five more slashes with the knife and it was all over.

The job done, he left as soon as he had changed out of his bloody clothes. Driving away, he congratulated himself on his foresight. If he hadn't thought to leave spare clothes and a knife in the back of the van, he wouldn't have been able to take advantage of the chance that had presented itself. As it was, he had been prepared. Even so, he remained on the lookout for any sign that he was being followed, and was nervous all the way from the fields back to the house he was renting on the outskirts of York. Although he had changed out of his bloody clothes, and was wearing clean jeans and an old blue jumper, he hadn't been able to scrub his hands completely free of all traces of blood before leaving the body.

Back in his garage he stripped and washed himself and the steering wheel thoroughly, put on a set of fresh clothes, rolled up the jeans and blue jumper, and stuffed them into a black bag along with the rest of the bloody evidence of that night's work. Two sets of black bin bags were now safely stored in the lock-up where no one would ever find them. It was nearly two o'clock in the morning by the time he finally closed his front door. But although he was exhausted, he was too psyched up to go to bed straight away. At last he fell into bed and lay still, reviewing what he had accomplished so far. His only slip-up had been allowing his first victim to scratch the back of his wrist while he was stabbing her. He had tried to scrape any traces of his skin from under her nails, but was sure the police would still be able to detect his DNA. He would not make that mistake again. That one slip could have been enough to finish him. But nearly a week had gone by since then, and the police still seemed to be clueless.

'Police are following several leads' the papers said, but they sure as hell weren't following the right leads. Because any useful clues were locked up out of sight in his garage. He couldn't help laughing whenever he thought about them running around like headless chickens. They must be panicking by now, unable to discover his identity. He particularly enjoyed reading speculation in the media about the mystery killer. He almost regretted not being able to reveal himself to the world, but of course he couldn't. Arrogance, like complacency, had been the downfall of others before him. He wasn't that stupid. He knew how to keep his mouth shut. Perhaps on his deathbed – if he ever knew when that was – he might blurt out the truth, but that was hopefully a long way off. He still had a lot to accomplish before then. His plan was only just beginning to unfold, and now he had worked out how to get away with it, there was no longer any reason to hold back.

This was just the beginning.

17

GERALDINE FELT A FLICKER of excitement. Something must have happened for her to be summoned before she had even set off for work. She put her coffee cup down and listened.

'There's another body. This one's a male, found out in the fields near Greenfield. It's about an hour's drive away, but Ian wanted you to go and see it before they move it. The SOCO team should be finished photographing it soon so...'

'I'll leave straight away,' Geraldine interrupted, reaching for her bag and slipping on her shoes. 'What else can you tell me?'

'It's another stabbing. That's all the information we've got so far, but we think the victim was involved in the investigation into Stephanie's murder.'

'Do we have an identity?' She had a horrible suspicion she already knew who it was.

'This has yet to be confirmed, but we think it could be Peter Edwards.'

'I was afraid you were going to say that. You know he came to Fulford Road yesterday?'

Within minutes she was manoeuvring her car out of the narrow exit to the car park underneath her block of flats. After speeding along the main Tadcaster Road, she drove as fast as she dared along icy country lanes, past trees and bushes sparkling in the early morning sun. Her destination was signalled ahead of her by the top of a white forensic tent appearing above hedgerows stripped bare by winter frosts.

Peter was unrecognisable, his eyes concealed beneath congealed pools of blood, his nose smashed almost flat. Even his fair hair looked different, streaked with dark splashes. With a shudder, Geraldine saw that his mouth had been slashed across into a ghoulish parody of a grin, just like Stephanie's. She wondered if the killer was intending to leave a macabre calling card, taunting the police for being unable to find him.

'What happened?' she asked, her voice muffled by its protective mask.

'You spoke to him, didn't you?'

She turned to see Ian's eyes gazing at her above his mask. He was pale, the skin under his eyes grey. He looked noticeably older. Knowing how the sight of bloody corpses made him nauseous, Geraldine tried to smile encouragement at him from behind her mask.

'He told me he was being stalked,' she said softly. 'He was frightened.' They stood side by side for a moment, gazing down at the dead man.

'Why didn't we do something?'

She shrugged. 'There was no evidence to back up what he was saying. Eileen thought he was being paranoid.'

'What did you think?'

She shook her head. 'What difference does it make? I'm just a sergeant. Who's going to listen to me or commit resources to following my hunches?'

Ian looked at her. His eyes were brighter than before but she couldn't read his expression, with most of his face concealed behind a mask.

'Next time speak to me.' It sounded as though he was talking through clenched teeth.

'And you're going to argue my case with Eileen, are you?' she asked.

He turned away without answering.

'Are we OK to move him now?' an officer asked. 'The mortuary van's here from York.'

'Was he already dead when he was brought here?' Geraldine asked.

'No, he was alive when he arrived. The attack took place right here. His blood has soaked into the soil beneath the body, and he doesn't appear to have been moved post mortem.'

Leaving the tent, Geraldine peeled off her mask and drew in a few deep breaths. Tiny puffs of fog floated out of her mouth into the freezing air. Visibility was limited in the heavy mist that hung over the fields so that, as Ian took a few steps further away from her, his outline grew hazy. When he turned back, his face was no clearer than that of the battered corpse. Realising her own features would be similarly obscure, Geraldine moved towards him. His face came into focus as she drew near, as though he was emerging from a misty lake.

'Are you OK?' she asked.

He grimaced. Not many people knew how uncomfortable he felt around dead bodies. As a detective inspector investigating murders, colleagues naturally assumed he was fine viewing victims of the cases he worked on. He wasn't the only officer Geraldine had worked with who felt physically sick at the sight of blood. She sometimes wondered if she was unusual. Dead bodies drenched in their own blood had never bothered her, however shocking their injuries. It was the suffering of those left behind that disturbed her. For every murder victim there were family members, friends and partners, violently bereft of someone they loved. It was the sight of their grief that kept Geraldine awake at night, not the memory of the dead who were past pity and compassion. As far as she was concerned, dead bodies cried out only for justice to be visited on their killers.

'It's…' he broke off and looked down.

'What?'

When he looked up again she was surprised to see he was smiling. 'Just that I've missed working with you.'

In an instant, all the stress Geraldine had been feeling since her arrival in York seemed to lift, like the mist rising above the surface of the muddy field.

'There are car tracks in the grass verge over there,' a scene of crime officer called out to them as they walked back together towards the road. 'A vehicle seems to have parked there, by the gap in the hedge, not far from where the mortuary van is now.'

'How many cars were parked there?' Ian asked.

'Just the one.'

'So it looks as though the victim and his killer came here together. Have we got a cast of the tyre tracks?' He glanced around at the police vehicles parked along the verge.

'That's already been done,' a SOCO said briskly. 'We got that done first thing, before all these cars arrived.'

'The road wasn't closed then,' Geraldine muttered.

'Well, if you've finished here, let's move the body and see what else we can learn. Come on, Geraldine, we'll get back to the station.'

'I'll see you there.'

There was barely time for Geraldine to write up her decision log and grab a coffee before she had to head to the incident room for a briefing. Eileen swept into the room just as Geraldine arrived.

'Another body,' she snapped, as though the assembled team were somehow responsible for the second murder. 'You spoke to him, didn't you, Geraldine?'

'Yes. I put in my report that he thought he was being stalked.'

'And we thought he was just being paranoid,' Eileen said.

Geraldine didn't reply.

'Well,' the detective chief inspector went on, 'it seems he might have been right that someone was out to get him, but let's not arrive at any conclusions about that just yet. Stephanie was stabbed in her flat in York and this murder took place out in the fields in Saddleworth, so it could be a coincidence they were killed within a week of each other.' She paused. 'Of course, this victim's connection to Stephanie is highly likely to be significant, but then again they weren't close, were they?

Although they were at school together, they hadn't seen much of one another since then, isn't that right?'

Geraldine nodded. 'Peter told me he hadn't seen her since they left school five years ago,' she replied. 'He had an alibi for the night of her death.'

'So two former schoolmates were both killed within a week of each other,' Ian commented.

'The fact that they were at school together could be irrelevant,' Eileen insisted.

Geraldine understood her reluctance to acknowledge a connection between the two murders. Dealing with isolated independent murders was less worrying than the prospect of investigating a double murder.

'The fact is, a lot of people living around here attended that school,' Eileen continued. 'Statistically it's not that unlikely that two unrelated murder victims would have been at the same school.'

'They were in the same class,' Ian said.

'Ian's right,' Geraldine said firmly. Briefly she described how both victims had not only been attacked in the same way, but had been cut across the mouth so that they appeared to be smiling broadly. 'This was no coincidence. They were victims of the same killer.'

Eileen raised her eyebrows. 'Very well. But for now, we share none of that. Details of the attacks do not leave this room. Is that understood?'

There was a murmur of consent. No one wanted the media to go wild with stories of a serial killer on the loose. Such publicity would not only make the job of the police more difficult, it could spur the killer to commit more atrocities.

Geraldine went with Ian to find out what had been discovered at the post mortem. Since his admission that he was pleased to be working with her again, without a word spoken they seemed to have teamed up once more. Geraldine couldn't have been more pleased.

Jonah went through the usual routine, telling them Peter's age, his general health which was unremarkable, and the cause of his death.

'This was another vicious assault,' he concluded. 'From the angle of entry, many of the wounds were inflicted when the victim was already lying on the ground, and several were made post mortem.' He paused to let his words sink in. 'Even after he was dead, his killer continued his attack,' he added, as though wanting to be sure they had understood what he was saying. 'It was an extremely ferocious attack that went on for some time.'

'So are you implying this was a different killer to the one who murdered Stephanie?' Ian asked.

'That doesn't necessarily follow. He would have been able to spend more time with Peter,' Geraldine pointed out. 'When he killed Stephanie he would have needed to get away as quickly as possible, for fear of being discovered. But this attack happened late at night, out in the fields, in foggy weather. He wouldn't have had to worry too much about being seen.' She turned back to Jonah. 'How many times was he stabbed?'

'Seven times in the chest. Twice while he was still upright.' He pointed to two bloodless gashes in the white flesh near the dead man's heart. 'The other three injuries were more forceful. The blade was driven straight down into his chest while he was lying on the ground. Then there are further incisions here and here.'

He indicated several lacerations on the dead man's neck, shoulders and forearm. With the blood cleaned away, the apertures looked surreal, like lipless mouths.

'What time was he killed?' Ian asked.

'It's difficult to give an exact time as he was lying outside overnight, but I'd say it was around midnight, give or take an hour or two either way. He'd been drinking quite heavily before he died, so you could check the local pubs in case anyone remembers seeing him. You might be able to find out who he was drinking with.' He paused. 'But it was the same killer, or, at least, the deaths are related. Look!'

With a flourish, he pointed to the dead man's mouth.

'I noticed that,' Geraldine said. 'It's in my report from the crime scene, and I've brought it to the attention of the DCI. She wants it kept quiet for now. We don't want the press getting hold of it.'

Jonah grinned at Ian. 'Your new sergeant doesn't miss much. You'd better buck up your ideas, or she'll be leapfrogging over you on the career ladder.'

Ian glanced at Geraldine as though to apologise for the clumsy comment, although of course Jonah could hardly be accused of insensitivity, since he knew nothing about her recent demotion.

'She'll do,' Ian replied gruffly and Geraldine laughed.

'So, is there anything else? Any DNA under his nails?'

'Not that we've been able to find. There don't appear to be any defence wounds at all. He must have been caught off guard, or perhaps he was too drunk to retaliate.'

The three of them stared at the dead man.

'Of course it doesn't help us to find out who the killer was,' Ian said slowly, 'but at least we can confirm that the victims were both killed by the same person. So we now know there's a connection between the crimes, and we also know the victims were at school together, five years ago. I think we should start there. Do you want to arrange a visit to the school tomorrow, Geraldine? What do you think?'

Geraldine was still staring at the body.

'Peter was right,' she replied miserably.

Whatever else happened, nothing could alter the fact that they had failed to protect Peter from a violent maniac.

'We weren't to know,' Ian said softly.

'We should have known. Isn't that our job, to protect people?'

18

THE SCHOOLS IN YORKSHIRE had not yet opened after the Christmas holidays. A borough intelligence officer told Geraldine that a new head had started at Saddleworth Secondary School two years ago. The previous head having remained in Uppermill, Geraldine decided to start her enquiries there. Susan Mulvey had been head of Saddleworth School for over fifteen years, her residency covering the two victims' final seven years at the school. There was a slim chance she might be able to shed some light on the case. Geraldine called to make sure she was at home before setting out, and the ex-head promptly responded by inviting her round for tea. She sounded as though she would be pleased of the company.

The journey to Uppermill was beginning to feel familiar. As she drew up outside Susan's house and climbed out of the car, Geraldine had an uncomfortable sensation that someone was watching her. She dismissed it as guilt at having failed to protect Peter when he had told her he was being stalked. All the same, she looked around uneasily. The side street where she had parked was deserted. Telling herself she was imagining things, she marched up to the front door and rang the bell. Turning suddenly, she thought she caught a glimpse of a figure in a long dark coat darting out of sight at the far end of the street, too far away for her to register any distinguishing features. She wasn't even sure that she had seen a human figure. It was the rapidity of movement that had caught her eye. She looked again but there was no one there.

Behind her she heard the click of a latch.

'Sergeant Steel?' a woman's voice enquired.

Geraldine turned to her with a smile. She was growing accustomed to her new title. In addition to the alliteration, it had a satisfying rhythm to it.

'Mrs Mulvey?'

'Yes. Come in out of the cold and let's get that door shut. And you can call me Susan. We're not at school now.'

There was something dogmatic in the woman's welcome. Generations of children must have been reassured or intimidated by her air of authority. She took Geraldine into a living room where pale blue curtains and carpet complemented wall paper patterned with tiny blue flowers. Three matching armchairs stood around a low coffee table on which a china tea set had been carefully laid out, complete with a cake that looked as though it might be homemade. A handful of newspapers and magazines had been placed neatly in a wooden rack. This was the home of a woman who appreciated order, a woman who liked to be in control.

'Now then, do you take sugar?' Mrs Mulvey asked, as though the sole purpose of Geraldine's visit was to join her hostess for tea. 'The seed cake's just come out of the oven.'

Once the tea had been poured and the cake cut, Geraldine went straight to the point of her visit. She handed the other woman a printout of the two victims' faces, taken from their passports.

'Do you recognise them?'

'What's this about?'

'I was hoping you would be able to tell me something about these ex-pupils of yours.'

Susan screwed up her eyes and scrutinised the sheet of paper. 'Just a second.' She stood up and returned a moment later with a pair of glasses hanging on a chain around her neck. Putting them on, she peered at the images again. Geraldine waited.

'This is the poor girl who was murdered last week. Yes, I

remember Stephanie. She can't have been more than about twenty-three. What a tragedy.'

'What can you tell me about her?'

'Well, it was a few years ago, and we have a lot of pupils passing through the school, but yes, I remember Stephanie.' She stared at the picture. 'So she was killed?'

'Yes. I'm sorry.'

'No, no, that's quite all right. I understand. We need to do everything we can to find out who committed this atrocity.' She peered at Geraldine over the top of her glasses. 'I heard on the radio there's been a second victim.'

'Yes, Peter Edwards. He was in the same class as Stephanie at Saddleworth School.'

Susan looked solemn. 'Yes, I seem to remember that.'

'In confidence, can you think of anyone who attended the school around the same time as them who struck you as potentially violent? Anyone who rang alarm bells?'

Removing her glasses, Susan shook her head. 'I'm sorry, Sergeant, but it's a while ago. I remember all the pupils who attended my school, but I can't be sure of the dates of their attendance.'

'Would it be possible for you to check the school records to see if anyone there at the same time as Stephanie displayed signs of psychological disturbance?'

'I guessed you might turn up here about the recent murders. I realised at once that the victims were both pupils at my school. I've been giving this a lot of thought, as you can imagine, Sergeant, since I heard about Stephanie, not just because my school's been mentioned in the media in connection with these murders, but because I knew the victims.'

'You knew them both?'

'I knew *all* my pupils, Sergeant.' She sniffed. 'As I said, I've been giving this matter a great deal of thought and I have to conclude that it's really not surprising both victims attended my school, given the killer is presumably also a local. We have nearly fifteen hundred pupils attending the school and send around two hundred out into society every year. So if a violent maniac is killing people in the area, the chances are the victims will have been pupils at Saddleworth School. I don't think you can read anything into this but a predictable coincidence. What's more concerning is whether this lunatic is likely to strike again. Are people actually safe, living here in Uppermill?'

Geraldine reassured her that neither of the murders had taken place in Uppermill. Stephanie had been killed sixty miles away in York, while Peter had been killed in the fields a few miles from the village. The conversation had strayed off at a tangent. Effortlessly taking control, the former headmistress had carefully steered the focus away from the original question. Geraldine slid the printout across the table so that it was right in front of Susan.

'We believe the two murders are linked. The victims knew one another. They were in the same class at school. Now, is there anything you can recall that might help us? Take your time. Please, this is important.'

Susan replaced her glasses and stared at the paper again. Once more she shook her head.

'I'm sorry, Sergeant, but I can't imagine who might have done this. I doubt it was a pupil from Saddleworth School. This kind of extreme behaviour would surely have manifested itself in some way during adolescence? And I really can't think of anyone who stands out as violent. But you're free to approach the current head teacher and request a check of the school records in case something has slipped my mind.' From her tone, she clearly didn't believe that she had could have overlooked anything. 'I have an excellent memory,' she added, as though to confirm what Geraldine was thinking. She didn't want to talk about it.

Since she had claimed to know all her pupils, Geraldine enquired about the two victims.

'What would you like to know?'

'We've seen copies of their school reports, but is there anything else you can tell me? Anything you remember about them.'

'It was a long time ago,' Susan hedged.

Geraldine nodded. She didn't entirely trust the retired head teacher's claim to have known all her thousands of pupils personally, until Susan continued.

'Stephanie Crawford was a pleasant girl. Quite sharp, but not the best student. She let nerves get the better of her when it came to exams. She was a quiet girl, not unpopular, tolerably pretty, but in no way remarkable. I can't tell you much more about her, I'm afraid. And I remember Peter Edwards, too. He wasn't a bad boy, but sadly lacking in ambition.' A fleeting smile crossed her lips. 'He was one of the lads. Not a ring leader, but he was involved in any high jinks that was going on. At the end of their last term, six of the boys managed to get hold of the school mascot and hang it from the roof.' She chuckled.

'You've got a good memory.'

'I saw what happened, on the news, and I recognised the names of the victims, so I went through some old school photos.' She sighed. 'They were very young. And you really think their deaths were related?'

She lowered her gaze, and Geraldine had the impression she was uncomfortable.

'Susan, is there something else? You can speak to me in confidence, unless you have something to tell me that has a direct bearing on my investigation, in which case I'll have to share it with my team, of course. I know you understand what I'm saying, and I can't help feeling you know more than you're admitting.'

The other woman stared at the floor. Geraldine waited. When Susan looked up again she let out a sigh.

'Yes,' she said, 'we did have a little trouble at that time. There were a few incidents of bullying. But nothing out of the ordinary.' She scowled. 'These things go on all the time in schools. Oh, we held regular anti-bullying campaigns and sometimes we succeeded in putting a lid on it but it was never long before it started up again.' She fell silent and looked down at the floor again.

'What happened with Stephanie and Peter?'

'Oh, there was nothing particular involving them, but there was some bullying during their time at school that went on for quite a while. We never managed to pin down the culprits, but we knew there was more than one pupil responsible for what was happening, which always made it more difficult to identify and isolate the perpetrator. We never really did get to the bottom of it.'

'Who was the victim?'

Susan shook her head. 'You know, I've been wracking my brains ever since you came here asking questions, but I just can't remember. I'm not sure there was just one victim. It was... well, there was a group of boys who seemed to be doing it. We suspected Peter was one of the gang. But no one ever came forward and we never managed to find out who was behind it. I don't think Stephanie was involved at all. And now I'm afraid I really do have nothing more to tell you.'

All Geraldine could do was thank her and leave.

'You will let me know if you think of anything that might help us, and please, whatever you do, don't mention any of this to anyone else.'

Susan nodded. 'I understand.'

19

LEAVING UPPERMILL, GERALDINE DROVE straight to the neighbouring village of Greenfield. As soon as the door opened, it was obvious Peter's landlady knew what had happened.

'Do you know who did it?' She was clutching a tissue and dabbed at her eyes and sniffed as she spoke. 'The poor boy. I heard he had stab wounds all over his body. The thought of it's going to give me nightmares for the rest of my life. He was such a nice quiet young man. Who could have done such a thing?'

'Who told you he suffered multiple stab wounds?' Geraldine answered the question with another.

'That's what I heard,' Peter's landlady mumbled. 'Is it true?'

'He had a fatal wound in his chest. Whatever else you may have heard is merely speculation passed around by people who know even less about what happened than you do. I wouldn't pay any attention to idle chit chat like that.'

'You saw him though, didn't you? You know what happened. Tell me everything, please. I want to know. We weren't related, but he lived here in my house with me. He was like a son to me.' Her voice broke into a sob. She pressed her tissue against her lips and stared at Geraldine. 'Please,' she whispered, 'I want to know what happened.'

Geraldine sighed. 'We're still trying to find out the details and discover who did this. I was hoping you might be able to help me clear up a few questions.'

'Yes, yes, of course.'

They went inside and sat down. 'Now please, I have to know. Is it safe living here?'

Geraldine took a deep breath. 'We believe Peter was targeted.'

'Targeted?'

'This doesn't appear to have been a random attack. So there's no reason to suppose anyone else might be at risk.' Apart from other pupils who were in his class at school, she thought. 'But I'd be vigilant...'

'Vigilant? What do you mean?'

Geraldine chose her words with care. In a village her words might be broadcast effectively without any interference from the media. This investigation was assuming a very different feel to the cases she had worked on in London. If she could enlist local support that would almost certainly help her, but the close community was equally likely to cause problems. She was already wondering whether to pursue Susan Mulvey's mention of bullying. Once news of that leaked out, the issue was likely to start appearing in the media and the number of spurious and malicious calls to the police would mushroom.

'With two people killed in the area, it might be sensible not to wander around at night on your own in the dark. That's all I meant.'

'Two people?'

Geraldine mentioned Stephanie.

'But she was killed in York, wasn't she? It's different in the city,' the landlady said, as though Stephanie moving to York explained her death.

Geraldine decided not to press the point. Instead, she questioned Peter's landlady about the company he had kept while he was living with her. Apart from going to the pub with a few of the locals, it seemed that Peter had done little other than go to work in a local garden centre. He had led a very quiet life.

'What about family?'

'I was his family,' she replied, breaking down in tears again. 'The only family he had.'

'But not related?'

The landlady shook her head. 'No, but we might as well have been for all the support he got from his parents.'

'Do they live locally?'

'His mother died while he was still at school. It was the cancer. And his father moved south to Birmingham to be with his new partner soon after Peter left school. Peter didn't want to go with them so he stayed put, right here. I don't blame him,' she added, 'although if he'd gone with his father...' she broke off again, shaking her head, too overcome with emotion to say any more.

'Do you know when his father left the area?'

She shook her head. 'About three years ago. Maybe longer. Peter's been living here with me for three years,' she added, anticipating Geraldine's next question.

'Did he ever mention Stephanie?'

'No. He never spoke about much really. We talked about the weather, and his dinner – I cooked for him every evening and he was always very appreciative. He always thanked me. I used to care for my mother, but since she died I had no one else to look after. That's why I thought I'd take in a lodger, have someone else in the house. Peter was the first lodger I took in.' She sighed. 'I don't think I'll have another lodger. Not now. Not after what's happened.'

Even though he had lived under her roof for three years and they had been close, in a way, she actually knew very little about Peter. Perhaps there wasn't much to know, Geraldine concluded after calling in at the garden centre where he had worked. The manager there was in his fifties, short and wiry and softly spoken.

'He was a quiet lad,' he said. 'We were all shocked to hear what happened to him. He wasn't the sort you'd expect to be in any trouble. What was he doing out there at night anyway?'

'We don't know.'

'It said in the news he was killed in the early hours in the field where they found him.' The manager frowned. 'Do you think someone deliberately took him out into the fields to kill him?'

Geraldine shook her head. 'We don't yet know what happened. There are a number of possibilities. It could have been an accident,' she hesitated. The media hadn't yet revealed the extent of the dead man's injuries, but that was only a matter of time. 'It's possible it was a random attack. But we're currently exploring the idea that he might have been deliberately murdered. If there's anything you can think of that might help us to get to the bottom of this, please don't hold back. Anything you say will be treated in confidence. I mean, no one will find out the source of the information. So, can you think of anyone who might have wanted to harm Peter? Anyone he'd argued with or upset?'

The manager shook his head. 'Like I said, he was a quiet lad, more likely to be overlooked than to provoke any sort of a reaction. To be honest, he wasn't the sharpest tool in the box, but he was obliging and he seemed to enjoy working here. He wasn't what you'd call a top salesman, but he made himself useful. Between you and me, I think he was happiest when he was with the plants. I'm not sure I didn't hear him talking to them when he thought no one was listening. I think he preferred them to people.' He shrugged. 'Can't say I blame him for that.'

Geraldine had a word with all the other employees there. Everyone she spoke to described him as an inoffensive young man. They all said they were devastated at what had happened, and couldn't believe anyone would want to harm Peter.

'He was such a nice young man,' was the general view expressed. 'How could anyone do that to someone like Peter?'

Geraldine had no answer; amiability was no protection against a violent maniac.

20

ALTHOUGH GERALDINE DIDN'T RETURN to Fulford Road until early evening, way past the time when most of her colleagues would normally have gone home, the police station was humming. With a double murder investigation on their hands everyone was working hard, and very few people were complaining about the additional hours. Geraldine was quickly brought up to speed. All of Stephanie's former classmates and work colleagues had been questioned. A few possible leads had emerged. Geraldine studied the reports in preparation for the next briefing the following morning.

Two years younger than Stephanie, her brother lived at home with his parents in their family home in Uppermill. No one had yet spoken to him, as he had been out when Geraldine had visited his parents. Geraldine didn't think it was likely to be significant that Stephanie had rowed with her brother shortly before she had moved out. As siblings, they probably argued all the time. Even so, Geraldine wondered whether the boy might have something to add to what they already knew about his sister. Certainly he ought to be questioned.

Eileen was thinking along similar lines because she brought the subject up almost straight away at the briefing the next morning.

'You spoke to Stephanie's parents?' she barked, looking at Geraldine.

'What did they say about their son?'

'Nothing much,' Geraldine replied. 'He wasn't in when I visited them.'

Eileen frowned. 'Why didn't you ask them to summon him home while you were there?'

'He plays the guitar in a local boy band and was out at a gig,' Geraldine explained. 'He wasn't deliberately avoiding me. They were playing in a pub in Leeds and his parents said he wouldn't be home until late.'

Geraldine had done nothing wrong, yet Eileen's tone sounded accusatory.

'And why didn't you arrange to see his parents when he was at home?'

Instead of defending herself against the implied criticism, Geraldine kept quiet. New to the force, she hadn't yet earned the right to argue with her senior officer.

Eileen grunted. 'We need to speak to the brother.'

'I'll go,' Geraldine said straight away.

Her eagerness would probably be interpreted as an attempt to curry favour, but the truth was that she was curious to hear what Stephanie's brother had to say.

She called ahead to say she wanted to speak to Mr and Mrs Crawford and their son.

'You'd best come over in the afternoon. He's never up before midday.'

'I'll be round this evening.'

'Come early, or he'll be out drinking with his mates.'

'Please ask him not to go out until I've spoken to him.'

Mrs Crawford responded sourly that she had no control over her son. With the self-absorption of a twenty-year-old, it seemed he would happily ignore a request from a police officer investigating his sister's murder if it interfered with his social life.

'Please make sure he knows I want to speak to him,' Geraldine insisted. 'If he refuses to see me at home that's going to raise serious questions, meaning my senior investigating officer is likely to arrange for him to come to the police station in York. Obstructing a murder enquiry isn't very sensible.'

'I'll do my best to keep him here,' Mrs Crawford agreed grudgingly.

Instead of waiting until the evening, Geraldine decided to arrive at four. She had already spoken to Stephanie's parents, who had in addition spoken to several other officers. No one had yet questioned the dead girl's brother, Freddie. He was the person she was most interested in seeing. If he went out she would have to chase around looking for him, and it might be more difficult to get much sense out of him once he had started drinking.

Mrs Crawford looked surprised to see her. 'I thought you said you were going to be here this evening.'

Geraldine nodded. 'I decided to come earlier.'

Without any further explanation she asked to see Freddie. Mrs Crawford showed her into the neat front room again and a few seconds later Geraldine heard her yelling up the stairs for her son to 'get down here now!'

There was a muffled buzz of someone calling back an answer. Mrs Crawford shouted again. After a few more exchanges, Geraldine heard footsteps clomping down the stairs and a young man burst into the room. Cut short above his ears, his straw-coloured hair had been left to grow longer on top of his head and hung down over his eyes in a style fashionable with some youngsters. He peered suspiciously at her through his fringe.

'What?' he demanded, a stereotype of a sullen teenager.

'Please sit down.'

'I'll stand thank you. And can we make this snappy as I'm going out soon.'

Geraldine was tempted to request that he accompany her to the police station in York for questioning. But he wasn't a suspect, and for all his posturing he must have been deeply distressed by his sister's murder. Besides which he was only twenty, and clearly frightened.

'Please sit down,' she repeated quietly. 'I'm sorry for your loss. I'm here as part of the investigation into your sister's death. We're all very sorry about what happened.'

The boy grunted. She wondered if she had got through to him.

'I came here to ask if there's anything you can tell us that might help us to find out who committed this terrible act?'

There was a pause. The young man perched on the arm of a chair.

'Was she raped?' he blurted out. 'They won't tell me anything, and the media just spouts all sorts of shit. What happened?'

Geraldine told him his sister would have died quickly. 'She wouldn't have known anything about it after the first stab wound.'

His eyes narrowed. 'Are you just saying that to make me feel better?'

She shook her head and he paused, thinking. She waited.

'So what do you want with me?' he asked at last.

'We know what happened to your sister, but we don't know who did it. And we believe the killer might have claimed another victim.'

'That guy Peter.' Geraldine nodded. 'I saw it on the news. I wondered if it was the same killer. Everyone's saying it was. They're saying there's a serial killer in the area.'

'Freddie, is there anything you can think of that might help us?'

He dropped his eyes and shrugged, clamming up.

'Anything at all. Can you think of anyone who was angry with your sister?'

Without warning he jumped to his feet. 'I didn't know that guy Peter. We had a row, she was always bugging me. But it was nothing to do with me. I was here in Uppermill. You can ask anyone. And anyway I wasn't angry with her, not any longer, not after she'd gone to live in York. You want to know the truth? I wish she'd never gone there. I'd rather have put up with her living here than what happened. She was stupid, all right, but she was my sister. I would never have done anything to hurt her.'

'Freddie, no one's accusing you of being involved in what happened to your sister.'

'But you're all thinking that if I hadn't been here, she might never have gone to York.'

'Nonsense. She was ready to move out, that's all. It was nothing to do with you.'

Freddie looked sceptical. 'That's what *they* think,' he muttered angrily, sitting on the arm of the chair again.

Geraldine pressed him but he said he couldn't think of anyone who might have wanted to kill his sister.

'It's crazy to think anyone did it deliberately,' he said. 'She wasn't that sort of person.'

'What sort of person?'

'The sort of person anyone would want to kill. She was way too boring. She was…'

He covered his face with his hands, but not before Geraldine had seen tears glistening in his eyes. His air of bravado vanished, he slipped off the arm of the chair on to the seat without uncovering his face, and sobbed. After a few moments he sat up, rubbing his eyes with his fists, like a child.

'Sorry,' he mumbled, embarrassed by his display of emotion. 'But she was my sister.' His voice rose in anguish. 'I'm on my own now. There's no one else…'

His mother came into the room, and sat beside her son, rocking in her seat and wailing. Feeling helpless, Geraldine slipped away. There was nothing she could say that would alleviate their grief or soften the finality of their loss. But she would do everything in her power to track down the person who had caused their cruel suffering.

21

ASHLEY WAS SURPRISED WHEN one of her former school friends, Beth, phoned to invite her round to another old school friend's flat the following evening. It seemed an inappropriate time to throw a party, not to mention very last minute, but Beth was insistent.

'Sorry Beth, I'm just too tired to be sociable right now. I've not been feeling up to anything much since...' she hesitated. 'You heard what happened to Steph?' Her voice wobbled as she said her dead flatmate's name. 'To be honest, partying is the last thing on my mind right now.'

Beth muttered that she knew about it. 'That's why we have to meet. It's not a party. We need to talk about what happened to Stephanie and Peter.'

'I don't want to talk about it.'

'Listen, Ashley, you *have* to come. Everyone who still lives in the area and was in our class has to. It's all organised. Leah's in touch with Robin and he said he'll give you a lift. He lives near York and he's driving over here for the meeting.'

Ashley's head was spinning. 'What are you talking about? What's been organised?'

'You know me and Leah are both still living here in Uppermill?'

Ashley mumbled something.

'And there's you and Robin in York. There are bound to be a few more of our year group still living in the area, but if the killer is focusing his attacks on our class, we can't just wait around like sitting ducks. We need to get together and talk about what's happened.'

Ashley thought she understood, but she wasn't keen on that kind of amateur group therapy.

'Listen, Beth. I appreciate what you're trying to do, really I do, but my GP has referred me for bereavement counselling if I need it, so I'll leave it at that. I'm sorry, but I just don't think us all getting together is going to help. You don't know what it was like for me, finding her like that...'

'This isn't some kind of support group. I mean, in a way I suppose it is. But we need to talk about what we're going to do. What if one of us is next?'

Ashley felt a sudden rush of blood to her head. 'What are you talking about?'

Beth explained that she and Leah were concerned there might be a connection between the two recent deaths. If that was the case, it might have something to do with their time at school.

'I know it sounds unlikely, put like that, but we're worried someone might be targeting our class, picking us off one by one. I don't want to sound melodramatic, especially not after what you've been through, but Leah thinks we might all be at risk. If there's even the slightest chance she's right, we need to talk about what we should do. The others agree with me. So we're meeting to discuss the situation and decide what we're going to do about it.'

'What do you mean?'

'Maybe between us we can think of a reason why someone seems to be targeting our old classmates. We have to put our heads together and try anyway.'

'You don't think it's coincidence, both of them being in the same class as us?'

'Well, it could be, but we thought we should get together to discuss what's happened, just in case we can come up with something. So you'll be there at Leah's, won't you?'

Ashley hesitated. 'Shouldn't we leave all this to the police? What can *we* do?'

'Of course it's a matter for the police, but they don't know anything about *us*, do they? If we can come up with a plausible reason why this is happening we'll go straight to the police. We're not suggesting we try and deal with a homicidal maniac ourselves! But the police have questioned me and Leah and asked us if we can think of anyone who might have had a grudge against Stephanie and Peter.'

'Well? Can you? What did you say?'

'Neither of us could come up with anything just like that. How about you?'

'Same.'

'But Leah thinks – that is we both think – if we all get together we might be able to think of something. It's got to be worth a try anyway.'

Ashley wasn't keen, but Robin had offered to give her a lift so there was no good reason for her to refuse.

'Great. I've given Robin your address and he'll pick you up on his way. Can you be ready about seven?'

'OK.'

'See you tomorrow then.'

Ashley regretted having given in as soon as she hung up but there was no way out of it, short of pretending to be ill. If she did that it would be obvious she was just making an excuse. The following evening she showered and changed, and was ready by half past six in case Robin was early. She sat on her bed, nervously checking her reflection and wondering what everyone else would be wearing and then hating herself for caring what her former classmates would think of her. It was only a week since Stephanie had been horribly killed and here she was, fretting over her own appearance. It made her feel like a monster. Regretting having allowed herself to be bullied into accepting Beth's invitation, she struggled to hold back her tears.

As it turned out, she needn't have worried because Robin never showed up. Too late she realised he must have gone to the wrong flat. She hadn't mentioned to Beth that she was staying with a neighbour. If she had been watching through her front window in her bedroom, she would probably have seen his car draw up. 'Freudian slip,' she thought with miserable satisfaction. She hadn't wanted to go anyway. Beth and Leah were right. The killer could be targeting her class. But if that *was* the case, there was no guarantee the killer wasn't one of the people going to Beth's flat that evening. The thought was terrifying. She wondered who else was going to be there, and what conclusion they would draw from her absence. She hoped they wouldn't suspect her.

22

'WELL, THIS IS A complete waste of time,' Leah burst out, following Beth into the kitchen.

'I wouldn't say that,' Beth replied.

'For a start, Ashley hasn't showed up.'

Beth squirmed and looked away. She knew very well Leah blamed her for what had happened.

'Didn't you even think to ask her for her address?' Leah demanded, her plump face reddening with barely controlled anger.

Beth made a feeble attempt to defend herself. 'That *is* her address.'

'Well she isn't living there any more so no, it isn't.'

'But everyone else is here.'

Leah grunted. 'We need Ashley here. She was sharing a flat with Stephanie which means she's the only one of us who knows more than the police are telling us. We need to hear what she has to say.'

Beth tried to convince Leah that Ashley had been reluctant to join them and would probably have found a reason not to turn up anyway, but Leah was having none of it. Privately Beth thought that even if Ashley had been there, the evening would have been a disaster. Robin and Ned didn't appear at all worried about their own safety, following the deaths of their two former classmates.

The two girls were more or less in agreement that they ought to be concerned, although Leah was far more strident. 'There are, that is, there *were*, seven of us living in the area,' she said.

'Two of them – of us – have been murdered. That's more than thirty per cent of us. You can't just ignore that.'

'Twenty-eight per cent,' Robin corrected her. 'Two out of seven is actually twenty-eight point five per cent.'

He was equally dismissive of the idea that the rest of them might be in danger.

'But what are the chances that two people from the same class would both be killed in the same week?' Leah insisted.

With Robin and Ned both convinced the closeness of the two deaths was a coincidence, Leah's suggestion they all put their heads together and try to think of any reason someone might be targeting their class fell flat. Beth and Leah threw a few ideas around, while Robin and Ned drank beer and swapped jokes as though this was any ordinary social gathering.

'I don't know about you,' Leah said, 'but I'm scared to go to work next week.'

Beth thought about what to say. Admittedly Leah had a tendency to overdramatise things, but Beth had already annoyed her by failing to find out where Ashley was staying. She didn't want to provoke Leah further by openly disagreeing with her.

'I think we should be OK during the day, but I'm not going to go out alone after dark,' she fibbed, backing Leah up. 'Not until they catch the killer.'

'We don't know if anyone else from our class has been killed. We only know about the two who still lived around here,' Leah pointed out. 'I think it's time we insisted on police protection.'

'It couldn't do any harm,' Beth agreed.

Robin continued to scoff at their fears. 'For goodness sake, don't be so naive. Don't you think the police have enough real crimes to deal with? They're not going to take any notice of any of us.'

Ned nodded. 'You can't report a crime that hasn't been committed and expect the police to do anything.'

'So you think we should just wait until someone else – one

of us – gets killed before we go to the police for help?'

'Have any of us received any death threats? I know I haven't. Have any of you?' Robin asked.

They all shook their heads.

'Exactly. So where's your evidence that you're in any danger, any more than everyone else with a killer running around the area?'

'That's hardly the point,' Leah said.

'That's exactly the point,' Robin told her firmly.

'Two people have been killed, both from our class at school,' Leah insisted, her voice rising in frustration. 'How much more of a threat do you want before you start taking this seriously?'

Robin put his glass down. 'Listen, Leah, there's nothing to suggest those murders were related in any way, and no reason to suppose they were connected to any of us. I honestly think you're getting in a tizz over nothing and winding yourself up needlessly.'

Robin and Ned left soon after. With a sigh, Leah opened another can of beer. 'So it's down to us to find out what's going on,' she said.

'There's not a lot we can do.'

'We need to be thinking about how to protect ourselves,' Leah continued, ignoring Beth's interruption. 'And we need to find out who's doing this, and why, so the police can track him down and lock him up.'

Beth said nothing. She was beginning to think that Leah was getting unnecessarily worked up all over again. Of course it was deeply shocking that Stephanie and Peter had been killed, and it was natural that Leah would be in a state about it. They were all upset. Looking back on the evening, it seemed to Beth that everyone had been venting their emotions in different ways. But she agreed with Robin that Leah was exaggerating the danger to the rest of them, and becoming hysterical in the process.

'Robin's right, none of us has actually been threatened,' she ventured.

Leah rounded on her. 'So you're siding with them now, are you? Do you think whoever's doing this warned Stephanie or Peter about what was going to happen to them? We're not talking about someone who goes around making threats. We're talking about someone who actually goes out and kills people. I can't believe you're taking this so calmly. We have to do something to stop this killer before he gets us, too.' She paused. 'I've been making enquiries.'

'What do you mean? What sort of enquiries?'

'We have to protect ourselves.'

'What are you talking about?'

Leah hesitated before jumping up and leaving the room. She returned a moment later, holding a brown paper bag.

Beth couldn't help laughing, she was so surprised. 'What's that going to do? Are you going to put it over your head so the killer can't recognise you?'

She stared in disbelief as Leah took a small black gun out of the bag. 'What the hell are you doing with that? You have to get rid of it, now! Someone could get hurt.'

'Well, it's not going to be one of us. I'm going to make sure of that.'

'You don't even know how to use it.'

Leah smiled. 'I lived on a farm until I was ten. I know how to protect myself. No one's going to come here and stab us to death.'

'You're insane.'

'No, I'm being sensible.'

Leah slipped the gun back in the bag. 'You mustn't tell anyone about this. Promise me you won't.'

Beth shrugged. 'If you say so.' She didn't intend to carry on arguing with a lunatic holding a gun.

23

WHEN NAOMI INVITED GERALDINE to join her for lunch in the canteen she thought it might sound churlish to refuse, even though she was in the middle of writing up a report on Freddie Crawford. The job wasn't urgent, and it was important for her to get to know her colleagues in York. Naomi chattered easily as they made their way to the canteen, keen to tell Geraldine about the interesting sites in York. She said nothing that couldn't be found in any guide book, but Geraldine listened politely, responding when appropriate. When they were sitting down over soup and salads, the conversation drifted to the investigation.

'There's still the unidentified DNA,' Geraldine pointed out. 'That has to be the key to this whole thing.'

Naomi nodded. No one could deny the significance of the DNA they had found.

'But without a match, there's nothing we can do,' Naomi said.

'I think we ought to take a sample from everyone who was at that school with the victims,' Geraldine answered. 'Pupils and teachers.'

'That would be a massive undertaking.'

'But necessary. We'd only need to look at the ex-pupils who are still living in the area. How many of them can there be? And the teachers who were there with them, most of them have probably moved away by now.'

Naomi nodded. 'You're right. We need to start taking samples from everyone who was at school with them. We could spread the search even wider, to everyone who might have come in contact with them. I expect Eileen will get on to that. To be fair, we have only just discovered they were in the same class at school.'

After they had been eating in silence for a moment, Naomi asked how Geraldine was settling in.

'I've only ever worked around here, first in Northallerton and then I recently moved to York. I love the area, but it must be exciting in London?'

Geraldine nodded, refusing to be drawn on the reason for her move.

'Well, you'll find we're a sociable bunch. I'm sure you'll soon feel as though you're among old friends here.'

'Yes, and I've worked with Ian before.'

Naomi looked up. 'When was that?'

Geraldine told her that she had worked with Ian in Kent, before he had been promoted to inspector and moved to York. Naomi put down her knife and fork and leaned forward. Lowering her voice, she intimated that she wanted to ask a question about Ian.

'I'm just thinking that, as you've known him for a while, you might know the answer. Don't tell me if you don't want to, or if you don't know, but I heard a rumour that he's married and I wondered if that's true.'

Geraldine wasn't surprised to discover that Naomi was interested in Ian. He was an attractive man. If she had been younger, she might have made a play for him herself, but she was five years older than him and besides, they knew each other too well as old friends for him to ever see her in a romantic light. Geraldine was surprised that he hadn't responded to Naomi's advances. Slim and blond and pretty, she was not unlike his estranged wife, Bev, although not as beautiful. Her make-up was too heavy, and her skirts too short, for a woman in a serious professional role. Yet she was undoubtedly attractive, combining her flirty attire with an air of confident efficiency that smacked of someone who knew how to do her job, and do it well. She listened attentively as Geraldine explained that Ian was estranged from his wife who was living with another man, back in Kent.

'I don't think she ever really settled here, and she wasn't happy being married to a police officer. The unsocial hours were a problem for her.'

Naomi nodded. 'It happens,' she said. 'But do you think they might get back together?'

'I don't think so. She's living with someone else and they've started a family. It's the other man's baby, which makes it complicated.'

'Was he very cut up about it?'

Geraldine nodded. 'He adored her. She was really stunning, and I think she broke his heart, as the saying goes.'

'Oh, poor Ian. What about you? Have you ever been married? Any family?'

Geraldine told Naomi that she had never been married, and went on to talk about her adopted family.

'So Celia and I weren't that close when we were growing up. We're much closer now, but she's a long way away. And then...'

About to tell Naomi about her twin, a recovering addict in London, she changed her mind.

'What about you? Have you ever been married?'

Naomi laughed. 'I'm only twenty-six.'

All at once, Geraldine felt very old. Returning to her desk, she realised that she had told Naomi quite a lot about herself, but had learned very little about her young colleague. She must be lonelier than she had appreciated, to talk so much about herself. She had said nothing about the person who was uppermost in her mind, but as soon as she arrived home that evening, she phoned the clinic to find out what was happening. Three days had elapsed since she had last spoken to her twin sister, and agreed to pay her rent. Since then she had heard nothing, and she was beginning to worry. Her concern grew when it seemed to take a long time for the clinic to find Helena and put her on the phone. For once Geraldine's fears seemed unfounded. Helena sounded both sober and cheerful.

'I think I done it this time,' she said.

'Done it?'

'Yeah, I finally kicked the habit. I tried before, you know, only it never come to nothing. I tried a few times and never got anywhere close. But this time – well, they tell me it's one day at a time, but I'm telling you, I'm feeling good. I never felt this good in my life before.'

Geraldine was cautiously optimistic. 'That's great!'

'I'm not saying I'm expecting it to be easy. But I've got started and I'm not going to screw it up this time.'

They discussed the arrangements for Helena's move back to her apartment. This time when Geraldine repeated her determination to pay the rent directly, Helena agreed without demur. She even thanked Geraldine for helping her to stay clean. At least that area of life seemed to be moving forward in a positive way. But Geraldine had too much experience of addicts to feel confident that Helena wouldn't relapse. After hanging up, she wondered whether she ought to have suggested Helena come and live in York, where Geraldine would be able to keep an eye on her. It might be a good idea for Helena to move right away from her existing contacts. But if she wanted to resume her habit, she could do so anywhere. While Geraldine was deliberating, her phone rang.

'I haven't spoken to you for days,' Celia said.

'I know. I've been really busy.'

'You're always busy.'

Geraldine sighed. Her adoptive sister was still upset with her for moving away from Kent, where Celia still lived.

'York? Are you joking? York?' Celia had spluttered. 'York's miles away. It's right up in the north of England. It's nearly in Scotland. Why on earth would you want to go there? I can understand you wanting to be in London. Like you said, it's a good career move. But how can it be a step up to go from London to York? It doesn't make sense. I suppose you've been promoted. Does this mean you're a detective chief inspector? Even so, is it really worth it? You'll be hundreds of miles away...'

Aware that she should have confessed she had been demoted to sergeant, Geraldine had bottled it. 'No, I haven't been promoted,' was all she had said.

Now Celia sounded frosty when she asked how Geraldine was settling into her new post.

'It's OK,' Geraldine replied. 'Early days, you know.'

Celia sniffed as though to say she really didn't know what Geraldine meant.

'More important, how are *you*? It must be what, eight weeks to go?'

As she spoke, she was conscious that she hadn't phoned her pregnant sister for over a week. Anything could have happened in that time. She wasn't even sure without checking how long it was until the baby was due.

'You are still OK, aren't you?' she added in sudden panic.

'I'm fine, just fed up. And missing my sister.'

Geraldine understood that Celia was likely to be emotional, with her hormones in turmoil. Even so, she felt uncomfortable when Celia burst into tears.

'You know I'd come round if I could,' she said feebly.

'When am I going to see you?' Celia sniffed.

'Tell you what, why don't I come down tomorrow? It's Sunday and I'm due a day off.'

'But aren't you busy with an investigation? I wouldn't want to get you in trouble.'

It was just as well Celia couldn't see Geraldine's sour expression. With her demotion and enforced relocation, she could hardly be in much worse trouble at work.

24

LEAH HAD SPENT THE evening with her belly dancing group which had gathered for a post-Christmas celebration. It had proved impossible to find a time they could all make in December. As soon as the term ended, several of the group, including their teacher, had gone away for Christmas and the New Year, so it was well into January before they were all able to go out together. The date had been agreed weeks before Stephanie had been killed. Under normal circumstances, Leah wouldn't have thought twice about walking home alone through the village. She needed the exercise. That was the reason she had signed up for a belly dancing class in the first place, after all. Since they had fixed the date, circumstances had changed.

Thinking about the killer loose on the streets, she nearly made an excuse to stay at home. But as the class had arranged to meet at a pub in Uppermill, she felt obliged to go. Besides, the others were good company and she didn't want to miss out on spending an evening with them. The pub wasn't far from her flat, and it wasn't as if the police had issued a warning for people not to go out alone after dark. No one else was curtailing their activities on account of the recent murders. Stephanie had been killed miles away in York, and Peter hadn't been attacked in the village. Perhaps Beth and the others were right, and she was being needlessly anxious. She resolved not to let fear govern her life. In the end she decided to compromise by going to the dinner, and taking a taxi home.

Her courageous decision not to be cowed by what had happened to Stephanie and Peter didn't embolden her, however, and she was too anxious to enjoy the evening. No one else so much as mentioned the subject of the local murders. Yet all the time her friends were exchanging Christmas horror stories, she was preoccupied with thinking about her journey home. Reluctant to leave before anyone else, she took the first opportunity to clamber to her feet when someone else said she had to get home for her babysitter.

When Leah stood up to a chorus of surprise at her leaving so early, she said she could feel a headache starting.

'I thought you weren't your usual self,' someone remarked.

Leah felt like an old frump, going home early while the others were ordering another round of drinks, but she didn't want to stay any longer than she had to. She thought she would soon be home, but the cab company told her that they wouldn't have a car available for at least an hour, unless she had booked one in advance. She prevaricated for a moment, but she had already left the pub and didn't want to go all the way up the stairs again. In any case, the others might leave before her taxi arrived and she didn't want to end up sitting alone in the pub. There was nothing for it but to walk home as quickly as she could.

The cold air made her shiver as she walked out into the foggy night. As she passed a row of shops, she caught a glimpse of her reflection in a shop window. A wide pale face stared back at her before it disappeared in a swirl of fog, making her look like a ghost. She hoped it wasn't a bad omen. Still, she didn't have far to walk. Involuntarily she quickened her pace. The main road through the village was fairly busy, with people out drinking on a Saturday evening. Revellers spilled out on to the pavement outside a club, the centre of Uppermill's nightlife. Many older residents complained about the hubbub emanating from the place on Saturday nights. Leah was briefly buoyed up by the crowd of local people, a few of whom she recognised. But the knowledge that any one of them could be the killer undermined her fleeting surge of confidence.

Thick fog that had descended during the course of the evening seemed to grow denser as she turned off the main road. She felt as though she had entered a tunnel, silence enveloped her so abruptly. With the moon and stars obscured, street lamps offered the only illumination, barely visible at intervals through the gloom. She hurried from one diffuse pool of light to another, all her senses alert to any sound of pursuit. She couldn't believe she had been stupid enough to go out on her own after dark. Listening intently, she thought she heard an echo of her own footsteps tapping on the pavement. Or it could have been the sound of someone following her. Already walking fast, she began to trot. Hardly able to breathe for apprehension, she kept her eyes fixed straight ahead. Not only would it slow her down to look over her shoulder, but she might be paralysed by the sight of a figure at her heels. Involuntarily she broke into a run, panting at the unaccustomed exertion, and almost lost her footing. She could feel her heart racing as she regained her balance.

Her building was in sight. A light was on downstairs. She sprinted forwards. With a final burst of energy she dashed through the gate, nearly slipping over again as she raced up the short path to her door. Reaching the doorstep she had to pause while she rummaged desperately in her bag, cursing herself for not having fished her keys out when she left the restaurant. Her fingers found the keys and fumbled to insert the right one in the lock. As the door swung open, she looked around, ready to scream if her pursuer lunged at her on the doorstep.

Peering through the darkness, she couldn't see any sign of movement. The fog was so thick she had managed to evade her pursuer and reach home safely. She flung herself inside, slammed the door, and ran up the stairs ready to blurt out her story to her flatmate, but the apartment was empty. Physically trembling with delayed shock, she busied herself making a mug of tea. Until Beth was home she couldn't put the chain on the door. Still shaky, she phoned her. There was no answer.

She tried again. The fourth time she rang, Beth answered.

'What's up? I saw your missed calls.'

'Where are you?'

'I'm out, in the village. Where are you?'

'I'm at home. Beth, I think you should come back right now. And for God's sake be really careful. It's not safe out there.'

'What the hell are you talking about?'

Leah could hear muffled noise in the background: loud music, voices and laughter.

'Where are you?'

She cursed under her breath on learning that Beth was at the club she had passed only about fifteen minutes earlier. If she had known, they could have walked home together. As it was, she had nearly been attacked on the street and now Beth would be facing a similar danger on her way back.

'Beth, it's not safe out there. I'm pretty sure someone followed me home. He might be out there waiting for you right now.'

She couldn't be certain, but it sounded as though Beth was talking to someone else.

'Beth, are you listening to me? You need to come home now. And don't walk back on your own. Ask someone to come with you. Someone who wasn't in our class at school,' she added, as a precaution.

'I can't really hear you. I'll be back later. See you.'

Beth rang off before Leah could protest. When Leah tried to call her back she didn't answer. Leah's terror gave way to anger. If Beth wanted to risk her own life, that was her look out. Leah had done her best to warn her of the danger. Frustrated and emotionally exhausted, she burst into tears.

25

IT WAS GOING TO take at least four hours to drive to Celia's, even on a Sunday. By leaving early Geraldine hoped to arrive by mid-morning. She considered going by train, but it probably wouldn't save much time, and taking the car meant she could leave whenever she wanted. If she hadn't been on a case, she would have stopped off overnight in London and gone to see her twin sister to find out for herself how she was getting on. It had been on her mind to go to London and see her, but with Celia nearing the end of her pregnancy, Geraldine had decided to prioritise her. She set off, still uncertain whether she had made the right decision. Due to leave the clinic soon, Helena might be in more urgent need of support. Geraldine resolved not to say anything to Helena about her trip to Kent, instead sticking to the claim that she was unable to leave York at such a critical time in the investigation.

Celia's joy at seeing her confirmed that she had made the right decision. While Helena might or might not be pleased to see her, Celia greeted her with open arms.

'Geraldine! It's been so long! Come in, come in. I'll put the kettle on, and then I want to hear all your news.'

Geraldine had admitted to her adopted sister, Celia, that she had been compelled to move to York, after a problem she had encountered in London. She hadn't gone into details about having to leave the Met after putting herself on the wrong side of the law trying to protect her birth twin, Helena. With hindsight it had been a rash effort, with failure probably inevitable. After meeting Helena for the first time as an adult, she had allowed her emotions to overrule all common sense. Now she was suffering the consequences, one of which was that she had been obliged to move further away from Celia.

As usual, Celia wasn't interested in hearing Geraldine's detailed news but was happiest when talking about herself. Geraldine didn't mind. Celia was on her own for hours every day and needed company. Besides, it saved Geraldine having to talk. Apart from issues of confidentiality, she didn't really like telling Celia about the cases she was working on. Celia could never get past the shock of hearing that people had been murdered and Geraldine could tell her sister was uncomfortable hearing her talk dispassionately about the victims. Celia briefly brought up the subject of Geraldine's work.

'I read about your case,' she said. 'It was in the news. That poor girl was only in her early twenties, and the boy wasn't much older. How terrible. Who would do such a thing?'

'That's what we're trying to find out,' Geraldine mumbled.

Celia's emotional response jarred with Geraldine. Sometimes she wondered if she was unnaturally callous, because she was able to deal objectively with her work while other people were overwhelmed with the horror of what had taken place. But that attitude went with the job. She was trained to study the facts of a case rationally, without indulging in any personal feelings beyond a hard anger that fuelled her determination to see the killers brought to justice. Not that sentencing was always appropriate. With a skilful barrister, a premeditated murder could earn a prison sentence of just a few years. But there was nothing Geraldine could do to influence the length of a prison sentence. All she could do was prepare as clear a case against the perpetrator as she possibly could.

Geraldine's brother-in-law and niece were both home in time for lunch and the four of them sat around the table in Celia's spacious kitchen to enjoy a traditional Sunday roast.

'I suggested we all go to the pub for lunch,' Sebastian said, 'but Celia insisted on cooking.'

'I'm not an invalid,' Celia grumbled. 'I can still cook.'

'And very good it is, too,' Geraldine said.

'It's yummy!' Chloe agreed.

Celia grinned. 'I'm glad you two are enjoying it,' she said pointedly.

Sebastian smiled. 'I'm not saying it's not good. It's fantastic, and nothing the pub can produce could match this, nowhere near. I just don't want you to overdo things.'

Celia rolled her eyes. 'I wish you'd stop trying to wrap me in cotton wool. I'm perfectly OK.'

Geraldine and Chloe exchanged a grin as they tucked into their roast lunch contentedly. They had both heard a similar conversation between Celia and Sebastian many times over the past six months.

It was gone five and already dark by the time Geraldine left. Celia tried to persuade her to stay the night and set off in the morning but that was clearly impractical. Apart from the fact that Geraldine had to be at work early the next morning, the traffic would be far heavier on a Monday. Besides, the roads were safer after a day of traffic and winter sunshine than at the end of a freezing night. Promising that she would drive carefully and return soon, she left, reassured that Celia was fine.

Feeling slightly guilty that she had enjoyed her break from the stress of moving along with the pressures of a double murder investigation, she drove home through a light but steady sleet. She had made the right decision to leave early. In a few hours slush on the roads would turn to ice. Leaving London behind her, she felt a pang of regret that she was going so far north, instead of returning to the flat in Islington where she had been happy. Leaving London had been a wrench. She had joined the Met with no intention of quitting her job until she was forced to retire. Her commitment to life in London had been absolute, until she had been abruptly uprooted against her wishes. Although she knew she would break the law again to save her sister's life, she wondered if York would ever replace London for her. It was certainly a long drive home from Celia now.

26

LEAH HAD BEEN WAITING up for Beth the previous evening. It had hardly been a pleasant end to Beth's night out. After making her way back through the thickest fog she had ever seen, she had been relieved to reach home safely. The fog itself hadn't bothered her much. In fact, she would have quite enjoyed the walk if it hadn't been so cold, but her jacket didn't offer her enough protection and she had been pleased to finally get home out of the bitter cold. Her relief had evaporated at the sight of Leah standing in the living room, her round face streaked with tears. Arms crossed, she had scowled at Beth, demanding to know where she had been. Beth was tempted to ignore the question.

'I told you, I was at the club this evening. Not that it's any business of yours.'

As she spoke, it had struck her that she was sick of sharing a flat with Leah.

'What's happened to you, Leah? You used to be fun, you know. Now – well, it's like living with my mother. Worse.'

Leah began blubbering, mumbling about being stalked and killed. The histrionics went on for a while. Beth had tried not to listen. She was fed up with Leah's attention seeking. It was one thing sharing her feelings, but Beth had heard enough of Leah's anxieties. Apart from the fact that she had nothing new to say, if she was right then Beth had just as much reason to be scared as Leah did, if not more. Because if what Leah was telling her was true, not only was their home under surveillance by a murdering lunatic, but Beth was living with a woman who kept a gun in her bedroom. It made Beth nervous about getting up to go to the loo during the night in case Leah heard her and mistook her for an intruder. It was all well and good Leah saying she wasn't going to shoot Beth, but if she was panicking in the dark she might not recognise her flatmate until it was too late.

'You have to get rid of it,' Beth said to her as they sat having a late lunch together in front of the television on Sunday. 'It's not safe to keep it here.'

'I got it precisely because I don't think we're safe here.'

'What are you talking about?'

'He's watching us.'

'Who is?'

Leah lowered her voice and hissed. 'The killer. He's watching us.'

Beth stood up and went over to the window to look out. The fog had cleared on a crisp cold day. Frost sparkled on the branches of a tree. A car drove by. Apart from that the street was deserted.

'There's no one outside,' she said.

'Just because you can't see him doesn't mean he's not there,' Leah replied sharply. 'Of course he's not going to let us see him.'

'Then how do you know he's there?'

'I don't know why you're laughing. It's not funny. I know he's there because I saw him, but that was before he realised we were on to him. Now he knows, he's keeping out of sight. That's why you can't see him. But he's still out there, watching us.'

Beth wanted to laugh again but Leah was so earnest, she hesitated. There was no doubt her flat mate was genuinely scared. Until all this had happened, Leah had been fun, bubbly and frivolous. She would collapse in giggles at the slightest provocation, sometimes for no apparent reason. This anxious Leah was unfamiliar and unwelcome. Not wanting to spark off another row, Beth decided to humour her friend.

'What makes you think we're being watched?'

Leah shook her head. 'I've seen him, standing out there. And I told you, he followed me home last night.'

'Well, he's not there now, and no one followed me. I don't know how you could even tell, in all that fog. Look, you might have seen someone out there at some point, I'm not saying you didn't.'

'I know what I saw.'

'Yes, I believe you. If you say you saw someone outside, then I believe you. But even if there was someone out there, so what? There's no reason to suppose he was watching us. Listen, Leah, everything that's happened with Stephanie and Peter, it's unnerved everyone. We're all on edge, not just people who were in our class. No one likes the thought of a killer living somewhere in Yorkshire. It's really scary. But having a gun really isn't a good idea. We're more at risk of being accidentally shot than being stabbed to death by a stranger. You have to get rid of it.'

They discussed the situation for a while, but Leah remained adamant that she was keeping hold of the gun.

'It cost me a fortune,' she said.

'Well, can't you sell it?'

'I'm not getting rid of it, and that's final. I don't feel safe at night without it.'

In the end Beth gave up trying to argue with Leah. There was no point in them both getting heated about it. She would have to deal with the problem herself. Once she had thrown the gun away, there would be nothing Leah could do about it, but she was going to have to think carefully about how to dispose of it. For a start she would have to find a hiding place no one could stumble across accidentally. If a child were to get their hands on it, the possible consequences didn't bear thinking about. In addition, she would have to make sure the gun never found its way to the police who might be able to take fingerprints or DNA, and trace it back to her and her flatmate.

Leah would be furious, but she had never consulted Beth

before bringing a gun into their rooms so she could hardly complain if the same treatment were handed out to her in return. And once Leah calmed down and recovered from her panic, she was bound to agree that Beth had done the right thing. Having made up her mind what she was going to do, Beth settled down to watch television. Unless Leah decided to go out that Sunday evening, which was unlikely, it would be impossible to slip the gun out of the flat without her seeing. Although she wasn't comfortable with the thought of spending another night in the flat with the gun beside Leah's bed, Beth was resigned to waiting until Monday to deal with the problem. Somehow she would contrive to leave work early so she could pop home and leave again, with the gun in her bag, before her flatmate came home.

About six o'clock Leah said she was going to take a shower. As soon as she heard the water running, Beth nipped into her flatmate's room. It was a mess. Stepping over clothes scattered on the floor, she tiptoed to the bedside cabinet. Silently she opened the drawer. Her hand trembled as her fingers closed around the gun. Too late she realised her fingerprints would be on it. Dropping it in her bag, she hurried back into the living room and grabbed her jacket and hat.

'I'm just going out,' she called out.

Without waiting to check whether Leah had heard her, she left. Her heart pounded as she hurried down the path to the street, furious with Leah for having put her in this situation. She was tempted to go back inside and threaten to shoot her flatmate with the bloody thing. It would serve Leah right to give her a scare like that. If anyone looked in her bag, Beth would be in serious trouble. Her breath came in short gasps when she thought about what she was doing, but she had no choice. Because of her flatmate's crazy paranoia, she was having to walk around the village with an illegal gun in her bag. She had never been so terrified in her life before, and it was all Leah's fault.

27

DRIVING BACK WAS A slower journey than travelling down to her sister's had been. Tired and peckish, even though Celia had given her a huge lunch, she had stopped for a bite to eat at a motorway services and didn't reach home until past ten o'clock. She fixed herself a mug of soup, and sat down in her living room to study the notebook where she recorded her private thoughts. In addition to her official decision log, together with all the reports and interviews, forensically gathered evidence and other information gleaned from witnesses and all the people who had known the victims, she was keeping a note of her own impressions and theories. It wasn't a strictly factual account but rather her own thoughts arising from the evidence, all hand written to eliminate the risk that anyone else might come across her jottings. She had only started doing this since her arrival in York.

The other members of Stephanie and Peter's class at school bothered her. She suspected at least one of them would be able to offer a theory about who might have killed them, but Eileen had decided, quite rightly, not to reveal evidence suggesting they had been victims of the same murderer just yet, for fear of starting a panic.

'Once the media get to hear about it, it could spark a storm of unhelpful speculation from all sorts of people, which would only put us under more pressure.'

Along with the majority of her colleagues, Geraldine agreed. The last thing they wanted was to fuel a public panic about a vicious serial killer. The media loved stories like that. What worried Geraldine was that, if the killer had been a member of the victims' class at school, they would have traced him quite easily through the DNA left at the crime scene. Yet this killer had succeeded in committing two murders within a week, and they still had no idea of his identity. That hadn't happened by chance. Whoever they were looking for was disturbingly intelligent.

Finishing her mug of soup, she began to study her notes in earnest. So far no one she had encountered had struck her as in any way suspicious. Stephanie's flatmate and boyfriends had all seemed genuinely shocked and bewildered by the murder. None of them could offer any ideas about who might have carried it out, apart from Ashley's inconclusive reference to an unknown ex-boyfriend of the victim. Pursuing that line of enquiry had come to nothing. In her notes, Geraldine had suggested that Stephanie might have fabricated a violent ex-boyfriend to make herself sound more interesting to Ashley. It was all discouragingly vague.

Unable to shake off the feeling that Stephanie and Peter's former classmates held the key to the murders, she decided to speak to them all again herself. Turning to her iPad, she set about rereading the reports posted by other officers who had spoken to them. There were four of them still living in the area, two women and two men. The rest of the class had moved away. A team of constables had been checking public transport and CCTV on the roads, but no evidence had been uncovered to show that any other member of their class had returned to the area recently, other than a few who had come back to visit family in the area over Christmas and the New Year. It was lucky the murders hadn't been committed then, as the number of suspects would have increased dramatically. It was just as well the killer hadn't thought of that.

Every adult male living in the local area was being approached for a DNA sample, along with all the past pupils from the victims'' class, but no match had yet been found for the DNA they had discovered, and that was the only clue so far to the killer's identity. Eileen had set up a search for everyone who had attended the school at the same time as the victims, regardless of where they were now living, and the initial search had been widened to the surrounding areas of the county. Police throughout the UK were deployed to track down each individual who had been at school with Stephanie and Peter, including anyone who had taught them, and DNA samples were obtained and tested. The massive undertaking could take months to complete, but it had to yield a result eventually. They just had to hope there would be no further attacks while the search was underway.

'No one is exempt,' Eileen said. 'If we can't find our killer here, we'll extend the search overseas. A few of their former classmates are living abroad, but people can travel.' She looked around the room, a fixed determination in the set of her jaw. 'Wherever this killer is hiding out, we'll find him. There will be no escaping our search, no slipping through the net.'

Eileen spoke as though she was addressing a press conference. Geraldine thought she might be rehearsing for one. They were nowhere near closing the case, and Geraldine wasn't the only one convinced the murders had been thought out very carefully and deliberately. The fact that the killer had carried them out so successfully suggested premeditation. The more Geraldine thought about the case, the more troubling it became. If the killer was living in the area, he was making sure he avoided being approached for a sample of his DNA. That, too, suggested the murders had been meticulously planned in advance.

It was nearly two when she finally fell into bed, exhausted, but she couldn't sleep. No sooner had she stopped thinking about the case than her thoughts drifted to her twin sister, and her deep-seated anxiety about how Helena was coping with the prospect of leaving the clinic. She would need a great deal of help to move on from her previous lifestyle, but Helena's community was peopled with drug dealers and addicts. In the morning, Geraldine resolved to call the clinic and contact social services to check what assistance was in place for Helena once she quit the clinic. It might have been because she was tired, but Geraldine's characteristic optimism seemed to have deserted her.

28

COMPARED TO SATURDAY EVENING, the village was like a ghost town. As Beth walked down the main street, a buzz of voices reached her from the yard outside the pub where a group of youngsters had gathered to smoke. They must have been freezing, huddled together around a patio heater. She scurried past. A fine sleet began to fall and the smokers vanished into the pub. Glimpsing warm lights inside, Beth felt a pang of regret, but she couldn't join them. Not yet. Before she could do anything else she had to get rid of the gun. There was no one else on the pavement as she crossed the road and reached the path that led down to the canal. A car sped by and she froze beneath the trees, waiting until it passed. Standing still she wouldn't be spotted there. After a few seconds she carried on walking.

In the pale moonlight it was just about possible to make out a faint mist hovering above the water. Beth was glad of it. The worse the visibility, the less chance there was that someone would witness her disposing of the gun. It would disappear beneath the surface of the canal with barely a ripple. She glanced around but there was no sign of movement. In the summer people often strolled along the tow path between bridges, but on a cold winter's evening no one would be taking a walk there. Only someone with a specific reason to visit the canal might discover her. Not only was the place deserted, but the path was out of sight from passing cars. In addition to the mist hovering over the water, the canal was set apart from the road by a grassy plot bordered by trees. The branches might be bare but in the darkness she would be invisible from the road. She took a few steps along the tow path, away from the village.

Stopping, she gazed down at the water, shimmering darkly in the moonlight. There was no sign of the ducks that swam around on the canal in warmer weather. She wondered if they migrated to a milder climate in the winter. Their absence made the place feel lonely. It wasn't a great stretch of the imagination to picture herself as the only creature left alive on the planet after an apocalyptic disaster. If she carried on scaring herself like this, she would end up even more disturbed than Leah. She had heard that mental illness could be contagious. Certainly other people's moods affected the way she felt, and Leah could hardly have been more agitated lately.

With a shiver, Beth dismissed her miserable thoughts. The spooky setting by the black water was making her scared. In a few minutes she would be back on the main street, nipping into the pub over the road for a quick drink before setting off home. Leah was going to be annoyed with her for going out anyway, as if it was any of her business what Beth did with her time. An extra half hour or so wouldn't make any difference, and Beth deserved a drink after what Leah had put her through. Leah had told her she had spent a lot of money on the gun. More fool her. It served her right that she was going to lose it. This horrible situation Beth found herself in was entirely Leah's fault.

In the silence, the click when she undid the clasp on her bag was startlingly loud. As she opened the bag, she hesitated. Another noise had caught her attention, as though someone had drawn in a breath nearby. She listened intently.

Silence.

'Who's there?' she called out in a voice that trembled, even though she was alone. 'Is anyone there?'

Leah's stupid jitters had upset her more than she had realised. She waited.

Silence.

She turned her attention back to her bag, desperate to get this over with quickly before anyone could discover what she was doing. While she fumbled to take the gun out of her bag, she thought she heard a faint footstep, as though someone was approaching quietly. She looked around again but it was impossible to see far in the darkness. She cursed under her breath, realising what was happening.

'You know I can hear you,' she said. 'Leah, I know it's you. Why the hell are you following me? There's no point. You're not going to stop me, so you might as well piss off.'

She knew why Leah had followed her. She wanted her gun back. Shaking with cold and anger, Beth walked further along the path until she was nearly at the next bridge. There was no sound of pursuit. Now that Leah knew Beth had heard her, she might give up trying to retrieve the gun. Beth glanced around, but she couldn't see her flatmate. Cautiously she drew the gun out of her bag. As she did so, a hand gripped her roughly by the elbow and pulled her backwards so she could neither drop the gun in the water, nor raise her arm to throw it in.

'Let me go!' she cried out furiously. 'Leah, this isn't funny. The gun could go off! What are you doing? Stop it, you idiot.'

Another hand grabbed her round the face, the palm slapped roughly against her mouth to silence her. She tried to resist, her cries muffled by the hand pressing against her lips. Her eyes flicked frantically from side to side but she couldn't see far through the thick night air. In the struggle her head twisted round. She caught sight of a man's face grinning down at her, ghastly in the pale moonlight.

29

ON MONDAY MORNING, GERALDINE was pleased to be back at work. Her trip to Kent had been more tiring than she had anticipated and although she had been pleased to see Celia and her family, she had been drained of energy by the time she reached home. It was actually a relief to slip back into the routine tasks that came her way as a sergeant. That afternoon, regardless of her work commitments, she was determined to call the clinic to enquire about Helena. Having made that decision, she settled down to work.

Eileen had a meeting early on, but late morning the team gathered to discuss the case. Eileen was interested in the possible significance of the two victims having attended the same school, in the same class. Ian still wasn't convinced that was important.

'They had to go through the education system,' he pointed out. 'And coming from the same village, the chances are they would attend the same school.'

'In the same class though? What are the chances of that?' Geraldine asked.

Although Eileen agreed with Ian that a lot of local people went to that school, nevertheless she was keen to press on with obtaining DNA from all the people in the victims' class. While they waited, hoping the forensic team would come up with a lead, there were reports to write and procedures to follow. Geraldine was quietly getting on with her job, trying not to worry about Helena, when she received a message about a hysterical call from Leah.

'Please repeat that,' Geraldine said.

As soon as she put the phone down she went to advise Eileen about this new development.

Eileen drew in a sharp breath and looked helplessly at Geraldine. 'Sweet Jesus, don't tell me there's going to be another one. Do you think something's happened to Beth?'

'All Leah said was that Beth went out yesterday evening and didn't come home. There could be all sorts of reasons why a young woman might stay out all night.'

'You'd best get over there as quickly as possible and see what's really going on. Let's hope Beth will have turned up by the time you get there.'

Geraldine seemed to be spending a lot of time on the road, but she didn't mind. Once she left York the countryside was beautiful, even in the bleak winter, and it was better than being stuck in traffic in London.

An anxious voice responded when she rang the bell, calling to her through the door. 'Who is it?'

Geraldine answered, giving her name and rank. 'Detective Sergeant' rolled off her lips without any hesitation.

The door opened slightly and Geraldine saw the chain was on.

'Show me your identity card!'

Geraldine held it up. A moment later the door was opened by a plump girl who had clearly been crying.

'You called us about Beth,' Geraldine began.

'Yes, yes, come in. Beth's not here. It's just me, on my own.'

'When do you expect her back?'

Leah let out a sob. 'She should be here now, but she didn't come home last night. We had a row and she went off in a huff leaving me here alone.'

'Do you know where she is?'

Leah shook her head. Geraldine couldn't tell if she was genuinely worried about her flatmate, or just concerned about her own situation.

'No, I told you, she's buggered off and left me, in spite of everything that's going on. She knows I don't feel safe here on my own. I thought you might have come here to talk about offering us police protection,' she added plaintively.

'Police protection?'

'Yes. We need protection from the killer. He's already killed two of our class at school.'

Geraldine wasn't surprised to learn that Leah had been thinking along those lines. But before she engaged in any discussion of Leah's situation, she wanted to find out what had happened to Beth.

'Where did she go?'

Leah looked sulky. 'I told you, I don't know. She didn't tell me. She went off in a huff.'

'Why in a huff?'

Leah shrugged. 'We had a row yesterday evening and she went out and she hasn't been back since. And before you ask me again, I don't know where she went. She didn't tell me. She probably met some guy in the pub and went home with him. She does that all the time. And when I called her to tell her to come back, she wouldn't answer her phone. That's what she's like when she gets in a mood. She knows I don't want to be here at night on my own, especially without...' she broke off abruptly. 'Without anyone else here,' she concluded.

Geraldine had the impression she had been about to say something else.

'Can you call her now and ask her where she is?'

Leah tried but Beth didn't answer.

'What did you argue about?'

Leah frowned and muttered something about having fallen out with Beth, without attempting to explain why. When Geraldine pressed her, she became tearful. She was upset, but more than that she seemed frightened.

'It was nothing,' she insisted, 'just a stupid row, but now she's gone off and she's refusing to answer my calls and I'm stuck here on my own.'

Geraldine asked again about the cause of the argument.

'It's none of your business what we argued about,' Leah said at last, with a flash of temper.

Increasingly bothered, Geraldine questioned her about her flatmate's movements. If Beth really had disappeared, that raised all sorts of questions. None of the possibilities that occurred to Geraldine were reassuring.

'Please, Leah, it's important that we find her. Can you think where she might have gone?'

Geraldine could contact Beth's parents and work colleagues, but Leah was more likely to know who the missing girl might have gone to see. Although she was at pains to avoid worrying Leah, she was already thinking of her flatmate as a missing girl.

'Which pub did she go to yesterday?' she asked.

'What? Are you going to go there and ask who she was with?'

Geraldine nodded. That was exactly what she was planning to do. If Beth had gone home with a man she had met up with in the pub, it should be relatively easy to track her movements. But when Geraldine's own phone rang, she answered it with a sinking feeling that she might not need to spend time searching for Beth after all.

'As it happens, I'm already in Uppermill,' she said when Ian had finished speaking. 'I'll be right there.'

'What are you doing in Uppermill?'

'I've been talking to Leah.'

'What does she have to say?'

'I'll tell you when I see you.' She rang off and turned to Leah. 'I have to go, but I'll be back tomorrow. In the meantime, try not to worry.' It was a futile comment, in the circumstances.

She wanted to leave at once, before Leah had a chance to ask her what had happened. It wasn't so much that she was reluctant to have to deal with an emotional outburst from Leah, but rather that she was keen to speak to the girl who had found Beth's bag as soon as possible. With every moment that passed, her memories would become hazier. A forensic team had already been despatched to examine the site where the bag had been discovered. The sooner they could examine the scene, the better their chances of finding out exactly what had taken place before any evidence deteriorated further. With what could be a crime scene exposed to winter conditions, every moment's delay was significant. A diving team were on standby if the go-ahead was given to dredge the canal.

'Something's happened to her, hasn't it?' Leah blurted out as Geraldine stood up. 'What's going to happen now? Who's going to keep me company if Beth doesn't come home?'

Ignoring Leah's bleating, Geraldine hurried from the room. After all, the best way she could protect Leah was by finding out what had happened to her flatmate. Only when she was at the front door did she stop to warn Leah to keep the chain on the door. Slamming it behind her, she checked it was properly closed and was reassured to hear the chain being slid across.

30

BETH'S BAG HAD BEEN handed in to the local police station by a girl called Sarah Byrne who lived in a terraced house just off the main road in Uppermill. Geraldine went straight to her house. A man of around forty opened the door and smiled easily as he ushered her in out of the cold.

'Was it you that spoke to me on the phone?'

'That's right. About a bag handed in to the police by your daughter.'

'Yes, that's right. Sarah!' he called out to his daughter as he closed the front door. 'There's a policewoman here to see you. My daughter will be very excited to meet you,' he added, still smiling.

A moment later a girl of about twelve came galloping down the stairs. Catching sight of Geraldine, she halted halfway down the stairs and turned to her father.

'Who's she?'

He laughed. 'She was expecting to see a uniformed police officer,' he told Geraldine. 'It must be something important to bring you here,' he added.

'I'm sorry to disappoint you both, but this is just routine,' Geraldine lied. 'Sarah, I want you to tell me exactly what happened when you found the bag.'

The young girl hesitated and looked at father who nodded encouragingly at her.

'I was there with my dad, but it was me that found it. He would've walked straight past it.' She glanced at her father again.

'I met Sarah from school and we were walking back together. I work from home,' he added, with an embarrassed shrug.

Geraldine guessed he was out of work.

'I have to come home along the main road if I'm on my own,' Sarah explained, 'but when dad meets me we take a short cut along the canal path.'

Geraldine nodded. 'So you were walking along the canal path,' she prompted Sarah. 'What happened then?'

'Yes, and dad was going on about homework and stuff and I was just looking at the water. But it's boring, except in spring.'

'She likes watching the ducklings,' Mr Byrne explained.

'They're so cute!' Sarah cried out, suddenly animated.

Geraldine waited patiently. Finally the girl reached the point in her narrative where she had stumbled on the bag.

'It was just there,' she said, 'lying in the mud. I'm not surprised no one had seen it. I almost didn't see it and I've got really good eyesight, haven't I, dad?'

'Yes, you have.'

Gently Geraldine pressed her to describe exactly where she had found it and learned that the bag had been lying right by the water's edge. The immediate concern was that Beth had fallen in the canal, but until the area had been examined by scene of crime officers there was no way of knowing whether that was true. If it was, forensic examination of the scene would establish whether she had slipped or been pushed.

'Do you think she fell in the canal?' Sarah asked, wide-eyed.

'We don't know what happened to her,' Geraldine replied. 'But we're hoping she's fine, and I'm sure she'll be pleased to get her bag back.'

After reporting her findings, Geraldine drove through the village and parked near the lane leading down to the canal. The area had been cordoned off to members of the public, and a group of them had gathered by the entrance to the path. As Geraldine made her way through the crowd, a woman blocked her way and began haranguing her. Other voices joined in.

'What's going on here?'

'Why is the path closed?'

'Has someone drowned?'

'We have a right to know what's going on in our own village!'

Without stopping to answer any of their questions, Geraldine pushed her way through the assembled onlookers. A constable stood aside to let her pass. It was early afternoon, not yet dark but overcast and freezing cold. Quickly she pulled on shoe covers and protective clothing before entering the forensic tent. The canal side was being treated as a crime scene, even though no body had been found. A girl from Stephanie and Peter's class at school had gone missing, without her bag. It was looking grim.

Several white-suited officers were scrutinising the tow path, taking photographs under bright lights, and collecting evidence. Geraldine approached one of them.

'What was in the bag?'

The other woman straightened up. 'You'll need to ask Jed.' She pointed to a tall officer standing nearby.

Geraldine approached him and posed her question again. Straightening up, Jed listed the contents from memory.

'There wasn't much in it. There was a purse with nearly thirty quid in notes and coins and a couple of bank cards: a debit card and a credit card, house keys, a comb, a mobile phone, a few cheap biros, and a make-up bag containing a tube of concealer, a small jar of foundation, mascara, red lip gloss, and some other cosmetics.' He paused in his recital. 'You'll have to check the report if you need to know more details of the contents, but there was nothing unusual in there, nothing you wouldn't expect to find in a woman's bag.'

Geraldine thanked him. Another officer had been examining footprints. It was quite muddy alongside the canal, but in the cold weather the ground had hardened with frost and become icy in patches. As a result there were very few footprints, and little to suggest there had been a struggle. The grass had been flattened in places but that was inconclusive, many of the footprints having been made by the girl who had found the bag. She and her father had apparently trampled all over the spot where the bag had been lying. Having learned as much as she could, there was no point in hanging around in the forensic tent where she felt she was getting in everyone's way, so Geraldine went back outside and gazed around the gloomy scene.

In the summer it would be a picturesque corner of the world, with an arched brick bridge spanning the canal. Ducks might be scudding around, with birds in the trees, and people walking their dogs along the towpath or leaning on the parapet of the bridge to gaze out over the water. But in winter the whole area was deserted, apart from the small crowd that had gathered on the pavement trying to find out what was going on. Down by the water, the white forensic tent was the only sign of life.

It was cold and miserable standing around there. Just as Geraldine was thinking about leaving, Ian arrived, his cheeks ruddy from the cold.

'Well?' he asked by way of greeting.

His brusque manner reminded Geraldine of her own approach to colleagues when she had been an inspector, conscious of the weight of responsibility that attached to her position. As a sergeant her work was equally important, but somehow she didn't feel under quite so much pressure, perhaps because she could no longer harbour any ambition to progress in her career. Short of behaving in a manner that was criminal or negligent, her position was secure. The worst had already happened.

'There's no sign of a body,' she told him, 'but Bethany Carr has disappeared. She went out yesterday evening and hasn't been home since. I've spoken to the girl who found her bag, and it doesn't look as though she left it here it intentionally. Apart from money, her keys were in it, and other personal bits and pieces, like her phone and make-up.' She frowned. 'A girl in her twenties would never discard her phone and make-up, not to mention her purse with her credit card.'

She paused. Ian scowled at the implication of her words. Having the canal dredged would be an expensive undertaking, but there was no other option.

'We need to circulate her picture as widely as we can, and get the diving team here as soon as possible,' he said.

'That's what I was thinking.'

He nodded. 'They'll have to do as much as they can while they can still see enough. Then, if they've not found her, we'll pick up again in the morning, at first light.'

Geraldine appreciated the urgency. If the missing girl's body *was* in the canal, the longer it remained in the water the less evidence it was likely to yield, evidence that could be degenerating with every passing moment.

31

BETH'S PHOTOGRAPH HAD BEEN sent to all the local police stations, constables were speaking to her former colleagues at work and a further team had been tasked with knocking on doors in her street to enquire whether anyone had seen her leaving the flat on Sunday evening. The weather had been very foggy, so it was hardly surprising that no one remembered having seen her out in the village that night. Time seemed to crawl by until late in the afternoon, when Eileen gathered the team together. A hush fell over the assembled officers as the detective chief inspector looked around with an expression even grimmer than usual. Her eyes had almost disappeared beneath her lowered brows and her thin lips were pressed closed. Even the most insensitive of the officers present must have realised Eileen had summoned them to pass on bad news. Geraldine suspected she knew what they were about to hear.

A young constable standing next to Geraldine mumbled something about Eileen losing the plot. Another officer barely out of his teens agreed. It wasn't the first time Geraldine had noticed the absence of deference the younger officers seemed to show towards their senior officers. It had been very different when she had been new to the force. Before she had time to reproach either of her young colleagues for their lack of respect, Eileen cleared her throat and began. She spoke fiercely, as though the news infuriated her. Perhaps it did. Certainly they were all frustrated at the lack of progress in the investigation to discover who had killed Stephanie and Peter.

'I've called you here because there's been another one.' She paused and drew in a deep breath.

Seeing her senior investigating officer visibly moved, Geraldine wondered how she herself might have behaved if she had ever found herself in a similar position. She had to accept that she would never face that challenge now. At one time, she had virtually taken her promotion to detective chief inspector for granted. But at least she was still alive to experience the frustrations and regrets of her career.

'That is, another member of the same class at school has been found dead. I'm sorry to inform you all that Bethany Carr's body has been discovered in the canal. Given recent events, we're treating this as a suspicious death for the time being, although nothing has yet been confirmed.'

'So this could have been an accident?' someone asked.

Eileen inclined her head. 'Yes, it's certainly possible this was just a terrible coincidence. I know you'll all join me in hoping that will prove to be the case. Of course, it's a dreadful tragedy, whatever the circumstances. The poor girl's dead. But we have to remember that Stephanie and Peter were both stabbed to death in similar attacks. Beth drowned in the canal, which is a very different matter. All the same, three deaths in ten days...'

There was silence for a moment. More than two murders would be very serious news indeed. No one wanted to be dealing with a serial killer. And the media would be driven into a frenzy if this turned out to be another victim of the same killer.

'For the time being there is to be no hint to the media that this third death could be related to the others. Hopefully they haven't yet caught on to the fact that Bethany was in the same class as Stephanie and Peter. We want this to be reported as a tragic accident. Let's hold off speculation about a serial killer for as long as possible. It only gets in the way of us getting on with the job if we keep being pestered for press releases.'

'And a lot of hype in the media could encourage a serial killer, if that *is* what we're dealing with,' Geraldine added quietly.

Eileen frowned.

'A drowning could be a suicide,' Naomi pointed out.

'Yes, that's possible.' Eileen gave a forced smile.

No one really doubted that they were looking at a third murder.

'Three deaths in ten days,' one of the young constables repeated.

'That's one every three days,' another youngster added.

'Let's not go jumping to conclusions,' Eileen said, but she looked weary and her voice lacked its usual sharpness.

The detective chief inspector seemed to have lost her bounce. Usually a forceful presence in the room, she now stood with shoulders bowed, looking older than her years, as though all her energy had drained away. Geraldine was faintly bothered. At a time like this a senior investigating officer needed to be on top of her game, driving her team to greater efforts. She ought not to be overwhelmed by the pressure of a desperate struggle.

As soon as the meeting finished, Geraldine and Ian set off for the mortuary. The post mortem had not yet been completed, but Jonah had contacted the police station to let them know he was ready with his initial findings. As they drove to the hospital, Ian expressed his surprise at the peremptory summons.

'He usually wants to complete his examination before speaking to us,' he said.

'Perhaps he's found something unusual.'

They went straight to the examination room without pausing to exchange pleasantries with the anatomical technology assistant. Geraldine thought Avril looked slightly disappointed as Ian hurried past her with a cursory nod by way of greeting.

'Ah, good, you're here,' Jonah said, looking up with a broad smile. 'That was quick. I'm glad you've come because I've got something here that I think may interest you. The body was pulled out of the canal this morning, the supposed victim of a drowning. What you want to know is whether the death was accidental, or the consequence of foul play?'

Ian explained that they were worried someone might be targeting the members of a particular class that had attended Saddleworth School. It could be coincidence, two of them being murdered within a week of each other, but three in less than a fortnight suggested the victims had been deliberately selected.

'Ah yes,' Jonah agreed, 'three coincidental deaths does stretch credibility.'

At her side Geraldine heard Ian swear softly. She stared at the bloated white body lying on the cold metal table. The day after Bethany had gone missing Geraldine had gone to her flat to speak to Leah about her disappearance. She might already have been dead by the time Geraldine arrived in Uppermill. It was even possible she had been dying at the very moment Leah was telling Geraldine her flatmate had gone out the previous evening and not come home again. Although it made no sense, she couldn't help wondering whether this death might have been prevented if she had gone to see Bethany one day earlier. It was possible the dead girl had known something about the killer but had been reluctant to go to the police with her information. Perhaps that was why she had been killed. Someone should have approached her sooner. As soon as they had finished at the mortuary, Geraldine resolved to go and speak to the other members of Stephanie and Peter's class straight away. Whatever else happened, they had to do everything they could to prevent any further deaths as quickly as possible.

'When did she die?' she asked.

'She died on Sunday night, some time between six and midnight. It's impossible to pin it down exactly as she was in the water for about thirty-six hours.' He paused and glanced first at Ian and then at Geraldine, as though to check he had their full attention. 'Now, the interesting aspect of this death is that she didn't drown.'

Geraldine leaned forward to look more closely at the body, but could see no gashes in the chest marking it as similar to the other recent murder victims.

'I can't see any stab wounds,' she said.

'Did I say she was stabbed?' Jonah asked. 'Guess again.'

'Can we please not play games,' Ian broke in irascibly. 'You're not making sense. What do you mean, she didn't drown? She was pulled out of the canal. What the hell did she die of, if not drowning?'

Jonah shook his head, making a tutting noise. 'Do I detect a temper, Ian? Now that *does* surprise me. And just for that, I'm going to keep you in suspense a little longer. You're going to have to guess what killed her.'

Out of the corner of her eye Geraldine could see Ian was uneasy. He concealed his feelings well, but when they had first worked together he would have had to leave the room to throw up when faced with a disfigured corpse. She wondered whether she would have realised how queasy he was if she had only just met him. Jonah seemed oblivious to Ian's discomfort. With Ian temporarily incapable of banter, she took up Jonah's challenge herself.

'She didn't drown, and she wasn't stabbed,' she said slowly, studying the body. 'There are no signs of any injury that I can see, no signs of bruising around the neck, although it's difficult to be sure, with the skin so mottled and swollen.'

'But possibly there are signs that you can't see,' Jonah replied.

'She was poisoned?' Geraldine hazarded a guess.

Jonah nodded at his assistant. Together they gently turned the body over so he could point out a whitish blemish between the dead girl's shoulder blades. It wasn't easy to spot, but on close examination Geraldine could see the skin was puckered around it. She frowned and shook her head to indicate she didn't know what it was. It looked like a bullet wound.

The pathologist spoke solemnly now. 'There's no exit wound, which suggested the bullet was still inside the body.' He reached for an evidence bag which he held up, with a flourish. 'And here it is! I found it lodged in her heart. There was barely any water in her lungs. She must have been unconscious when she entered the water, but still breathing for a few seconds at most, maybe one inhalation. She couldn't have shot herself in the back,' he added lightly.

'So this is definitely another murder,' Ian said heavily. 'It looks like we'll have to dredge the canal after all.'

Jonah looked uncharacteristically sombre. 'I hope you find it.'

If the gun wasn't in the canal, it could still be in the hands of the killer.

32

THE CAUSE OF DEATH having been established, they were waiting for the results of the toxicology report. The forensic lab were checking skin samples in hopes of finding traces of the same DNA on Bethany's body as had been found under Stephanie's nails. With Bethany having been underwater for over thirty hours, it was unlikely they would find such evidence even if there had been any physical contact between the victim and her killer. Meanwhile the dead girl's parents were due to arrive that evening to make a formal identification. Jonah had a few hours in which to try and make her face appear presentable.

'This isn't going to be easy,' he said.

Geraldine looked at the bloated and discoloured flesh, swollen and grey, and felt a wave of compassion for the victim's parents. In addition to suffering the unimaginable pain of hearing that their daughter was dead, they now had to view her ravaged face.

'I'm sure you'll do a great job,' Ian said.

Geraldine didn't see how that was possible, but she didn't say anything. It wasn't important anyway. The girl was dead. Her appearance no longer mattered. With a pang she remembered the make-up and mirror found in Bethany's bag. Whatever she looked like now, her parents had lost her. This hideous lump of grey flesh could bear little resemblance to the daughter they had known.

On the way back to the police station Geraldine tried to initiate a conversation.

'Do you think we should speak to the other members of the class, and warn them they could be in danger?'

There was no need to explain what she meant by 'the class', or that the investigation had just taken a serious turn for the worse. It seemed they were hunting for a serial killer who had somehow acquired a gun. Ian merely grunted. Understanding that he needed time to recover from viewing the body, Geraldine kept quiet.

After a few moments, he replied. 'You're right. They could be at risk. Let's talk about it when we get back.'

Geraldine was pleased that Ian agreed with her, as did Eileen when they discussed it back at the police station. There had been seven former classmates living in the area. Now there were four.

'You spoke to Leah, didn't you, Geraldine?'

She nodded.

'Well? What did she have to say for herself?'

Geraldine only hesitated briefly. She didn't have much to add to what she had already recorded but was uncertain whether Eileen had yet had time to study her report. She decided to recap, just in case, and described Leah's anxiety about being followed.

'Yes, I saw that,' Eileen said. 'But what was your impression, Geraldine? Was she actually being stalked, as she claimed?'

Geraldine shrugged. It was impossible to draw a definite conclusion from someone who was hysterical.

'Go and speak to her again,' Eileen said. 'See if you can find out anything concrete. And once you've finished with her, you can pump the other former members of the class and find out if they can shed any light on all of this.'

While Geraldine set off to talk to Leah, Ashley, Robin and Ned, Ian was busy trying to trace the gun, looking into where it had come from and, more urgently, what had happened to it since the shooting. With luck, it was lying concealed beneath the dark waters where Beth had been found. At the same time as the canal was being dredged, Ian was organising a team to investigate sales of guns in the area both physically and online, cross-referencing anything that came up with people who had attended Saddleworth School while Stephanie, Peter and Bethany had been there. It was a massive undertaking. Not a single transaction must be allowed to slip through the net. The gun had probably been acquired illegally so the borough intelligence unit, the drugs squad, and other local officers were also investigating, calling in favours and exerting as much pressure as possible on all their informants.

Calling up and finding Leah was at home, Geraldine drove straight to Saddleworth. In a heated car, she removed her jacket. Only when she stepped out of the car did she pull her jacket tightly around her as she walked carefully to Leah's front door, keeping an eye out for icy patches. The last thing she wanted to do was to slip over and injure herself, miles away from a home that wasn't even her home.

Leah must have been listening out for Geraldine because the door opened as soon as the bell rang.

'Where's Beth?' she asked before Geraldine was even over the doorstep. She looked past Geraldine, her round cheeks pale beneath red-rimmed eyes, scanning the corridor. 'When's she coming back?'

The dead girl's parents were on their way to identify the body but Leah hadn't yet been told what had happened.

'Let's go inside and sit down. It's freezing out here.'

Once they were seated, Geraldine gently explained that Bethany wouldn't be coming back.

'She's dead, isn't she?' Leah asked and burst into tears.

Having given the girl time to regain her composure, Geraldine leaned forward in her chair and studied Leah's expression closely as she began to question her.

'Did Bethany say anything about who she was going to meet, on the night she died?' she asked.

'What happened to her?'

Geraldine hesitated, afraid of provoking another bout of crying. 'Nothing's been confirmed yet,' she replied vaguely.

'Does that mean there'll be an autopsy?'

'I'm not able to discuss any details about the investigation.'

'But she was my friend. I have a right to know what happened to her.' Leah's narrow eyes widened. 'I could be next.'

'We're doing everything possible to find out what happened to her. We need you to give us as much help as you can.'

Leah nodded.

'Do you know where she was going on Sunday evening?'

For a moment, Leah seemed unaccountably flustered. Any final vestiges of blood seemed to drain from her pale face. 'She was – she took – I mean – I don't know – I was in the shower when she went out. I didn't see her go.'

She finished speaking in a voice so firm that it struck Geraldine as forced. It wasn't clear what was bothering Leah, but Geraldine was convinced she was lying.

'Leah, is there something you're not telling me? It really won't help if you keep anything back.'

Leah shook her head. 'No, no,' she protested earnestly.

'If you'd like to tell me anything else, here's my direct line. Or if you'd prefer to talk to someone else...'

'No, no, it's not you. It's just that – well, I haven't got anything else to say to you.'

Geraldine held back from warning Leah that her life could be in danger. The girl was already nervous to the point of hysteria. It would serve no purpose to worry her even more. Instead Geraldine decided to organise a constable to keep the street under surveillance. She left soon after, perplexed and frustrated, certain there was something Leah was refusing to disclose even though her flatmate had been murdered. But she couldn't force Leah to confide in her.

33

NED THOMSON WAS THE next former classmate of the three victims Geraldine was going to visit. He lived with his parents on their family farm in Saddleworth, set in grassy hills not far from Greenfield station. Passing a caravan site and a shop, she drew up outside a sprawling farmhouse. A skinny middle-aged woman opened the door. Her welcoming expression grew wary when she saw her visitor's identity card. Quickly Geraldine explained that she was working on the investigation into a recent murder in the area.

'Oh yes. And what has that got to do with us?'

'You must be aware of the recent tragedies. The victims were at school with your son, Ned. This is just routine. We're speaking to everyone who knew them at school who's still living in the area, to see if they can shed any light on what's happened.'

'It's got nothing to do with Ned. He's got nothing to say to you.' She started to close the door.

'He was at school with the victims…'

'So were a lot of people.'

Ignoring the interruption, Geraldine continued. 'He knew them. We're hoping he might be able to offer us some information that will help us to find out what happened. Anything he can tell us could be helpful.'

She hesitated to reassure Mrs Thomson that her son wasn't a suspect. At the moment, anyone living in the vicinity could be the killer.

'We're concerned that other members of his class might be

at risk. We need to track down whoever's done this. I'm sure Ned will be keen to give us any help he can.'

Mrs Thomson grunted. 'He'll be up on the top field with his father.'

'Can you call him, please?'

The woman nodded grudgingly. 'You'd best come in then. But none of this has got anything to do with Ned. He'd never lift a finger to hurt anyone.'

She was so desperate to protect her son, she had succeeded only in arousing Geraldine's suspicions. She showed Geraldine into a spacious room that looked as though it was furnished for greeting guests. One end was set out as a living room with sofas and armchairs, while at the other end of the room there was a large wooden desk and upright chairs. After ushering Geraldine over to a sofa, Mrs Thomson disappeared. A few moments later the door opened and a tall young man entered. He was wearing thick socks, and his trousers were splashed with mud above a neat line just below his knees. He must have removed wellington boots before coming into the house. Flicking a dark fringe off his high forehead, he sat down opposite Geraldine and smiled sadly at her.

'This is about Steph and Peter, isn't it?' He spoke very slowly in a low drawl, as though he was reluctant to speak and was thinking very carefully about his words, forming them in the back of his throat and forcing them out of his mouth. 'I thought someone would be coming here to ask me about it because we were all at school together. I know it was a long time ago, but it's still a coincidence, isn't it?'

Realising he hadn't heard about Bethany's death yet Geraldine hesitated, but he would find out soon enough. She might as well be the one to tell him.

'I'm afraid I have some more bad news for you.'

He nodded as though he wasn't surprised to hear what she was saying, but when she told him about the death of another of his former classmates, he looked genuinely startled.

'Seriously? Bloody hell. Sorry, I don't know what to say...' He shook his head, as though to shake the news away. 'I thought you were going to say you knew who had done it and were looking for someone. I didn't think you'd come to tell me Beth's dead too. That makes three, doesn't it?'

'I came here to see if there's anything you can tell us that might assist us in our investigation.'

'Yes, of course. Was she – was it the same? Another murder?'

He seemed fairly harmless, simple even. All the same, Geraldine was aware that he could be a homicidal maniac. Murderers were often unintelligent. Living on a farm he would certainly have access to firearms and, besides, he might not be as gormless as he appeared.

She nodded. 'We're still looking into what happened, but we believe it's possible she was murdered.'

'I understand you can't tell me anything. But how can I help you with your enquiries?'

Ned recited the question as though he was copying the wording. Geraldine wondered if he had heard it on television, and whether he watched a lot of crime programmes. But if everyone who watched crime series on television became a suspect in a murder enquiry that would include the majority of the population.

'Can you think of anyone who might have held a grudge against your classmates at school? Perhaps another pupil who was unfairly treated?'

He frowned. 'You mean, was there a kid everyone bullied, who might have come back to get his revenge?'

Geraldine shrugged. That might be a start.

He smiled weakly. 'That would probably be me. I was always very tall and I...' He broke off, frowning. 'I was six foot when I was thirteen.'

'That must have been hard.'

'The other kids used to call me beanpole, and – and other names, but my parents were happy enough with me.' His anxious face broke into a genuine smile. 'My dad used to tell me I could do the work of a man. That wasn't really true, because I was skinny and not very strong back then, but it made me feel good about myself, enough to ignore the stupid idiots at school. My mum used to tell me the other boys were jealous.' He paused. 'I wasn't unhappy as a kid. I certainly wasn't a tortured victim who spent his time plotting revenge.' He gave a shy smile. 'I spent my school days waiting for the day when I could leave and work on the farm full-time. My dad lets me help run the caravan site,' he added proudly.

Personable and apparently even-tempered, Ned didn't seem mentally sharp, but Geraldine reserved her judgement.

'I want you to think very carefully, Ned. Was there anyone in your school who struck you as odd in any way? It could have been a pupil or a teacher. Anything you tell me will be treated in confidence. Was anyone there capable of losing their temper, or being cruel?'

'That would be most of the teachers.' He gave a sad smile. 'I haven't been much help, have I?'

34

THE FINAL MEMBER OF the class still living in the area was an accountant who was buying a terraced house in Clifton, on the outskirts of York. Robin was very different to Ned, in appearance as well as intellect. Barely taller than Geraldine and slightly tubby, his fair hair was cropped short and his face had a boyish appeal. He gave Geraldine a worried smile when she introduced herself.

'Police, eh? I take it you're here about the recent murders? Well, it wasn't me.'

In an effort to appear relaxed he gave a fake laugh which only made him sound nervous. From inside the house came the sound of a baby crying.

'Can I come in?' Geraldine asked.

Apart from any other consideration, it was freezing outside. Robin nodded and led her into a square living room which gave the impression of being smaller than it really was due to the amount of clutter everywhere, mostly baby clothes and brightly coloured plastic toys. Robin moved a packet of disposable nappies off an armchair so she could sit down, but before she could question him a blond woman came in carrying a wriggling infant in her arms. She barely looked at Geraldine.

'Someone from the police is here,' Robin said. 'But don't worry. It won't take long.' He glanced at Geraldine.

'I hope not,' the blond woman replied. 'I'll start on his bath myself then, shall I?'

She sounded irritated, and didn't seem at all curious about what Geraldine was doing there. A moment later they heard her going upstairs with the baby, which had begun wailing loudly.

'He's only eight months,' Robin said, as though he felt he ought to explain why the baby was crying.

Briefly Geraldine outlined the reason for her visit. Like Ned, Robin looked shocked.

'Three members of our class have been murdered now,' he muttered, speaking more to himself than to Geraldine. 'And what's being done about it?'

'What makes you think Bethany was murdered?'

'I just assumed it, because Stephanie and Peter were both murdered.' He looked concerned. 'That's three victims now in two weeks, isn't it? It can't be coincidence, can it? It's not like this is America. Nothing like it. People don't get killed very often around here. I can't remember the last time it happened. And now you're saying there have been three murders in two weeks, and all the victims were in my class at school.' He glared at Geraldine, and she suspected he was more frightened than she had realised at first. 'I'd like to know what's being done about it.'

Geraldine pumped him for information about his former schoolmates and teachers, but although he kept saying he wanted to help, it seemed he had nothing to tell her. He was adamant that no one who had attended school at the same time as him could have wanted to kill his classmates.

'It doesn't make sense,' he kept repeating. 'It just doesn't make sense.'

When Geraldine questioned him about whether there had been any bullying at school, he shook his head.

'I honestly can't remember anything like that. I mean, there were the cool kids, and the geeky ones, and a few weirdos, of course, but there wasn't anything that could be described as in any way out of the ordinary, and certainly no serious bullying. We used to squabble and scrap, of course we did, like any group of boys do. But there was nothing that you wouldn't expect to come across in any group of kids. Nothing that might lead to a spate of murders, years later.' He rolled his eyes. 'That would have to be a seriously insane grudge from a complete maniac. And there was no one like that in our class at Saddleworth School. We were a decent enough bunch. Normal. And the teachers were mostly OK, too. The only nasty piece of work that I can remember was the school caretaker. He probably wasn't that bad, he just seemed scary to us kids.'

'What was his name?'

He frowned again. 'I can't remember. We called him Mr Hooligan, but that wasn't his real name, of course. I can't remember what he was called.' He looked anxiously across the room at Geraldine. 'You don't suppose someone's out to get the whole class, do you? I mean, you don't think there's any risk the killer might come looking for the rest of us?' He glanced at the door. 'I've got a baby here.'

Geraldine did her best to reassure him, while at the same time urging him to be careful.

'What do you mean?'

'I just mean that it would be sensible to remain vigilant. Keep an eye out for anything strange, and if you become aware of anything unusual, contact us at once.' She handed him a card with her phone number on it. 'If you're at all concerned, call us.'

'So was Beth definitely killed by the same person?'

'No, not necessarily. We don't yet know whether her death's in any way related to the other two.'

Along with most of the team, Geraldine was convinced the three deaths were part of the same investigation, but that information had not yet been officially confirmed.

She had done her best, but none of the surviving members of the class had been able – or willing – to give her any information that might assist the investigation. The only mention of anyone unpleasant had been Robin's reference to the school caretaker. Although all the academic and ancillary staff were being approached for samples of DNA, along with former pupils at the school, Geraldine made a note to have the caretaker checked. She decided against going back to her desk that evening, and instead went straight home. She was hungry, and tired, and dispirited that her evening's questioning had come up with no new information. Back at her flat, she settled down to write up her notes from her evening's work before turning her attention to supper.

She was not only tired, but also feeling uncharacteristically lonely. As a rule she was at ease in her own company and enjoyed spending time by herself, but tonight she found her solitude overwhelming. She wished she had a companion to share her supper, someone who could distract her from a case which was going nowhere, and snap her out of her dejection. Miserably she poured herself a glass of red wine. She had been making a conscious effort to cut down on her drinking, but there were evenings when she felt she needed something to help her relax.

35

SMALL AND LIGHT, IT was hard to believe something that looked so innocuous could be so destructive, and with so little fuss. Although in some ways not as satisfying as a blade it was far more efficient, as long as there was no one around to hear the explosion. He stared, mesmerised by the shiny hard surfaces of the gadget lying on his palm, its dimensions smaller than the area of his hand held out flat. He couldn't take his eyes off it. Although nothing much to look at, its latent power imbued it with an irresistible beauty. He wondered if it would look as interesting to someone ignorant of its function. In any case, by itself it was a mere lump of metal. His was the force that could transform it into a lethal weapon.

With a gun in his hand, he was truly invincible.

It was time to find a clever hiding place for it, somewhere no one else would think of looking. There was no urgency, because he never had any visitors. It had only ever been the two of them until she had disappeared, leaving him on his own. All the same, he had to accept the possibility that someone else might come snooping around. The police weren't complete idiots. They must have realised by now that his three victims to date had been at school together, in the same class. Eventually they might stumble on the right connections. Already they had been going from house to house, questioning local residents.

Fortunately he had foreseen that problem, and had taken the precaution of moving into a derelict house at the end of his road, three doors along from his own house, where he figured it would be relatively easy to keep a low profile. He had cancelled his mail, and dropped a note to his neighbours to say that he was going away. He didn't think anyone was likely to recognise him with a beard and moustache and the glasses he now wore, and he was careful to avoid being spotted going in and out of the abandoned house. It was a dangerous strategy, but he was up for the challenge. Staying put he would have risked the police demanding a sample of his DNA and once they had that, he would be done for. As with everything else in his life, it was only a matter of being prepared. Fortunately he possessed the foresight to pre-empt difficulties, and the intelligence to circumvent them. With such attributes he really couldn't fail.

Even so, despite all his efforts, he half-expected someone would have knocked on his door by now, questioning him about his association with the victims. He had rehearsed his replies, trying to be ready for anything they might ask him. The police wanted to question everyone who lived in the area. Whatever happened, if they caught up with him he mustn't do anything to arouse their suspicion. And that included storing the gun out of sight. It was small enough to be concealed almost anywhere but he wanted to keep it hidden somewhere special because, although he had only just acquired it by chance, it had immediately become his most treasured possession. Holding it gave him a thrill that reminded him how he had felt as a child playing with a small wooden box he had converted into a trap. Recalling how curious he had been about watching someone die, he smiled. He had come a long way since then.

The second murder had been reported in the local news for days. By the third death his exploits had attracted the attention of the national media which was gratifying, even though his notoriety possibly increased his chance of being caught. There was a great deal of speculation about whether the recent murders were linked, which made him smile. The police really didn't have a clue what was going on. Using a different weapon had been a touch of inspiration. Even though it hadn't been his idea to change his means of killing, he had been clever enough to take advantage of the gun being there. That alone should have baffled the police, as if they weren't confused enough already. Carrying out his plan was going to be easier now he had acquired a gun. He gazed at it lying on his outstretched palm. It hardly seemed to weigh anything. He would struggle to use it as a cosh it was so small and light. Yet with one touch of the trigger he could blow someone's brains out.

He smiled because his luck had returned with a vengeance. The beauty of it was that the gun could never be traced back to him. It was possible that Beth had acquired it illegally, so the police might never discover where the weapon had come from. Not that it mattered, as long as they never found out where it had gone. Getting his hands on it like that really had been the most amazing stroke of luck. Before she had a chance to turn and threaten him, or worse, he had snatched the gun from her. He had the impression she wouldn't have known how to use it anyway.

He wasn't sure, but he thought she was probably dead before she slipped from his grasp and vanished beneath the surface of the canal. His disappointment had been fleeting. He had waited for a few moments in case she rose to the surface, thrashing and flailing her arms, but the water had remained still, as far as he could see in the darkness, and there had been no sound of splashing or crying out. Satisfied she was dead, whether shot or drowned, he had left feeling somehow cheated at not having watched her die. Still, she had been a member of the class he was targeting, so her death would help intensify the atmosphere of terror he was building. And he now had a gun. That alone made her death worthwhile. All in all, it had been a very satisfactory night's work. And it wouldn't be the last.

36

THE NEXT MORNING GERALDINE overslept and arrived at work just after the daily briefing began. Cursing under her breath, she slipped into the incident room. With a third death connected to the other two the team had grown, with officers drafted in from surrounding forces. When Geraldine entered the crowded room everyone else was facing away from her, towards Eileen. The detective chief inspector herself was looking down at a document. When she had been working for the Met as an inspector, Geraldine couldn't have arrived late at a meeting without anyone noticing. As one of several sergeants, she was easily overlooked. For once, the anonymity of her position worked in her favour.

'It's completely different,' Eileen was saying. 'Stephanie and Peter were stabbed. Bethany died from a gunshot wound. The third incident was completely different to the other two. Where's the evidence that her death was connected to the other two?'

They all knew the detective chief inspector was desperately trying to convince herself they weren't investigating a third murder by the same killer. If they were, this would no longer officially be a double murder case, but a hunt for a serial killer, as the media were already claiming.

'They were in the same class at school,' Geraldine answered Eileen's rhetorical question.

'Yes, yes, we've established that,' Eileen cut in impatiently. 'And so were a few dozen other people. But there's nothing else about this third death that links it to the other two.'

'It has to be significant that they were together at school,' Geraldine insisted. 'They were in the same class at school, and now they're all dead. We can't just ignore the connection.'

She went on to report that she had learned nothing new from Robin or Ned, other than Robin mentioning the nasty caretaker. As all the former staff were being checked, that was already covered.

Ian joined in the discussion. 'What about the evidence of the killer's DNA we found on Stephanie?'

None had been found on either of the other victims.

'There was probably no time for Bethany to attempt to defend herself before she was shot,' Geraldine said.

It was a fair point, but Eileen remained adamant that they had to remain open to the possibility that Bethany might not have been killed by the same person. 'We're looking for hard evidence, not circumstantial speculation. Why would this killer suddenly start shooting? The previous victims were both stabbed.'

'Maybe he's only just got his hands on a gun.'

It was a chilling suggestion. There was a brief silence while everyone considered the horrific implications of this idea. When it was time to allocate responsibilities, Eileen asked Geraldine to question Leah again. As Bethany's flatmate she must have some idea about where the latest victim was likely to have gone the night she died, and Geraldine had already spoken to her several times.

'She's more likely to trust a familiar face,' Eileen said.

Geraldine wasn't convinced the detective chief inspector was right in this instance, but she was pleased with the task she had been given. Her only consolation for having been demoted was that she could spend less time sitting at her desk worrying about budgets and expenses claims, and more time playing an active role in the investigation. Despite having a sample of his DNA, they were still no closer to finding the killer. All they knew was that he was Caucasian, with dark hair and brown eyes. The need to close the case was growing more urgent with every passing hour. Everyone on the team was concerned about the reaction from the public when news of the shooting spread. There was no way they could keep it quiet.

'At least the shooting means the media can't start banging on about this being the work of a serial killer,' Eileen said.

Geraldine glanced at Ian and raised her eyebrows a fraction. He looked away almost at once, but she knew he had registered her scepticism. As an experienced officer, Eileen was well aware that the media could be cavalier with facts when it came to composing a story. And once one media outlet started broadcasting news of a serial killer, they would all rush to join in.

As the team dispersed after the briefing, Ian approached Geraldine.

'Had a wild night?' he asked quietly.

For a second she didn't understand what he meant, then she realised he had seen her arriving late.

'I suppose an early night with a mug of cocoa counts as wild when you get to my age,' she grinned with an impulsive wink.

He gazed at her with such a severe expression she thought he was going to reprimand her. As his inspector, she had been his mentor back when he had been a new sergeant. Now that he had become her superior officer he had every right to pull rank on her, but the prospect that he might do so was painful. Before she had moved to York she had regarded him as one of her closest friends. They had known one another for a long time and had formed what she had considered a strong bond during their working partnership in Kent. It seemed now that he hadn't shared that opinion. Gregarious by nature, his relationship with her was apparently unimportant to him, while he had played a significant role in her life.

'I suppose that depends what you put in your cocoa,' he replied and she laughed, hugely relieved by his feeble quip. 'Blimey, if you think that's funny, I should try out some of my jokes on you,' he said.

Eileen called a press conference in a vain attempt to scotch any rumours that the three murders had been carried out by the same killer. Predictably, when she was asked whether Stephanie Crawford, Peter Edwards and Bethany Carr were all victims of the same killer, she had to resort to fudging her answers. Her responses, 'There is no evidence to suggest that is the case', and 'We have reason to believe the murders are in no way all related', only fuelled further claims that the 'Slasher' had got hold of a gun. Initially dubbed 'The Yorkshire Slasher', Bethany's shooting had cranked up the hyperbole, but the tag stuck. 'Yorkshire Slasher in Sharp Shooting' was one hysterical headline, and a local paper ran the more succinct but equally alliterative headline: 'Slasher Shoots'. All the news items concluded by criticising the police for failing to apprehend the killer.

In a way it was unfortunate, as the public inevitably found reports of a double murder less disturbing than reports of a serial killer. Still, the police couldn't really blame reporters for milking the situation. In any case it could hardly make matters much worse. They already knew they were hunting for a man who had killed three times in less than two weeks, and was almost certain to kill again unless he was stopped.

37

LEAH MUNCHED ON A crisp and stared miserably at the others.

'I don't understand why you insisted we all come over here again this evening,' Ned said, sitting down and stretching out his long legs.

'You know I've left my family to come here,' Robin chimed in.

Both men were clearly disgruntled. Ashley, who had reluctantly agreed to accept a lift from Robin, looked resigned.

'So what's the big panic?' Ned asked.

Reaching for another crisp, Leah burst into tears, her face turning puffy and red. 'You don't understand,' she wailed. 'Why won't anyone listen to me?'

Ashley rolled her eyes. 'We *are* listening. But you haven't said anything. What's your problem?'

Leah's face turned a darker shade of red. 'What's my problem?' she spluttered, 'What's my problem? Are you seriously asking me what my problem is?' She became incoherent in her sobbing.

'Leah, what's wrong with you?' Robin demanded impatiently. He and Ned exchanged irritated glances.

'Three of our classmates have been murdered and you're asking me what's wrong? You know very well what's wrong. You were sharing a flat with Stephanie, Ashley. How can you sit there and pretend you don't know what's wrong? You all know what's wrong as well as I do. What *isn't* wrong?'

Ashley shrugged helplessly at the two men before answering. 'Listen, Leah, we're all upset about what happened, of course we are. You're not the only one with feelings, you know. Stephanie was my best friend.' Her voice wobbled and she paused, then continued firmly. 'But we can't do anything about it. We just have to hope the police find out who killed them. There's nothing else we can do. And in the meantime I see no point in the four of us getting together to talk about what's happened. Talking won't bring them back.'

Robin glanced at his watch and stirred in his seat. 'Ashley's right. What's the point in our coming here? Anyway I need to get home soon.'

Leah shook her head and flapped her hands in the air, unable to speak for a moment.

'Oh for heaven's sake,' Robin burst out. 'If you've got something to say, just spit it out.'

Leah gulped. The others waited for her to regain her composure sufficiently to speak. At last she stopped crying, dabbed at her eyes with a tissue, and sniffed several times.

'It's not just that I'm upset about Stephanie and the other two. Of course I am, but there's more to it than that. I'm scared. The thing is, three people who were at school with us have been murdered. Hasn't it occurred to you that someone's out to get the people who were in our class? Someone wants us all dead.' She gave a sob and gulped, biting her bottom lip. 'Any one of us could be next.' She looked at the others.

'Oh, for goodness sake,' Robin said. 'You've been watching too many teenage horror films.'

Ned frowned. 'What's happened to make you think their deaths have got anything to do with us?'

'Oh, only three people who were in our class have been murdered. That's all that's happened.'

Ashley frowned. 'Leah, I get it that you're upset, but there's no reason why any of *us* should feel threatened. The murders weren't carried out in the same place. Steph was killed in York, Peter was out in the countryside, and Beth was right here in Uppermill.'

Leah gazed anxiously at them. 'It's not just that,' she said in a low voice, barely louder than a whisper. 'I'm being stalked.'

While Robin muttered sceptically about 'hysterical bollocks', Ashley and Ned looked anxiously at Leah.

'What makes you think that?' Ashley asked.

'I don't just *think* I'm being stalked. It's happening.' In a trembling voice Leah described seeing a man on the street outside her flat.

'A man in the street?' Robin repeated in a dismissive tone. 'I dare say there are often men in the street. So bloody what?'

'You can try and brush it off, but he was watching me, I know he was. And I'll tell you another thing. One minute he was there, and the next minute he was gone. Vanished into thin air.'

'The invisible man,' Robin sniggered.

'You can laugh, but I know he was there. I could sense him!'

'It does sound as though you're imagining it,' Ashley told her, not unkindly. 'It's understandable. We're all on edge with everything that's been going on. But if you're really being stalked you should go to the police.'

'I can't.'

Ned frowned. 'This is getting silly. Listen, why on earth would anyone think Beth's death wasn't an accident? She must have gone for a walk down by the canal and fallen in. Maybe she slipped on a patch of ice...'

Leah interrupted him. 'Beth would never have gone off for a walk by herself in the dark, not with a killer on the loose. We were scared.'

'You're scared,' Robin said. 'It doesn't mean she was. You're not scared, are you, Ashley?'

'If she'd gone anywhere, Beth would have gone to the pub. It was freezing outside,' Leah insisted. 'She wouldn't have gone out for a walk along the canal. It was dark. No, someone took her there deliberately and killed her.'

'Well, it wasn't the same killer because according to the

news, Beth was shot,' Robin said. 'They're hardly going to make that up.'

'So it wasn't an accident,' Ned said. 'But if she was shot, it means it wasn't the same killer.'

'Exactly,' Robin agreed. 'It's not the same killer because Stephanie and Peter were stabbed. Think about it, if it's the same killer, and he has a gun, why would he wait until now to use it?'

'Maybe he didn't have a gun when he stabbed them,' Leah suggested.

'Oh, and suddenly he does. Very convenient. And very unlikely,' Robin said. 'He just happened to get hold of a gun without anyone knowing. I don't think so!'

Leah cleared her throat. She looked nervous. 'It might sound unbelievable, but it could be true.'

'Oh please, let's not get carried away,' Robin replied. 'I suppose you're going to tell us next that you handed the killer a gun yourself?'

Leah's face flushed with anger at his derogatory tone. 'In a way, yes, I did,' she answered with a flash of defiance.

'Oh stop talking rot,' he snapped.

The others stared in disbelief as Leah blurted out that she had got hold of a gun, for protection, and Bethany had run off with it the night she was killed.

'She didn't want it in the flat. She was afraid it might go off. She said she'd be scared to get up at night in case I mistook her for an intruder.' She broke off, tears welling up in her eyes. 'We argued about it. Then, on Sunday evening, while I was in the shower she went out, and when I went in my room the gun had gone. She took it and – and she never came back, because... because that was the night...'

For a moment no one spoke as the others registered the significance of what they had just heard.

At last, Robin spoke. 'Oh my God, you're telling us it's the same killer, only now he's got a gun?'

'I can't believe you didn't go straight to the police,' Ashley added, horrified.

'No, no,' Leah burst out, 'they mustn't know. Promise me you won't tell them. Don't say anything to anyone, please.'

While the others were in agreement that she ought to tell the police, Leah remained adamant she wasn't going to do that.

'I had the gun illegally. If the police find out about it I'll be in serious trouble.' She glared around the room. 'So don't try and split on me, because if you do I'll say I was lying and made it up to impress you.'

'Well, you have to tell them,' Robin announced. 'This puts a different complexion on everything. Like you say, that's three of our class killed, and we now know the killer has a gun. We need protecting. I've got a family. They could be at risk.' He stood up, his stocky figure looking slight beside Leah's. 'You've got to tell them.'

'There's no way I'm going to the police...'

Robin was already making for the door.

'Robin's right,' Ashley said uncertainly as she too stood up. 'The police will know what to do. We have to tell them everything we can, and then let them sort it out.'

Ned had offered to give Ashley a lift to the station and the two of them followed Robin out of the flat, leaving Leah on her own.

38

'I WANT YOU TO be really careful, Katie,' Robin said, trying to sound serious yet calm. 'Promise me you'll be careful.'

The last thing he wanted to do was worry his young wife, but he had to impress on her how important this was. He paced across the living room, watching with growing irritation as she picked up the baby and chattered to it.

'Promise me you'll be careful,' he repeated, determined to make her listen to him.

'I've no idea what you're talking about,' she replied. 'How can I be more careful?'

He flung himself down on the sofa beside her. 'Look, I'm not trying to worry you...'

'Well, thanks very much. Rob, what are you talking about?'

'Listen, love, you know there have been three murders in the area recently?'

He paused, feeling helpless. It was difficult to know what to say.

'Yes, I know. It's been in the news.'

'Well, the murderer hasn't been caught.'

'So what? The murders weren't all around here. Yorkshire is a big place.' She turned back to the baby.

'Listen to me,' Robin insisted. 'This is serious. There's a dangerous killer on the loose...'

'Oh for goodness sake. Listen to yourself. You sound like Mel.'

'Who's Mel?'

'You know, Melinda, from the antenatal class. She's always

making a drama out of something. It's like she's got some sort of anxiety disorder, what do they call it? Anyway, she's worried about the recent murders, but honestly, these things go on all the time. The media love it. They make a whole hoo-ha about it. And Mel tells us all about it in great detail. But so what? It's got nothing to do with us. She ought to stop fussing about what's going on in the news and focus on looking after her child.'

'I need you to listen to me,' Robin said.

He stood up and began pacing the room again, trying to decide how much to tell her. Kneeling on the floor, she put the baby down on his playmat and looked up, frowning. Rob sat down again and gazed miserably at her.

'You'd better tell me what's going on,' she said quietly. 'If you know anything about these murders...' Her voice tailed off and her blue eyes suddenly filled with tears. 'You can talk to me, Rob. No secrets, remember? If you're in some kind of trouble...'

He laughed harshly. 'I haven't been running around killing people, if that's what you're worried about.'

'Don't be silly. That's not what I meant. But something's wrong and you have to tell me what it is. This isn't fair, Rob. What the hell's going on? You can't drop hints and then not explain what you're talking about.'

He nodded. She was right.

'OK,' he said heavily. 'There have been three murders: Stephanie Crawford, Peter Edwards and now Beth Carr.'

He paused, lost in thought.

'You make it sound as though you knew them.'

'I did. Oh, not recently,' he added quickly, seeing her shocked expression. 'We were at school together.'

'Oh my God, I had no idea. Were they all friends of yours?'

'No, not really. I mean, we were in the same class and I knew them. I was actually friends with Peter for a while. We used to kick a football around together. I remember he was shorter than me for a while.' He laughed. 'I guess that's why I wanted to be friends with him.'

The shortest boy in the year, Robin had been desperate to be as tall as his peers.

'I'm so sorry you lost your friend like that,' Katie said. 'What was he like?'

'He was OK. We weren't that friendly. It was a long time ago anyway. But that's not the point.'

'What do you mean?'

Robin looked at his wife. Slim and pale, she looked very different to the girl he had first met three years ago when they were both at university in Liverpool. He sometimes wondered what he might have done with his life if Katie hadn't fallen pregnant so soon after they had graduated but she had, and now they were here, bringing up a son.

'What do you mean?' Katie repeated. 'What are you talking about?'

This was it. He would have to tell her all about it. Cautiously he explained that someone appeared to be targeting the members of his class at school, trying to kill them all. He did his best to make sure she took him seriously, while at the same time trying not to worry her. For once she heard him out without interrupting.

'Do you think you're being paranoid?' she asked when he had finished. 'And anyway, the third victim was shot. I know there was speculation in the media that the three murders were related, but it turned out that wasn't true. The first two were stabbed and the third one was shot.'

The baby began to cry. She swept him up in her arms and Robin felt a surge of tenderness for them both. If anything were to happen to them, he wouldn't want to live. Reluctantly he recounted what Leah had told him.

'So you're telling me the same person killed three of your classmates, and the killer has a gun?'

He had succeeded in making her anxious, but for the wrong reason.

'You're the one who should be careful,' she said, her face stretched taut with fear. 'I wasn't in your class at school. This is about you, not me, Robin. You're the one who's in danger. Surely the police can carry out a massive hunt for the gun and find the killer that way?'

'And how do you suppose they can track down the gun? Talk about looking for a needle in a haystack.'

'They could search the home of every member of your class for a start. They have to do something.'

With a shrug he told her that the police didn't yet know that Bethany's killer had recently acquired a gun. Leah didn't want anyone else to know.

Katie was horrified. 'She has to tell them.'

'We tried to persuade her but she flatly refused. She got hold of the gun illegally.'

'So she's prepared to withhold evidence that might help to find a killer who's already claimed three victims and is quite possibly threatening more people, including you. That's crazy. Anyway, if she won't tell the police, you have to.'

'She didn't want us to.'

'So?'

He shook his head. 'I was thinking of going straight to the police but I don't want to get involved. She made us promise not to say anything.' He bit his lip.

'Well, *I* never promised.'

Robin nodded. 'You know I would never stop you doing anything you want to do. But until they find this killer I want you to be – well, careful.'

'What do you mean?'

'Promise me you won't go out alone after dark...'

She gave an angry laugh. 'You want to impose a curfew on me?'

Before he could answer the baby began to cry again, and

she turned her attention to feeding him. Robin watched her for a moment, wondering whether to try and continue the conversation. On balance he decided it was best to leave it to her. Katie might be obsessed with the baby, but she wasn't stupid. If he knew his wife, she would be at the police station first thing in the morning.

'Well, there's no immediate danger,' he said at last. 'And hopefully this'll soon blow over. The police will sort it out. That's their job.'

Katie didn't answer.

39

As GERALDINE WAS ABOUT to leave her desk, her phone rang. Glancing down, she saw the number of the clinic where Helena was in rehab. With a sinking feeling in her stomach, she answered.

'I can't talk for long right now. Is everything all right?'

A stranger replied in an uninterested tone, informing her that Helena was ready to leave the clinic.

'I'm sorry, I can't give the arrangements my full attention at the moment. I'm at work and just about to go to a meeting. Can I call you back?'

'Don't worry, there's nothing for you to do right now. We just wanted to inform you. It helps if there's someone around to offer support.'

'Yes, of course. I'll come and collect her on Sunday morning and take her home. Please make sure she waits for me.'

Ringing off, Geraldine hurried to an interview room where a blond woman of about twenty was waiting for her. She was wearing a bright blue anorak and a red scarf. From her lap a small infant raised his head and stared curiously at Geraldine, as though trying to work out whether he recognised her. After a few seconds he lost interest in her and threw himself backwards to look up at the woman who was holding him. The young mother sat stiffly on the chair staring across at Geraldine, her face impassive. Only the expression in her eyes and her tightly clasped fingers betrayed her anxiety.

Geraldine gave her a reassuring smile. 'How can I help you, Mrs Jones?'

The woman continued to stare at her without speaking.

'What was it you came here to tell us?'

The young woman shifted awkwardly on her chair and cleared her throat. She seemed unable to meet Geraldine's eye.

'It's about the recent murders,' she said at last, and hesitated.

'If you have some information you think might help us, please tell me what you know.'

'I'm married to Robin Jones.'

Geraldine waited quietly for Robin's wife to explain herself in her own time.

'My husband was at school with the three recent murder victims. They were in the same class.'

Geraldine listened without speaking.

'He's afraid he might be next. He thinks the rest of the class might all be at risk. Do you think that's crazy?'

Geraldine shrugged and waited for the girl to continue but Katie paused, waiting for a response.

'It's very unusual for someone to target victims on such a large scale,' Geraldine replied cautiously. 'At this stage we're not ruling anything out but Bethany Carr was shot and the other two victims were stabbed, which suggests there's a different killer involved.'

'Yes I know, the killer's got a gun now, but it's the same killer,' Katie blurted out, her voice rising in agitation. 'He got his hands on a gun when he killed Bethany. That's what happened. But it's the same killer,' she insisted.

'We don't know that...'

'No, listen, that's what I came here to tell you. Leah was afraid to tell you because it was illegal, but you ought to know. Because it means it's the same killer. And if anything happens to Robin...' she broke off, her voice shaking. Taking a deep breath, she went on. 'And if there's anything that might help you find the killer, it's insane not to tell you. I don't know what they're thinking. They should have come to you straight away, all of them. It's crazy. I told him.'

To begin with Geraldine struggled to work out what the girl was telling her.

'And you're sure that's what happened?' she asked when she finally understood.

'That's what Robin told me, and he wouldn't make up something like that. Bethany took the gun, and I guess she was going to chuck it in the canal, only the killer caught up with her before she could get rid of it. If she hadn't had the gun on her, maybe she would have escaped alive... and now he's got a gun and he wants to kill Robin.' She raised tearful eyes to Geraldine. 'You have to stop him. You have to!'

After thanking Katie for coming forward, and reassuring her as best she could, Geraldine filed her report and looked for Eileen. The detective chief inspector was in a meeting so Geraldine went to talk to Ian instead. He smiled when he saw her enter his office.

'Geraldine, how's it all going?'

'I know how the killer got hold of a gun,' she said, without pausing to return his greeting.

Ian's welcoming smile vanished and he sat forward in his chair. 'Go on.'

Briefly she summarised what Katie had told her. 'Leah was reluctant to come forward because she got hold of the gun illegally,' she concluded.

Ian swore. Leah's decision to keep herself out of trouble meant the truth had been concealed for days. When Ian congratulated Geraldine for having unearthed what had happened, she pointed out that Katie had come forward of her own volition. Nevertheless she was gratified by Ian's praise. She wondered if he had been similarly pleased by her praise whenever *she* had commended *his* efforts as *her* sergeant. It seemed like a long time since they had worked together, their positions reversed. She wondered if he was also finding their new situation strange.

At last Eileen returned and summoned Geraldine and Ian

to her office to discuss the latest development. Quizzing Geraldine about Katie's account, the detective chief inspector was as incensed as Ian.

'Leah's so worried about being caught out in possession of an illegal firearm that she's prepared to withhold crucial information from the investigation. Is she a complete moron? Geraldine, never mind second- and third-hand information, go and speak to Leah. Make up whatever story you like to account for how you know about her taking a gun back to the flat, or don't explain it at all. Frankly right now I don't care about how or where or why she got hold of it. We can deal with that later. For now, we just need confirmation that Bethany took a gun with her on the night she was shot, and that Leah's gun was the one that fired the shot.'

'We don't know it wasn't Leah who shot her,' Ian pointed out. 'She said they had an argument.'

'It could have been Leah all along,' Eileen agreed. 'It almost looks likely, doesn't it? No, I know she's unlikely to have stabbed two people to death,' she added, seeing Geraldine's expression, 'but if you were to tell her that we're thinking along those lines, do you think it might help persuade her to start telling us the truth?'

40

'WHAT DO YOU WANT?' Leah called through the door once Geraldine had announced herself.

'I'd like to talk to you.'

There was a pause.

'Leah? Can you open the door please?'

There was another pause.

'Leah? You know I know you're in there.'

There was another pause before the door opened a fraction, with the chain across.

'Leah, you can see it's me. Open the door please.'

'I'm just going to bed.'

Geraldine began to lose patience but she spoke softly. 'Leah, I haven't driven all this way only to be turned away. I just want to come in for a quick chat. I don't understand why you don't want to let me in – unless you have something in there you don't want me to see? Come on now, open the door. I only want to ask you a few questions. It won't take long. Let's get it over with and then you can go to bed, and I can go home.'

The door opened. Leah was wearing a faded pink towelling dressing gown that fitted her snugly and was slightly too long for her. Beneath it her plump white feet were bare.

'What do you want?'

'Shall we go in and sit down?'

'I thought this wasn't going to take long?' Leah grumbled as she turned and led the way.

There was a bowl of sweets on a low coffee table in the sitting room. Leah reached for one and unwrapped it noisily as Geraldine asked her where she had been on the night her flatmate was killed.

'It was only five days ago,' Leah said, her eyes suddenly filling with tears. She sniffed loudly. 'I still can't believe she's gone. Why don't you find out who did it? Until you do, no one's safe. I could be next.'

Geraldine assured her firmly that the police were doing everything they could to find the killer. 'Tell me again what happened that evening. What time did Bethany go out?'

Leah shrugged. 'I don't know. I told you, I was in the shower when she left. It was probably around six or seven. I didn't look at the time.'

'So you heard her go out?'

'No. How could I, when I was in the shower? I didn't know she'd gone until I came out of the bathroom and discovered she wasn't here.'

'Tell me exactly what you did after you had your shower. Think carefully, and please don't leave anything out.'

'I came out of the shower and I went in my room and...' she broke off, frowning.

'Yes, you went in your room, and what happened then? Did you see something that told you she'd gone out?'

Leah's face reddened.

'What was it, Leah? Had she taken something of yours?'

For a moment Leah didn't answer. When she spoke, it wasn't what Geraldine was hoping to hear.

'She hadn't been in my room, as far as I knew. When I was dry I went into the living room and she wasn't there, so I called her and knocked on her door to see if she wanted to watch telly with me. That's when I discovered she'd gone out.'

'So you're saying she hadn't taken anything of yours with her?'

Leah's eyes narrowed slightly. Her mouth opened but she made no sound. Her stricken eyes closed and tears slid silently down her cheeks. Geraldine gave her a few seconds.

'Please,' Leah whispered without opening her eyes, 'please just go away and let me grieve for my friend in peace. You have no right to come here and harass me like this.'

'Leah,' Geraldine said gently. 'If there's anything you're not telling me, you need to tell me now. It's understandable that you'd be frightened about the killer and want to protect yourself. If you did something illegal, no one's going to be interested in that right now. All we want to do is find this killer and lock him up.'

A faint frown flitted across Leah's face as she opened her eyes. 'I don't know what you're talking about. I haven't done anything illegal, and you've got no right to come here making accusations like that. I'd like you to go now.'

Despite Leah's firmness, Geraldine wasn't convinced. She was inclined to think Katie had been telling the truth.

'Are you sure there's nothing else you want to tell me?'

'What do you mean?'

'What happened on Sunday evening? Tell me again, right from the beginning, because something doesn't add up. Did you and Beth argue? Was that why she went out?'

Leah described how she had urged her friend to stay indoors as it might not be safe to go out after dark, with a killer targeting their classmates, but Bethany had ignored her advice. They had quarrelled about it.

'What did you do after you discovered she'd gone out?'

'I stayed at home and waited for her to come back.'

'Where did she go?'

'How many times do I have to tell you? I don't know.'

'Did she often go out without telling you where she was going?'

'Yes, of course she did. We weren't joined at the hip. We weren't married. And anyway, I already told you we'd had a row. But I don't know where she went, and I didn't follow her, if that's what you're thinking, and I didn't kill her.'

Abandoning any hope that Leah would tell the truth freely, Geraldine spoke sternly.

'Leah, it's an offence to conceal information from police conducting a murder enquiry, so think carefully before you answer my next question. And remember, I'm here to track down a killer. I'm not interested in *anything* else.' She leaned forward in her chair. 'Have you at any time owned a gun, for self-defence? Tell me the truth, Leah. We don't want to leave the killer at liberty for a moment longer than we have to. So tell me the truth. Did you have a gun here in the flat at any time?'

'No, no, I never have. I never would. I wouldn't know where to get hold of one.' Leah lowered her face in her hands and burst into tears.

Disappointed that her questioning had done nothing to aid the investigation, Geraldine left. She suspected Leah was lying about owning a gun, but there was nothing she could do to compel the girl to tell her the full truth. While she had been talking to Leah, the canal was being dredged and the towpaths and shrubbery along both banks searched. It was still daylight when she left so, before setting off back to York, she stopped by the path down to the canal. The whole area was still cordoned off. A stout middle-aged couple were talking to a constable on duty as she approached. Bundled up in thick sheepskin coats, they looked angry.

'I'm sorry, sir,' a constable was saying to the irate villagers, 'but we're not letting anyone through.'

'And how long is this going to go on for?' the red-faced man demanded. 'We've not been able to get down here for the best part of a week now.'

'And no one seems to be able to tell us when the path is going to be open again,' his companion added. 'This is our village...'

'And this is our crime scene, for as long as we need to search it,' Geraldine interrupted. 'Listen,' she went on more gently, 'you must know that a girl was killed down here a week ago. Well, there's just a faint chance that the murder weapon might still be here somewhere.'

'If you let us through, we could help you look for it,' the man suggested.

Geraldine shook her head. 'We can't risk children stumbling across a firearm.'

The local couple withdrew, still grumbling. They couldn't argue with what Geraldine had just said. She made her way past the cordon to the sergeant in charge. With a shrug he told her there was no sign of a gun anywhere. Footprints and disturbance on the ground confirmed the suspicion that there had been a fracas on the canal bank at the point where Bethany had slithered into the water. Apart from that, the search had come up with nothing, and so far the dredging had found only mud and sludge and a haul of detritus. Seeing the mess of used condoms, chewing gum, an old wellington boot, and other random junk that had been retrieved from the canal, Geraldine felt an unexpected stab of pity for the girl who had been killed and tossed into the dirty water like so much discarded rubbish. She hoped Bethany had died from a gunshot wound and not drowned in the filthy canal.

'I think Leah was telling the truth about not seeing Bethany again after she went out,' Geraldine said at the meeting with Eileen the following morning.

'She has no alibi,' Naomi pointed out, seemingly in agreement with Eileen.

'Nor do a lot of people,' Geraldine retorted more sharply than she had intended.

Naomi looked surprised.

Eileen raised her eyebrows slightly. She turned to Ian. 'You're very quiet, Ian.'

'I've worked with Geraldine before. I've never known her to be wrong about something like this,' he said quietly.

Geraldine felt an unexpected rush of happiness knowing that at least one person had confidence in her judgement. It wasn't easy having spent years building up her reputation, as well as her status, only to be demoted and largely dismissed as an unknown sergeant who had yet to prove her worth. The fact that Ian had stood up for her to Eileen made the support all the more welcome. He was the only one of her current colleagues who actually knew her at all.

41

AFTER AN UNEVENTFUL SATURDAY, on Sunday morning Geraldine caught an early train to London, arriving at the rehabilitation clinic a couple of hours after her sister had left. When she expressed her irritation that Helena hadn't waited for her, the manager of the clinic immediately became defensive. Her carefully permed curls twitched every time her head moved as she explained that Geraldine's sister had been free to leave whenever she wanted.

'I'm aware of that, and I'm not criticising you. It's just that I asked her to wait for me and she didn't. That's all. It's not your fault. She should have waited for me.'

But the damage had been done. The manager pursed her lips and glanced up at a clock on the wall. Geraldine understood that the clinic must be under frequent attack from disappointed relatives of patients. A guarded stance must be second nature to the staff. She was annoyed with herself for having made it virtually impossible to quiz the manager about how Helena had been feeling when she had left. In her professional life Geraldine was experienced at dealing with members of the public. She had acquired the skills necessary to cope with people in every possible stage of intoxication or emotional distress. Yet where Helena was concerned she descended into complete ineptitude. Miserably she thanked the manager for taking care of her sister, and left.

When she reached Helena's address, she hesitated on the corner of the street, but she hadn't come all that way only to turn round and go back to York. The worst that could happen would be that Helena would reject her advances and shut the door in her face. That was, after all, what their mother had done every time Geraldine had tried to approach her. Now that Geraldine had settled the bill at the clinic, and had agreed to pay Helena's rent in her flat, there was perhaps no reason why Helena would want to see her again. Of course Geraldine could stop paying her sister's rent once the six months' agreement came to an end, but Helena knew that Geraldine would be reluctant to do that. Any stress might send Helena straight back to her habit – if she hadn't reverted already.

'Who's there?' Helena sounded sober.

'It's me, Geraldine.'

The door opened. 'I suppose you've come to give me a hard time about leaving the clinic?'

'What? No. You were due to leave today weren't you? And anyway, when you left was always your decision.'

'Like fuck it was,' Helena grumbled, but she stood back to let Geraldine enter. 'Come on into my palace. Nice, innit?'

The front door opened straight on to a small square living room furnished with a two seater sofa, and two small matching upright chairs upholstered in a faded green fabric. The walls were painted a grubby yellow, and there was a large grey smudge on the ceiling that looked like smoke damage. Grey nets at the window looked as though they hadn't been washed for a long time. Beside them hung thick lined curtains of some velvety material that must once have looked smart but were now soiled with mildew. It wouldn't have taken much effort to improve the place. A quick coat of paint and new curtains would have made a huge difference, and the stains on the carpet could have been covered with a rug, if they wouldn't come out. Geraldine wondered whether her mother had ever sat on one of the threadbare chairs but she didn't ask.

'Nice, innit?' Helena repeated

Uncertain whether her twin was being sarcastic or not, Geraldine gave a noncommittal grunt.

Helena sat down on one of the chairs and crossed her skinny arms over her flat chest. In a tight black jumper and short denim skirt she looked painfully thin. Geraldine was slim but Helena was little more than half her size. Yet even though Helena's hair had grown and looked shaggy, and she wasn't wearing any make-up to mask her blemished complexion, her resemblance to Geraldine remained striking. Staring at her skinny twin was like looking in a joke mirror at a funfair.

'Sure it's not as nice as what you're used to,' Helena added. 'But it's home.' She gave a lopsided grin.

Once again Geraldine wasn't sure whether her sister was being serious. Accustomed to spending her time interpreting other people's words, it seemed strange that she would struggle to understand her own twin.

'It's mine,' Helena added with undisguised glee.

Geraldine tried to imagine what life must have been like for Helena. From the little she had let slip, it was apparent that she and their mother hadn't got on well. Their mother's distress about Helena's habit had caused considerable friction between them. Geraldine sympathised with her mother's attitude to Helena's drug addiction. What she couldn't understand was why her mother had steadfastly refused to meet her until she was dying. Together they could have organised the help Helena needed a long time ago.

'How are you?' she asked.

Helena shrugged. 'I'm getting a cold.'

Geraldine smiled. Helena knew very well that wasn't what she meant.

'It's OK,' Geraldine said. 'You don't have to talk about anything unless you want to.'

Helena snorted. 'You paid for it so you want to know you got your money's worth.'

Geraldine shook her head. That wasn't the case at all, but there was no point in trying to explain her motivation to Helena. She wasn't even sure she understood it herself. Helena was a stranger to her. They had only met recently. Until their mother's death seven months ago, Geraldine hadn't even known she had a birth sister.

'How are you settling in?' she asked.

Helena shrugged. Given that she had been living there, on and off, for a while, it was a stupid question.

'Without mum, you mean?'

Geraldine nodded, embarrassed by her own crassness. 'I suppose so,' she mumbled.

Helena laughed. 'It's great, innit? No one to nag me and tell me what to do all the time. I can do what the fuck I like. You didn't know mum like I did. She was a right cow.'

Helena's face twisted in an effort to hide her emotion, but Geraldine saw tears in her eyes. As Helena turned her head away, Geraldine felt a pang of jealousy. At least her sister had known their mother.

'Helena...'

'Oh fuck off, will you? Who asked you to come poking your nose in my business? This is my life. It ain't got nothing to do with you so you can just fuck off. What you want to come here for anyway?'

Geraldine waited until her sister's anger had subsided before she spoke again.

'I just wanted to make sure you're all right.'

'Well, I'm fine, so you can save your questions for your interrogations. I don't keep asking how you are, do I?'

'Maybe you should,' Geraldine retorted with a sudden flash of anger. 'Or don't you care about me enough to bother?'

Helena looked startled. To Geraldine's surprise, her sister reached out and took her hand. Neither of them spoke. A moment later Helena withdrew her hand, but she couldn't take away the gesture.

42

THE FOLLOWING MORNING GERALDINE sat down at her desk in the busy office she shared with several of her colleagues. A phone was ringing, just behind Geraldine two constables were gossiping about something that had happened at the weekend, and there was a general background buzz of tapping on keyboards and muted conversation. Somewhere a door slammed. Outside the open window a car engine revved. With a flicker of nostalgia, Geraldine thought of the office in London which she had shared with one other detective inspector, while she herself had still held that rank. Both she and her colleague used to work quietly side by side, their peace interrupted only when one of them had been on the phone.

Doing her best to block out all the noise, Geraldine tried to focus on reading reports that had been recorded while she was away visiting her twin sister. Fully intending to study at least some of them the previous evening, by the time she had reached home she had been too tired and upset to work. Now she was doing her best to catch up with any new information before the meeting scheduled for later that morning.

What she saw first took her aback. Eileen had arranged for Leah to be brought into the police station in York for questioning. Unable to find Ian, Geraldine went over to Naomi's desk to ask her about the latest development.

'Oh, don't you know what's going on?' Naomi sounded genuinely surprised. 'You know about the shooting? Yes, of course you do. And you know we were given information that the gun was Leah's?'

Geraldine nodded. She was the one who had reported that.

'So,' Naomi went on, 'it looks as though Leah's involved somehow.'

Before Geraldine could enquire any further, they had to go to the incident room for the meeting. Eileen was already there, looking more relaxed than Geraldine had yet seen her, and Geraldine soon gathered that the detective chief inspector had arrived at the obvious conclusion that Leah was the murderer. Certainly what had happened pointed to her being guilty.

'So, it seems that after stabbing Stephanie and Peter, she acquired a gun – sadly all too easy to do.'

There was a murmur of agreement around the room.

'And then she shot Bethany,' Eileen went on. 'So now it's imperative we find out what she's done with the gun. Once we've got that, any defence she tries to pull off will be useless.' She smiled. 'The search team are bound to find the weapon soon, and when they do it'll be covered in her prints. Officers are all over her flat and the surrounding area, and searching the undergrowth around the canal again, this time focusing specifically on finding the gun. In the meantime, let's see what Leah has to tell us.'

Seeing Naomi mutter something to Ian, Geraldine suppressed a flicker of jealousy. It was none of her business if Ian chose to be friends with a young constable. She ought to start getting to know her new colleagues herself, but she had been thrown into an investigation before she had a chance to get to speak to most of them. Once the case was over, she would start making an effort to be sociable.

When the briefing finished, Geraldine made her way back to her own desk in the busy office and sat down to plan her day's tasks. Behind her she could hear a constable talking about her recent marital spat.

'So I said to him you can just pack your things and go, if that's your attitude.'

The speaker glanced up and noticed Geraldine seated nearby. Nodding to her colleague, she moved further away and continued her monologue, her voice too low for Geraldine to hear what she was saying. None of her married colleagues appeared to be particularly happy. She had often thought she was probably better off alone. A long time ago she had planned to get married, but she had been very young then, in her early twenties. After that break-up she had never been in a serious long-term relationship. It wasn't that she wanted to live alone, but she had been preoccupied with her work and somehow the right opportunity had never arisen again. With a sigh, she turned her attention back to her work.

One more murder and the dead locals from that class at school would outnumber the living. While they were waiting for the scene of crime officers to finish going through every blade of grass in the vicinity of the latest crime scene, and the forensic team were examining every possible scrap and trace of evidence, Eileen had decided that Leah was the most likely suspect. With officers drafted in from the surrounding area to conduct door-to-door questioning of everyone who lived in the same street as each of the victims, it was time to start putting pressure on the surviving members of the class. Geraldine's first task was to go and speak to the diminishing group of people who had been at school with the victims, while Eileen and Ian questioned Leah.

'It's time to find out exactly what she was doing with a gun in the first place,' Eileen said briskly.

Geraldine said she thought Leah had been concerned to defend herself. 'Even if she did get hold of a gun after Stephanie and Peter were killed, because she was afraid she might be next, that doesn't mean she used it to shoot Bethany.'

'If Robin's wife was telling the truth – and there's no reason to suspect she wasn't – then Leah lied to you,' Eileen said. 'And if she lied about getting hold of a gun, she could be lying about having used it.'

'Not necessarily,' Geraldine said, but Eileen didn't appear to hear her.

43

LEAH STARED AT THE square-jawed woman. Everything about her emitted an aura of uncompromising solidity and power, from her short iron-grey hair, through her hard grey eyes and thin lips, to her broad shoulders and large red hands. Leah wondered if this was an image the woman facing her across the table had deliberately cultivated, or if she was a naturally cold bitch. It was hard to believe anyone could be so unremittingly severe. Even the dark-haired police sergeant who had been to see Leah at home had shown her more sympathy. Leah wished that sergeant was there now instead of the chief inspector. She was due some support after three of her former classmates had been brutally murdered, including her own flatmate. She dropped her eyes, unable to meet the other woman's steady gaze, and decided that the detective chief inspector's ruthlessness must be an act. No one could be that harsh.

A tiny spider had time to crawl all the way up the wall while the grey-haired woman read out a seemingly interminable speech telling Leah her rights. She had been briefly introduced to the flabby man sitting beside her whose ostensible role was to safeguard her interests. But although everyone was busily declaring their concern to protect her, she didn't feel in the slightest bit safe stuck in a cramped room in a police station with two detectives watching her across the table, and a sweaty stranger fidgeting at her side.

Once the preliminaries were over, the interview itself seemed to drag on interminably. The woman kept asking her where she had been on Wednesday, and where she had been on Sunday, throwing days of the week and dates at Leah, one after another in rapid succession, trying to catch her out. Had anyone seen her? What had she watched on the television?

'I was at home,' she kept repeating. 'I can't remember what was on the telly. Just what's always on. I'm generally at home in the evening. I don't really go out much except on Saturdays. I used to go out with Beth…'

It was vital she stayed in control of herself so she could be careful to avoid saying anything stupid that might incriminate her in the eyes of the police, but in spite of her efforts to maintain her composure, she felt tears trickling down her cheeks. The fair-haired man looked at her with a sympathetic expression, but the woman's face remained impassive. Good cop, bad cop. Leah wondered if they sometimes swapped roles.

The detective chief inspector cleared her throat noisily. 'So you were alone each time one of your former classmates was killed?'

Blinking angrily, Leah took a deep breath. 'I wasn't alone when Stephanie and Peter died. Beth was at home too.'

'You must miss her,' the other detective said.

The kindness in his voice dissolved the vestiges of Leah's self-control, and she broke down in tears. Stirring in his chair at her side, the lawyer spoke for the first time, requesting a break. With a shrug of her broad shoulders, the detective chief inspector paused the interview. A few moments later Leah was sitting on a hard bunk in a small whitewashed cell, staring miserably at the metal lavatory. Her lawyer stood gazing down at her, a complacent expression on his round face, his pudgy white hands folded across his rotund belly. It was all right for him. He was free to leave whenever he wanted.

'When can I go home?'

He gave a smug smile. 'They can't hold you for long. Don't worry, you'll soon be released.'

'But I haven't done anything wrong. They've got no right to keep me locked up here like this. I want to go home,' she wailed. 'It's horrible in here. I want to go home. Please, tell them to let me go home. I've done nothing wrong.'

The lawyer nodded. 'Yes, of course. I understand. Now, you rest for a few minutes and then we'll finish off the interview and you'll be free to go. But first, is there anything else you'd like to discuss with me? Remember you can speak to me in complete confidence. I'm here to help you.'

Leah shook her head. 'No, no. There's nothing else. There's nothing to tell. And you're not helping me. Please, I just want this to be over.'

She tried not to cry again, but she couldn't help it.

'My client is very upset,' the lawyer said when they were seated in the interview room again. 'She's very distressed about the recent murders and this unnecessarily heavy-handed approach is causing her a great deal of further stress. So if there's nothing else, I suggest you send her home for the time being. It serves no purpose keeping her in custody.'

There was some more discussion in which Leah didn't participate. She sat quietly, biting her lip and struggling to control her emotions. At last the detective chief inspector rose to her feet. For such a bulky woman she moved with surprising grace.

'Can I go home now?' Leah asked.

But instead of being released, she was accompanied back along the corridor to her cell.

'Sit tight,' her lawyer said. 'We'll soon have you out of here.'

Leah didn't trust him. Intending to reassure her, he was irritating, since he was clearly powerless to help her. He hovered in the cell for a few minutes, uttering fatuous platitudes about keeping her spirits up and being patient. She didn't answer. When he finally left her alone she lay down on the hard bunk bed and closed her eyes, trying to pretend she was at home. But it was impossible to relax, knowing where she was. No longer needing to control herself, she let tears slide down her cheeks unchecked.

When Bethany died, Leah had thought that was surely the most terrible experience she would ever have to go through. To be questioned as a suspect in the murder case was even more terrifying. She didn't know how much longer she could bear to remain locked up in there before she lost her mind. In a frenzy of despair she began banging on the door, demanding to be let out, until her voice grew hoarse and her throat was sore. She might as well have saved her breath, because no one came in answer to her hysterical summons. For all she knew, the apocalypse could have arrived, leaving her as the only survivor on the planet. If war had broken out, or there was some other drastic reason to prevent anyone from unlocking her cell door, she would starve to death in there, all alone. Her self-pity was overwhelmed by fear and she lay rigid on her bunk, praying that someone would come and put an end to this horrible waking nightmare.

44

THAT EVENING BEFORE GERALDINE left work, her phone rang. It was Ned's mother.

'There's something Ned would like to show you,' she said.

It could have been the phone line, but her voice sounded curiously cold and tinny.

'What is it?'

'Please, can you come round? He won't tell me what it is, but he's very upset.'

'Can I speak to him?'

Mrs Thomson didn't reply straight away. Geraldine thought she might have gone to fetch her son, but instead she heard his mother's voice again. 'He doesn't like talking on the phone. It makes him nervous. You know he was profoundly deaf as a child?'

'No, I didn't know.'

'No, of course, why would you know that? You can't tell now, not really, not unless you listen really closely to him speaking. He had cochlear implants fitted in both ears when he was a teenager but he's never really caught up. He's not as dim as he seems.'

'He didn't strike me as dim,' Geraldine lied.

'And now something's happened, and he won't tell me what, but he said he needed to talk to you and then he locked himself in his room and he's refusing to come out.'

'I'll be with you as soon as I can.'

In little more than an hour, Geraldine was driving up the lane past the caravan site and farm shop to the large farmhouse.

Ned opened the door and ushered her inside quickly.

'What was it you wanted to show me?' Geraldine asked.

'You'd better come with me.'

He led Geraldine up a wide wooden staircase and along to a door at the end of the landing where he opened the door to a small bedroom with a desk in one corner. Taking an envelope from the top drawer, he handed it to Geraldine.

'This arrived in the post yesterday.'

The typed letter addressed to Ned Thomson had been posted in York with a first class stamp. It was a cheap envelope, and the contents were printed on a sheet of A5 lined paper with two holes punched in the margin. The four-word message typed in large capital letters said simply: YOU COULD BE NEXT.

'Ned, I want you to think very carefully. Do you have any idea who might have sent this to you?'

Ned shook his head. 'I don't know what it means. What do you think it means? It says I could be next. Is it from the killer?'

For answer Geraldine slipped the letter into a plastic bag and explained that she was going to have to take it away for forensic examination.

'This letter could be significant to our investigation. It will be returned to you as soon as possible, should you want it back, but you understand it could give us vital evidence that might lead us to finding the killer.'

'Oh my God,' Mrs Thomson burst out. She was standing in the doorway of the narrow room, listening. 'You think it's from the killer, don't you?'

'It could be.'

'Does this mean Ned's life is in danger?' Pressing her fist against her mouth, she glared anxiously at Geraldine.

'Until we find out who's behind all this, Ned is going to have to be vigilant.'

'What do you mean, vigilant?' he asked. He looked very pale.

Geraldine advised him not to leave the house alone, and not to go anywhere unaccompanied.

'My son should be given police protection,' Ned's mother said.

'I don't think that'll be necessary as long as he's careful not to go out by himself. With this new evidence you've just given me, we should be able to catch whoever is behind all this even sooner than we thought. But in the meantime, Ned, it would be wise for you not to go out unaccompanied. You work with your father, don't you? Can you stay close to him?'

'That message is a threat,' Ned's mother said. 'He isn't safe, and you know it.'

'He'll be safe as long as he's careful not to go out alone.'

Geraldine hoped she was right, but she knew police resources wouldn't stretch to twenty-four hour surveillance of Ned and all his former classmates, any one of whom might be a potential target for the killer.

'What do you mean, he should be careful? It's your job to protect people. You should be out there arresting whoever wrote that letter, not telling innocent people to protect themselves because you can't or won't.'

Ned's mother was almost in tears.

'We're doing our best,' Geraldine assured her gently.

'What exactly have you been doing? It seems to me you're not doing anything at all,' Mrs Thomson protested.

'We're following several leads and we hope to be making an arrest very soon. This letter will help.'

'Who is it?' Ned wanted to know, his eyes bright with curiosity. 'Who killed them? Who?'

'I'm afraid I can't tell you any more than that.'

If the killer *had* sent the message, as seemed likely, there was a chance he or she had left at least a partial print, or a trace of DNA, on the paper or the envelope. With the plastic bag safely tucked in her jacket pocket Geraldine left, Mrs Thomson's words still ringing in her ears. As she drove away, her phone rang. With a sinking feeling, she answered.

The reception on her phone was poor. If Geraldine hadn't seen the message Ned had received, she wouldn't have been able to make sense of what Robin was saying about a letter, and something about him being next.

45

LEAH HAD BEEN IN custody when the letters had been posted, and Ashley hadn't received one.

'Not yet, anyway,' Ian said.

'Maybe the killer doesn't know where she lives,' one officer suggested.

'The killer might have written to her, and his letter could have got lost in the post,' Ariadne said, eliciting a general murmur of agreement.

There was a stultifying atmosphere at the police station, with nothing much to do but wait for results of forensic tests. The two letters had been sent away for examination but so far scrutiny of the letters and envelopes had revealed nothing about the killer's identity. Determined to make sure nothing had been overlooked, Geraldine went to speak to the forensic officer, Archie, who had examined the letters. Although his report was detailed and thorough, a face-to-face encounter might yield some ideas. Tall and skinny, with a prematurely receding hairline, he gave her the eager smile of an enthusiast before launching into his report.

'There are minute traces of regenerated cellulose on one of the envelopes, visible under magnification, which suggests the envelopes were sold in a cheap cellophane wrapper.'

'Can that give us any indication where they came from?'

Archie told her they were the sort of envelopes that were available at just about every retail stationery outlet, as well as from online suppliers.

'We can't say where they come from, but there's a lot we *can* tell,' he added quickly, sensing her impatience. 'By analysing dating markers like fibres, synthetic brighteners, pulping chemistry, paper additives, adhesive components and surface treatments, it's possible to determine the likely age of the paper with reasonable accuracy. The precise formula for paper varies enough for it to be possible to identify the company that manufactured a particular sheet, by comparing different samples.'

His eyes glowed with enthusiasm, but Geraldine wasn't sure she was going to learn anything that might help move the investigation forward. She had a suspicion she was wasting her time, listening to an expert lecturing her about his own area of interest. And all the time they were talking, a vicious killer remained at large and she was helpless to do anything about it.

'So what can you tell me that might help us find whoever wrote these letters?'

Archie shrugged. 'It was all in my report. The writer used relatively cheap white Basildon Bond envelopes, peel and seal which they mostly are these days, so the flaps have no traces of saliva. And there are no finger marks on the envelopes. They were handled with rubber gloves, leaving traces of white latex but no identifiable finger marks. It can't have been easy, separating them with gloves on,' he added with something like admiration in his voice. 'Whoever sent these letters took a lot of trouble not to leave any identifying clues.'

Geraldine frowned, but her irritation did nothing to dampen her companion's enthusiasm.

'Is there anything else you can tell me?' she asked, struggling to hide her impatience.

But tracking down where one packet of envelopes had been bought at an unspecified time in the past, from a supplier anywhere in the world, was an impossible task, even with all the resources at her disposal.

'OK,' she said. 'So the envelopes are a dead end. What about the message itself? Does that offer any indication about who might have written it?'

Archie shook his head, his long face suddenly lugubrious. 'Not really. If you want my opinion, it would be pointless to speculate.'

Hearing the response she had been expecting, Geraldine's disappointment was stupid.

'The messages are identical,' Archie continued. 'They could all have been printed on the same simple printer, an Epson XP 432, or something similar. Like the paper and the envelopes, those sorts of printers are available everywhere. None of this gets you anywhere, does it? I'm sorry I can't be more helpful. But don't look so glum,' he added, forcing a smile. 'I'm sure you'll get your man in the end.'

His breezy enthusiasm made Geraldine feel uncomfortably jaded. It seemed a very long time since she had felt a similar youthful optimism.

'So there's nothing more you can tell us?' she asked. 'Anything at all that might narrow down our search?'

'I'm afraid that's it. If we find anything else, you'll be the first to know.' When Geraldine returned to the police station, she went to find Ian in his small office. He looked up when she opened his door, his expression despondent.

'It's early days,' Geraldine said. 'There's no need to look so fed up.'

'We have three victims and we're getting nowhere.'

He was right. They needed to start making progress, before there was another murder.

'What about your paper man?'

She shook her head. 'Nothing.'

Ian called up an image of the letters on his screen and nodded at her to stand behind him so they could stare at it together. Beside her cheek, close enough to touch, his fair hair glinted in the light streaming through his window. Momentarily distracted by a faint scent of aftershave, she forced herself to focus on the words on his screen: YOU COULD BE NEXT.

'He's not giving much away,' Ian grumbled. 'I've been staring at those four words for hours and I'm still no wiser.'

'It's a warning.'

'But why alert his potential victims? Surely he wouldn't want anyone to be expecting an attack. That's only going to make it more difficult for him to carry it off.'

'So he's arrogant. He thinks he can succeed whatever the odds against him. But in any case, they're already on their guard. He's just killed three of their class. How much stronger a warning could he have given them?'

'He's toying with them to taunt us.' Ian sounded angry. 'He knows we're not on to him yet.'

'And he's supremely confident he'll get away with it,' Geraldine added. 'Of course it might have nothing to do with us. He could be threatening them because he wants to frighten them. But why?'

'It must be some kind of payback.'

'But for what? The answer must lie in their school days.' She paused. 'Unless his intention is to terrorise one of them – Leah or Ashley, perhaps? All of this could be aimed at one of them.'

Sunlight glistened on Ian's hair as he shifted in his seat. 'You're suggesting he's killed three random people just to frighten someone else?'

'Yes, why not? And they're not random. They all know one another. He's threatening her with what he'll do to her if she doesn't give him what he wants. It's possible.'

'No. That's crazy. Do you really think anyone would kill three people, just to make a point?'

'Well, he *has* killed three people, and whatever his motive, it's certainly crazy.'

Ian shook his head. 'You need to go home and get some sleep. You're not thinking clearly.'

Geraldine went home that evening feeling thoroughly dejected. Seeing as she was feeling so low anyway, she decided she might as well phone her sister. Helena could hardly make her feel much worse. Besides, she might be making good progress, which would cheer Geraldine up.

'Hi, it's Geraldine. How are you doing?'

'OK.'

'What have you been doing today?'

'Not much. I went shopping.'

'What did you get?'

'Not much.'

It was a stilted exchange. After a few minutes, Geraldine gave up the attempt to engage her sister in conversation. She said goodbye and rang off, hoping there wasn't a reason for Helena's reluctance to talk to her. Having slept badly, she woke early next morning with a pounding headache. After a strong coffee she felt slightly better and set off for work, pausing briefly to check her post box in the entrance hall on her way out.

She didn't register anything unusual about the typed address, but as soon as she slipped the letter out of the envelope she recognised the message. Feeling sick, she hurried to the car park, keeping an eye out for anyone loitering outside her block of flats. Apart from an occasional car passing by, the street was deserted. Driving into work she considered her options. She was strongly tempted to keep quiet about the letter she had received, knowing that reporting it would result in her being taken off the case. She couldn't bear to be removed from the investigation and almost certainly have to leave the area. Withholding such significant information would land her in trouble if it ever came to light, but if necessary she could deny having received it. No one could prove it had actually reached her letter box. As Ariadne had mentioned only the previous day, it wasn't uncommon for letters to be lost in the post.

Then there was the issue of keeping information from the team. If her letter added anything to what they already knew about its sender, she wouldn't hesitate to report it. But as far as she could tell, the letter was the same as the others they had seen. Even so, it was possible the writer had slipped up and left a fingerprint or clear trace of DNA on this one. Since it hadn't been addressed to her by name, she could take it to Archie and have him check it without anyone else finding out about it. She would make up some story about having forgotten to put it through the system, and ask him to make an unofficial check. If he discovered anything useful, she would have to reveal what had happened. If not, she could keep quiet with a clear conscience.

Finally she had to consider the implications to her personal security. She definitely wasn't happy knowing the killer had discovered her address. Either he had hacked into her private accounts, or else he had followed her home. She would have to be vigilant. There was CCTV in all public areas of her building meaning that no one could reach her front door unobserved, and her own alarm system would automatically trigger an alert at the police station should anyone enter her flat uninvited. So, considered objectively, the threat to her personal safety was actually minimal. It was a difficult decision, but she decided to keep quiet about the letter she had received, at least until she had asked Archie to check it out.

For the first time she realised that she desperately wanted to stay in York where she was beginning to feel settled, and make friends. And she was working with Ian again.

46

ON HER WAY INTO work Geraldine dropped her letter off, sealed in an evidence bag, with clear instructions that Archie was to contact her directly if he discovered any clues as to the sender.

'It's entirely my fault,' she confided with her best pretence at an embarrassed smile. 'I left this one behind. I could get in serious trouble for that, and I've already got myself into hot water recently, so I'd really appreciate it if you didn't mention this to anyone else. Just call me with any feedback you have and I'll come and see you straight away.'

That morning Leah was released, the search of her flat and the surrounding land having failed to yield any result. They had to either charge her or let her go, and without any evidence to back up Eileen's suspicions, there was no point in initiating formal proceedings. She had been in custody when the letters had been posted, and there was no sign of her having travelled to York on the evening Stephanie had been murdered, or of her driving out of Uppermill on the night Peter's body had been deposited on the Tadcaster Road.

Eileen determined they should focus their attention on tracking down the gun that had been used to kill Bethany. This was, without doubt, their most pressing task for more reasons than one.

'It must be somewhere,' the detective chief inspector barked, glaring around the room as though the assembled officers could be bullied into revealing where the gun was hidden. 'We need to find out where it came from, and crucially where it is now.'

Geraldine watched a pale and shaky Leah collect her

belongings and walk out of the police compound looking dazed. Leaving the building, she blinked and lifted her face to the open sky and stood perfectly still for a moment to feel the fresh breeze on her skin. Through the window, Geraldine thought she saw tears glistening on Leah's cheeks as she shuffled out of the police compound. Geraldine wondered if life was more difficult for someone who surrendered easily to their emotions, or whether the challenge was greater for people who suppressed their feelings. Geraldine's own self-control was a combination of a natural predilection for privacy, and her strict training in concealing her feelings. She couldn't imagine what it must be like to constantly break down in tears.

Most of the team, including Eileen, were convinced that Leah must be guilty, yet, despite their best efforts, they had been unable to find any evidence that placed her at any of the crime scenes. Meanwhile she continued to insist that she had been at home on all of the evenings when the murders had been committed. Having observed her closely, Geraldine really couldn't believe Leah capable of killing someone in the heat of the moment, let alone of carrying out a series of cold-blooded premeditated murders. She kept her opinion to herself, aware that she was in the minority.

'If it was her, we'll get her,' Eileen grumbled. 'It's only a matter of time. We'll just have to hope there aren't any more victims before we stop her.'

Naomi nodded solemnly and a few other colleagues muttered, frowning.

'Someone must know what she's done,' Eileen went on. 'We need to persuade people to start talking. So let's get on to everyone who knows her, and see what we can dig up about her past. Is there any history of violence?'

'You mean like drowning kittens when she was a child?' a young constable piped up.

Eileen ignored the interruption. 'And in the meantime, I

want her kept under twenty-four hour surveillance. If she does try anything else, we'll be there to catch her in the act and prevent any more fatalities.

With so much expense about to be thrown at Leah, Geraldine could no longer remain silent. 'I just don't believe a hysterical girl like Leah would be able to keep quiet about her activities, not if she's really been running around killing people. The idea of her being discreet just doesn't ring true. You've seen how little self-control she has.'

'People who lack self-control are more likely to snap,' Naomi replied promptly.

'These are not the actions of someone who just snapped,' Geraldine said. 'These were carefully thought-out attacks. How else would the killer have got away with committing three murders?'

'And there are the letters,' Ariadne said.

'We don't know the letters were sent by the killer,' Naomi pointed out.

That was true.

'Have we made any progress with finding out who sent them?' Eileen asked.

Geraldine kept quiet.

Having been unable to establish where the letters came from, Eileen decided it was time to question all the local people who had known the victims, including the surviving members of that ill-fated class at school, the headmistress, and any other members of staff who had been at the school when the victims and the surviving classmates had been at school together. One of them might come up with a lead as a result.

Ian set to work co-ordinating a team to question all the staff and former staff of the school again, while Geraldine went to see Ashley. She hadn't spoken to her for about a week and was taken aback at the change in her appearance. No longer in shock, Ashley was attractive, with soft blue eyes and light blond hair that fell in loose curls down to her shoulders. She was slim and undeniably pretty, with that kind of quiet beauty that seemed to suggest she had a sympathetic nature. Although Geraldine liked her at once, she was fully aware that outward charm was no guarantee of decency or even sanity. She had encountered too many psychopaths with a similar engaging warmth to set any store by appearances.

Ashley was still staying with her neighbour, Gloria, in the flat above the one where she had been living with Stephanie. Gloria opened the door and smiled a welcome.

'Ashley's still here,' she confided, as though Geraldine didn't know that. 'My daughter's away at college, so I'm happy to put the poor girl up for as long as it takes. They've finished searching her flat, but she doesn't feel ready to go back there yet, poor thing. We're all in shock. And to think it happened here.'

She continued chattering, turning the conversation to her own daughter and how well she was doing in her studies, as they walked along the corridor to the living room where Ashley was watching television.

'We're watching *The Chase*,' Gloria said as Geraldine sat down. 'Now, can I get you anything?'

Geraldine shook her head. 'That's very kind of you, Gloria, but I'd like a private word with Ashley, if you don't mind.'

'No, no, that's fine, don't mind me,' Gloria said, sitting down.

Geraldine turned to Ashley. 'Can we go to your room? I would like to talk to you for a few moments on your own.'

'Oh, I see.' Gloria stood up, flustered. 'I didn't realise, I don't want to be in the way. If you want me to go...' she glanced uncertainly at Geraldine who nodded.

In a murder case, the demands of the investigation had to override any niceties, and it was important the details of the deaths be shared with as few people as possible. Once Gloria had left them, and the television was muted, Geraldine asked Ashley if there had been any instances of bullying when she had been at school.

'You need to speak to Ned.'

'I'm asking you. Ashley, if you know anything that might help us to trace this killer, you have to tell me. Refusing to share what you know, or even suspect, is not only against the law, it might lead to more deaths that could have been avoided. You do understand that, don't you?'

Ashley shook her head. 'Ask Ned. He's the one who was bullied,' she repeated, insisting that she didn't know who had been responsible.

Ned was one of the potential victims who had received a threatening letter. Somehow, the more information the police gathered, the less sense the case made. Worried about what Ashley had told her, and why she had refused to say more, Geraldine set off for Ned's farm.

47

AFTER A MILD START to the winter, bitter weather was forecast. Beneath a glowering grey sky, thick clouds looked low enough to reach up and touch, and it began to rain as Geraldine drove out of York. The rain turned to sleet that fell almost horizontally, blown across desolate fields by a cutting north wind. She glanced over her shoulder to check she had remembered to throw her fleecy jacket in the back of the car. Once she stepped outside, she would freeze without it. It looked as though she would soon have a chance to test the manufacturer's claim that her new woolly hat was waterproof.

Ned was out at the caravan site when Geraldine arrived at the house. Turning the car round, she drove back down the lane. Had the weather been warmer she would have walked the short distance, but the ground was wet and icy and although her shoes were waterproof she would have needed decent hiking boots to walk comfortably along the lane in this weather. The gate to the caravan site was shut but not locked. It only took a minute to jump out of the car and drag it open. Even so, she was glad she had pulled on her jacket before leaving her heated car. Driving through the open gate of the caravan site, past a sign advising visitors of opening hours, she drew up outside the main building and gazed around. In the summer it would be a lovely place for families to stay, and she could easily picture the place bustling with children and noise and activity. Now it had echoes of a scene from a Hitchcock film, with wisps of dry grasses blowing across the bleak landscape.

The whole place looked deserted as she walked past the

closed-up general store, but there were lights on in the office beside the shop, and the door wasn't locked. A middle-aged man was sitting behind a desk, staring at a computer screen. He looked up at her with a puzzled smile.

'Can I help you?'

Geraldine returned his smile. 'Thank you. I'm looking for Ned Thomson.'

'And you are…?'

She showed her identity card.

'I'm Albert, Ned's father. My wife told me you're investigating the recent murders.'

As he stood up, Geraldine saw there was a strong family resemblance between him and his son, although the father was completely bald. Like Ned, the man behind the desk was tall and he had a long face and gentle eyes which gazed warily at Geraldine.

'What do you want with Ned? You must know he's not…' he paused, searching for the right words. 'He's been very upset about the recent deaths. He knew all the victims, you know.'

Geraldine adopted what she hoped was a sympathetic expression. 'I'm so sorry to trouble you like this, Mr Thomson, but I really do need to speak to your son and I think it would be much better if I could see him here, in familiar surroundings where he feels comfortable, without any fuss.'

Ned's father nodded. 'I understand,' he answered heavily. 'And there's really no need to threaten me, or my son, with any kind of bother. Believe me, we're keen to see the end of all this. But Ned's easily upset and he's already told you everything he can.'

Carefully Geraldine explained that while nothing new had come up, there was a question that Ned might be able to help them with. She regretted that she was unable to divulge any details, but she did need to speak to Ned. With a shrug, Mr Thomson phoned his son, and Ned arrived soon after receiving his father's summons. Out of breath, his legs splashed with mud, he smiled anxiously at Geraldine as he pulled off his thick leather gloves.

'My dad said you were here. Have you found out who did it?'

Without answering she went and stood beside him so that his father couldn't hear what they were saying. Quietly, she asked Ned if he could remember any bullying at school. He shook his head.

'Are you sure?'

'Not really what you'd call bullying,' he replied slowly. 'Some of the other boys used to tease me a bit, because my hearing was bad, but they weren't being mean. I mean, my voice was odd in those days and kids pick on anyone who's different, don't they? Why do you ask?'

He stared at Geraldine, his candid blue eyes wide open. She had a feeling he might be lying.

'What is it?' Mr Thomson asked.

Geraldine explained that the question was only for people directly involved in the investigation. She said she hoped she could rely on Ned's discretion.

'It's very important that as few people as possible know about it,' she added.

Ned nodded solemnly. His father looked faintly disgruntled, but there was nothing he could do about it.

'Can you tell me about it?' she asked.

Ned looked anxious. 'No, I can't,' he said, his voice rising. 'It was a long time ago and I don't really see the point in talking about it now. It's over and done with.'

Geraldine was sure there was more he could have said if his father hadn't been present, but he lowered his eyes and remained silent.

'I hate to press you,' she persisted, 'but it's very important you tell me everything you can.'

Ned's father stepped forward to stand at his son's side. 'Is there anything else you can tell the policewoman, son?'

Ned shook his head.

'Are you sure?' Geraldine asked.

'There's nothing else,' Ned repeated.

Short of taking him with her to the police station for questioning, there was nothing more Geraldine could do to force him to talk.

'If I find you've been hiding something from us, Ned, you could be in serious trouble. You do understand that, don't you?'

He nodded solemnly, his eyes fixed on hers. Mr Thomson took his son by the arm.

'It's all right, Ned, the policewoman's just leaving. You're not in any trouble.' He turned to Geraldine. 'My son's told you all he knows.'

As she walked back to her car, Geraldine glanced back at the two men who were standing motionless, side by side, watching her go.

The following morning when the team assembled to discuss how the investigation was progressing, Geraldine suggested the killings could be related to a history of bullying at the school.

'According to Ashley, Ned was the victim of bullying. He dismissed it as insignificant, but Susan Mulvey suggested there was a sustained campaign of bullying,' she explained. 'She told me she couldn't remember who the target was, but I suspect she knew who it was.'

'In your report you said Ned denied it was serious,' Eileen replied.

'I know, but I had a feeling he might have known more than he was letting on,' Geraldine said quietly.

It was difficult to be certain, and she could hardly force Ned to talk to her. It wasn't as if he was a suspect.

'If he's withholding information that could help us, we ought to be putting pressure on him,' Naomi said.

The trouble was, Geraldine wasn't sure if he really did know more than he had admitted.

'It was only an impression I had,' she explained. 'There's no way of knowing what he knows, unless he decides to tell us. And his father was almost aggressive in his defence of his son. I guess he's had to be. That's why I didn't make too much of it in my official report. I'm just telling you because we're here talking about the case and throwing ideas around. If there's a possibility Ned's somehow involved in all this, then perhaps the others might know something, and one of them might be more inclined to talk to us. It's just an idea, but I think it's worth checking out.'

Ian agreed with Geraldine and so it was decided that she would ask the other three surviving classmates.

'It'll be interesting to hear what Leah has to say about this allegation of bullying,' Eileen said sharply. 'I darcsay she'll jump at the chance to throw suspicion on someone else.'

48

OVER A WEEK HAD passed since he had acquired a gun. It should have made his life easier, but the gun had actually created more problems than it solved. For a start, he had to be more cautious than before. If anyone caught so much as a glimpse of the gun, everything would be over. And meanwhile, there were three people still to dispose of. On reflection he decided it had probably been a mistake sending out threatening letters, but his intentions had been sound. The purpose of his campaign had always been to cause fear, and he had certainly accomplished that by now, if the media were anything to go by.

He was disappointed when the policewoman failed to panic, as he had intended. So far as he could tell, she had turned up at the police station in the morning as though nothing had happened. He was afraid her letter hadn't arrived yet. If she still hadn't reacted after a few days he would assume her letter had gone astray and come up with something more definite for her. Meanwhile, by now the girl who had caused all of this must have realised who was behind the murders, and understood that anyone she befriended would be eliminated. The people she had been at school with were only the beginning, but removing them might be enough to convince her that he was not prepared to share her with anyone else.

With hindsight he could see that it had been a mistake to let her continue working, because exposure to other people had made her less dependent on him. The idea of leaving him couldn't have come from her, which meant that someone else had put her up to it. If he could find out who that person was, he would rip their face to shreds with his bare hands. But they had been happy together before, and would be so again. Only this time, no one else would be allowed to interfere in their lives. Once they were married, she would never leave his house again.

Leaning back against his pillows, he stared uneasily at the gun. It certainly made the task easy, but it was too quick. One click and a person was dead. He closed his eyes and tried to relive the delicious sense of anticipation he had felt as a child, when he had slammed the lid of his homemade box shut on a quivering mouse. Shooting was altogether different. Cheated of the thrill, he didn't really feel like he had killed at all because it was the gun, not him, that meted out the sentence.

Now the gun lay there, black against his pale blue duvet cover. The benefit of such a weapon was to bestow power on whoever held it. With a gun in his hand, any feeble idiot could command instant obedience. It was an efficient but impersonal shortcut that stole the pleasure out of controlling other people. He picked it up and stroked the barrel with the tip of one finger, willing himself to feel an affinity with this uncompromising gadget, but he felt only resentment. The gun meant there was no need for him to even come close to his victims. It stole any intimacy from the act of killing, reducing it to a mere termination of physical function.

With a cry of rage he flung the gun away from him. It slid across the carpet and came to rest, clattering softly against the skirting board. He didn't want the wretched thing. It had come his way purely by chance, after he had been watching Bethany and Leah for a few days. Fortunately they had lived together, which had doubled his chances of finding one of them on their own. After only two deaths, the media had already started reporting his activities, throwing out wild claims about the dangers of walking the streets without company. Before long it would become impossible to carry out an attack. So when he had seen Bethany going out alone after dark one Sunday evening, the opportunity had been too good to miss.

He had followed her down to the canal where, before he had time to draw his knife, he had spotted a gun in her hand. Catching her off guard, it had been pathetically easy to overpower her and wrest the gun from her. But the killing itself had been a bitter disappointment, over in an instant, with an ear splitting explosion that he thought would bring the whole village out. There had been no time to witness her struggle, no observing her features slacken as her eyes grew glassy and her limbs flopped. As she collapsed into the water with a loud splash, he had sprinted away.

The memory of the incident still made him angry. The gun had spoiled it, removing the exhilaration of the kill. With cold detachment he acknowledged that although it was necessary for him to eliminate his victims, he also relished the thrill of the deed. It was like an addiction. But at least he had removed her, and it had been fast and efficient which was surely a good thing, even if it had been over too quickly for him to enjoy the experience.

He turned his attention to the immediate question of what to do with the weapon. Although he was keen to get rid of it, he realised that doing so might not serve his overall plan. There could well be an occasion that called for a quick kill. It would do no harm to hang on to the unlooked-for gun for a while. He didn't have to use it. Resigned, he crossed the room to retrieve it. Pushing it under his mattress, he lay down on the bed again and tried to concentrate on selecting his next victim.

Robin presented a challenge. Working in an office and living with a wife, he might prove unassailable in the short term. Ned would be easier to attack. Out in the fields he would be working alone, as long as his father wasn't hanging around. Ned's parents were annoyingly protective and the hype in the media was bound to make them worry about their son even more than usual. Thinking about Ned and his parents, he regretted having sent out threatening letters. It had seemed a good idea at the time, but had actually served only to make his task more difficult. But not impossible.

The easiest target was Leah, now living by herself. Before long she would find another flatmate to replace Bethany, or else she would move, so he needed to act quickly. He smiled, imagining her shocked expression and flailing arms.

Alone with her in her flat, after dark, he would whisper, 'If you scream, I'll kill you.' And then he would kill her anyway.

To make up for his disappointment by the canal he would use his knife in Leah's flat, and he would take his time killing her.

49

Inside the house a baby was crying. When Robin's wife opened the door she didn't look pleased to see Geraldine. Instead of greeting her, she gave a helpless shrug as though to say, 'You can hear the baby needs attention. What are you doing coming here when he needs feeding?'

Sure enough, her first words were: 'The baby's crying. Can't you hear him?'

'I'm sorry to disturb you. It's your husband I need to see.'

'Why? What do you want with him now? He's already told you everything he knows.'

'Really?' Geraldine did her best to hide her annoyance. 'What makes you so sure of that?'

Katie scowled. 'Well, I know my husband, and I know he's keen to help you. But I need to see to the baby before he works himself up into a state.'

Geraldine suspected she was too late to prevent that.

Katie's voice wavered, her anger overwhelmed by concern for her husband. 'You'll want to come in then?'

There was no need for an answer. Katie led Geraldine along the hallway to the kitchen where Robin was sitting, red in the face, trying to feed the baby with a spoon. The highchair and floor were splattered with dollops of mustard-coloured mush, which was smeared over the baby's face. Katie darted forward and grabbed the plastic spoon from the baby who instantly began wailing loudly again.

'Welcome to our haven of domestic bliss,' Robin said as he stood up, smiling miserably at his wife.

'That's easy for you to say,' she replied with a tired smile. 'You don't have to put up with this all day every day, and just look at the mess you've made.'

As the baby's screeching intensified, Robin ushered Geraldine back along the narrow hall to the living room, muttering about teething. They sat down, with the door closed to muffle the noise from the kitchen.

'Well? Have you got to the bottom of this yet?' he asked.

'We're following several leads. We think the killer was someone you knew at school. Think carefully, Robin. Can you remember anyone there who might have held a grudge against other members of the class? Perhaps someone with mental problems? Or someone involved with drugs?'

Robin smiled uneasily. He understood from her questions that the police were casting around, with no idea who had killed his former classmates.

'Robin, is there anything you're not telling me?'

For an instant, Geraldine held her breath, thinking he was about to offer her a new lead. But instead he shook his head.

'What about bullying? Can you remember much of that going on when you were at school?'

'Nope,' he said after a brief pause. 'I can't say there was. Nothing more than the usual, kids having a lark. I haven't got the foggiest idea why you're asking me about that. Can't you tell me what's happening now? You must have found out something. Have you got the gun?'

'Not yet.'

Robin pulled a face. 'Don't you think your time would be better spent trying to find out who's got it?'

Before Geraldine could respond, they heard his wife calling him.

'I have to go,' he said, standing up. 'I'm supposed to be on duty this evening.' He jerked his head towards the kitchen with a grimace.

Geraldine urged him to contact her directly if he remembered anything that might help them. Geraldine's next visit was to Ashley who was still living with her neighbour.

'I think Gloria's getting a bit fed up with me,' she confessed to Geraldine as they took their seats in the living room. 'But I don't think I can bear to move back into the flat where – where it happened. I know it's been cleaned up but I couldn't go in the kitchen and cook, as though nothing had happened.'

Geraldine gave a sympathetic response, before going through the series of questions she had just asked Robin.

'Ned was the weird one...' Ashley said.

'Was he badly bullied for it?'

Ashley stared at the floor without answering.

'Who bullied him, Ashley?'

Again Ashley sat silent.

'You don't seem to appreciate what a serious offence it is to withhold information from the police in a murder enquiry,' Geraldine said, with a twinge of guilt about the letter she had concealed, even though nothing useful had so far been discovered from it. 'You could face a custodial sentence, apart from which the killer might strike again unless you tell me everything you know about Ned.'

'Is he the killer?' Ashley whispered.

At last, after some further persuasion, she began to speak. 'I understand. The thing is, when we were kids, at school, Ned struggled to keep up with the rest of us because he was hearing impaired, you know? He had a special teacher for a while but then he had cochlear implants put in, kind of hearing aids that connected to his brain. They worked, but his speech wasn't great even then.' She paused again. 'So yes, he used to get bullied, quite a lot in fact.'

Geraldine nodded. She had suspected as much.

'How is that relevant to your investigation?' Ashley asked.

'Tell me more about the bullying.'

'Some of the boys used to leave messages about him on the whiteboards. They never mentioned him by name, but we all knew who they meant. They'd write insults, "N is a dummy" and things like that, only some of them were far worse and quite obscene. The teachers never understood what the messages meant, or at least they pretended not to. Perhaps their hands were tied and they needed evidence before they could do anything.'

Geraldine nodded. She knew how that felt.

'Anyway,' Ashley went on, 'the teachers carried out this massive investigation that went on for a whole term, but no one exposed the bullies. There were probably too many of them.' She gave an embarrassed laugh. 'We all thought it was funny, because the teachers didn't understand what was going on. We assumed they didn't know who N was, and we did. I guess they must have realised, but we all thought it was our secret. And the teachers were desperate to know who was writing the messages and they couldn't find out what we all knew. We were only children, and anyway Ned didn't seem to care so it wasn't like we were hurting anyone. That's what we told ourselves anyway. It went on for ages. Everyone knew that N meant Ned, and eventually just about all of us were joining in, writing rude messages on the white boards.' She gave an embarrassed smile. 'It seemed like fun at the time.'

Geraldine asked her who had been responsible for starting the trend for writing the messages on the board, but Ashley insisted she didn't know.

'It was all so long ago,' she apologised. 'I really can't remember that much about it all, but I do remember seeing the messages on the board. I remember there were lots of rumours flying around, but we never found out who started the messages, at least I never did. We used to find it hilarious.' She paused. 'I never knew if Ned understood what was going on but as a child I didn't care and I don't think anyone else did either. It was just a joke.'

She seemed to be talking a lot. Driving away from Ashley, Geraldine pondered the significance of her nervous chatter, rather than what she had actually said. She suspected that Ashley had been lying to her when she had claimed not to know who had bullied Ned at school. That suggested the bully was now a friend of hers, whom she was keen to protect. The fact that she had not received one of the threatening letters seemed to bear out that suspicion. It was hard not to think about the deaf boy who had been bullied at school and wonder whether he had been pushed too far. He seemed harmless enough, but it was all very inconclusive.

50

AFTER HER FRUSTRATING CONVERSATION with Ashley, Geraldine drove straight to her next visit. It was growing late by the time she arrived, but Leah opened the door at once without even asking who was there and they went and sat in the living room.

'They were here going through everything,' Leah said as Geraldine reached for her phone. 'What's going on? I don't understand. I'm a victim, you know. It was my flatmate who was killed, and I've been questioned and questioned about where I was that night, when I told you right from the beginning that I was here, on my own, and as if that wasn't enough, you had to lock me up in a cell overnight! It's disgusting the way I've been treated, as if I was the guilty one, when I'm a potential murder victim! And now I've got to sleep here, in the flat where she was living before it happened.' She burst into tears.

Geraldine considered pointing out that Leah was lucky Bethany hadn't been killed at home, like Stephanie. Ashley hadn't been allowed back into her flat for days while it had been processed as a crime scene, and she still didn't want to return there. At least Leah had been able to stay put. But she didn't say any of that. Instead, she went through her prepared questions once again. Unlike Ashley, Leah was ready to answer at once.

'Bullying? I should say there was. As soon as we hit puberty it all kicked off. Although I used to get bullied even before that, because they sense weakness, don't they, the bullies? Not that I was weak, but I've always been sensitive, and bullies pick on that, don't they? Yes, I was badly bullied at school, especially as an adolescent, because I was a bit overweight back then. Lots of girls are,' she added as though defending herself for putting on weight. 'It was just puppy fat. Anyway, no one ever did anything about it. So what are you doing, coming here again? You've got some front, after all you've put me through. Have you done anything to catch this killer? Look what he sent me while I was banged up.'

Still crying, she stood up and left the room, returning a moment later clutching a grubby envelope.

Geraldine recognised it at once. 'Basildon Bond,' she muttered.

'Who? Don't tell me you know who the killer is, finally?'

'I'm talking about the envelope.'

Slipping on a latex glove, Geraldine held out her hand and removed the letter from the envelope. She knew what was written on it without looking: YOU COULD BE NEXT.

Leah stared at Geraldine, her eyes inflamed and glistening with unshed tears.

'What does it mean?' she whispered, her aggression overshadowed by fear. 'Am I going to be killed?'

Either Leah was a first-rate actress, or she was genuinely scared by the letter. Geraldine studied the envelope. The postmark was indistinct, and in any case, if Leah was the author of the threatening letters, she could have asked someone else to post them while she was in police custody, in an attempt to provide herself with an alibi. The date of postage established nothing, just as Leah receiving a letter didn't prove she hadn't sent the letters out herself.

'What are you doing with it?' Leah asked as Geraldine put the letter in an evidence bag and slipped it into her bag.

'I need to take it away for forensic examination. Why didn't you call us straight away?'

Leah shrugged. Geraldine explained that similar letters had been sent to Ned and Robin.

'But not to Ashley, of course,' Leah replied sourly.

'What makes you say that?'

It was Leah's tone rather than her words that interested Geraldine.

'Oh, no reason, really. It's just that everyone always loved Ashley.'

'The boys, you mean?'

'She was so pretty, and blond, and delicate, you know.'

Geraldine contemplated dumpy Leah with her face blotchy from crying, and wondered how far jealousy might have driven her. But that wouldn't account for her killing three other members of their class at school, and leaving Ashley untouched. She wondered if Leah herself had been infatuated with Ashley and had wanted to eliminate her friends. The idea was ridiculous, especially after so long a gap, but not impossible.

She returned to her questioning. 'Do you remember someone in your class called Ned?'

'Of course.'

'He's hearing impaired.'

'Yes, I know. The deaf boy who lived on a farm.'

'Were you close to him at school?'

'I knew who he was, we all did, but we weren't exactly friends. I never really spoke to him. He was probably a perfectly nice guy, but I used to think he was weird, because of the way he spoke. Don't tell me he's the killer!'

'Would that surprise you?'

'Well, he seemed pretty harmless, but I suppose he did live on a farm so they must have guns and things.' At the mention of guns, she reddened.

'What about Robin?'

Leah's blush deepened. 'He was in my class too, but he was one of the cool guys, you know? He wasn't interested in me.'

That wasn't what Geraldine had asked. Robin was fairly

short, but he was good looking. She wondered if Leah had fancied him.

'What about Ashley? Was she friendly with Ned or Robin?'

Leah's face twisted into a sour grimace. 'She was friendly with all the boys. At least, all the boys were after her. I'm not saying she was flirty. It was the opposite, really. She was very quiet. She just let them all run after her and compete for her attention.'

'That must have been hard for the rest of you.'

'Not really,' Leah brushed off the suggestion a little too readily. 'None of us wanted to go out with any of them. They weren't exactly God's gift, any of them.'

'Did Ashley go out with any of them?'

'She was interested in someone else.'

Still tearful, Leah gave a mischievous smile. Geraldine waited, confident that she was keen to share her gossip. Having lost her flatmate, she was bound to be feeling lonely, and ready to talk to anyone, even a police officer. Sure enough, Leah blew her nose and cleared her throat, preparing to pass on what she knew.

'She was seeing someone but no one was supposed to know, apart from us, of course. But no one else knew. We were all sworn to secrecy. Oh, it's all right, we were in the sixth form, but he was older than her and she didn't want her parents to find out.'

'How much older?'

Leah shrugged. 'I don't know. He was just older than her. She didn't tell me everything. It wasn't like I was her best friend,' she added bitterly.

'Who was close to her?'

'There were four of them who used to go around together. Nicole and her family went to live in America soon after we left school.'

'And the others? You said there were four of them who used to hang out together.'

Somehow Geraldine wasn't surprised to hear that Ashley's other two best friends at school had been Stephanie and Beth.

'Was she friendly with Peter?'

'I don't think so. I mean, not that I knew about.'

'Leah, I'm not here to gossip, but this is important. Who was Ashley's boyfriend?'

'I don't know. You'll have to ask her.'

'When did they stop seeing one another?'

Leah shrugged. 'I told you, I wasn't her best friend and when we were in the sixth form we didn't really mix that much. She had her clique and – and I had my own friends. Once we left school we didn't socialise at all. She moved away and I don't know who she was friends with, or who she was going out with.'

Geraldine returned to her earlier question. 'Do you remember Ned being bullied at school?'

'No, not especially.'

'What do you mean, not especially?'

Leah looked uncomfortable. 'Well, he was deaf, although he could hear, but he had a funny voice. Oh, you know how it is, kids will pick on anything. But he seemed quite happy. I don't know if he really knew what was going on. He didn't seem bothered by it.'

Geraldine tried to find out details of the bullying but all Leah admitted to recalling was that other pupils used to mutter insults at him behind his back. She was fairly certain he hadn't even been able to hear them. When Geraldine asked about messages written on the whiteboard in class, Leah said she had no recollection of that at all. There didn't seem to be anything else Leah could tell her, and it was too late to call on Ashley again, so Geraldine drove home and wrote up her decision log there.

Mulling over what she had learned about the victims' time at school, Geraldine had a frustrating sense that in all the snippets of information she had heard that night there had been a clue that might unravel the whole case, if she could only spot it. Sitting back on her sofa with a glass of red wine in one hand, and the remote control in the other, she flicked through television channels without really registering what was on. For no apparent reason, her gut feeling was screaming out to her that Ashley held the key to the mystery. Details about her school days flickered in and out of Geraldine's consciousness like myriad pieces of a vast jigsaw. The problem was, Geraldine didn't have a picture to guide her how to put the pieces together, and singly they made no sense at all. She would have liked to set up a team dedicated to discovering everyone who had known Ashley when she was in the sixth form at school, but as a sergeant she didn't have the same powers as she had enjoyed during her time as an inspector. She was only just beginning to appreciate the limitations of her new post. Resolving to talk to Ian first thing in the morning, she went to bed and dreamt she was dragging a dead woman out of the canal. The wet skin was slippery and every time Geraldine pulled the woman from the water and lay her down on the bank, the body slipped back down the slope into the canal. Only after several failed attempts did Geraldine glance at the dead woman's face and recognise her sister, Helena.

51

A BLEARY-EYED GLORIA OPENED the door in her dressing gown. 'Bloody hell,' she blurted out, 'do you know what time it is?'

'I'd like a word with Ashley. I came early so I could catch her before she goes to work.'

'You did that all right. She's probably not even up yet.'

Gloria glowered at Geraldine, but she stepped aside to let her in.

'Have you arrested anyone?' Ashley wanted to know as soon as she came into the front room.

'No. And don't worry, this won't take long,' Geraldine assured her. 'I want you to tell me about the man you were going out with when you were in the sixth form.'

'What man?'

'You were seeing an older man, someone you didn't want your parents to know about.'

Ashley gave an awkward laugh. 'I don't think so,' she replied. 'Who told you that?'

'Are you saying you never dated an older man while you were at school?'

'It's hardly the kind of thing I'd forget. Whoever told you that must have confused me with someone else. No, I'm sorry but I didn't have a boyfriend when I was in the sixth form. At that time the only boys I really knew were local ones from school, and I can't say I fancied any of them. I mean, no offence and all that, but we probably knew each other too well.'

Puzzled, Geraldine asked a few more questions before leaving without finding out what she wanted to know. That was in keeping with the investigation, which seemed to be floundering. She wasn't alone in feeling frustrated. The detective chief inspector's foul mood wasn't helping. Geraldine struggled not to compare Eileen's conduct with how she herself would have striven to behave had she been promoted; a senior investigating officer's role was to encourage her colleagues, not chastise them. But it was easy to criticise other senior officers, especially now she would never face the challenge of leading a team herself.

'The killer's got to slip up sooner or later,' Eileen said.

She spoke in a controlled tone, but the tension in her voice was clear to everyone. Even her wording seemed all wrong to Geraldine, implying as it did that their success depended on the killer making an unforced error, rather than on their own intelligence and hard work.

'How many more people are going to be killed before he makes a mistake?' Ian muttered.

Eileen glared at him. 'We're not exactly sitting around waiting for him to screw up. We're going to track him down through the DNA he left at the crime scene. It's only a matter of time now.'

But although DNA had been collected from local residents on a massive scale, processing the samples had not yielded a possible match with the partial DNA profile recovered from Stephanie's body. Insisting that 'someone somewhere must know something,' Eileen had organised appeals for information through the media. There was no longer any point in trying to conceal the fact that the three murders were connected and the media was buzzing with reports of a violent serial killer. The news had spread as far south as Kent, and Celia had rung Geraldine, agog to hear about the investigation. Her concerns for Geraldine's safety unwittingly reminded her about the threatening letter she had received. Archie had reported that nothing had been found on either the letter or the envelope. He had cunningly protected Geraldine's role in submitting the letter for examination so she was able to stay silent, assuring herself she could do more to help track down the killer if she continued working on the case than if she was sent away for her own protection. But she wasn't confident she was right to keep quiet about it.

'I owe you,' she had told Archie and was surprised when he blushed.

'It's all part of the job,' he had blustered. 'To be honest, it's not every day I get approached by a detective to play a part in a major murder investigation. It was quite exciting, really.'

Slipping back into the police station, Geraldine had felt a spasm of anxiety in case her absence had been noted and was going to be queried, but no one had paid any attention to her.

Naomi was grumbling. 'The nonsense they broadcast, you'd think there's a killer running amok on the streets brandishing a knife in one hand and a gun in the other, assaulting everyone he sees. It's hardly our fault we haven't caught him yet. We're certainly doing everything we can.'

Accustomed to dealing with criticism from the media, Geraldine shrugged off the reports. 'They're just trying to sell their papers.'

'At our expense. They're turning public opinion against us, making out we're a bunch of incompetent idiots wasting tax payers money. Next thing you know, there'll be more cuts. You wait and see. This is playing right into the hands of the hatchet men in government. As if we haven't got enough to contend with.'

Geraldine sighed. Reporters in general were only too eager to generate panic in order to attract interest to their particular news story. It might be irresponsible journalism, but drama and tragedy sold papers and boosted audiences for radio and television channels. The trouble was, Naomi was right. Harsh criticism of the authorities turned members of the public against the police, making people less likely to come forward with information. At the same time, all the publicity might discourage people from going out alone after dark, which was probably a good thing while this killer remained at large. She had a strong suspicion he wasn't finished with his killing spree yet.

'We just have to wait for the results of the tests,' she said.

'So you're saying there's nothing else we can do?' Naomi asked.

'We can think,' Geraldine replied. 'If we can work out who might have a motive...'

'A motive for senseless killing?' Naomi replied. 'I don't think so. You can't get inside the mind of a maniac. Not unless you're insane too.'

Geraldine was about to quip that perhaps she was, when Eileen came over.

'Let's not get carried away with speculation,' the detective chief inspector said. 'The only way to nail a killer is through hard forensic evidence. Even confessions can be false.'

'We've been told that Ashley was seeing an older man when she was in the sixth form. We could try to find out who he was.'

'According to Leah she was seeing someone,' Eileen agreed, 'but Ashley's denied it.'

'Yes, I know, but she could be lying.'

'More likely Leah was spinning a yarn, trying to deflect suspicion from herself.'

Geraldine accepted the sense in that remark. None of them were convinced Leah was trustworthy.

'All I'm saying is that it will be easier to find the right evidence if we know where to look.'

Eileen bristled. 'We're looking everywhere,' she said, as though addressing an audience at a press conference. 'The killer won't escape. We get results by working thoroughly and efficiently, not by chasing hunches.'

Geraldine didn't answer. She knew her approach to detective work was sometimes considered controversial but, in the absence of hard evidence, she believed it could be useful to follow a hunch. And she had a feeling Ashley was hiding something about the man she had been seeing.

52

NEARLY TWO WEEKS HAD elapsed since Geraldine had last visited her adopted sister, Celia, and a phone call from Geraldine was long overdue. Guilt and a sense of duty, rather than love, had prompted Geraldine to respond when Celia had first turned to her for support after the death of their mother. Similar to their mother in appearance and inclination, Celia had always been closer to their mother than Geraldine. Only after their mother's death did Geraldine discover the shocking truth that she had been adopted. After giving birth to her only natural daughter, Celia, their mother had been unable to have more children. She had adopted Geraldine so that Celia wouldn't be an only child.

Since their mother's death, Geraldine and Celia had grown closer than before, but now she hesitated to pick up her phone and make the call. She anticipated her sister complaining that she hardly ever saw Geraldine, which was true now more than ever. It wasn't that Geraldine was reluctant to see her sister, but she was preoccupied with the case, and Celia lived a long way away from her. Not only was the journey tiring, but she didn't want to travel so far from the centre of the investigation.

The conversation this evening started out cheerfully enough.

'Geraldine! It's great to hear from you. I guess you must still be working on that dreadful case. It's been all over the news, even here. How many people have been killed now? Honestly, I know I've said it before, but I don't know how you can bear to hear all about it, and see those bodies! It makes me shudder just reading about it. I suppose they're keeping you hard at it?'

'Yes, everyone here's busy working on it. All leave's been

cancelled,' Geraldine added, in an attempt to preempt any demands for a visit.

'I guessed as much. So, how are you?'

'That's what I called to ask you. It can't be much longer to go now.'

Celia laughed. 'I look like a hippopotamus and I feel even worse. Honestly, Geraldine, if I get any bigger they'll need a hoist to get me out of bed in the morning.'

Celia described the progress of her pregnancy, and Geraldine listened to the details of her latest scan, and the functions her unborn baby was already able to perform, and how strong its heartbeat was. She could imagine Celia had chattered like this to their mother every day during her sister's first pregnancy. Feeling a pang of guilt that she was unable to offer her sister more support, she reminded herself that Celia had a husband and a daughter, and a circle of local friends she had grown up with. Geraldine had problems too, and she was on her own, living in an unfamiliar city. After a while the conversation shifted from Celia's pregnancy to news of her older daughter, Chloe. It was a relief to engage in such normal conversation, with no mention of bodies or evidence.

'So when do you think you're going to be able to come and visit us?' Celia enquired at last. 'If you don't come soon, the baby will be here before you!'

Geraldine hesitated. She was hoping to fit in a visit to her twin sister in London, but had decided to keep that area of her life private at least until after Celia had given birth.

'I'm planning to come over as soon as I can get time off,' she hedged.

'And when's that going to be?'

'I'm not sure. I'm sorry to sound so vague, but it just depends on work.'

'You know Chloe's desperate to see you,' Celia went on, with a hint of condemnation in her voice.

They both knew that wasn't true. The last time Geraldine

had gone to Kent, Chloe had been far more interested in texting her friends than talking to her aunt. It was Celia who wanted Geraldine to visit them.

'I want to see her too,' Geraldine replied. 'But I just can't get the time off right now.'

The telephone conversation lasted over an hour and by the time she rang off, Geraldine felt worn out. Even though her sister seemed perfectly happy with her life and really didn't need Geraldine around, she always made her feel guilty for having moved away. It would probably have been easier on them both if Geraldine had admitted the truth right from the start and told Celia that she had been given no choice about moving to York, if she wanted to continue working. But she hadn't even told Celia that she had discovered she had a birth sister, an identical twin, a heroin user who had been the cause of her expulsion from the Met.

Apart from her determination to protect her adopted family from any contact with Helena, it was all too difficult an emotional mess to dump on Celia while she was pregnant. Eventually, Geraldine supposed, she would have to tell her, but the longer she allowed Celia to continue in ignorance, the harder it would be when she finally told her the truth. She could imagine Celia's dismay on learning that she wasn't Geraldine's only sister. And that wasn't all. While Celia and Geraldine were sisters by virtue of adoption, Helena and Geraldine were not only birth sisters, but identical twins. Celia was bound to feel ousted from her comfortable perch as Geraldine's only close relative.

With more immediate concerns to occupy her, Geraldine turned her attention away from her personal issues to the man the papers were calling The Slasher. He was probably plotting his next attack, and they still had no idea where to look for him. The DNA which had given them such high hopes was worthless without a matching sample on the database.

'We must redouble our efforts to find him,' Eileen had urged the team at their last briefing.

At her side Geraldine had heard Ian muttering about needles and haystacks. All they knew from the partial and unidentified DNA profile was that the missing man was Caucasian, with dark hair and brown eyes. Extensive and time-consuming examination of automatic number plate recognition on the main roads into the area had failed to come up with any vehicle arriving and departing at times which matched the times of the murders, and a concentrated study of CCTV on public transport had proved equally unproductive. It was possible the killer might be living in the vicinity, although even that inference was inconclusive. So far all they had to go on was supposition based on tantalising fragments of evidence. And the letter Geraldine was concealing hung over her. Not only might she land herself in trouble again, but there was a chance the threat to her life might be genuine.

53

SHE WOKE ABRUPTLY IN the night and lay on her back, rigid with fear. Now that she was awake and consciously listening, everything was silent. She told herself she must have imagined hearing noises. Even before Beth had been killed, she had hated being in the flat on her own. Making an effort to breathe slowly, she closed her eyes and tried to go back to sleep.

A creak, followed by a soft grating sound. Someone had crept across the loose floorboards in the living room and opened the door.

Feeling tears trickle down her cheeks, she gritted her teeth and suppressed a whimper. Every muscle in her body tensed. Once her ordeal was over she could collapse in hysterics, but right now she had to remain calm if she was going to have any hope of surviving. She stretched her eyes wide open, as though that might help her to hear better. In the darkness she could make out the shape of the window in her room, almost completely blacked out by the curtain. Cautiously she turned her head towards the door and waited, her breath a series of mute gasps.

The silence should have been reassuring. Perhaps she had only imagined hearing an intruder in the flat. Nevertheless she lay motionless and terrified, gripping the edge of the duvet so tightly, her fingers hurt. Gingerly she relaxed her hands and forced herself to breathe slowly. She did her best to persuade herself she couldn't have heard anyone walking around. It must have been gurgling pipes, or a car revving outside, that had disturbed her sleep. During the night there were all sorts of strange noises in the flat. None of them meant anything.

Another faint creaking. This time she wasn't mistaken. There was someone else in the flat.

She had a pressing need to pee. Weighing up her options as calmly as she could, she resigned herself to wetting the bed if she had to. In the meantime, she would have to try to hold it in. Sometimes the urge went away if she took no notice of it. Doing her best to ignore her physical discomfort, she listened. There were only two possible reasons why an intruder might be wandering around in the flat at night. The first was that a random thief had broken in and was searching the place for valuables to nick. That would be terrifying enough. The burglar might become violent, or be off his head on drugs. But the second possibility was even more alarming. Because this might be no random burglary, but a carefully planned intrusion. She had already been warned that someone might be looking for her, and she thought she knew why. The anonymous letter had told her that she could be next to die.

Silently she reached for her phone before scrambling across the mattress, away from the door, and lowering herself down off the bed. After the soft warmth of her duvet, the carpet felt scratchy against her cheek, and the room was chilly. Careful not to make a sound, she dragged herself across the floor. It was awkward squeezing under the metal rim of the bed base. For a horrible moment she was afraid she might get stuck. She pictured the intruder coming in and sitting down on the bed, lowering it so that she was well and truly wedged. Some of the springs in the bed base were broken and the weight of a man's body on the mattress might crush her if he decided to lie down and wait for her.

Squirming, she wormed her way right underneath the bed and lay there listening, trying to breathe silently. She couldn't hear anything. As long as the intruder didn't come in the room she might be able to call for help, but it was awkward trying to use her phone when she couldn't turn her head to see what she was doing. Although she felt as though hours had passed since she had woken up, in reality it couldn't have been much longer than a few minutes. Even so her arms and legs were stiff. Aching all over from lying in an uncomfortable position unable to move, she strained to listen while she fiddled blindly with the phone screen, trying to guess where the different numbers would be on the keypad so she could turn it on without looking.

The door of her room must have opened silently, because there was an unexpected click. She nearly cried out in surprise as the light came on. Faint footsteps on the carpet were accompanied by the sound of soft breathing. She saw a pair of black trainers approach her hiding place. Whoever was there, was standing right by the bed. She stared in horrible fascination at feet that looked enormous from that angle. She could see the bottoms of faded jeans, but that was all. A person, probably a man, in black trainers and old jeans was hardly a useful description to give the police if she managed to escape alive, but there was no way she was going to stick her head out for a better look.

Without warning the bed quivered and jolted and a man's voice let out a curse. She hardly dared breathe for fear of being heard. She supposed he must have pulled the duvet back expecting to find her cowering beneath it.

'What the fuck!' he cried out.

She didn't recognise his voice.

A few seconds elapsed before the feet turned and walked away. A moment later, she heard the door close. She waited, wondering what was happening. Her left arm and leg felt completely numb, but she didn't dare stir. She waited. At last she felt she would go insane if she stayed there another moment, trapped in the narrow space beneath her bed. Unable to turn her head, cautiously she slid her phone across her body, from one hand to the other, so that she was holding it on the side she was facing. At once she saw the 'Emergency' icon at the bottom of the screen. She wouldn't need to turn the phone on in order to summon help.

'I need the police,' she whispered urgently. 'There's an intruder in my flat. My name's Leah Rutherford.' As she gabbled through her address, her self-control vanished. 'Please hurry! He's going to kill me!'

With the police on their way she had only to wait, but she wasn't sure she could stay under the bed much longer. Besides, she was desperate for the toilet. Knowing the police would be there very soon gave her courage. Careful not to make a sound, she dragged herself sideways. Peeping out, she squinted all around, but could see no sign of the black trainers. Holding her breath, she dragged herself out from underneath the bed, on the side opposite the door. She didn't stand up straight away, but raised her head gingerly, craning her neck to peer over the bed. She was alone in her room with the door closed. She could have cried with relief. She glanced at her phone. It was half past three. She had no idea how long she had been hiding under her bed. Her hips gave agonising stabs of pain when she tried to move her legs, and her shoulders ached. Finally she managed to pull herself upright. Hobbling over to the door, she put her ear against it and listened.

Silence.

She wondered whether it would be suicide to open the door when the intruder could be standing just the other side of it, waiting for her, but she was desperate for the toilet. She cast about for a weapon. If the intruder had left the flat, so much the better. If not, she would just have to fend him off until the police arrived. She opened the door a crack and peeped out. The overhead light had been switched on in the living room, but there was no sign of anyone there. While she stood prevaricating, there was a very loud banging and a voice called out, 'Open up! Police!'

Before she could stop herself, Leah felt a warm sensation

trickle down her legs, quickly turning chilly. As she shuffled to the front door, she hoped no one would notice she had wet herself. But she didn't really care. She was alive and safe, at least for now.

54

'THIS WHOLE SITUATION IS getting out of control,' Eileen fumed, her square face flushed beneath her lowered brows.

Geraldine shared the detective chief inspector's agitation. If Leah was telling the truth, someone had entered her flat unlawfully during the night. With the chain on, no one could have entered through the front door. Damage to a window frame suggested it could have been jemmied open. The window was at the back of the block, out of sight of any security cameras. Although there was no sign of anyone turning up in the night carrying a ladder, they already knew this killer was cunning. Window cleaners had been there the previous week, and it was possible a ladder had been hidden in nearby bushes in preparation.

Nothing had been stolen, which seemed to suggest that if there had been an intruder, he had been looking for Leah herself. Admittedly the story sounded quite far-fetched not least because, according to Leah, she had found the presence of mind to hide. Not only that, but she had managed to squeeze her ample frame right underneath the bed. Geraldine went straight round to the flat where Leah related everything that had happened to her during the night at great length.

'I couldn't help it,' she concluded tearfully. 'I just couldn't hold it in any longer. I've never done that before.'

'Why didn't you call the number I gave you? This was exactly why I gave it to you.'

Sobbing, Leah explained she had been under the bed in the

dark, unable to use her phone properly. She had struggled to find the emergency number.

'I couldn't hang around. I wanted the police to get here straight away.'

Geraldine nodded. Leah's account made sense. Afraid for her life, she hadn't wanted any delay while she fiddled about with her phone, barely able to move in a cramped space. Given her emotional nature, it was surprising that she had managed to think at all. Having learned all she could from Leah, Geraldine handed her to a scene of crime officer. By establishing which surfaces the intruder might have brushed against, they would be able to identify what he had been wearing. Wherever he had been standing, he would have left traces of his presence impossible to spot with the naked eye. Once they had eliminated any known DNA, they should be able to isolate that left by the intruder. They had plenty to work on. Even so, the possibility that the killer had been in Leah's flat the previous night, and they had missed him, was almost unbearable.

Leaving Leah with her colleague, Geraldine went to see Ashley. DNA had been obtained from everyone still in the UK who had been at the school at the same time as the victims, but a match for the killer had not yet been found. It was beginning to look as though they would have to start looking elsewhere.

Checking through her records, Geraldine spotted something that she remembered had troubled her at the time. It had only been a passing comment, but when Geraldine had first spoken to her, Ashley had mentioned that she and Stephanie had once compared notes about violent ex-boyfriends. No one had managed to unearth anything about a violent ex-boyfriend of Stephanie's. Then Leah had mentioned an older man Ashley had been seeing when she was at school. Putting these two random comments together, Geraldine wondered if perhaps it was Ashley, not Stephanie, who had been in a relationship with a violent boyfriend. Ashley had denied that she had been seeing an older man. Now, with Stephanie gone, and Leah ignorant of the details, only Ashley could reveal the truth.

Three weeks after Stephanie's murder, Ashley had finally left Gloria's flat. Geraldine wasn't sure whether she had volunteered to find alternative accommodation or had been asked to leave. Whatever the circumstances leading to her move, she had found herself a room in a house in Bootham Row in York.

'It's not much,' Ashley apologised, as though Geraldine might care about the size of her room. 'But I can't go back to the flat where Stephanie was killed, and Gloria's daughter was due home, and I have to live somewhere. What do you want?'

'Can I come in?'

'I suppose so.'

Entering the room, Geraldine could see why Ashley had described it as small. There was barely space for the two of them to sit side by side on the single bed, which made it more difficult for Geraldine to observe Ashley's expression as she questioned her. Twisting herself sideways, she began.

'Ashley, we know you had a boyfriend while you were still at school.'

'So do most girls.'

Geraldine nodded. 'He was older than you, wasn't he?'

Ashley didn't respond.

'He was white, with dark hair and brown eyes,' Geraldine went on.

Once again Ashley didn't react in any way but stared straight ahead, stony-faced. Gently Geraldine explained that a man's DNA had been discovered on the body of Ashley's dead school friends.

'We need to speak to that man, to eliminate him from our enquiries if he's innocent.' She paused to allow the information, and its implications, to sink in. 'The problem is, there's no match for this individual's DNA on our database.'

'Well, there wouldn't be, would there?'

'What makes you say that?'

Ashley had spoken bitterly. Now she looked flustered. 'I just meant that if you knew who it was, you'd have caught him by now.'

'You do understand that it's vital we find this man, don't you? There's a chance he could be the killer. And if he's not, at the very least he'll be able to help us with our enquiries. What's his name, Ashley? It's time for you to start co-operating with us, before someone else is killed.' She paused, waiting. 'You do know it's a very serious offence to withhold information from the police during the course of a murder investigation?'

For the first time, Ashley turned to look directly at Geraldine. All the colour had drained from her face and there was a strange haunted expression in her eyes.

'I don't know where he is. I haven't seen him for years, not since we left school. I can't tell you anything. I don't know where he is.'

'You can start by telling me his name.'

Ashley shook her head.

'If he's innocent he has nothing to fear, but if he's guilty and you're deliberately protecting him...'

Geraldine broke off, startled, as Ashley spun round to face her, eyes blazing.

'I'm not protecting him,' she hissed.

'Why won't you tell me his name then?'

'Because I don't know it. I never knew his full name.'

'You must have had a name for him. You must have called him something.'

'We weren't together very long.' She hesitated. 'He told me his name was Tom.'

Geraldine wasn't sure whether she believed her.

'What do you mean, he *said* that was his name? Was it his name or not?'

Ashley just shrugged. 'I've told you everything I know.'

Geraldine questioned her further but she was unable to learn anything else. Dissatisfied, she left with next to nothing to go on, convinced that Ashley knew more than she was prepared to say.

55

IT WAS CURIOUS HOW Geraldine's personal and professional lives often seemed to mirror one another. Having reached an impasse in the investigation, she decided to spend the rest of the day on trains, travelling to London and back, to check that her twin sister was coping on her own. But when she called Helena there was no answer. She tried several times before giving up. It looked as though Helena had forgotten to charge her phone. It was too far to travel on the off chance that she would find her sister at home. It wasn't as if Geraldine was at a loose end, exactly. There was always work to be done when a murder investigation was ongoing. She spent the afternoon rereading notes, tidying up her reports, and attempting to research a man called Tom. It was a futile task.

The mood at the Monday morning briefing was edgy. DNA matching the sample found on Stephanie's body had been identified in Leah's flat, which seemed to confirm her story, and suggested her intruder was in fact the killer they were hunting for. But for all that, he had slipped away unseen. Examination of CCTV from the entrance to the flats showed a shadowy figure making his way to the back of the building at three in the morning, twenty minutes before Leah had summoned the police. The picture was indistinct, visual image enhancement revealing only that the intruder's features were almost completely hidden between a hood pulled low over his eyes, and a scarf that covered the bottom part of his face.

'He made sure we couldn't recognise him,' Eileen grumbled. They stared at the blurred image for a moment. Leah had been lucky to survive the break-in. Next time she might not be so fortunate. In the meantime, her flat had been placed under police surveillance.

'He won't get away again,' Eileen vowed. 'But he's a slippery customer.'

They all knew what she meant. It was unlikely they would be given a second chance to catch the killer breaking into Leah's flat. He was too clever for that.

The remainder of the meeting was spent discussing reports about the progress of the team gathering DNA samples from anyone who had been associated with Saddleworth School during the victims' time there. It had been a massive undertaking, but everyone they had been able to trace who had attended the school in the relevant period, either as a pupil or on the staff, had now been tested and eliminated from the list of potential matches.

'We've managed to contact all the ancillary staff, as well as the teachers,' Naomi concluded her report.

'Without finding a match,' Eileen pointed out.

'I have a possible lead,' Geraldine said, speaking up for the first time that morning. 'It's extremely tenuous.'

'Tom?' Eileen repeated, frowning, when Geraldine had finished. 'It's not much to go on. A man called Tom, who was living in the area, and seeing a school girl.'

'She probably wasn't underage,' Geraldine said. 'At any rate, Leah said Ashley was seeing this man when she was in the sixth form so she would have been over sixteen, possibly even eighteen, and he might only have been a couple of years older than her. At that age even two years can seem like a lot, especially if he was working and they were still at school. Leah described him as "an older man" but she didn't know how much older. She said it was only a secret because Ashley didn't want her parents to know about the relationship.'

'Why not?' Eileen asked.

Geraldine shrugged. 'Teenage girls,' was all she said.

A sympathetic murmur went round the room from a few middle-aged officers, presumably parents of teenagers.

'We need to find this man Tom,' Eileen said. 'Geraldine, if we bring Ashley in for questioning do you think we can persuade her to tell us who this man is?'

'We could try, but for some reason she's clamming up. She didn't even want to give me his first name.'

'Do you think she's protecting him?' Eileen asked.

'I wondered about that, but I don't think so. She told me she hasn't seen him for years, but there's definitely something stopping her from talking about him. I think she's frightened.'

'Maybe she doesn't know where he is now,' Naomi suggested.

'Yes, that's what she said,' Geraldine said.

'Couldn't Leah tell you anything more about him?' Eileen asked.

'Leah didn't seem to know anything about him, apart from the fact that he was older than Ashley. She didn't even know his name. According to her, Ashley had two close friends who were in her confidence. Unfortunately Leah wasn't one of them.'

'But I'm guessing the two friends who might have known about this man were Stephanie and Bethany,' Eileen scowled.

Geraldine nodded.

'Well, get Ashley back in and find out who this man was. Thank goodness someone's been beavering away and unearthed a new lead,' Eileen said, giving Geraldine a rare smile.

With Ashley back at work in York, it was a simple matter for Geraldine to go to the bank and ask to speak to her. Once again, Ashley refused to co-operate.

'I don't believe you can recall nothing about this man except his first name,' Geraldine insisted.

Ashley just shrugged.

'He was your boyfriend. You must remember what he looked like.'

'He had brown hair.'

Geraldine tried every means at her disposal to persuade the girl to open up, but she remained obdurately silent on the subject of her former boyfriend. Realising she was wasting her time, Geraldine left. She was on her way back to the police station when it struck her that she had met one woman in the course of the investigation who not only had a good memory for names and details, but was willing to divulge what she knew. Instead of returning to Fulford Road, she set off in the direction of Saddleworth, hoping that Susan Mulvey would be at home.

The retired head teacher answered the door at once and welcomed Geraldine with a smile.

'I don't know how you do it, Sergeant, but you must have read my mind. I was just about to put the kettle on.'

She refused to answer any questions until she had made a pot of tea, leaving Geraldine no choice but to wait impatiently. When they were finally settled with tea and fresh scones which her hostess admitted she had made herself, Geraldine posed her question.

Susan shook her head.'No, I don't remember any of the girls having a boyfriend called Tom.'

When Geraldine urged her to think carefully, Susan answered with a question of her own.

'Are you sure you don't mean Tim? I remember one of the girls was seeing a man called Tim, and I think it was Ashley. In fact, I'm sure that's who it was.'

Controlling her sudden excitement, Geraldine asked about Tim.

'I know he was older than Ashley, and he had a car. But I'm afraid that's all I can tell you. I never saw him. But she made no secret of it. She wanted her friends to know that her boyfriend was older than all of them. It's immature, of course, but having an older boyfriend is very much a status symbol for young girls.'

'How much older than her was he?'

'I really don't know.'

'What *can* you remember about him?'

'Not much, to be honest. I'm sorry.'

Geraldine's spirits began to sink, but she pressed on. At least she had discovered Ashley had given her the wrong name in what must have been a deliberate lie. That in itself might be significant.

'Try to think. What else can you remember about him?'

'Well, I do remember there was something a bit off about him. One of her friends came to see me about it to express her concern. She thought he sounded strange.'

Geraldine no longer tried to hide her excitement. 'Strange in what way?'

Susan spoke slowly, frowning with the effort to remember. 'According to her friend, Ashley wasn't happy with this man. I called her in and had a talk about resisting unwelcome sexual advances, the usual patter. I seem to remember she wasn't very receptive. I had the impression she didn't really like him, but she wanted to keep hold of a boyfriend who had a car. As I said, she was very young.'

'Can you remember Tim's other name?'

'Yes. It's all coming back to me now. He was called Tim Hathaway. I remember wondering whether he could be a descendant of Shakespeare's wife.'

Geraldine smiled as she thanked Susan for the information, and the scone. Now they had a name, it was only a matter of time before they traced Ashley's former boyfriend. The likelihood was that he had already given a DNA sample and been eliminated from the enquiry. But there was a faint chance she might have just discovered the identity of the killer.

56

EILEEN IMMEDIATELY ASKED THE question that had been troubling Geraldine.

'If his name's Tim, why did Ashley tell you he was called Tom? Surely she can't have forgotten her own ex-boyfriend's name. So why did she lie about it?'

Geraldine shook her head.

'Well, never mind about that for the time being,' Eileen went on briskly. 'Our priority is to find Tim Hathaway. I'll organise a team to track him down, and meanwhile I'd like you to bring Ashley in and see what she has to say for herself.'

Eileen smiled at Geraldine. Now that they had a firm lead, the detective chief inspector seemed to have recovered her drive. Accustomed to analysing the conduct of her senior officers in preparation for her own anticipated promotion, Geraldine found herself privately criticising Eileen for letting her energy levels drop when the investigation had appeared to be floundering. But of course Geraldine no longer needed to concern herself with her own professional development. She wasn't even an inspector any more, and would never find herself leading a team from her own office. With a sigh, she returned to the busy open-plan room she shared with several other colleagues.

For the second time that day Geraldine entered the bank where Ashley worked and asked to speak to her.

'I'd like you to accompany me to the police station. We think you might be able to assist us in identifying a potential suspect,' Geraldine explained, taking care to be as generic as possible in her explanation.

Ashley's set expression didn't alter, but her eyes blazed. Rather than looking frightened, she seemed furious.

'There's nothing to be concerned about,' Geraldine added kindly. 'But we really do need your help. I trust you can spare her for a few hours?'

'Of course,' the manager replied at once. 'Don't worry,' he added, turning to Ashley. 'You can take the day if you need to. I'll make sure it doesn't come off your holiday entitlement.'

They drove to the police station in silence. Geraldine wasn't convinced it was sensible to try and put pressure on Ashley to open up. She was afraid the approach might have the opposite effect. If possible, Ashley seemed even more obdurate than when Geraldine had last seen her.

'Are you going to lock me in a cell?' Ashley asked as they stepped out of the car.

'No, nothing like that. We just need to ask you a few questions.' Geraldine gave what she hoped was an encouraging smile. 'As long as you've done nothing wrong, there's no reason why you should be locked up.'

'You locked Leah in a cell for days, and she hadn't done anything wrong.'

'No, she hadn't, but she was a suspect for a while.'

'And I'm not?'

Geraldine paused in her stride. They had not yet reached the entrance to the police station but were walking up the wide path towards it. She didn't want to stop as it was cold, and a fine drizzle had begun to fall. Yet to Geraldine's irritation, Ashley seemed ready to start talking. If this moment was allowed to pass, a similar opportunity might not arise again. Even the rooms used for informal interviews had an oppressive atmosphere, and whatever Geraldine said to try and gloss over the situation, there was no denying that Ashley had been brought into the police station for questioning. She might be more inclined to talk freely right now, outside, in the open air.

'No, not at the moment,' she replied. 'And hopefully you

never will be. But you do need to tell us the truth, Ashley. The more you beat about the bush, the more suspicious my senior officers are likely to become. You do see that, don't you?'

Ashley nodded.

'So don't you think it's about time you started telling us the truth?'

'I am telling you the truth. I've never lied to you.'

'I mean the whole truth,' Geraldine said. 'Why did you tell me your ex-boyfriend's name was Tom when we now know he's called Tim?'

'That's what I said to you. I said he told me his name was Tim. But he never told me his second name.'

The rain began to fall in earnest and they hurried towards the police station. Geraldine wasn't sure how she was going to crack Ashley. Far from flummoxed at being caught out in a lie, she was coolly acting as though Geraldine had made a mistake. They reached an interview room and sat down.

'You say that you didn't know your ex-boyfriend's surname, but your former head knew he was called Tim Hathaway,' Geraldine began. 'How would she have known that when you...'

'Hathaway!' Ashley interrupted her quickly. 'Yes, that was it. Hathaway. I'm hopeless with names, but I remember now. We used to joke that he might be a descendant of Shakespeare's wife, you know, Ann Hathaway. The others wanted me to ask him about it, but I never did.' She gave a faint laugh. 'It was just a silly idea they had.'

'Now we know his name, we're going to find him,' Geraldine said.

Observing Ashley's face closely as she spoke, Geraldine didn't add that she gave no credence at all to Ashley's pretence of having forgotten Tim Hathaway's name.

Ashley looked very pale and drawn. 'Yes,' she said softly. 'You can find him, can't you?'

'You can make it easier for us, Ashley.'

'How?'

Geraldine suppressed a sigh. 'By telling us where he lives.'

Ashley shook her head. 'I don't know. Listen, we didn't see each other for very long and I was still at school, still a kid. We went to his house a few times, but he drove us there in his car and I don't know where it was.'

'What can you remember about it?'

'It was a row of houses, somewhere near York, or it might have been in York, I don't know. I never paid much attention to where we were going. It was fun, you know, being in a car with a man, when I was only seventeen. It was something to tell the other girls. That's why I did it. We were never serious about each other, at least, I wasn't,' she added uncertainly. 'I can't speak for him.'

'You must remember something about his house.'

'It had a dirty front door, and the window sills were dirty, and you could hear the trains going past from the back garden. There was a big old tree in front of the house but I can't remember if it was in the garden or on the street outside. The place was pretty rundown inside and it smelt funny.'

'How funny?'

'Sort of damp and mouldy.'

'Was it near the station?'

Ashley shrugged. 'That's all I can remember. It wasn't – it wasn't a happy relationship.'

'What do you mean?'

'He wasn't a very nice man.'

'What did your friends say about him?'

Ashley shrugged and her cheeks flushed a deep red. 'They were impressed, because he was older and he had a car and a house and everything, even though it wasn't a very nice house. I didn't tell them that,' she added, with an embarrassed laugh.

'You wanted them to be jealous?'

'We were seventeen.'

'You said he wasn't a nice man. What you mean by that?'

Ashley shrugged. 'It doesn't matter now.'

'Did your friends agree with your opinion of him?'

'I don't know. They never met him.'

Geraldine frowned. Ashley seemed to be telling the truth at last, but her stilted confession hadn't really shed much light on the mystery.

'Do you think Tim Hathaway killed your friends?' she asked outright.

Something in Ashley's face changed, as though she had withdrawn into herself. She stared straight at Geraldine and spoke in a completely flat tone that didn't alter even when she posed a question. 'I don't know. I don't know. Why would he?'

She had voiced what was bothering Geraldine. What could have prompted Tim Hathaway to suddenly start killing the former classmates of his ex-girlfriend, a girl who claimed she hadn't seen him for several years. It was all really odd. And if something didn't make sense, it was probably untrue. She wondered whether they were following a false lead, after all.

57

GLANCING AT THE SECURITY screen that displayed activity in the street outside the house he had moved into, he noticed three cars drawing up, one after another. He had been waiting for this. However careful he was to cover his tracks, he knew the police were cunning. He would never make the basic mistake of underestimating his enemy. That kind of hubris had proved the downfall of many clever criminals. There was nothing to suggest these were police cars, but he wasn't taking any chances. He had been preparing for this, practising the gait he was going to adopt as part of his disguise. But he didn't have much time. Six people climbed out of the cars, all at the same time, and headed for his gate. This was it. They had found his house. But they hadn't caught him. While they were banging on his front door, he was watching from an apparently empty house three doors away.

Stopping only to seize the bag he had packed in case of such an emergency, he dashed for the back door. He felt the gun in his pocket and smiled grimly. If the police cornered him they wouldn't take him alive, and not all of them would walk away from the encounter either. Slipping out of the house, he listened for the Yale lock clicking shut behind him. If they traced him to the derelict property, leaving the back door unlocked would give them a clue about where he had gone, and he had no intention of making this easy for them. Crouching low, he struggled through bushes that proliferated along the side of the overgrown lawn, and hurried down to the end of the garden. It was the work of a second to push a loose fence panel aside and force his way through. Slithering down the steep bank to the railway, he darted across the tracks and sprinted along beside the line. In the distance he heard the roar of an approaching train and flung himself down in the undergrowth. Invisible to anyone sitting in the train, he used the time while it thundered past to pull on a dark cap which would prevent him shedding hair and dandruff.

By now the police would be in his house, searching for him. It was only a matter of time before they discovered signs of occupation in the empty property three doors along, and found the loose fence panel. He had to find shelter at a station before they widened their search. Glancing up at the sky, he wondered how long it would take the police to mobilise a helicopter. As though in response to his upward gaze, it began to rain. The slope might become too slippery to climb. Abandoning his plan to run until he reached a station, he began to clamber up the grass. A successful criminal had to be adaptable. Only then could he stay one step ahead of his pursuers.

As he struggled up the slope, he faced an even harder challenge – to control his anger that his identity had been discovered so soon. Because he wasn't ready to stop yet. With only three victims down, he still had much to do. But he had to control his rage and focus on finding somewhere to hide. He couldn't allow any other consideration to distract him from that immediate priority. Once he had given his pursuers the slip, he would continue with his plan, undeterred. In the meantime, worrying about how the police had traced him would have to wait. In terms of his overall scheme it wasn't really that important because, however hard they tried, they weren't going to stop him.

Now they knew who he was, the police would be setting up a massive man hunt, and they wouldn't hold back. It would be easy enough for tracker dogs to follow his scent along the railway line and up the slope. Somehow he had to circumvent his pursuers for long enough to reach the river without being spotted. As well as men and dogs on the ground, there would soon be helicopters circling and searching. There was no point in waiting until darkness fell, because the helicopters would have thermal imaging. He might even be easier to spot moving around at night.

Once he had crossed the river he would be safe, because the dogs would lose his scent. And as for the police, well, they would be looking for a man in his thirties. On the other side of the river, Tim Hathaway would vanish, and he would resume his activities unhindered. It was a pity, but from now on it might be best to simply shoot his victims. Admittedly it wasn't as much fun, but without access to his van all the blood from a stabbing would make things tricky. Plotting and scheming, he reached the top of the slope. He wasn't far from the river and safety.

He avoided quiet side roads and kept instead to the busier main road where no one paid any attention to an inconspicuous young man in a long black coat carrying a large holdall. He had always studied how to look unremarkable. Reaching Queen Street, he slowed his pace to a brisk walk and made his way to the station where he turned left to cross Leeman Road. Head lowered, he reached the river, aware that with every passing second his enemies were mustering their forces. He could imagine urgent calls going out to helicopter pilots and dog trainers. Really, with the police so focused on his capture, other criminals could be having a field day if they only knew.

Quickly he made his way past the railway bridge to a quiet part of the river. The weather was on his side, because there weren't many people around. But once the manhunt was under way, he would be unable to continue moving around under the radar. Time was running out. If he didn't escape soon, the chance would be lost. He hurried on until he reached his small motor boat. By moving fast, he should be able to cross the river without leaving any trail. A sunken boat carried no scent.

Humming to himself, he slithered down the slope beside the

bridge, out of sight of prying eyes. As he clambered into the boat and pushed off, he heard the roar of a helicopter. Sweating, he pulled on the cord to start the engine. Nothing happened. His heart pounding, he yanked it as hard as he could. This time the engine spluttered and whirred. Hardly able to breathe for fear, he lay low in the boat as it sped across the churning water. It wasn't far to the other bank, but he couldn't land immediately opposite his point of departure as the police were bound to take their dogs over the water to cast around for his scent on the other side. He pictured dogs circling, sniffing at the ground, and shivered.

The little craft was swift, and before long he found a suitable site for landing. Dragging the boat out of the water and on to the path underneath an overhanging tree, he tore at the planks with his gloved hands without making any impact. Fishing his knife out of the bag he slashed at the wood, ripping through it repeatedly until the bottom of the boat lay in splintered shreds. It would never float now. Glancing along the path in both directions, he shoved the ruined vessel into the water and wedged a large boulder under the engine. The boat hung on the surface for a moment before sinking slowly down out of sight, taking his scent with it.

Partly concealed by the branches of the tree, he replaced the knife in his bag and exchanged his dark cap for a shaggy grey wig. After putting on a pair of metal-rimmed spectacles with plain glass lenses, he turned his reversible raincoat inside out, and pulled on a pair of old wellington boots he had bought from a charity shop. They were slightly too large but he had never worn them before, and they would help mask the scent of his feet. For some time he had been preparing for just such an eventuality by washing his clothes and towels in baking soda, and showering with scent-eliminating soap and shampoo manufactured specifically for deer hunters, which he bought online. He hoped his precautions would suffice to protect him from pursuit as he shuffled rapidly back towards the town, where the profusion of human scents was likely to confuse any dog still following his trail.

Having left one river bank as a youngish man, he had emerged on the far side as a man in his late seventies who walked with a slight stoop. Not only was his disguise impenetrable, he had done all he could to avoid leaving a scent; and best of all he still had the gun safe and dry in his haversack. As though coming to his aid a light snow began to fall, making any scent even more difficult to pick up. The police had done well to find his house, but he was too clever for them. They wouldn't find him again.

58

EVEN THOUGH THEY LIVED close to the city centre, the growing popularity of Airbnb had impacted on Nell and Bert's establishment, and money was becoming increasingly tight. Added to that, there was always a quiet period between New Year and the annual Viking Festival in February. Not expecting any guests, Nell almost missed the bell when it rang. Answering the door, she found an old man on the doorstep. His grey hair was dripping on to the drenched shoulders of his beige overcoat, and she wouldn't have been surprised to discover that his socks were wet too. All in all he was a sorry sight.

'Yes? Can I help you?'

'Your sign says you have a vacancy?'

'Yes, yes,' she answered quickly, brightening up at the prospect of a guest. 'We do have a room available. Now come on in out of the cold and wet and I'll put the kettle on. It's perishing out there.'

As the old man shuffled inside, she noticed with approval how he wiped his boots very thoroughly on the welcome mat. She was even happier when he booked a room for a week and stumped up the cash in advance.

'I always think it makes life easier, paying bills in cash,' he explained almost apologetically. 'I can't be doing with credit cards. It doesn't feel like real money, does it? And besides, credit has caused a great deal of damaging uncertainty to the economy as a whole, as well as to individuals who can't always be relied on to behave responsibly when it comes to dealing with money. The problem with buying on credit is – well, I won't bore you with my opinions. I have a lot to say about it. In fact, I've written several books on the subject.' He gave a bashful smile. 'Suffice it to say that when I listen to the way the youngsters talk these days it worries me greatly, it really does. We can't keep on living on credit. Sooner or later we're going to end up in trouble. One chancellor after another has ignored the warning signs.'

He rambled on for a while in a similar vein as he drank his tea, but Nell hardly listened to the old man's lecture. As soon as she could get away, she hurried off to stuff the wad of cash in the safe before showing her new guest to his room.

'Are you all right with stairs?' she asked, panicking that she might lose the money she had just received.

'That's not a problem,' he was quick to reassure her. 'The Oxford college where I've been lecturing is positively riddled with steep narrow staircases. It's all rather antiquated, but it keeps me fit.'

Relieved, she returned his smile. Despite his white hair and stooping figure, he had a surprisingly youthful face. He must have good genes, she thought enviously as she led the way upstairs.

'Here you are. This is the room I was telling you about. I hope it suits you.'

He hadn't asked to see the room before parting with his cash, which was unusual. She supposed it was his age that made him naive, and besides, professors were notoriously absent-minded.

'This is fine,' he replied.

He didn't seem very interested when she told him about the breakfast arrangements, but he thanked her politely.

'I wish to be left alone while I'm working. Even when I'm not writing I'll be thinking, and I don't like to be bothered when I'm occupied with a book, so please make sure I'm not interrupted under any circumstances. I hope that's clear?'

'Yes, of course.'

He thanked her again. 'And please don't take any notice if you hear me leave the house at odd times. Walking helps me to concentrate, so I often go out, even at night. Looking up at the stars helps me think.'

Assuring the old man he wouldn't be disturbed, Nell left him.

'So what's he like, this new guest?' her husband enquired when they were settled comfortably in front of the television later that evening.

Nell thought before answering. The old man had seemed very friendly on arrival, but once he had seen his room he had made it absolutely clear that he didn't wish to be disturbed under any circumstances.

'He says he's writing a book,' she told Bert. 'And he wants to be left alone to get on with it. He doesn't want people bothering him.'

Bert grunted. 'A book, eh? What's it about then? Not one of your slushy romances, I bet.' He laughed easily.

'It was something to do with international economics. He did explain it to me, but to be honest I didn't have a clue what he was talking about. I stopped listening.'

'Oh well, as long as he's paying us, that's all the economics we need from him.' Bert laughed again.

'And he said he won't necessarily want breakfast, and he might go out at odd times,' she added. 'He said he likes to take a walk and he often goes out at night because the quiet helps him think.' She laughed. 'He seems to think the city's quiet after dark. Let's hope he isn't planning on going into town on a Saturday night.'

'He's not writing a book about hen parties, then?'

They both laughed.

'No, I told you, international economics, whatever that means. That's what he said, anyway. He seems a harmless enough old soul and he's certainly going to be quiet.'

The light was still on in the professor's room when they went up to bed.

'Writing his book, I expect,' she whispered.

'Let's hope he carries on writing it here for a long time,' he whispered back. 'We can certainly do with the money. See? Didn't I say all along there was no need to worry? I knew something would turn up.'

Passing his door they heard their new guest moving about in his room and hurried on up the stairs to their own room, careful not to make any noise. They didn't want to disturb him.

59

By THE TIME GERALDINE pulled into the kerb a few doors along from the address she had been given, the pavement in front of it had been cordoned off and two uniformed officers were standing guard. That was an encouraging sign, indicating that something significant was taking place inside the house. At last the investigative team seemed to be making progress, although what all this activity signified was as yet unclear. It was raining as she climbed out of her car, a cold steady sleet that was turning to snow. She had left her umbrella at home and the cold and wet were making her shiver. Holding her collar up around her neck with one hand, and thrusting the other in her jacket pocket, she hurried towards the house.

A small group of bystanders had already gathered. Huddled together in winter coats they were stamping their feet and watching in silence, apart from a strident reporter who seemed to have assumed the role of spokesperson. Geraldine studied the loudmouthed woman as she approached. In her late thirties, with peroxide blond hair and bright red lipstick to match her bright red jacket, she was standing at the front of the crowd of onlookers, waving a microphone at one of the uniformed officers who stood, impervious to her screeching.

'Who lives here? Who lives here? Who lives here?' she kept repeating as Geraldine drew near. 'Stop right there!' she cried out, pouncing on Geraldine as she was about to pass through the cordon. 'What's going on? Has there been another murder? Have you caught The Slasher? The public have a right to know!'

An aggrieved murmur from the crowd accompanied her demands.

'And the police have a right to get on with the job without being harassed,' Geraldine snapped, as she pushed past the reporter. 'You'll just have to wait for the press conference. We're not here to provide you with a scoop.' She uttered the last word with as pronounced a sneer as she could muster.

'The public have a right to know!' the blond woman insisted.

'The public have a right to be protected, and your interference is making that more difficult.'

Despite her intense irritation, Geraldine stopped short of threatening to have the reporter arrested for hindering the police in their work. The woman would no doubt have relished the opportunity to star in her own news story. As she walked through the gate, Geraldine heard one of the bystanders busily telling the reporter that she lived in the next house.

'And who lives here?' the blond woman asked.

Geraldine paused to listen.

'I can't say I know him. He's a very private person, keeps himself to himself.'

Seeing Geraldine standing by the gate, the reporter edged the neighbour further away, out of earshot. Geraldine shrugged. If they had really discovered where the killer lived, everyone in the street would be visited by police officers soon enough, asking for information about their neighbour. And in any case, whatever gossip the neighbour shared with the blond reporter would no doubt be available online soon enough, with whatever embellishments the reporter chose to add.

Before Geraldine stepped inside the house she was issued with protective clothing.

'There was no one here?' she asked, as she pulled on her white oversuit.

'No, the place was empty when we got here. We seem to have the right place. There's a cornucopia of incriminating evidence, but it looks as though he got wind of our arrival and scarpered in a hurry.'

'Is it a crime scene?'

A murder was always shocking. In the wake of three other victims, it would be devastating.

'No, we haven't found any bodies, not yet at least. They're outside checking the garden now.'

Geraldine nodded. 'So what have you found?'

'Loads,' he replied. 'Most of it's already been bagged up.'

'Did you find any weapons?'

'No, nothing like that, I'm afraid,' the officer replied, clearly thinking along the same lines as Geraldine.

Wherever the killer had gone, he had taken his gun with him.

Glancing up, Geraldine saw Ian's tall, broad frame picking his way carefully down the stairs, his feet protected by plastic shoe covers. He nodded when he caught sight of her in the hall.

'This is his house all right,' he said. 'We're waiting for confirmation from the DNA lab, but that shouldn't take long. And you won't believe what we found in the garage. Come on, I'll show you. We can talk as we go.'

The garage door was open. While Geraldine had been inside the house the pavement had been cleared to allow a tow truck to back into the drive. A vehicle covered in a tarpaulin was being attached to the truck, prior to being taken away for forensic examination.

'There goes his van,' Ian said. 'The back was full of black bin liners stuffed with bloodstained clothes. Three bags in fact, all tied up very neatly. I'm guessing we already know whose blood it is.' He paused. 'Give me three names.'

Geraldine nodded without speaking.

'All we need to do now is find the slippery bastard. How the hell did he manage to avoid giving a DNA sample? Oh well, we've driven him out of his lair, but where has he gone? He seems to have vanished.' Ian's voice was taut with suppressed fury. 'He's clever.'

'We have to find him soon,' Geraldine said. 'He can't have gone far.'

'Then where the hell is he?'

For a moment neither of them spoke. The silence between them was broken by the shrill voice of the blond reporter.

'What's under that cover? What are you hiding? My readers have a right to know!'

'Oh, do shut up,' Geraldine muttered under her breath. 'As if we haven't got enough to worry about.'

Leaving the scene of crime officers to continue their search of the property, Geraldine followed Ian back to the police station. It was bustling with activity. Everyone seemed to be on the phone, researching online sites, or typing up reports. For once, no one was standing around chatting. By the end of the afternoon confirmation had been received that the house where Tim Hathaway had been living was covered in DNA matching the unidentified traces they had already found. There could no longer be any doubt that they had found their killer's house. They just didn't know where he was.

'He can't have gone far,' Eileen said with grim satisfaction, echoing what Geraldine had said earlier.

Helicopters were circling the skies, sniffer dogs were pursuing the suspect's scent which was now readily available, and every station, roadside services, seaport and airport had been alerted, along with information circulated to every police force in the country.

'He won't get away,' Eileen repeated.

'What if he's not on the move at all?' Geraldine asked. 'What if he's in hiding somewhere nearby planning to stay out of sight until the search is called off?'

'The search won't be called off until we find him,' Eileen retorted sharply.

But they all knew they couldn't maintain such a labour-intensive manhunt indefinitely. And in the meantime the suspect remained on the run, and armed. He might kill again at any moment and they were powerless to stop him.

60

THERE WAS NOTHING MORE to be done that evening. Too tired to join Ian and Naomi for a drink, Geraldine went straight home. She was so exhausted, she wondered whether she was sickening for a cold or flu bug. Wrapped in a blanket and sipping a cup of piping hot cocoa, she felt warm for the first time that day. It was a few days since she had last spoken to her twin so she called her. Helena's phone went straight to voicemail. With a sigh, Geraldine turned on the television and tried to focus on a light-hearted quiz show, but she was too tired to take it in. The investigation wasn't over yet, but they had identified the killer and Eileen was right. It was only a matter of time before they caught up with him. The danger was all but over. She went to bed early and slept well for the first time in weeks.

Having breakfast in her flat the next day, she did her best to ignore a headache throbbing behind her eyes as she sat gazing out over the river. The buildings on the far side of the black water were almost hidden in an early morning fog, and she could see no activity on the river at all. She had no appetite but munched her way miserably through a bowl of cereal, determined not to fall ill. This was only her first investigation since her relocation to York and she was just beginning to make a favourable impression on her detective chief inspector. She couldn't afford to weaken now.

Before leaving for work, she tried Helena's phone again. Still there was no answer. Concerned that Helena might be struggling to cope after her period of rehabilitation in a drugs clinic, she called one of her ex-colleagues on the Met, who had been a good friend to her in London. Sam was surprised and pleased to hear from her, but clearly irritated to hear the reason for Geraldine's call.

'What do you want me to do about it?' she asked.

'I was hoping you might go round there and check she's all right.'

'Do you have any idea how stretched we are right now? Have you seen what's going on here? I don't have time to see my own family. I hardly go home these days. When am I supposed to find the time to visit your sister? Really?'

'It was just a thought. I wouldn't ask, but I'm worried about her.'

'And you can't go and see her yourself?'

Briefly Geraldine told her former colleague about the hunt for Tim Hathaway.

'Well, he can't have just disappeared,' Sam said.

'I know.'

'And once you track him down, you'll be able to go and see your sister for yourself. I'm sure she's fine. You'd have heard if there was a problem,' Sam went on, her initial indignation fading. 'Look, I'll call by there later on my way home and let you know how she is.'

Geraldine was almost too overcome to thank her. 'You know I wouldn't ask if I wasn't really worried. There's no one else I can ask. You don't know how much this means to me.'

'OK, OK, no need to go overboard. I'm not exactly competing with Mother Teresa here. I just said I'd call by on my way home.'

The police station was a hive of activity when Geraldine arrived, but the mood was not as upbeat as it had been the previous day. A sniffer dog had picked up Tim's scent by the railway and had tracked him as far as the river where he appeared to have jumped in a boat. The handler had searched for miles along the opposite side of the river and at last the dog had picked up the scent again on the bank. But although they had circled the area, the trail appeared to end there.

'We'll have to send a diving team down,' Eileen barked, her eyes alight with excitement.

'Let's hope he's fallen in and drowned,' someone said.

'Drowning's too good for him,' Ian grumbled.

There was a murmur of agreement from their colleagues. Given the choice, Geraldine would have preferred to see the killer face trial, but she wouldn't be sorry to learn he was dead, however it came about. At least if he had drowned he wouldn't be able to claim any more victims.

'They used to hang, draw and quarter criminals,' a middle-aged constable said.

'The good old days. You remember it well,' another constable called out and everyone laughed.

That evening Geraldine joined Ian and Naomi and a few of their other colleagues for a drink in the pub in Fulford Road, just a few yards along from the entrance to the police station compound. Everyone seemed relaxed, sipping their pints at the end of a day's work. Even though the killer was still at large, the general feeling seemed to be that they would soon have him behind bars.

'It won't be long now,' was the phrase her colleagues kept repeating.

Geraldine seemed to be the only one who felt anxious, but she kept her concerns to herself. Ian challenged her about her long face.

'I'm just thinking I need to phone my sister,' she replied.

That wasn't exactly a lie. She *was* worried about Helena, but she had actually been thinking that a psychopath with a gun could effect a lot of damage in the space of a few minutes. They might catch the killer soon, but possibly not in time to prevent further fatalities.

Ian nodded sympathetically.

'If she's anything like my sister, I'm not surprised you're looking down in the dumps,' one of the older constables joked.

His remark prompted a spate of terrible quips about siblings that quickly degenerated into even worse jokes about mothers-in-law. Geraldine glanced at Ian wondering if he would be upset by the references, seeing as he was currently going through a messy divorce, but he seemed to revel in the banter and high spirits. Naomi was sitting beside him, laughing heartily. For no particular reason, Geraldine felt a wave of loneliness. She was in cheerful company, but she barely knew most of her colleagues. Ian was the only one she could really call her friend, and he hardly seemed to notice her. Quietly she made her excuses and stood up to leave. She wasn't sure whether to feel pleased when Ian followed her out on to the street.

'Geraldine, I wanted to ask you how your sister's getting on,' he said as they walked back to the police station car park together.

'Which one?' she asked. 'You know Celia's pregnant?'

'No, I didn't know,' he answered, although she was sure she had told him. 'I was asking about your twin, Helena. She's out of rehab isn't she?'

'I think she's OK, but…'

'But?'

Geraldine told him she hadn't been able to get hold of Helena.

Ian frowned. 'That must be worrying, but it's only a day since she hasn't been answering, and she's probably just forgotten to charge her phone.'

'Yes, I expect you're right.'

Geraldine told him that a friend of hers on the Met had promised to look in on Helena that evening, and asked him how his divorce was progressing.

'Oh God, these things take forever,' he replied. 'Even when everyone's in agreement.'

Before he could say any more, they heard someone calling them. Naomi had followed them out of the pub. She caught up with them just as they entered the car park, and asked if they were going out to eat.

'I think I'm going to head home,' Geraldine replied. 'I'm a bit tired and I've got a few calls to make. But it's a nice idea. Another time.'

'Sure,' Naomi said.

Geraldine walked off alone towards her car. She didn't look back.

When she reached home, she put off calling Sam for as long as she could, first fixing herself some supper and opening a bottle of particularly nice red wine she had bought before the investigation had begun, to celebrate her move – or perhaps to console herself. Sam answered her phone straight away.

'Hi Geraldine, I was going to call you later. How's it going?'

'Fine, I think, but what about Helena? Did you manage to…'

Sam interrupted. 'Look, I'm sorry, but I just didn't have time to get round there today. I'll go along tomorrow without fail.'

After a brief desultory exchange of news on their respective cases, Sam said she had to go. Promising to call Geraldine the following evening, she rang off. With a sigh, Geraldine put her feet up and took a sip of her wine. It didn't help. Unable to relax, she tried Helena's phone number again but there was still no answer. Trying to reassure herself that a recovering heroin addict disappearing off the radar wasn't necessarily a harbinger of bad news, she poured herself another glass of wine.

61

UNTIL THE CURRENT SITUATION had arisen, the two girls hadn't seen each other since they left school, so when Leah called Ashley in tears, she was surprised as well as pleased when Ashley offered to come round after work on Friday.

'We could ask the landlord to change the mattress, if you like,' Leah suggested, 'if you feel weird about sleeping in Bethany's bed, that is. I mean, after what happened.'

Ashley said she was fine with the room as it was. 'It's not as if it's her bed now, is it? And anyway, it's only until Sunday. I've got to be back in time for work first thing Monday morning.'

Leah sighed. Ashley couldn't have made it clearer that she didn't intend staying for long, but at least she was going to be there for a couple of nights, which meant that Leah wouldn't be in the flat on her own. And by Monday, with any luck, the police would have got their act together and caught the killer. If not, Leah would have to try to persuade Ashley to move in with her for longer, although that would be difficult since she worked in York. Leah planned that they would watch a film together and she went out and bought plenty of snacks in readiness. But the visit was not going as she had intended.

'Are you sure you didn't imagine it?' Ashley asked when Leah told her all about her night intruder.

With a loud sniff, Leah wiped a stray tear from her cheek. 'I appreciate you're trying to be nice, but that doesn't make me feel any better.'

'Well, I don't know what else you want me to say,' Ashley replied.

She waved a hand in dismissal as Leah lifted a large bowl of crisps from the table and held it out to her.

'It's not as if we know who your intruder was, so I don't know what we can do about it,' Ashley said.

Leah popped a crisp in her mouth and crunched miserably. 'You keep saying "*your* intruder" as though this was just *my* problem, but any one of us could be next. You know Robin was sent a threatening letter as well as me, and there could be one on its way to you right now. It might arrive any day. And for all we know Ned might have received one as well. This isn't just about me. We've all got to take it seriously. You can't just wash your hands of it, because I'm telling you, he might come for any one of us at any time.' She sniffed again and reached for another crisp. 'The police are useless. They said they're going to keep a watch on the flat, but I haven't seen anyone outside. Did you notice anyone when you arrived?'

Ashley shook her head. 'You could to go back to them and complain if you're really worried.'

'Of course I'm worried. Aren't you?'

'Well, I don't understand what's going on, so I can't say.'

Leah shivered. 'Don't you get who the intruder was? Do I really have to spell it out for you? It was him, wasn't it? He killed the others and now he's coming here to get me. That's who broke into my flat.'

Glancing up at Ashley to see if she was listening, Leah was gratified to see that her guest finally appeared to be taking her seriously. Staring attentively at her, Ashley sat forward in her chair.

'Are you sure?' she asked. 'The thought had crossed my mind but it seemed so unlikely.'

'Well, I can't think who else it could have been.'

'Do you think he'll come back here?'

'Shit, I hope not!'

'But what if he does?' Ashley insisted.

'Well, like I told you, the police are supposed to be keeping a watch on the flat, whatever that means,' Leah replied. 'But I haven't seen anyone outside, and believe me, I looked. In any case, I don't suppose the police would notice if someone crept into the flat again at night. He's managed it once without being caught. And we're supposed to have CCTV here.'

'Well, you don't need to worry now I'm here,' Ashley said.

'Thank you. I really appreciate that you came.'

Shortly after that Ashley went up to bed, saying that she was too tired to start watching a film; she had been up early in the morning to get to work. Leah lifted the bowl and rested it on her lap so she could lean back comfortably in her chair and pop crisps into her mouth with the minimum effort. After a while she felt her eyes begin to close and her arm dropped by her side. It was still early but she decided to follow Ashley's example and go to bed. At least she should sleep well, for once, after a week of disturbed nights when she had imagined hearing strange noises in the dark.

Over breakfast the next morning, Leah came to the conclusion that she didn't really like Ashley very much. She had never realised before how spoilt her old friend was. To begin with Ashley spent ages in the shower, after which she used Leah's hair dryer without asking if she could borrow it. Then when they were finally able to sit down to breakfast, nothing Leah had in the flat was good enough for her. Ashley refused to eat anything that contained sugar, insisting that she had to watch her figure. So she sat sipping black coffee and watching Leah tuck into a plate of eggs and sausages, making her feel uncomfortable. Just as Leah felt she couldn't possibly eat any more under her friend's watchful eye, the bell rang.

Leah went over to the intercom and studied the tiny black and white image of an old man with bent shoulders staring back at her through metal-rimmed spectacles. She had no idea

who he was, but she had no qualms about opening the door
to so elderly a stranger, especially now Ashley was in the flat
with her. He was probably some religious fanatic, but it could
do no harm to find out what he wanted.

62

AT FIRST LIGHT ON Saturday morning the divers were in place ready to begin their search. It wasn't long before they came across a spot on the far side of river where the prow of a boat appeared to have butted up against the mud, suggesting it had probably been powered by an engine. Added to that, the vegetation at the water's edge had recently been crushed by someone stamping around. Examination of the surrounding area quickly revealed splinters of wood caught in the grass and river weed that could have come from a boat. One relatively large scrap had a fragment of dirty white paint on one side, clearly visible to the naked eye.

'It looks like he used a boat, at least partially painted white, probably with a motor,' a scene of crime officer said. 'That's how our man got away. But he didn't get very far,' he added. 'So where did he go from here, I wonder?'

The scraps of wood were being collected and bagged up to be taken away for examination under a microscope. All the signs seemed to suggest that a boat had arrived at that point after crossing the river, so it made sense for the divers to begin their search there. It didn't take them long to discover a small craft lying in the mud on the river bed, the bottom smashed to pieces. In addition to several jagged holes in the wood, when the divers attempted to haul the wreck up to the surface they discovered it had been weighted down with a large rock wedged in the engine. There was no longer any doubt that the boat had been deliberately scuppered.

Ian was already at the scene when Geraldine arrived. She

had been talking to Sam when she had received a message about the discovery.

'I said I'll try and get round there this weekend,' Sam had said.

'Sam, I'm sorry to put this on you, but there's no way I can get back to London right now. We're in the middle of an investigation...'

'You're not the only person who works,' Sam had interrupted her, sounding thoroughly exasperated.

'I know, I know, and I'm sorry. She's not your sister, I know, but you're there, in London, and I'm hundreds of miles away. It's impossible for me to get there.'

It had been an unsatisfactory conversation, made all the more difficult because Geraldine had to end it.

'I'm sorry, I've got to pick up a message.'

'Oh, it's different when it's you that has to work, isn't it?'

She was afraid she had annoyed Sam so much that she would change her mind about spending time going to check on Helena. Geraldine's sister wasn't *her* responsibility.

Now Geraldine stood at Ian's side while he brought her up to speed with what was happening. Standing around in the cold and damp did nothing to improve her mood as they watched from behind an inner cordon set up to protect the ground which had been contaminated by the inclement weather and the activities of the diving team. Scene of crime officers were busy photographing footprints and collecting potentially useful fragments. They watched in silence as a white forensic tent was erected over the scene.

'Better late than never,' one of the scene of crime officers called out cheerfully. 'But what with the sleet and you guys trampling all along the path, we'll be lucky to find any useful evidence out here.'

'At least we've got the boat he used,' another officer defended their activity.

'So now we know we're looking for him on this side of the river?'

'Unless he doubled back over one of the bridges.'

It could have been because they were working out in the open air, away from the claustrophobic atmosphere of the police station, but somehow they all seemed cheerful. Feeling excluded from the good-natured banter Geraldine found their camaraderie depressing, but Ian was happy to join in the noisy exchange.

'So we've narrowed the search down to this side of the river, or the other side of the river,' he said, and the other two men laughed as though he had cracked a good joke.

'Cheer up, love, it might never happen,' a white-coated officer said as he passed her.

Geraldine pulled her collar up and sneezed. There wasn't really any point in her being there. Not so long ago she wouldn't have missed this for anything, attending a scene where vital clues were being discovered that might lead to the arrest of a dangerous criminal. Glancing up at Ian, she saw the excitement in his eyes and knew that he was caught up in the thrill of the investigation as she would once have been. But it was damp and cold and she wanted to be at home asleep, instead of which she had been dragged out of bed to stand around near a grey river, watching her breath form tiny white clouds, while her feet and hands slowly froze. Maybe she ought to accept that she was burnt out, past her sell-by date, and it was time for her to retire. The thought made her feel like crying. Her job had always been the driving force in her life, but somehow, ever since she had attended her birth mother's funeral, she had been struggling against an underlying feeling that her existence was no longer merely difficult, it was pointless.

Wrapped in her own misery, she didn't register straight away that Ian was talking to her.

'You look half-frozen,' he said. 'Not used to the weather up here.' He grinned at her. 'You soft southerner.'

Touched that he had noticed her discomfort she smiled back

at him, and on the instant, her mood lifted. Cold and tired, she had allowed the weather to get the better of her.

'You're right,' she said. 'I'm bloody freezing. Look, there's nothing for us to do here, is there? I mean, you don't need me around, do you?'

To her surprise, Ian seemed momentarily lost for words. 'I... you...' he stammered, 'no, you go and warm up somewhere,' he concluded, regaining his composure. 'There's no point in you standing around here catching a chill. I'll see you later.'

Geraldine made her way slowly along the muddy path which was wet with icy patches. Once or twice she nearly lost her footing but at last she was safely back at her car. She was tempted to go home and have the breakfast she had missed, but instead drove to Fulford Road and had coffee and toast in the canteen at work. It wasn't as good as having breakfast at home looking at the view over the river, but at least she was at the police station and didn't have to drive through any more morning traffic. And she felt a lot better after having something to eat.

She had warmed up and was settled at her desk planning her day when her phone rang. After listening for a moment, she sprang to her feet and went in search of Ian who was back at his desk, on his phone. His shocked expression told her that he was listening to the same message.

'I don't believe it. Where did you say it was found?' he was saying.

She waited until he had finished on the phone.

'I know,' she interrupted him, as he started to tell her what had happened. 'I just had the same call. I came looking for you as soon as I heard.'

They stared at one another for a second. Geraldine guessed that her own stricken expression was mirrored in his face. She wanted to comfort him like a child, and had to restrain a sudden crazy impulse to reach out and put her arms around him, telling him that everything was all right. But everything was far from all right. Because while they had been running around by the river chasing clues, fooling themselves that they were finally getting somewhere, the killer had also been busy.

He had found another victim.

63

THEY MADE THEIR WAY to the mortuary in miserable silence. When they arrived, Ian got out of the car first and stood waiting while Geraldine fiddled with the zip on her jacket and pulled her hood up.

'Don't stand out here in the rain,' she scolded him as she joined him.

'I thought we could go in together.' He shrugged. 'It's only spitting.'

Geraldine scowled. 'That's an understatement if I ever heard one.' She had worked alongside Ian for long enough to know that he found the sight of a corpse distressing and suspected he was reluctant to go in and view another body so soon after Bethany had been pulled out of the river. But that was no reason to stand around outside in the rain.

'You could have waited for me inside. Come on, let's get indoors before we're both drenched.'

The door was opened almost at once by Avril who stepped back to admit them. Her face, already smiling a welcome, seemed to brighten even more when she met Ian's eye.

'Come in out of the rain,' she fussed, ushering them indoors.

'What is it with you women and rain?' Ian asked. He was laughing, but Geraldine knew him well enough to register his irritation. 'Anyone would think you dissolve if you get the slightest bit wet.'

'It's not a case of dissolving,' Avril replied, still smiling, 'but it's common knowledge that you're far more susceptible to colds and flu if you stand around in the cold and damp.'

'What a load of old poppycock,' Ian replied.

Laughing, Avril told Ian he could 'pop his cock' for her any time he liked.

'You're just worried the damp will mess up your hair,' he said.

Brushing her hand through her short hair, Geraldine interrupted their flirtatious banter, speaking more sharply than she had intended. 'Jonah wanted to see us.'

'Yes, of course,' Avril's smile didn't falter. 'He's waiting for you.'

They followed her along the corridor. Jonah looked up from his grisly work as they went in.

'You got here in double quick time,' he said, nodding and smiling at Ian. 'You'll be pleased to know I've got another one for you. That makes four in how long is it? Seems like only a few days since Stephanie was brought in.'

'It's four weeks,' Geraldine replied, keeping her voice even.

'Hmm. One a week. It's about time you guys sorted out this mess.'

'Who is he?' Ian asked, his voice taut with anxiety.

He stared down at the body lying stretched out on its back. Turning her attention away from her colleague to the body, Geraldine saw that this victim was a man, wiry and dark-haired, his skin as smooth and white as alabaster. His cold black eyes seemed to be staring up at the brightly lit ceiling, as though attempting to distance himself from the indignity of this physical examination. Ian looked away quickly, his normally good-natured features twisted in a peevish frown.

'Surely this can't be meant for us? I don't understand what we're doing here.'

He waved one of his hands dismissively in the direction of the corpse as he spoke.

Jonah shook his head. 'I would have thought it was obvious what you're doing here. You're detectives, aren't you?

Working on a murder case? And this is a dead body.'

Ian grunted.

'Yes, here we have a dead body,' Jonah repeated, accompanying his words with a theatrical flourish. 'So perhaps *you'd* like to tell *me* what it is you fail to grasp because, as I understand it, you're the brains around this table. I'm just a pathologist. All I do is gather evidence. I don't reach any conclusions. That's your job.'

Ian sounded vexed. 'You know perfectly well what I meant. I get it that you suspect this man here to be the victim of some foul play, but it's got nothing to do with the investigation we're working on, has it?'

He cast a sideways glance at Geraldine, perhaps hoping she would agree with him.

Jonah smiled archly and put his hands on his hips like an actor in an amateur pantomime. 'And what makes you so sure of that?'

'His age for a start.'

'What do you mean?' Jonah sounded genuinely surprised.

'He's too old.'

'Too old for what? I didn't know there was an age limit on being killed.'

Jonah laughed and Ian joined in.

'Ian means he's too old to be a victim in our case because the victims we're investigating were at school together in the same class. They're all in their early twenties. Your body here looks a lot older than that.'

'He was in his mid-thirties,' Jonah said. 'Although he wanted to appear older.'

As he spoke, he showed them an image of a white-faced old man with shaggy grey hair, his spectacles askew. He looked so different, it took Geraldine a moment to register that they were looking at a picture of the dead man.

'You're saying he was wearing a wig?' Ian asked, looking baffled.

'So he didn't want to be recognised,' Geraldine said, equally puzzled. 'But this man's about a decade too old to have been at school with our other victims. What made you think he was linked to them in any way?'

'DNA,' the pathologist replied.

'You mean you identified the same DNA on him as you found on Stephanie?'

Jonah inclined his head. 'Oh yes.'

Geraldine glanced at Ian and saw her own consternation reflected in his eyes. The pathologist appeared to be suggesting that the killer had begun selecting his victims from a larger pool of people.

Delicately Jonah took a scraping from the dead man's finger and held it up in front of them. 'It's the same DNA all right. And he was shot by the same gun.'

'This was another shooting,' Ian said slowly. 'How come you found the killer's DNA on the victim's finger? I don't understand what you're telling us.'

'He must have tried to push him away,' Geraldine suggested.

'But this time the killer had a gun,' Ian said. 'Thanks to our bungling,' he added under his breath.

'I could have taken a sample from anywhere on the body and come up with the same result,' Jonah told them, pointing at the body. 'This body is packed with your killer's DNA. It's in every cell.'

Geraldine stared. 'You mean...'

The pathologist nodded his head. 'You've found your killer.'

'But someone else got to him first,' Geraldine replied.

Jonah nodded. 'Yes. Someone's killed your killer.'

64

TIM HATHAWAY HAD BEEN discovered lying face down in the mud beside the path leading down to the canal, not far from the spot where Bethany had entered the water. An elderly woman had spotted the body and assumed the dead man was asleep, but suspecting that something was wrong, and concerned that the stranger might be suffering from hypothermia lying on the frozen ground, she had approached him and called out. When the man hadn't stirred, she had gone into the library to seek assistance. A volunteer librarian had gone outside with the old woman, accompanied by a retired nurse who happened to be in the library. The first woman had become hysterical on discovering the man was dead, but the nurse had called the emergency services and before long a police assessment team had arrived to take control of the situation.

By the time Geraldine arrived outside the library, a forensic tent was in place and the scene of crime officers were busy hunting for scraps of evidence.

'He wasn't killed here,' one of them told Geraldine. 'We're doing our best to work out how he was brought here, but we're having to do a bit of speculation. It looks as though he was dragged down the path. That much seems clear. We've followed the trail back as far as the road, and there are recent tyre marks. We can't be sure but it seems he was transported here in a small car – God knows how the killer managed to cram him inside. The body must have been moved pretty promptly, before rigor set in.'

'What about the killer? What can you tell us about him?'

'Her. At least, that's what we think. There appear to have been two women involved in depositing the body here, from what we can establish from the footprints around the area, although of course it's difficult to be certain as three other women walked all over it before the death was reported, and they managed to virtually obliterate any earlier traces. And one of them was a nurse. You'd think she would have known better.'

'You said you thought there were two women involved?'

'That's what we think, but we're still waiting for confirmation. We've sent details of all the footprints off to the lab for analysis, but from what we can see, there are still signs of two sets of prints that were made some time before the body was discovered this morning, and we don't think they match any of the three women who were here this morning when the body was reported to us.'

'Two women,' Geraldine repeated thoughtfully.

'Does that help?'

Geraldine shrugged. 'Let's see what the forensic examination throws up.' It must have been obvious that her cautious words were at odds with the excitement she was feeling, because the scene of crime officer grinned.

'We'll get that information to you as soon as we can.'

Back at the police station, Eileen summoned a meeting of the team, trying to make sense of what had happened. The latest victim had been identified at once as Tim Hathaway. As far as they had been able to discover, he appeared to have no living relatives, his father having died in a domestic accident when Tim was a child, and his mother following some ten years later, suffering from some sort of dementia. He had no surviving grandparents, no siblings, and both his parents had been only children.

'A bit of a solitary existence,' someone commented.

'Both his parents died prematurely,' Geraldine added thoughtfully.

Before they could continue, a message came through. The registration numbers of cars that had passed security cameras outside the two pubs beside, and across the road from, the library had been checked. One of them was registered to Ashley Morrison.

'What was she doing in Saddleworth?' Eileen asked.

'Two women,' Geraldine muttered. 'Leah Rutherford lives in Saddleworth. Could Ashley have been visiting her?'

'Where's that surveillance officer? He was supposed to be here,' Eileen barked.

A constable stepped forward. 'I'm on the surveillance team,' he announced.

'Well?'

'Well, yes, Ashley Morrison's car was parked in Leah's street. She arrived,' he checked his notes, 'on Friday, early evening. It's all in the report,' he added as though he felt the need to defend his team's work. 'She stayed there overnight and drove off on Saturday evening, soon after dark.'

'Where did she go from there?'

He shrugged. 'We were only tasked with keeping an eye on Leah's house.'

'Did you see anyone else?'

'Yes. Leah had another visitor while Ashley was still there, an elderly man who arrived around ten on Saturday morning.'

'What was he wearing?'

'A long light-coloured raincoat.'

'What happened then? Did he go inside?'

'Yes.'

'And when did he leave?'

Geraldine held her breath. The roomful of people waited in silence for the answer.

The constable looked uncomfortable. 'We didn't observe him leaving the property,' he replied.

'What do you mean?'

'We didn't see him leave.'

Eileen's voice dropped. 'And you didn't think that was odd?'

The constable frowned. 'We assumed he was staying there.' He hesitated. 'There is another maisonette in the house. He could have been a resident there.'

'That was Tim Hathaway, you idiot,' Eileen said quietly.

'Yes, I realise that now,' the constable replied. 'But there was nothing at the time to arouse suspicion. He was just an old man entering the building.'

Eileen nodded briskly. 'So,' she said, turning away from the red-faced constable, 'Tim Hathaway turned up at Leah's flat on Saturday morning. He knew we were looking for him, so he was travelling around disguised as an old man. What was he doing at Leah's flat?'

'He was probably expecting to find Leah there on her own,' Geraldine said. 'He'd already broken in there once. He might have worked out it might not be safe to break in again at night, so instead he rang the bell in broad daylight, confident he wouldn't be recognised. He was returning to finish the job he failed to complete a week ago.'

'But instead of killing Leah, he ended up being shot himself,' Ian said. 'Because he didn't find Leah on her own as he'd expected. She had company.'

Eileen nodded grimly. 'The killer who had murdered their three friends turned up threatening to kill them. Between the two of them, Leah and Ashley succeeded in overpowering him and disarming him, and they shot him in the chest in the scuffle.'

'Was it an accident, or an execution?' Geraldine asked grimly.

65

OFFICERS WERE DESPATCHED TO bring Leah and Ashley to the police station for questioning, but neither of them was at home. An alert was immediately issued to look out for both of the suspects, as well as for Ashley's car. With a few minutes to herself for the first time that morning, Geraldine was putting on her jacket ready to step outside to call Sam. But before she could leave the office, the desk sergeant sent a message to say that Leah had turned up at the police station. She was alone. Once she had been settled in an interview room, Ian and Geraldine went to question her about what had happened the previous night. Speaking to Sam would have to wait.

Leah refused to have a lawyer present. 'I don't mind if you record what I say. I came here to tell you everything that happened. I don't need a lawyer if I'm telling the truth, do I? It was all an accident. We've done nothing wrong.' She burst out crying and although she tried to speak, what with hiccupping and sobbing, she became completely incoherent. Geraldine and Ian exchanged a glance, Ian irate, Geraldine resigned. She handed the crying girl a tissue and a glass of water.

'Leah,' Geraldine said gently, 'we appreciate that you've come here voluntarily. But you have to tell us what happened. Now take your time and calm down so you can speak clearly. At the moment I'm afraid I can't understand a word you're saying. Now, we know Ashley was staying with you at your flat so let's start there.'

'Yes. She said she'd come and spend the weekend with me because I didn't want to be there by myself after the break-in, and she needed somewhere to stay. She didn't like the room she was living in.' She started crying but pulled herself together with a visible effort, and explained all over again how Ashley had come to be in her flat.

'And then yesterday morning, you had another visitor?'

Leah nodded.

'Tell us what happened.'

Leah's puffy eyes opened into wider slits. 'It was him. I didn't realise straight away. He looked so old, but it was him. The man who's been killing everyone. It was him. Ashley recognised him straight away, because she knew who he was but I'd never seen him before and...'

'How did she know who he was?'

'He's the man she went out with in the sixth form, the one I told you about.'

'The older man she was seeing while she was at school?'

'Yes.'

Geraldine nodded and waited while Leah blew her nose noisily and drank some water. After a moment, she prompted Leah again.

'So what happened yesterday morning, when he came to the flat?'

In between bouts of sobbing, Leah described how the old man had claimed he was looking for his niece who used to live in the flat Leah now occupied. He had appeared distressed on learning that she no longer lived there, and had asked if she might be kind enough to contact her landlord and see if he knew where the previous tenant had gone.

'I didn't see any reason not to let him come in. I didn't know it was him. I thought it was just some confused old man who had lost his niece's current address. So we went into the kitchen and he sat down on a stool.' She paused.

'And what happened then?'

'He was sitting in the kitchen and Ashley came in and saw him. He hadn't even seen her yet, but she threw herself at him and knocked him right off the seat. I didn't know what was going on but she kept yelling, "It's him! It's him!" I thought she'd gone mad. He'd landed on his knees on the floor and I still thought he was just some old bloke so I was going to help him when he pulled a gun out of his pocket.'

'Your gun,' Ian said.

'What? No!' Leah cried out. 'It wasn't my gun. It wasn't.'

'Never mind that,' Geraldine interrupted her impatiently. 'Let's get back to what happened yesterday. The killer was on his knees on the floor, Ashley was yelling, you were about to go and help him to his feet, and then he pulled out a gun. What did you do next?'

Leah shook her head. 'I didn't do anything. I was – I think I was screaming. Ashley lunged at him and they were struggling. I remember thinking he seemed pretty fast for someone that old, and then somehow she got hold of the gun. I think he must have dropped it when he fell off the chair. Anyway, she was holding the gun and the next thing I knew there was a loud bang and...' Leah dropped her head in her hands, sobbing. 'It was an accident. It was an accident. He was going to kill us. He was going to kill us all.'

'Why didn't you call for help? Leah, why didn't you contact the emergency services straight away? Ambulance? Police? Leah, your friend shot someone. By not calling for help you made yourself an accessory to her crime. You need to answer the question. Why didn't you call for help?'

Leah straightened up in her chair with a shiver. Her voice shook. 'Ashley said he was dead so a doctor couldn't help him.' She hesitated. 'I wanted to call the police, but Ashley said we'd both be done for murder, and anyway he had it coming and we shouldn't lose any sleep over his death. She said we'd be safe now.' She let out a sob, and clapped her hand over her lips to suppress another one. 'I just wanted to be safe. It's been a nightmare. A real nightmare.' She paused to blow her nose again. 'Ashley said all we needed to do was get rid of the body, get it out of my flat, and that would be that. She had her car outside, so...' she shuddered at the memory.

'What happened, Leah?'

'We cleaned the kitchen. It took hours. I didn't want to, but Ashley said we had to.'

'How did you move the body out of your flat?'

'We squashed him up and wrapped him in my duvet and tied it all up in a big bundle. Then we cleaned the kitchen and waited until dark before we shoved the body out through the back window, rolled up in my duvet. We'd tied the ends together so it couldn't fall out, and between us we managed to drag it to the car. It weighed a ton. Ashley was parked right outside the house, and there are no street lights just there so it was dark enough to put it in the car without anyone seeing.' She took a deep breath. 'And then we drove down to the town without any lights on in the car, and left it by the canal. There was no one around at that time of night so we untied the duvet and it just fell out... she said she'd get rid of the duvet. It had all the blood... she didn't even drop me back home,' she added. 'She said it was better if we didn't see each other again. She just drove off and left me.'

Geraldine frowned. 'You told me before that you and Ashley weren't the best of friends at school?'

Leah looked miserable. 'We weren't not friends, exactly, it's just that I wasn't one of her clique. You know how it is at school.'

'Why was she staying with you?'

'I told you, I was afraid the killer might come back, and she said she'd spend the weekend with me. It was nice of her. Although she only came because she didn't like where she was living. She was trying to find somewhere else in York.'

In any event, Ashley was the one who had pulled the trigger, and they needed to find her urgently.

'So where's Ashley now?' Ian asked.

Leah said she didn't know.

'You do realise it's vital we find her,' Geraldine said. 'And you know that we will. It won't take us long to discover where she's gone. Listen, Leah, this is important. We need to make sure she can corroborate your story, otherwise you might end up in prison, if a jury doesn't believe what you've told us.'

Leah shook her head, her face taut with fear.

'Not only that, but she has a gun and she's used it once,' Ian added.

They paused to allow his words to sink in.

'No, no,' Leah gasped. 'It was an accident. We never meant it to happen.'

Her plump face seemed to dissolve in front of them, quivering and twitching with the effort to regain control of her emotions. Watching her break down in tears again, Geraldine sighed. Ian suggested they take a break, and while a female constable took a cup of tea in to Leah, they went away to discuss what she had told them. They were inclined to believe Leah's account of the events of the previous day, but where Ian believed both girls must have been too terrified to know what they were doing, Geraldine wasn't convinced. She couldn't help wondering whether it had been coincidence that Ashley had arrived at Leah's flat just when it seemed possible that Tim might return there. And in the meantime, Ashley was at large and armed with a gun which she had just used to kill her ex-boyfriend.

'We have no idea of Ashley's mental state right now,' she said when they discussed the situation with the detective chief inspector.

Eileen turned to stare at her.

'She's disappeared, and we know she has a gun,' Geraldine went on.

'We'd better find her then,' Eileen snapped.

Geraldine and Ian exchanged a worried look. With the murder of their suspect, the investigation had taken a terrible twist.

66

ON HER WAY HOME that evening, Geraldine tried to call Sam but there was no answer. Either her former colleague was busy, or else she was avoiding speaking to Geraldine because she still hadn't been to visit Helena. Geraldine swore and hung up. A moment later her phone rang. Expecting to hear Sam's voice, she was surprised to hear who was on the line.

'I need to talk to you,' Ashley said.

'Tell me where you are and I'll send a car to fetch you right away.'

In the brief silence that followed, Geraldine was afraid Ashley had hung up.

'I need to talk to you,' Ashley repeated at last, 'but we've got to meet somewhere private, and you have to come alone.'

If the conversation hadn't taken place in the middle of murder enquiry, Geraldine would have been tempted to smile at Ashley's melodramatic demands.

'Why don't I come and pick you up and we can go along to the police station together, and then you can tell us about your ordeal?' Geraldine did her best to sound reassuring. 'We can arrange for you to have some support, if you feel you need it.'

'What do you mean, support?'

'Sometimes victims benefit from counselling after they've undergone a traumatic experience like you have. You and Leah were lucky to survive. I don't know if you realise how dangerous your visitor was.'

Ashley didn't answer, but she didn't hang up either.

'Are you still there?' Geraldine asked.

'If I tell you where to find me, you have to promise me you'll come alone.'

It was easy to agree to Ashley's condition, and truthful, as Geraldine was by herself in her car. What she didn't add was that she was going to request that several patrol cars meet her at the pub Ashley had mentioned. It wasn't far away so as soon as she set off Geraldine called for urgent assistance. If Tim's death had been an accident, Ashley would have her chance to prove her innocence. In the meantime, Geraldine wasn't taking any chances.

'Alert an armed response unit. The suspect has a gun which she's already used.'

There was a chance Geraldine would be first on the scene, since she was already close to the destination. Weighing up possible outcomes she decided not to wait for backup to arrive, for fear Ashley might change her mind and slip away before any of the police reached the pub. They couldn't afford to lose sight of her again. With the possibility that she was volatile, and the likelihood that she was armed, it was vital she was apprehended quickly and with minimal risk to the public. The immediate concern was that she could be sitting in a busy pub with a gun in her pocket. Drawing up in the pub car park Geraldine scanned the vehicles looking for Ashley's registration number. She spotted it easily, parked near the entrance. Preparing herself for the worst, she approached the pub.

The bar was full of young people, chatting and laughing, oblivious to the danger that threatened them. Ashley must have been looking out for her, because as Geraldine entered and looked around she saw her getting to her feet, one hand raised in greeting. Aware that Ashley was probably armed, Geraldine watched her make her way through the crowd of youngsters gathered around the bar. Waiting in the doorway, she wondered how she could persuade Ashley to step outside.

As long as they remained in the pub, innocent members of the public could be in danger.

As it turned out, Geraldine needn't have worried about the safety of the pub customers, because Ashley was also keen to leave. 'Come on,' she said, jerking her head in the direction of the door. 'Let's get out of here.'

Above the noise of traffic Geraldine heard the wail of several sirens, but her relief didn't last for long. Ashley slipped the gun out of her coat pocket. Concealing it beneath the long sleeve of her coat, she pointed it at Geraldine, and ordered her to walk towards the car park exit.

'Get in,' she snapped as they reached her car.

Geraldine climbed in just as two patrol cars sped into the car park and screeched to a halt.

'Give me your phone and get us out of here,' Ashley said.

'Ashley, you don't have to do this. We know Tim's death was an accident. You're not in any trouble. You can stop this now.'

'Drive!'

Geraldine weighed up her chances of surviving the encounter if she risked waiting for another car to come and block off the exit, but Ashley was growing increasingly agitated.

'I said drive! Don't think I won't use this. Now give me your phone.'

'You'll never get away with threatening a police officer,' Geraldine replied as she drove slowly out of the car park, with the two patrol cars on her tail.

She wondered if they could see the gun in Ashley's hand.

'Give me your phone. I need to get rid of those cars.'

'I can't reach my phone. It's in my pocket.'

Ashley stretched across with her free hand and felt for Geraldine's phone. With a gun pointing straight at her, Geraldine didn't dare risk trying to resist.

'Give me the number,' Ashley said.

'What number?'

'Stop playing games and give me the number to call!' Ashley repeated, her voice becoming shrill.

Reluctantly Geraldine gave her what she wanted and Ashley called the police control centre to make her demands clear.

'They want to talk to you,' she said.

'Do what she asks. She's armed,' Geraldine called out.

With a satisfied nod, Ashley dropped the phone out of her window. 'Now get us out of here!'

Conscious of the gun lying in Ashley's lap, Geraldine obeyed. Glancing in the rear-view mirror she could see the patrol cars had dropped out of view. 'No one's following us. You can put the gun away now.'

'Let's get out of the city first,' Ashley said. 'We want to go somewhere we can talk without being disturbed.'

They drove for a while without speaking. Geraldine wondered whether Helena would grieve for her if she was killed, and how Celia would cope with her loss.

'It was Leah's fault,' Ashley said suddenly. 'She shot him. She insisted on my going to stay with her, and then she shot him right in front of me. She set me up. I'm innocent.'

'All the more reason for you to come with me to the police station, and tell us everything that happened.'

'No way. How do I know I can trust you? It's her word against mine.'

Geraldine hesitated. It would be for a jury to decide whether Ashley was telling the truth or not.

'Ashley,' she said gently. 'You don't have to do anything you're not comfortable with. You're a victim in all this, and we want to offer you support. Everyone will understand you're acting bizarrely because you've been traumatised by your experience. You just witnessed a man being shot dead. You've already told me it was Leah who shot him, and I believe you. But in any case it was self-defence, so neither of you has anything to worry about. You've done nothing wrong.'

'I didn't do anything. It wasn't me. She did it. Not me.'

'OK, it's OK, I believe you,' Geraldine lied. 'Why would I say I believe you if I don't?'

'Because I'm pointing a gun at your head, ready to blow your brains out if you don't do what I want.' Ashley gave a curious bark of laughter. 'Now let's get away from here.'

67

THE MARKED POLICE CARS had been recalled. Geraldine kept glancing up at the rear-view mirror but she couldn't see any sign of pursuit. Overhead there was no roar of helicopters. To all appearances she had been abandoned to the whim of a maniac wielding a gun. Yet, far from deserting her, she knew that her colleagues would be doing everything in their power to save her, even if it meant taking Ashley's life. Police marksmen might already be in place waiting to take Ashley out the instant Geraldine somehow managed to distance herself from her captor. She looked in the mirror again, and all around. Still there was no sign that they were being accompanied as they left the built-up area of York, driving along the main road towards Leeds. The traffic was light now they had left the city. Although there were cars in sight, there were none nearby.

'Turn left here,' Ashley snapped suddenly. 'Now!'

Geraldine wondered what Ashley would do if her instruction was ignored and they continued along the main road all the way into Leeds. Ashley could hardly shoot her while they were driving at speed, but they would have to stop, or slow down, at some point, and when they did Ashley would be able to shoot her without risk of crashing. In the meantime, it was best to avoid upsetting her. Besides, if there was to be any shooting, it was better for it to take place on an empty road where there would be no other casualties. Above the hum of the engine she could just about make out the distant roar of a helicopter. She wondered if Ashley realised they were being observed from a distance as they turned off the main road on to a narrow lane.

'Don't slow down!' Ashley warned her, jiggling the gun in her lap.

'I have to. There might be something coming the other way.'

'I said don't slow down.'

With a shrug, Geraldine accelerated. At least she wasn't likely to be shot while they were travelling fast.

'There's a farm building about a mile along the road,' Ashley said after a while. 'There it is,' she added as the roof of a solitary barn came into view through a dip in the hedgerow. 'Turn off there and park the car inside.'

Driving through a gap in the hedge, Geraldine held her breath as they bumped along a muddy track. She was terrified that a jolt might cause the gun to go off, but they reached the cover of the barn without accident. Unusually for her, she could feel sweat trickling down her forehead. She wiped it away with her sleeve and as she lowered her arm she saw that her hand was trembling. She swallowed, hard. Her mouth felt dry and she was afraid she might cry. Struggling to suppress her emotions, she gazed around the barn. Open on one side, it offered shelter from direct sunlight and would have been pleasantly cool in hot weather. Right now, it was freezing in there.

Ashley's apparent reason for coming to the derelict barn was that the car would be out of sight there. Clearly she hadn't bargained on the barn itself being spotted from a helicopter. Now they were no longer driving, a powerful engine could be heard circling above them. Geraldine glanced at Ashley, but she seemed oblivious to the overhead surveillance team. Staring through the window behind Geraldine as though she had forgotten her presence, she kept the gun pointing steadily at her.

All at once Ashley's expression relaxed into a smile and she turned to Geraldine. 'There's no one there. Don't look so worried. The police aren't going to let you die. You're one of them, aren't you? You know they're going to do whatever it takes to save your life.'

'What do you want from me?'

'That's obvious, isn't it? You're going to negotiate for me.'

'Negotiate?'

'Yes. They have to give me what I ask for or else...' she jerked the gun and laughed. 'Come on, lighten up. We both know they won't risk it. They'll be only too happy to give me what I want in exchange for your life. I won't ask for anything they can't give me.'

Geraldine controlled the urge to tell Ashley that she would never get away with what she was doing. Instead, she resolved to do her best to humour her. If only she could get close enough to her captor to disarm her, the situation could be quickly resolved. Failing that, all she needed to do was keep Ashley talking until the police had the barn surrounded with police marksmen. Before long they would hear the voice of a negotiator, hailing Ashley through a megaphone. Meanwhile, time seemed to have slowed down. Now the engine had been turned off, the air inside the car was cooling down rapidly. Geraldine could feel the cold seeping through her jacket, and up through the soles of her shoes. There was nothing in the barn apart from the car itself and its uneasy occupants.

They waited, listening to the roar of the helicopter swell and recede as it circled around, until Geraldine felt as though she had been sitting at the wheel of Ashley's car for as long as she could remember. Her feet and hands were physically hurting from the cold. Still there was no sound of cars approaching down the track, or voices calling out instructions, only the distant roar of the helicopter. The tension inside the car was becoming unbearable.

'Where are they?' Ashley burst out at last. 'They must know we're here. Surely the helicopter spotted us. What's taking them so long?'

Trained to cope under pressure, even Geraldine was finding the waiting almost intolerable. Afraid that Ashley would crack, she looked directly at her captor and forced a smile.

'Do you want to talk me through your demands so I know

what to say when the time comes? We can discuss what's realistic...'

'What's there to talk about?' Ashley interrupted her. She sounded tetchy. 'They need to turn up and start negotiating. I know what I want.' She paused. 'I had to do it, you know,' she added.

'What do you mean?'

'You know what I mean.' There was a long pause. 'I knew it was him all along.'

'Are you talking about Tim?'

'Yes, of course I'm talking about Tim.'

'Do you mean you knew he was killing your friends?'

'Yes.'

'Why was he doing it?'

'To punish me.'

Geraldine frowned. 'If you knew it was him, you should have come to us.'

'You wouldn't have believed me. And anyway, what good would that have done?'

'He would have been arrested and tried for murder.'

'And after all that, how long would he have spent behind bars? He would have pleaded guilty on the grounds of diminished responsibility or whatever other trick he could have pulled, and with good behaviour he would have been free within a few years.'

'That would have been for the courts to decide.'

'What do they know? I'm telling you, he would have got away with it.'

'He wouldn't have got away with anything, not after killing three people.'

'He would have been locked up for a few years, that's all.'

'Ashley, whatever you think, you can't take the law into your own hands. We have a justice system to uphold the law.'

'That's not justice. And it wouldn't have protected *me*. Don't you understand? If the police had got hold of him, he would never have gone away. I had to end it. I had to be sure it was really over.'

'What was?'

'His obsession with me.'

'What do you mean?'

'He was so possessive, and violent. If I so much as looked at another man he threatened to lock me in his cellar again.'

'Again?' Geraldine seized on the word.

'Yes, he locked me in there sometimes.'

'Was this while you were still at school?'

'It started then, but we carried on seeing each other for years after I left, right up until I walked out and went to live with Steph in York. I thought he wouldn't find me there. I thought I could escape.' She gave a bitter laugh. 'He would have found me wherever I went. He was like that. I could never have got away from him, not unless...'

'I don't understand why he killed Stephanie and Peter and Bethany,' Geraldine said. 'Was it to frighten you, or punish you?'

'He did it to isolate me. He thought if he could take away all of my friends, I'd go back to him. He thought it would make me need him. The stupid thing is, Peter and Beth weren't even really my friends. I wouldn't have cared if I never saw them again as long as I lived. They were just people I knew at school. But Tim wanted to get rid of everyone I knew. He was like that. Completely mad.' She seemed to be talking to herself. 'I think he always was, only when I was younger I didn't realise it.' She laughed, but her cheeks were wet with tears. 'I was flattered by his single-minded attention. I didn't know then that it had nothing to do with love. It was insanity. It was only ever insanity.'

Geraldine wondered how much truth there was in what she was hearing. But Tim had killed three people before Ashley had shot him. That at least was undeniable. And although what Ashley had said about ending Tim's obsession with her was appalling, it did follow a terrible logic. With his death, her relationship with him really was ended, with a finality that couldn't be delivered by the legal system Geraldine served. Despite her fundamental belief that the law was the only rightful means of delivering justice, she acknowledged its limitations. Now Ashley had become the killer who would probably serve a relatively short prison sentence on the grounds of diminished responsibility. And when she was released, she would be free of her persecutor for life.

68

WATCHING THE PATROL CARS peel off, Ian maintained his distance, careful to keep at least one other vehicle between him and the car he was following. Once he almost lost them when he was held at a red light.

'Which way? Which way?' he demanded aloud, panicking that he had lost them.

A helicopter pilot directed him across a roundabout and out on to the Tadcaster Road where he overtook a couple of slow-moving vehicles. With the target in sight again, he eased off the accelerator and allowed another driver to overtake him. As long as there were no more than two cars between them, he could tail them effortlessly. He avoided allowing a van or lorry to get between them and block his line of vision. With the helicopter to guide him there was little chance of losing them, but he still felt happier when he could see the car himself.

Up ahead he saw them turn off. Reaching the entrance to the narrow lane where they had disappeared, he drew in beside the hedge and waited. After a few minutes he took his foot off the brake and allowed the car to crawl forward. When the roof of a barn came into view, he parked his car right up against the hedge and continued on foot. Pressing his back up against the shrubbery he edged forwards, one step at a time, aware that if he made any noise at all he might be responsible for a fatality that would haunt him for the rest of his life. Behind him the bushes rustled gently in protest at his movements, no louder than they might have done at a sudden wind whipping through their leaves.

The side of the barn facing the lane was open to the elements. The car had been driven in forwards, so that the people inside it weren't looking in his direction. Even so, he advanced very cautiously. Ashley had only to glance round and she would spot him at once, with the sun behind his back. He dropped down on to his front and hauled himself over the prickly grass as quickly as he could. Once he reached the threshold of the barn, he was below the car windows and no longer visible to the two women inside it. Slowly he pulled himself up until he was level with the back of the car. There he paused. He was within a few inches of Ashley, and he had no idea what to do next.

For the first time it occurred to him that he had followed the two women without any plan for what to do when he found them. He had been in many other dangerous situations, but this was the first time he had reacted in such mindless panic. If his own life had been threatened he would have remained calm but, in the heat of the moment, he had allowed his judgement to be clouded by his fear for Geraldine's safety. Shocked to discover how easy it had been to disregard his training, he forced himself to focus on his immediate predicament. Analysing his motivation for such reckless behaviour would have to wait. Right now he needed to concentrate on Geraldine's predicament.

As he appreciated the extent of the danger into which he had rushed, terror clutched at him until he was barely able to breathe. He crouched behind the car, clinging to the fact that he had seen Geraldine through the window, and she was still alive. He could hear a faint hum of voices which indicated the two women were talking. Geraldine would be doing her best to keep the conversation going until help arrived. He settled down to wait. The negotiator would soon be there, and once that kicked off, he would be ready to act if necessary. If not, he would roll underneath the car and stay out of sight until it was all over. Just being close enough to Geraldine to hear her voice was reassuring.

He felt a jolt. Peering round the edge of the car, he saw the passenger door had swung open. He pulled his head back sharply, just as Ashley looked out; another second and she would have seen him. Quickly he flung himself flat on the ground and pulled himself right underneath the car. Wedged between the freezing cold earth and the chassis he listened intently, trying to work out what was happening. He could hear raised voices above him, but the sound was muffled by the vehicle. It was excruciating having to lie there, helpless, not knowing what was going on, unable to do anything to help his colleague.

Above him the car began to bounce and he heard Ashley yelling, 'Put them on now!' A moment later she shouted, 'Get out! Get out!' At the same time, she climbed out of the car, almost close enough for him to reach out and grab her ankle. She was wearing faded jeans and pink socks, with dirty white trainers, but that was all he could see of her. A section of a second pair of legs appeared on the other side of the car. Ian watched Geraldine's black trousers and feet move slowly towards the exit, while Ashley's legs moved at the same speed in the same direction on the opposite side of the car. Ian waited. In a moment the two women would walk out of the barn, unaware of his presence. Before the negotiating team arrived, he might find an opportunity to seize Geraldine's captor from behind. Taking her completely by surprise, he would be able to overpower her before she knew what was happening. But if his plan backfired, Geraldine would be shot.

Hardly daring to breathe, he twisted around so he could look out without being seen. The two women were walking slowly around the car, one on each side. They met at the back of the car, in the entrance to the barn. Ian swore under his breath when he saw that Geraldine was handcuffed. He slid silently backwards to the space between the far wall of the barn and the front of the car. Pulling himself out from underneath the car, he crouched down to peer over the top of the bonnet.

'What was that?' Ashley asked.

Ian froze.

'What's what?' Geraldine asked, although she must have heard whatever sound had alerted Ashley to Ian's movement.

'I thought I heard something.'

'It's the countryside,' Geraldine replied. 'There's no one else here making any noise apart from animals and the wind.'

Knowing her as well as he did, to Ian's ears her casual tone sounded fake. He hoped her dismissive comment wouldn't arouse Ashley's suspicions. It was possible that Geraldine genuinely believed what they had heard had been the rustling of the wind, or movement of some animal through the grass. But her words made him suspect she was wondering whether anyone else was there, watching and waiting.

'There's no one here,' Geraldine repeated firmly, as though to confirm that she thought there probably was.

'What if someone's followed us?'

'Only a complete moron would go chasing after a woman with a gun. He could be shot if he was discovered.'

Geraldine replied so decisively that Ian was now convinced she suspected he was there. The two women moved out of the barn. If they kept walking, in a few moments they would come across his car parked by the hedge and know there was someone else there. It wouldn't take long for Ashley to scurry back to the barn, her gun at Geraldine's head. If she threatened to shoot unless he came out of hiding, he would have to stand up and show himself. He could imagine her lining the two of them up, too far away for them to reach out and grab her, close enough for her to shoot either or both of them with ease if they tried to move. In attempting to rescue Geraldine, he had probably only managed to ensure he died alongside her at the hand of an enraged killer. It wasn't much consolation to know that if Ashley managed to survive, she would spend the rest of her miserable life behind bars.

69

GERALDINE EYED HER CAPTOR warily. Without the use of her arms, her only means of attack were her feet and head, neither of which was very helpful against an enemy waving a gun. Her adopted mother used to tell her and Celia that they should 'Be thankful for small mercies.' Now Geraldine took scant comfort from the fact that her wrists were secured in front of her. Had the handcuffs been snapped shut behind her back, her shoulders would have been aching horribly.

'What now?' Geraldine asked as Ashley looked around.

'We just wait until they come and exchange you.' Ashley gave a worried smile. 'You're my bargaining chip.'

She was about to say something else when the peace of the rural setting was shattered by a blur of chaotic sensations. It began with a deafening roar overhead as a helicopter swooped past, circling the barn. The noise of the engine faded as the helicopter wheeled at the furthest point on its manoeuvre. At that moment a man's voice rang out from a loudspeaker.

'Ashley Morrison, we have the area surrounded. You can't get away. Put down your weapon and step away from the sergeant with your hands raised above your head.'

While he was speaking, Ashley darted behind Geraldine and grabbed her around the neck, ramming the gun against the side of her head.

'Back off!' she shouted. 'Back off or I'll shoot her!'

Unable to move her head, Geraldine swivelled her eyes wildly, trying to look around. There was no one else in sight. The team must have assembled behind the barn.

'I'm handcuffed,' Geraldine called out.

She twisted her head as far as she could and repeated herself, aware that her words would be carried away by the wind. It was important that her colleagues knew she was unable to use her arms. No one answered. She didn't know if anyone had heard her. There was a long pause which seemed to last for hours, before a woman's voice called out through the loudspeaker system.

'Let's all stay calm and take this one step at a time. Ashley, we know you don't want anyone to get hurt. No one wants that. We know what happened, and we understand how upset you must be feeling. The victims were your friends. We're here to help you get through this traumatic experience. We're not here to cause you any more trouble. We don't want that any more than you do. Now put your weapon down so we can talk calmly about the situation.'

Feeling the gun pressing against the side of her head, Geraldine stood as still as she could. Her arms were beginning to ache from being held in one position for so long, and she could feel her legs trembling. Cautiously she rotated her shoulders to prevent them stiffening.

'Keep still,' Ashley snapped at her.

Geraldine stopped moving her shoulders.

'What is it you want?' the negotiator asked.

Ashley let out a deep breath. 'That's more like it,' she said softly. Raising her voice, she answered. 'I'll need a car with a full tank, and ten thousand pounds in cash, and twice as much again in euros, and some more ammunition. I've only got – a few bullets left.'

She was careful not to reveal how many, but it would only take one to end Geraldine's life.

'If you shoot me, you'll have nothing left to bargain with,' Geraldine said quietly, relieved to hear how steady her voice sounded.

The helicopter was hovering some distance away so they could hear one another more easily.

'Put the gun down and we'll talk,' the negotiator's voice floated across the grass.

'Where are you?' Ashley called out. 'I can't see you.'

'I can see you.'

'Are you up there in the helicopter?'

'No, we're standing very close to you.'

'Stand where I can see you. I can't talk to empty air.'

'When you put the gun down I'll come and talk to you.'

'That's not going to happen until I get what I want.'

'We can wait,' the negotiator said. 'Are you hungry? We can fetch you something to eat if you like.'

Ashley glared at Geraldine. 'Is this a trick?' she asked.

Geraldine decided she might as well answer truthfully. 'No, it's not a trick. They think you might be easier to deal with if you have something to eat. It's nothing personal,' she added quickly. 'Most people are liable to become short tempered if they're hungry, and the last thing they want is to stress you out.' It was an effort of will not to glance at the gun in Ashley's hand. 'You've had enough to upset you lately as it is. I know you don't want to believe me, but we really do all want to help you get through this. You've had a terrible time of it lately.'

'Lately?' Ashley interrupted bitterly. 'What do you know about what I've suffered – for years? He was a monster.'

'You're free of him now.'

'Yes, but not free of you.' Ashley's voice rose.

Without warning something hit Geraldine with tremendous force, throwing her sideways. Unable to break her fall by putting out her arms, she jarred her shoulder painfully as she crashed to the ground.

A single shot rang out.

One tiny splinter of metal was all it had taken to end her life. She wondered who had produced the bullet that had torn a path through her vital organs. It must have been mass produced along with thousands of other bullets, churned out of some diabolical machine. Her last thought was of Helena. Their mother's dying request had been that she would take care of her sister. Now Geraldine was abandoning her as well, leaving no one to look out for Helena.

'I'm sorry,' she whispered as she lost consciousness. 'I'm sorry I'm leaving you.'

She couldn't have been unconscious for more than a second before she became aware of an agonising pain in her shoulder. She knew what had happened, but something about the shooting didn't feel right. Ashley had been aiming at her head. The impact that knocked Geraldine off her feet had hit her squarely in her right side, which made no sense. What was even more baffling was that the pain she was now experiencing was in her left shoulder, where she had hit the ground. For an instant her thoughts whirled in turmoil. Calling on all her training to calm herself down, she drew in a deep breath before opening her eyes and glancing around. What she saw took her by surprise.

A man was lying spreadeagled on top of Ashley who was thrashing around beneath him, clawing at the ground, desperately trying to reach the gun which was lying on the ground just out of her reach. Clambering to her feet, Geraldine staggered over to the gun. She half-expected all this would turn out to be a dying hallucination, but the gun was real enough. Gingerly she crouched down and picked it up in one shackled hand, carefully holding it pointing downwards. As she straightened up, a host of uniformed armed officers appeared, seeming to spring from the ground. They surrounded Geraldine and the two figures still wrestling on the ground.

'Come on now, settle down, there's no point in struggling,' Ian panted. Having subdued Ashley he hauled her to her feet, holding both of her wrists behind her back in one of his large hands. Within seconds a couple of uniformed female officers had stepped forward to handcuff her and escort her away down the lane to where the police vehicles were parked. Geraldine handed the gun to a firearms officer, who bagged it as evidence.

While they were talking, the armed response team withdrew as abruptly as they had appeared.

Satisfied the gun was no longer a threat, Geraldine turned on Ian, unable to contain her fury.

'Where did you come from? What the hell are you doing here? You realise you could have been killed.'

When Ian responded by putting his arms around her, she was mortified to feel tears welling up in her eyes.

'I had to do something,' he said. 'I couldn't leave you here alone with her.'

'Try explaining that to Eileen,' she replied, and felt his chest shaking against her cheek as he laughed.

Only later did it occur to her that he could have been shaking with relief.

70

AFTER A SLEEPLESS NIGHT, Geraldine called Sam.

'I'm sorry if I was being unreasonable,' she began, but Sam interrupted her.

'No, it was my fault,' she said. 'It can't be easy for you, worrying about your sister from a distance. Anyway, there's no need to stress over her, at least not for now. I was going to call you when I had a moment. I saw her yesterday evening. I tried to call you but you weren't answering. Is everything OK with you? Only it's not like you not to call back.'

'I lost my phone.'

'What?'

'Well, to be precise, it was thrown out of a moving car. It was found, but only after it had been crushed by passing traffic. Several heavy lorries, by the sound of it.'

'Did you say you threw it out of a car while it was moving?'

'At speed. It's a long story. But how was Helena?'

'She was OK, but she's seriously annoyed with you.'

'With me?'

'Yes.' Sam laughed. 'She said she tried to call you about twenty times last night. I can believe it as well. She's...' she paused. 'Your sister's pretty full on, isn't she?'

'You mean neurotic?'

'That's one way of putting it.'

'I'm sorry if she gave you a hard time.'

'Oh no, she was fine with me. In fact, I rather liked her. She's quite a character, isn't she? She's a remarkable woman, considering everything she's been through. But I wouldn't want to be in your shoes when she catches up with you. She's going to give you a real ear bashing. She thought you were going to see her yesterday, and she's feeling really let down. You're going to have to make it up to her.'

Geraldine nodded. Trust Helena to exploit any opportunity to make Geraldine feel guilty.

'I'll call her later,' she said. 'I've got to get to work now. But if you speak to Helena, you can tell her that I didn't call her yesterday because I'd been kidnapped at gunpoint by a psychopath...'

'I don't think you can invent any traumatic experience that will match what she's been through,' Sam said.

'It's not a competition,' Geraldine heard herself retort, as though she and Helena were children vying for Sam's attention.

Vexed with herself, she hung up. Somehow Helena seemed to bring out the worst in her.

Still annoyed with herself, she drove into work where she joined Ian outside Eileen's office. He looked thoroughly dejected.

'Why the long face?' she asked. 'Tim Hathaway's dead and we've got Ashley in custody. I'd say we did a good job, in the end.'

Ian's expression brightened. 'Yes.'

Before Geraldine could say anything else, they were summoned into the detective chief inspector's office.

'So,' Eileen said, as Geraldine entered, 'I hear Ashley had you locked in your own handcuffs?'

Geraldine wasn't sure, but she thought the detective chief inspector was laughing at her. She nodded. There was no shame in having acceded to the demands of an armed killer.

'She's in a cell under twenty-four hour surveillance while we're waiting for a psychiatric assessment,' Eileen went on.

'Which means she'll get a reduced sentence,' Geraldine muttered crossly.

'Not necessarily. But that's for the courts to determine.'

Geraldine remembered Ashley's complaint that the justice system would one day have released Tim back into society, a free man. Ironically Ashley was now going to try and exploit the courts herself by persuading them that she had never intended to kill Tim.

'His death wasn't an accident,' she said. 'Ashley as good as told me she planned his murder. That's why she went to stay at Leah's flat, because she thought he'd go back there.'

'What are you saying?'

'Ashley was hoping Tim would return, because she was fixated on putting an end to his pursuit of her. She was looking for an opportunity to kill him. But she wanted to get away with it. I think she was hoping he'd break in again at night, so she could claim they were defending themselves against an intruder. Only of course he worked his way in disguised as an old man and she panicked after she killed him, and persuaded Leah to help her get rid of the body. If she can succeed in convincing a jury that they killed Tim as an act of self-defence, and they only tried to get rid of the body afterwards because they were in a state of shock, she might get off with a reduced sentence, or even manslaughter.'

'What happened to "innocent until proven guilty"?' Eileen asked. 'How do you know it wasn't an accident Tim was killed? We can't even be sure whether Leah or Ashley shot him, because they're both accusing each other of having pulled the trigger.'

Before Geraldine could answer, the detective chief inspector turned on Ian.

'And what on earth do you think you were you doing, running around between an armed killer and an armed response unit? If you're so keen on being shot, why don't you join the army? I've got no place on my team for maverick officers who rush off on their own like that. Did you think you'd be welcomed back as a hero and given a medal for risking your life? You're lucky I'm not issuing you with a written warning.'

Geraldine bristled. 'That's not fair,' she blurted out.

Eileen turned to her. 'Not fair?' she repeated, raising her voice. 'Not fair? I'll tell you what's not fair. I've been saddled with an inspector who's prepared to abandon all his training and go off gallivanting on his own, for no good reason.'

'How can you say it was for no reason when he just saved my life,' Geraldine protested. 'Ashley was about to lose control when he barged into her and knocked the gun out of her hand. If he hadn't been there, she might have killed me.'

'Are you saying the team that was put in place wasn't up to the job?' Eileen's face had gone very pale.

Conscious that she was probably about to put the kibosh on her career once and for all, Geraldine met Eileen's glare with a frown of her own. This wasn't fair either. If she hadn't messed up and Eileen had, their roles could easily have been reversed. Knowing that her damaged career was probably already over, she found it unexpectedly liberating to speak her mind, heedless of Eileen's reaction. She was too angry to care what the detective chief inspector thought of her.

'I'm saying that Ian saved my life,' she replied, lowering her voice and speaking very quietly. 'I'm not suggesting his actions deserve any particular acknowledgement, but nor should he be criticised for doing his job. And his action saved my life. Doesn't that count for anything?'

Eileen stared at Geraldine. 'Ian is a good officer,' she conceded. 'And loyalty is an underrated virtue. Just be sure that's all it was.'

'If you're going to report that Ian saved my life in an act of some sort of glory-grabbing heroics, you'd be misrepresenting what he did.'

'He risked his life to save yours, so you're repaying him by putting your career on the line to protect his?' Eileen gave a curious grunt.

'Geraldine, this isn't necessary,' Ian muttered angrily. 'I can fight my own corner.'

'Finally, one of you seems to be talking sense, of a kind,' Eileen said, turning to him. 'Because you're quite right. This isn't necessary. And nor is your ridiculous talk about fighting your corner, Ian. No one's attacking you here. We're all on the same side, remember? And we achieved the result we needed, even if your methods were unconventional, to say the least. This was an extreme situation,' she glanced at Geraldine. 'So I'm going to overlook your flagrant disregard for orders. But I'm warning you, unofficially, to watch your step in future. From now on you do things strictly by the book, however high the stakes.'

Ian nodded. 'Yes ma'am,' he said. 'And thank you.'

71

GERALDINE AND IAN WERE sitting at a corner table in the pub with Naomi, going over the details of the events leading up to Ashley's arrest.

'And she actually made you put on your own handcuffs?' Naomi asked.

She sounded outraged, but Geraldine had an inkling she was trying not to laugh. Several of her other colleagues had made no attempt to conceal their amusement at the incident.

'She had a gun,' Geraldine replied, struggling to hide her annoyance. 'Which she'd already used to kill Tim.'

'We don't know for certain Ashley was responsible for his death. She's saying it was Leah who shot him. But it's only natural for you to want to place the blame for that on Ashley,' Naomi went on quickly, as Geraldine began to protest. 'I'd feel exactly the same in your position. Believe me, you have my sympathy on this. After all, Ashley did nearly kill you. But don't worry. She'll go down for what she did to you, if nothing else.'

Geraldine shrugged. If Naomi believed she was accusing Ashley of having murdered Tim out of some misguided desire for revenge, so be it. She was tired of arguing that Ashley was guilty of premeditated murder.

'It doesn't matter what we think,' she said. 'The outcome will be decided in court by strangers who weren't there, on the basis of whatever Ashley's lawyer instructs her to say. The truth behind the facts will be buried...'

As if trying to lighten the mood, Ian interrupted cheerfully.

'You haven't thanked me properly yet for saving your life.'

'I still don't understand what you were doing there,' Naomi said. 'There was a whole armed response unit, a negotiating team, and God knows how many more officers swarming around the place. What on earth possessed you to go charging in like that? I'm surprised Eileen hasn't thrown the book at you.'

Ian laughed. 'She did rap me over the knuckles,' he admitted.

'Serves you right. What were you thinking?'

Ian shook his head, his expression troubled. 'If it's the truth you're after,' he glanced at Geraldine, 'I don't really understand what the hell I was doing. And I certainly can't tell you what I was thinking at the time because my brain seemed to have stopped working altogether. It's like I was in a daze. Do you think I need to get help?'

'I think what you need is a drink,' Naomi replied. 'And I wouldn't let on to Eileen that you fell apart under pressure. Listen, Ian,' she leaned forward and put her hand on his arm. 'You saw a colleague was in danger, so you went to help. Because that's what we do, we help people. It's why we do this bloody job in the first place. You would have done the same for anyone. It just happened to be Geraldine you rescued. It could have been me. And for what it's worth, I think you were very brave.'

'It's never happened to me before,' he said, moving his arm to raise his glass. 'Do you think I'm losing it? Seriously?'

'I think you need another drink,' Naomi repeated firmly. 'It doesn't do to dwell on these things.'

She stood up and made her way over to the bar.

'Alcohol's probably not the best answer,' Geraldine said quietly.

Ian turned to look at her. 'Do you think I was brave?'

She considered the question for a moment. 'You did what you thought you had to do.'

He nodded. 'All that mattered to me in those confused

moments was that *you* were in danger. It's like nothing else existed. Do you think I'm losing it? Be honest with me, because I need to know.'

'You've been under a lot of pressure lately, with your divorce and the case. What you need is a holiday.'

'I need a drink, I need a holiday,' Ian repeated irritably. 'Why are you women always trying to tell me what I need?'

She gazed into his troubled blue eyes. 'No one else can tell you what you need, Ian. That's something you're going to have to figure out for yourself.'

He was so still, Geraldine wondered if he had noticed that, without thinking, she had put her hand on his arm.

GERALDINE STEEL WILL BE BACK IN

DEATH ROPE

LEIGH RUSSELL

eBook available
26 July 2018

Print book available
22 November 2018

noexit.co.uk/deathrope

READ ON FOR A PREVIEW OF
GERALDINE'S NEXT CASE...

Prologue

Reaching her in waves, the shrill sound seemed to come from somewhere inside her head. It was a few seconds before she realised she was listening to her own screams. For an instant she stood transfixed, a helpless spectator, before she ran outside, bawling for help. Thankfully the gardener was there, and he followed her back into the hall where her husband was hanging from the banister. As she fell silent, she could hear him grunting with the effort of supporting the body. His arms clasped around her husband's legs, he struggled to stop the rope from pulling taut. Above them, Mark's arms swung limply, and his head hung at an odd angle. She was aware of the gardener's mouth moving before she realised he was yelling at her to call an ambulance. Trying to nod, she couldn't move. Her eyes were glued to a ghoulish caricature of a familiar face, bloated tongue protruding between dry lips, tiny red dots of blood speckling the whites of bulging eyes. She stared, mesmerised, at a drop of saliva crawling down his chin, trying to work out whether it was still moving.

The gardener glared at her, and she realised he was still shouting at her to call for help. As if in a dream, she reached for her phone and dialled 999.

A voice on the line responded with unreal composure, assuring her that help was on its way.

'What does that mean?' she gabbled. 'When will they get here?'

'They're on their way.'

Time seemed to hang suspended, like the body.

They waited.

Looking down, she struggled to control an urge to salvage her shopping: tomatoes had rolled across the floor, along with other soft foods she had carefully packed on top of packets and tins. One tomato had already been trodden into the carpet. While she was dithering she heard a siren, followed by hammering at the door, and then her own voice, oddly calm, inviting uniformed men into the house.

Of course they were too late to save him. She had known that all along.

1

Geraldine smiled at her adopted sister. Despite her complaints about disturbed nights, Celia looked happier than Geraldine had seen her in a long time. Her month-old baby snuffled gently in his sleep as she rocked him gently in her arms.

'Would you like to hold him?' Celia asked.

Still smiling, Geraldine shook her head. 'It might wake him up. Anyway, I really should get going.'

'It's still early,' Celia protested. 'Even you can't pretend you've got to get back for work tonight. It's Sunday, for goodness sake. Why don't you stay overnight and go home tomorrow?'

As a detective sergeant working on murder investigations, Geraldine's job was no respecter of the time of day, but she wasn't on a case just then. All the same she shook her head. Even though there was no pressing reason for her to hurry away, she had a long journey ahead of her, and she was back on call in the morning.

'He's lovely,' she repeated for the hundredth time. Privately she thought that her tiny new nephew resembled a pink frog. 'Don't get up. We don't want to disturb him.'

Celia gave a sleepy smile. 'You'll come back soon?'

Geraldine was quick to reassure her sister that she would return as soon as she could. She made good time, and reached home in time for supper. She had been living in York for nearly three months and, after a miserable winter, she was starting to feel settled. She was even thinking of selling her flat in London and buying somewhere in York, putting a stamp of permanence on her move. The transformation in her feelings seemed to have taken place almost overnight. One evening she had gone to bed feeling displaced and lonely. The following morning she had woken up unaccountably at ease in her new home. Driving to work her spirits had lifted further on seeing a bank of daffodils, bright against the deep velvety green slope below the city wall. Already early groups of oriental visitors were beginning to throng the pavements. She wasn't looking forward to an influx of summer tourists clogging up the bustling streets of a city that unexpectedly felt like home.

A few weeks had passed since then, and she was still undecided what to do. Celia would be disappointed if Geraldine decided to make her move to York permanent, but the idea of settling there seemed increasingly appealing with every passing week. She had to live somewhere, and York was as good a place as any. She liked it there. Besides, her oldest friend and colleague lived there. She wondered how Ian Peterson would react if he knew she was considering him in making a decision about where she wanted to spend the rest of her life. Mid-morning on Monday, Geraldine was summoned to an interview room where a member of the public was waiting to lodge a complaint. As an experienced officer, Geraldine was used to fielding vexatious accusations. With a sigh she made her way along the corridor to the room where the irate woman was waiting for her. Stocky and square-jawed, with short grey hair, she sat with trousered knees pressed together and fleshy arms folded across her chest.

'What seems to be the problem, Mrs Abbott?' Geraldine asked as she sat down.

The grey-haired woman's eyes glittered and her voice was unsteady. 'I want to talk to someone about my brother's murder.'

'Are you saying your brother's been murdered?'

'Yes, that's exactly what I'm saying.'

'And is this a murder case that's under investigation? What's your brother's name?'

The woman shook her head, and her ruddy face turned a deeper shade of red.

'No, no, no. You're not investigating it. No one's investigating anything. Look, my brother was found hanging from a banister nine days ago.' She leaned forward and lowered her voice. 'They said it was suicide, but that's simply not true.'

Geraldine frowned, and tried to look interested. She found it was usually best to let aggrieved members of the public have their say.

'Perhaps you'd better start at the beginning. What makes you suspect your brother's death wasn't suicide?'

'It's more than a suspicion. I know my brother – that is, I knew him. There's no way he would have taken his own life. He wasn't that sort of a person. He was – he was a robust man, Sergeant. He loved life.'

'Circumstances can have a devastating effect on people, even those we think we know well –'

'Please, don't dismiss this as the ramblings of a grieving woman. I knew my brother. He would never have killed himself. He was blessed with a cheerful disposition, and, before you say it, he didn't suffer from depression, and he didn't have money worries, or any problems with drink or drugs. There was nothing in his life that might have prompted him to end it. And hanging's not the kind of death that can happen by accident. No, he was murdered, I'm sure of it. I waited as long as I could before coming forward because I thought no one would believe he killed himself, but now she tells me they're burying him on Wednesday, so we don't have much time. I came here to plead with you to look into what happened, before it's too late.'

Geraldine did her best to pacify the distressed woman, wondering whether Amanda was simply trying to cause trouble for her brother's widow.

'Do you have any evidence that your brother was murdered? At the moment, all you've given me is supposition.'

Amanda shrugged her square shoulders. 'I wasn't there, but I know – I knew my brother. Why would he have suddenly done away with himself?'

Geraldine was faintly intrigued. Amanda didn't strike her as the kind of woman who might be given to hysterical delusions.

'So if he didn't commit suicide, and it wasn't an accident, what do you think happened?'

'My sister-in-law did it,' Amanda answered promptly. 'It's obvious. They never got on. And now she gets her hands on everything he worked for.'

'How long were they married?'

'Over twenty-five years.'

'That's a long time for a couple who don't get on to stay together,' Geraldine said quietly.

'And she finally had enough of him and killed him, only she made it look like suicide so she could get away with it. I'm convinced that's what happened. Nothing else makes sense.'

Geraldine almost dismissed what she was hearing as a family disagreement, but Amanda was so insistent that she agreed to look into Mark Abbott's death.

'Please, you have to find out what happened,' Amanda said. 'He was my brother and I'm not going to sit back and see her get away with it, not if I can help it. Will you keep me posted?' she enquired as she stood up, 'or can I come back to see how you're getting on?'

Geraldine promised she would do her best to find out whether there might have been anything unlawful about the death. Having seen Amanda off the premises, she went to speak to her detective chief inspector, Eileen. A large woman, about ten years older than Geraldine, she had dark hair greying at the temples, sharp features, and an air of solidity that was both reassuring and overbearing at the same time.

'It sounds like family politics,' Eileen said, when she had listened to Geraldine's account. 'The sister of the deceased is going out of her way to make trouble for his widow. Perhaps she was expecting to be mentioned in his will and is disappointed to have been left out of it?'

'That's what I thought. But there's one more thing. The deceased took out a fairly hefty life insurance policy with a two year suicide exclusion clause.'

Eileen nodded. 'And you're telling me the two years ran out –'

'A week before his death. Of course, that doesn't mean he didn't kill himself. He might have waited so his wife would benefit from the policy,' she added, speaking more to herself than to her senior officer. 'But there's something about it that doesn't feel right.'

'If you want to make a few discreet enquiries, that's up to

you. I can't see we've really got anything to investigate, but you can take a look if you like, as long as it doesn't distract you from your work here.' Eileen paused. 'If every widow was accused of murdering her husband when she inherited his estate, we'd have more suspects than police officers.'

2

Sometimes Charlotte forgot about her new circumstances. After more than thirty years of marriage, she still woke up expecting to hear her husband snoring beside her. She was used to lying awake at night, listening with growing irritation as each sonorous inhalation was followed by a brief hiatus before the sigh of air released from his lungs. Now it was the silence that disturbed her sleep. Somewhere overhead a pipe rattled and wheezed, a faint echo of the noise she had endured every night for decades, ever since they had moved into their spacious property. She flung one arm out sideways, savouring the empty expanse of bed beside her, the sheets cool and unwrinkled. Tentatively she stretched her leg out as well, until she was occupying half of her husband's share of the mattress. It didn't matter. There was no one to kick her back onto her own side of the bed. There were no longer any sides. The whole bed was hers.

The funeral had been set in motion. In two days' time mourners would gather to mumble hymns, someone would recite a eulogy, and everyone would talk about what a devoted husband and father Mark had been to her and Eddy. The thought of it irritated her, but there was no point in exposing his occasional lapses now he had gone. No one would want to hear about her dead husband's philandering, least of all his son. She drew her arm and leg quickly back onto her own side of the bed and wrapped her arms around her body, wondering who would attend the ceremony. Her stepson, Eddy, would be there, of course, accompanied by his wife. Her own sister was unable to travel all the way over from New Zealand with her family, but they had all sent their condolences.

A few of Mark's work colleagues would show up out of a sense of duty, as would the handful of friends she and Mark had kept in touch with over the years. She wasn't close to any of them, but they had all known one another for a long time and that counted for something. It was partly pride that had prompted her to contact them. She didn't want people thinking she had no friends now that Mark was gone, although the truth was that she had no real friends of her own. She never had. But the main reason she had invited as many people as she could was that it would be easier to avoid her sister-in-law in a room full of people. Much as she hated the prospect of seeing her, she could hardly have kept the news about Mark's death from his only sister.

'I suppose Aunt Amanda will have to be there,' Eddy had said, voicing his mother's feelings.

'Don't worry,' Charlotte had told him. 'I'll deal with her.'

She had felt nowhere nearly as confident about speaking to her sister-in-law as she had pretended. An overbearing woman, Amanda had understandably been shocked on hearing the news of her brother's death.

'But I don't understand,' she had barked, as though it was impossible to believe that an overweight man in his sixties could possibly have died. And that was before she had learned about the circumstances surrounding his death.

Charlotte could almost feel her sister-in-law glowering at her down the phone line. She hesitated, but there was no easy way to answer the question. Her one word reply prompted a cry of outrage.

'Suicide?' Amanda had repeated, her voice rising in a horrified shriek. 'What do you mean, it was suicide? How could it be? Mark would never have killed himself. I don't believe it.'

Charlotte had drawn in a deep shuddering breath and tried to sound sympathetic. Of course it was terrible for Amanda to lose her brother in that way, and Charlotte was devastated to have to pass on such terrible news. But she couldn't help feeling the tragedy was far harder for her to cope with. Not only had she lost her husband of over three decades, but she had been the one to find him, suspended from the banister. For the rest of her life she would be haunted by the memory of his swollen face, his dead eyes glaring at her in wordless accusation.

She had gritted her teeth as Amanda proceeded with her enquiries. Doing her best to avoid focusing on the horrible memory, Charlotte had tried to describe what had happened in a detached way, as though she was talking about a scene in a film. Amanda had a right to know and besides, until she was satisfied, she would never stop bombarding Charlotte with questions. Amanda had never been sensitive to other people's feelings. As accurately as she could, Charlotte described how she had found Mark hanging in the hall and had rushed outside, screaming for help, and how the startled gardener had dropped his rake, narrowly missing injuring himself. To his credit he hadn't hesitated to run all the way up the length of the garden to go inside with her. Although clearly shocked, he had taken control of the situation, yelling at her to call an ambulance while he righted the upturned chair, clambered onto it, and flung his arms around Mark's legs to support him. All the time he had continued shouting at her to summon help.

'Why didn't you call an ambulance straightaway?'

For an instant the question had hung between them unanswered, then Charlotte began babbling about shock, and the urgent need at the time to free Mark from the noose. She didn't add that for a moment she had been unable move. Instead of calling for help she had stood, rooted to the spot, staring at the two men entangled in their macabre one-sided embrace. After that, she could remember nothing more until the pounding at the front door had shattered the silence. Even then the gardener had been forced to shout at her to open the front door, or the police would have smashed their way in.

'But I don't understand,' her sister-in-law had repeated when Charlotte finished speaking. 'It doesn't even make sense. How could he have reached the upstairs banister? Not Mark. I can't believe it of him.' She had sounded close to tears.

The last thing Charlotte wanted to do was talk about what had happened, but she supposed she might as well get it over with or Amanda would never let it rest.

'We think he went upstairs and tied the rope around the banister up there and then threw the end of the rope over, so he could reach it from the hall. Then he must have gone downstairs, climbed up on a chair, and... '

Her voice had tailed off. Surely Amanda wouldn't want her to continue.

'I see,' Amanda had replied curtly, too upset to continue.

'So I'm sorry,' Charlotte had resumed after an awkward pause, 'but –'

'I don't understand,' Amanda interrupted her. 'What could

have driven him to do it? Mark wasn't the sort of man to take his own life. Something must have happened to make him do it, if it really was suicide, which I doubt.'

Charlotte hadn't replied to what sounded like a veiled accusation. Whatever vile conclusion Amanda chose to draw was of no consequence. She hadn't been there, and Charlotte had. The police were convinced that Mark had taken his own life, and nothing Amanda could say was going to change their minds. It was over, and Mark was gone.

3

Geraldine hadn't worn her long black jacket since her birth mother's cremation. It was hard to believe nearly a year had passed since then. Giving the jacket a shake, she pulled it on over black trousers and a grey shirt, an appropriate outfit to wear to a stranger's funeral. Fulford Cemetery was not far from where she worked, and easy enough to find, but all the same she was nearly late. The car park was three quarters empty as she parked her car and hurried into the prayer hall. Although the front rows were only half full, she slipped into a seat near the back of the hall. She had barely sat down when the funeral cortège arrived and everyone shuffled to their feet. As the coffin was brought in, Amanda caught sight of Geraldine and her expression tautened with recognition. Other than that, no one seemed to notice the stranger in the back row.

It was a dreary service, even for a funeral, with a dull and generic eulogy. Geraldine was reminded of her birth mother's funeral, where no one had spoken apart from the celebrant who had never met the dead woman or her family, and had taken no trouble to find out anything about her. The ceremony seemed to drag on interminably, but at last it drew to a close and the congregation filed outside to gather in clusters in the chilly spring sunshine. Observing the mourners, Geraldine could see nothing to arouse suspicion.

The widow's grief was evident but restrained. At her side a man, presumably her son, stood stiff and dignified. A young woman was holding his arm, a solemn expression on her face. Her hair was as black as Geraldine's but hung down to her shoulders, while Geraldine's was short. A few people hovered near them, looking slightly awkward. It wasn't clear whether they belonged to their group or not.

The dead man's sister stood a few feet away from the widow and her party. After a brief hesitation, Geraldine joined her.

'That's his family,' Amanda said, nodding her head in the direction of the group. 'That's his widow, Charlotte, with my nephew, Eddy, and his wife, Luciana.'

If Geraldine hadn't heard Amanda accuse her sister-in-law of having murdered the dead man, she might have been startled by the hostility in her voice. But there was nothing Geraldine could do to question any of them, or to look into the circumstances of this death, and nothing about the funeral that prompted her curiosity. Amanda had been so insistent, Geraldine had allowed her own judgement to be overruled and had consequently wasted her time attending the service.

She was uncomfortably aware that she had only been tempted to investigate the death because it offered her an opportunity to assume some responsibility for her work. Having been recently demoted from detective inspector to the rank of sergeant, she was struggling to contain her frustration at waiting for tasks to be allocated to her when she had been accustomed to running her own team. Still, in attending the funeral, at least Geraldine had done her best to satisfy Amanda that her accusation had been taken seriously. With luck that would pacify her for a while, hopefully until she recovered from the shock of her brother's suicide – if he really had taken his own life.

Geraldine was about to return to her car when a portly man accosted her.

'Are you a relative?' he enquired.

About to reply that she had worked with the deceased, Geraldine hesitated. 'I used to be a neighbour,' she muttered vaguely. 'I kept in touch.'

It was as well she had been circumspect, because she learned that her interlocutor had been working with Mark Abbott until his death.

'It came as a shock, I can tell you,' he added, lowering his voice. 'I still can't believe it. Did you know him well?'

Geraldine shook her head and mumbled something appropriate.

'He was the last person I'd expect to go and do anything like that,' the man went on. 'Not that there is anything quite like that, is there? But I mean, Mark of all people. You knew him, didn't you?'

Geraldine mumbled quietly.

He glanced around, probably to check the close family weren't within hearing. 'I thought it was a wind up when I first heard the news. I mean, it would have been in pretty poor taste if it had been, but I simply couldn't believe it. He just wasn't that kind of person, was he?'

'No, he wasn't,' Geraldine agreed. 'Still, you never know.'

'True,' he nodded. 'You think you know someone and then –' he shrugged. 'What gets me is that we were out the night before it happened, and he was right as rain then. Well,' he hesitated, 'that is to say, he seemed all right. He told me he was planning a holiday, and we arranged a game of tennis for the weekend. We used to knock up once in a while, you know? Nothing too serious. Not like when I was younger and could move around the court.' He smiled ruefully. 'But it's hardly what you expect a chap to be talking about the night before he tops himself, is it? Oh well, you never can tell.'

He wandered off. Geraldine watched him go and talk to the widow and her son, before she turned to make her way back to the car park. Before she had left the forecourt, Amanda came over and barred her way.

'I'll be coming to see you again,' she announced. 'I'm not letting this go.' She leaned forward conspiratorially and went on, without lowering her foghorn of a voice. 'They think I'm going to give up, but I know what happened and I'm not going to stop until you find out who did it.'

'Oh for goodness sake,' Charlotte interrupted her sister-in-law, stepping forward and hissing at her in a furious whisper. 'Can't you ever shut up? This is his funeral.' She burst into tears and her son and daughter-in-law bustled her away, throwing angry glances at Amanda as they moved away.

'Oh yes, they'd like nothing better than to shut me up,' Amanda told Geraldine. 'Her and her crocodile tears.' She turned to glare at Geraldine. 'I'll see you tomorrow.'

'I'm not likely to have anything new to tell you tomorrow,' Geraldine said.

With a grunt, Amanda strode away. Nothing in the mourners' demeanour had borne out the accusation that had been levelled against them. But now a second person had cast doubt on the idea that Mark Abbott had killed himself, and the dead man's colleague from work was hardly likely to be harbouring a personal grudge against the widow. Aware that the dead man's sister might be acting maliciously, Geraldine had to acknowledge that the funeral had raised a further question over Mark Abbott's death. However hard she tried to ignore her unease about his suicide, she couldn't shake off the suspicion that something was wrong.

Returning to the police station, she shelved her curiosity about the alleged suicide, and settled down to work. It had taken her a few months to learn her way around York and get to know her colleagues at the police station in Fulford Road, but now her new place of work had become familiar, and she had struck up a friendship with a couple of her colleagues. Ted Allsop was a stocky man nearing retirement who had befriended Geraldine right from her first day at Fulford Road. She soon realised that he was equally sociable with everyone, but that only made her warm to his broad smile all the more. Another colleague who looked set to become a friend was a raven-haired woman called Ariadne, who had a Greek mother and an English father. She was about the same age as Geraldine and also single. Apart from that they had very little in common, but it was enough. If Geraldine could make just one real friend at work, she would be satisfied. Besides the relationships she was hoping to forge, her old friend, Ian Peterson, worked in York. His presence hopefully meant she was going to feel less lonely. Conscious that she could never return to London, she tried to focus on the positive aspects of her new life.

DETECTIVE GERALDINE STEEL

'YOU'RE JUST PLAIN
GOING TO LOVE HER'
JEFFREY DEAVER

OVER ONE MILLION COPIES SOLD WORLDWIDE

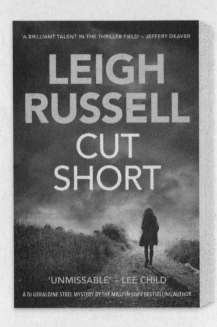

CUT SHORT

Meet Detective Inspector Geraldine Steel: fierce, dependable, and committed to her job. Relocated to the quiet town of Woolsmarsh, she expects respite from the stresses of the city; a space where she can battle her demons in private. But when she finds herself pitted against a twisted killer preying on young women, she quickly discovers how wrong she is...

Can Geraldine save the lives of the town's young women – or will she become the killer's ultimate trophy?

noexit.co.uk/cutshort

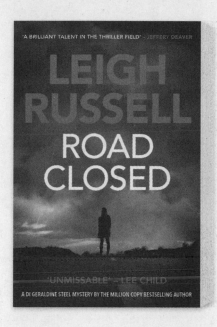

ROAD CLOSED

When a man dies in a gas explosion, the police suspect arson. But the case takes on a new and terrible twist when the prime suspect, a local felon, is viciously attacked. As police enquiries lead from the expensive Harchester Hill estate to the local brothel, their key witness dies in a hit-and-run. Coincidence? Or cold-blooded murder?

With so many lives lost already, DI Geraldine Steel must put her problems aside, to protect others. After all, in the race for justice, sacrifices must be made.

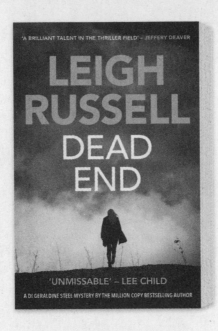

DEAD END

Headmistress Abigail Kirby is dead. A potential witness has been murdered. And for DI Geraldine Steel, the stakes have been raised yet higher. Abigail's teenage daughter, Lucy, is missing, believed to have run away with a girl she met online. Time is quickly running out for Geraldine before her naivety costs Lucy her life.

But with a serial killer on the loose, Geraldine's own life is in danger, and though her Sergeant Ian Peterson makes a shocking discovery, could it be too late to save her from a dreadful fate?

noexit.co.uk/deadend

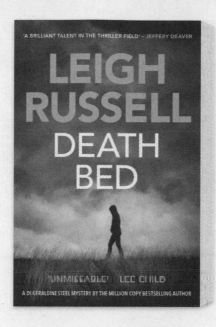

'A BRILLIANT TALENT IN THE THRILLER FIELD' – JEFFERY DEAVER

LEIGH RUSSELL

DEATH BED

'UNMISSABLE' – LEE CHILD

A DI GERALDINE STEEL MYSTERY BY THE MILLION COPY BESTSELLING AUTHOR

DEATH BED

When the bodies of two black girls are discovered in North London, the pressure is on to find a killer before the case divides the local community. But motive seems to go far beyond race in DI Geraldine Steel's first investigation in the nation's capital.

Two teeth were extracted from each victim, and when this information is leaked to the press, there is a media frenzy over the unusual MO. As the police pursue their lead suspect, a third girl goes missing.

With the death toll mounting, time is running out for Geraldine as she hunts for the elusive killer the media are calling 'The Dentist'.

noexit.co.uk/deathbed

STOP DEAD

When a successful businessman is the victim of a vicious murder, all evidence points to his wife and her young lover. But then the victim's business partner suffers a similarly brutal fate and when yet another body is discovered, seemingly unrelated, the police are baffled. The only clue is DNA that leads them to two women: one dead, the other in prison.

With rumours growing of a serial killer in the city, the pressure to solve the case is high. But can Geraldine find the killer before there's yet another deadly attack?

noexit.co.uk/stopdead

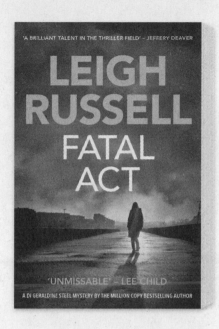

'A BRILLIANT TALENT IN THE THRILLER FIELD' – JEFFERY DEAVER

LEIGH RUSSELL
FATAL ACT

'UNMISSABLE' – LEE CHILD

A DI GERALDINE STEEL MYSTERY BY THE MILLION COPY BESTSELLING AUTHOR

FATAL ACT

How far would you go to find a murderer? DI Geraldine Steel, known for pushing the boundaries of her position in the name of justice, is on the hunt for a conviction, even if it threatens her life. A glamorous young TV soap star dies in a car crash but despite the severity of the incident, the driver of the second vehicle has somehow survived – and is now missing.

When an almost identical case occurs resulting in the murder of another young actress, Geraldine finds herself on the hunt for a serial killer. With mounting evidence, the killer's identity seems within her reach. But with her sergeant's life on the line, Geraldine has a sacrifice to make.

noexit.co.uk/fatalact

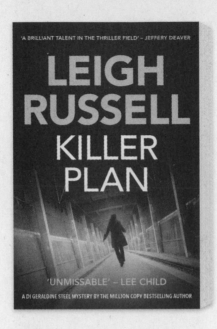

KILLER PLAN

Caroline's husband is killed, but she can't turn to the police without implicating herself in his murder. When one of her 10-year-old twins is kidnapped, the desperate mother is forced to resort to drastic measures to get him back.

As time runs out, Geraldine realises she has a secret that might just help solve the case, but the truth could destroy her career. Faced with the unenviable decision of protecting herself or the widow she barely knows, Geraldine must grapple with her conscience and do the right thing before the death count mounts any further.

noexit.co.uk/killerplan

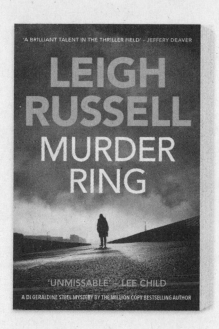

'A BRILLIANT TALENT IN THE THRILLER FIELD' – JEFFERY DEAVER

LEIGH RUSSELL

MURDER RING

'UNMISSABLE' – LEE CHILD

A DI GERALDINE STEEL MYSTERY BY THE MILLION COPY BESTSELLING AUTHOR

MURDER RING

The dead body of unassuming David Lester is discovered in a dark side-street, and DI Geraldine Steel is plunged into another murder investigation. The clues mount up along with the suspects, but with the death of another man in inexplicable circumstances, the case becomes increasingly complex. As Geraldine investigates the seemingly unrelated crimes, she makes a shocking discovery about her birth mother.

noexit.co.uk/murderring

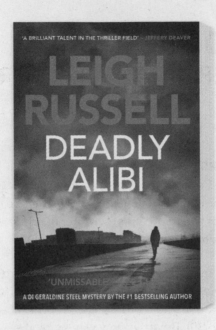

'A BRILLIANT TALENT IN THE THRILLER FIELD' – JEFFERY DEAVER

LEIGH
RUSSELL

DEADLY
ALIBI

'UNMISSABLE'

A DI GERALDINE STEEL MYSTERY BY THE #1 BESTSELLING AUTHOR

DEADLY ALIBI

Two victims and a suspect whose alibi appears open to doubt...
Geraldine Steel is thrown into a double murder investigation
which threatens not only her career, but her life. When her
previously unknown twin Helena turns up, her problems threaten
to make Geraldine's life turn toxic in more ways than one.

noexit.co.uk/deadlyalibi

NO EXIT PRESS
UNCOVERING THE BEST CRIME

MEET NO EXIT PRESS, the independent publisher bringing you the best in crime and noir fiction. From classic detective novels, to page-turning spy thrillers, our books are carefully crafted by some of the world's finest writers and delivered to you by a small, but mighty, team.

In our 30 years of business, we have published award-winning fiction and non-fiction including the work of Pulitzer Prize winner **Robert Olen Butler**, British Crime Book of the Year 2016 *Dodgers* **by Bill Beverly**, and winner of the Governor General's Award for Fiction *The Last Summer* **by Andrée A. Michaud**. We are the home of crime and noir legends **Robert B. Parker** and **James Sallis** whose novel *Drive* was made into the iconic film starring Ryan Gosling. And we pride ourselves on uncovering the most exciting new or undiscovered talents such as **William Giraldi**, **Ausma Zehanat Khan**, **Howard Linskey**, **Luke McCallin** and of course, **Leigh Russell**.

We are a proactive team committed to delivering the very best both for our authors and our readers. Want to join the conversation and find out more about what we do? Catch us on social media or sign up to our newsletter for all the latest news from No Exit Press HQ.

f | No Exit Press   **noexit.co.uk/newsletter**

A LETTER FROM LEIGH

Dear Reader,

I hope you enjoyed reading this book in my Geraldine Steel series. Readers are the key to the writing process, so I'm thrilled that you've joined me on my writing journey.

You might not want to meet some of my characters on a dark night – I know I wouldn't! – but hopefully you want to read about Geraldine's other investigations. Her work is always her priority because she cares deeply about justice, but she also has her own life. Many readers care about what happens to her. I hope you join them, and become a fan of Geraldine Steel, and her colleague Ian Peterson.

If you follow me on Facebook or Twitter, you'll know that I love to hear from readers. I always respond to comments from fans, and hope you will follow me on **@LeighRussell** and **fb.me/leigh.russell.50** or drop me an email via my website **leighrussell.co.uk**.

That way you can be sure to get news of the latest offers on my books. You might also like to sign up for my newsletter on **leighrussell.co.uk/news** to make sure you're one of the first to know when a new book is coming out. We'll be running competitions, and I'll also notify you of any events where I'll be appearing.

Finally, if you enjoyed this story, I'd be really grateful if you would post a brief review on Amazon or Goodreads. A few sentences to say you enjoyed the book would be wonderful. And of course it would be brilliant if you would consider recommending my books to anyone who is a fan of crime fiction.

I hope to meet you at a literary festival or a book signing soon!

Thank you again for choosing to read my book.

With very best wishes,

Leigh Russell

About Us

In addition to No Exit Press, Oldcastle Books has a number of other imprints, including Kamera Books, Creative Essentials, Pulp! The Classics, Pocket Essentials and High Stakes Publishing > oldcastlebooks.co.uk

For more information about Crime Books > crimetime.co.uk

Check out the kamera film salon for independent, arthouse and world cinema > kamera.co.uk

For more information, media enquiries and review copies please contact marketing > marketing@oldcastlebooks.co.uk